# DAISY DARKER

## ALICE FEENEY

**MACMILLAN**

First published 2022 by Macmillan
an imprint of Pan Macmillan
The Smithson, 6 Briset Street, London EC1M 5NR
*EU representative*: Macmillan Publishers Ireland Ltd, 1st Floor,
The Liffey Trust Centre, 117–126 Sheriff Street Upper,
Dublin 1, D01 YC43
Associated companies throughout the world
www.panmacmillan.com

ISBN 978-1-5290-8981-3

1 3 5 7 9 8 6 4 2

A CIP catalogue record for this book is available from the British Library.

Map artwork by Hemesh Alles

Typeset by Palimpsest Book Production Ltd, Falkirk, Stirlingshire
Printed and bound by CPI Group (UK) Ltd, Croydon, CR0 4YY

Visit **www.panmacmillan.com** to read more about all our books
and to buy them. You will also find features, author interviews and
news of any author events, and you can sign up for e-newsletters
so that you're always first to hear about our new releases.

For Diggi.
You fixed my broken heart and saved my life more than once.
I will love you always, and miss you forever.

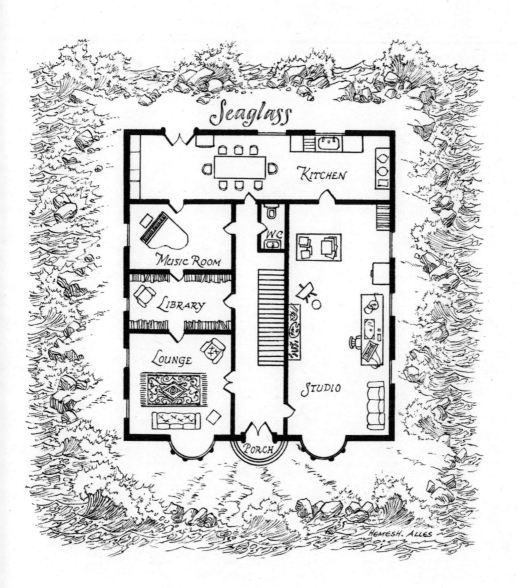

Seaglass

Kitchen

Music Room

Library

Lounge

WC

Studio

Porch

HEMESH. ALLES

*A note from the author's agent:*

I received this novel just after Christmas last year. It was wrapped in brown paper tied with string, and had been hand-delivered to my office in central London. I do not know who by. There was no cover letter, not even a note. Inside the parcel, I found a manuscript. Most writers send their work by email these days, and I do not accept unsolicited material, but the name on the title page took my breath away. Because the author of this novel had been dead for some time. I have never believed in ghosts, but neither can I offer a rational explanation. I knew the author well enough to know that nobody else could have written this book. After a great deal of consideration, I decided that this was a tale that deserved to be told. The publishers of this novel have changed the names of some of the characters for legal reasons, but not one word of the story. If it is a story. I confess I fear that at least some of what you are about to read might be true.

# One

I was born with a broken heart.

The day I arrived into this lonely little world was also the first time I died. Nobody spotted the heart condition back then. Things weren't as sophisticated in 1975 as they might be now, and my blue colouring was blamed on my traumatic birth. I was a breech baby, to complicate matters further. The weary doctor told my father to choose between me or my mother, explaining apologetically, and with just a hint of impatience, that he could only save one of us. My father, after a brief hesitation he would spend the rest of his life paying for, chose his wife. But the midwife persuaded me to breathe – against all their odds and my better judgement – and a hospital room full of strangers smiled when I started to cry. Everyone except for my mother. She wouldn't even look at me.

My mother had wanted a son. She already had two daughters when I was born, and chose to name us all after flowers. My eldest sister is called Rose, which turned out to be strangely appropriate as she is beautiful but not without thorns. Next to arrive, but still four years ahead of me, was Lily. The middle child in our floral family is pale, and pretty, and poisonous to some. My mother refused to name me at all for a while, but when the time came, I was christened Daisy. She is a woman who only ever has a Plan A, so none of us were given the contingency of a middle name. There were plenty of other – better – options, but she chose to name me after a flower that often gets picked, trampled on, or made into chains. A mother's least favourite child always knows that's what they are.

It's funny how people grow into the names they are given. As though a few letters arranged in a certain order can predict a person's future happiness or sorrow. Knowing a person's name isn't the same as knowing a person, but names are the first impression we all judge and are judged by. Daisy Darker was the name life gave me and I suppose I did grow into it.

The second time I died was exactly five years after I was born. My heart completely stopped on my fifth birthday, perhaps in protest, when I demanded too much of it by trying to swim to America. I wanted to run away, but was better at swimming, so hoped to reach New York by lunchtime with a bit of backstroke. I didn't even make it out of Blacksand Bay and – technically – died trying. That might have been the end of me were it not for the semi-deflated orange armbands that kept me afloat, and my ten-year-old sister, Rose. She swam out to save me, dragged me back to shore, and brought me back to life with an enthusiastic performance of CPR that left me with two cracked ribs. She'd recently earned her First Aid badge at Brownies. Sometimes I suspect she regretted it. Saving me, I mean. She loved that badge.

My life was never the same after I died a second time, because that's when everyone knew for sure what I think they already suspected: that I was broken.

The cast of doctors my mother took me to see when I was five all delivered the same lines, with the same faces, as though they had rehearsed from the same sad little script. They all agreed that I wouldn't live beyond the age of fifteen. There were years of tests to prove how few years I had left. My condition was unusual and those doctors found me fascinating. Some travelled from other countries just to watch my open-heart surgeries; it made me feel like a superstar and a freak at the same time. Life didn't break my heart, despite trying. The irregular ticking time bomb inside my chest was planted before birth – a rare congenital glitch.

Me living longer than life had planned required a daily cocktail of beta blockers, serotonin inhibitors, synthetic steroids and hormones to keep me, and my heart, ticking over. If that all sounds like hard work and high maintenance, that's because it was, especially when I was only five years old. But children are more resilient than adults. They're far better at making the most of what they have, and spend less time worrying about what they haven't. Technically, I'd already died eight times before I was thirteen, and if I'd been a cat I would have been concerned. But I was a little girl, and I had bigger things than death to worry about.

Twenty-nine years after my traumatic arrival, I'm very grateful to have had more time than anyone predicted. I think knowing you might die sooner rather than later does make a person live life differently. Death is a life-changing deadline, and I'm forever in debt to everyone who helped me outstay my welcome. I do my best to pay it forward. I try to be kind to others, as well as to myself, and rarely sweat the small stuff these days. I might not have much in terms of material posses-sions, but that sort of thing never really mattered to me. All in all, I think I'm pretty lucky. I'm still here, I have a niece who I adore spending time with, and I'm proud of my work – volunteering at a care home for the elderly. Like my favourite resident says every time she sees me: the secret to having it all is knowing that you already do.

Sometimes people think I'm younger than my years. I've been accused of still dressing like a child on more than one occasion – my mother has never approved of my choice in clothes – but I like wearing dungaree dresses and retro T-shirts. I'd rather wear my long black hair in intricate braids than get it cut, and I'm clueless when it comes to make-up. I think I look good, considering all the bad things that have happened to me. The only visual proof of my condition is carved down the middle of my chest in the form of a faded pink scar. People used to stare if I wore something that revealed it: bathing suits, V-neck sweaters or summer dresses. I never blamed them. I stare at it too sometimes; the mechanics of my prolonged existence fascinate me. That pink line is the only external evidence that I was born a little bit broken. Every couple of years during my slightly dysfunctional childhood, doctors would take it in turns to open me up again, have a look inside, and do a few repairs. I'm like an old car that probably shouldn't still be on the road, but has been well looked after. Though not always and not by everyone.

Families are like fingerprints: no two are the same and they tend to leave their mark. The tapestry of my family has always had a few too many loose threads. It was a little frayed around the edges long before I arrived, and if you look closely enough, you might even spot a few holes. Some people aren't capable of seeing the beauty in imperfection, but I always loved my nana, my parents and my sisters. Regardless of how they felt about me, and despite what happened.

My nana is the only person in my family who loved me unconditionally. So much so, she wrote a book about me, or at least about a little girl with the same name. If mine sounds familiar, that is why. *Daisy Darker's Little Secret* is a bestselling children's book, which my nana wrote and illustrated. It can be found in almost every bookstore around the world, often nestled between *The Gruffalo* and *The Very Hungry Caterpillar*. Nana said she chose to borrow my name for the story so that – one way or another – I could live forever. It was a kind thing to do, even if my parents and sisters didn't think so at the time. I suspect they wanted to live forever too, but they settled for living off the book's royalties instead.

Nana had more money than she knew what to do with after writing that book, not that you'd know it to look at her. She has always been a generous woman when it comes to charity and strangers, but not with herself or her family. She believes that having too much makes people want too little, and has always hesitated when asked for handouts. But that might be about to change. Many years ago, long before I was born, a palm reader at a fair in Land's End told my nana that she wouldn't live beyond the age of eighty. She's never forgotten it. Even her agent knows not to expect any more books. So tomorrow isn't just Halloween, or Nana's eightieth birthday. *She* thinks it's her last, and *they* think they might finally get their hands on her money. My family haven't all been in the same place at the same time for over a decade, not even for my sister's wedding, but when Nana invited them to Seaglass one last time, they all agreed to come.

Her home on the Cornish coast was the setting for my happiest childhood memories. And my saddest. It was where my sisters and I spent every Christmas and Easter, as well as the long summer holidays after my parents got divorced. I'm not the only one with a broken heart in my family. I don't know whether my parents, or my sisters, or even Nana's agent take the palm reading about her imminent death seriously, but I do. Because sometimes the strangest things can predict a person's future. Take me and my name, for example. A children's book called *Daisy Darker's Little Secret* changed my family forever and was a premonition of sorts. Because I do have a secret, and I think it's time I shared it.

# Two

*30 October 2004 – 4 p.m.*

S eeing Seaglass again steals my breath away.

It normally takes at least five hours to drive from London to Cornwall, slightly less by train. But I always enjoyed swapping the hustle and bustle of the city for a network of twisted memories and country lanes. I prefer a simpler, slower, quieter way of living, and London is inherently loud. Navigating my way back here has often felt like time travel, but my journey today has been quicker than expected and relatively pain free. Which is good, because I wanted to get here first. Before the others.

I'm pleased to see that nothing much has changed since my last visit. The stone Victorian house with its gothic turrets and turquoise tiled roof appears to have been built from the same granite rocks it sits on. Pieces of blue-green glass still decorate some of the exterior walls, sparkling in the sunlight and gifting Seaglass its name. The mini mansion rises out of the crashing waves that surround it, perched upon its own tiny private island, just off the Cornish coast. Like a lot of things in life, it's hard to find if you don't know where to look. Hidden by crumbling cliffs and unmarked footpaths, in a small cove known locally as Blacksand Bay, it's very much off the beaten

track. This is not the Cornwall you see on postcards. But aside
from the access issues, there are plenty of other reasons why
people tend to stay away.

My nana inherited Seaglass from her mother – who allegedly
won it from a drunken duke in a card game. The story goes
that he was an infamous bon viveur, who built the eccentric
building in the 1800s to entertain his wealthy friends. But he
couldn't hold his liquor, and after losing his 'summer palace'
to a *woman*, he drowned his sorrows and himself in the ocean.
Regardless of its tragic past, this place is as much a part of
our family as I am. Nana has lived here since she was born.
But despite never wanting to live anywhere else, and making
a small fortune writing children's books, she has never invested
much in home improvements. As a result, Seaglass is literally
falling into the sea and, like me, it probably won't be around
much longer.

The tiny island it was built on almost two hundred years
ago has slowly eroded over time. Being exposed to the full
force of the Atlantic Ocean and centuries of wind and rain
have taken their toll. The house is swollen with secrets and
damp. But despite its flaking paint, creaking floors and ancient
furnishings, Seaglass has always felt more like home to me
than anywhere else. I'm the only one who still visits regularly;
divorced parents, busy lives, and siblings with so little in
common it's hard to believe we're related, have made family
gatherings a rather rare occurrence. So this weekend will be
special in more ways than one. Pity fades with age, hate is lost
and found, but guilt can last a lifetime.

The journey here felt so solitary and final. The road leads
to a hidden track on top of the cliff, which soon comes to an
abrupt dead end. From there, the only two options to get down
to Blacksand Bay are a three-hundred-foot fall to certain death,

or a steep, rocky path to the sandy dunes below. The path has almost completely crumbled away in places, so it's best to watch your step. Despite all the years I have been coming here, to me Blacksand Bay is still the most beautiful place in the world.

The late afternoon sun is already low in the hazy blue sky, and the sound of the sea is like an old familiar soundtrack; one I have missed listening to. There is nothing and nobody else for miles. All I can see is the sand, and the ocean, and the sky. And Seaglass, perched on its ancient stone foundations in the distance, waves crashing against the rocks it was built on.

Having safely reached the bottom of the cliff, I remove my shoes and enjoy the sensation of sand between my toes. It feels like coming home. I ignore the rusty old wheelbarrow, left here to help transport ourselves and our things to the house; I travel light these days. People rarely need the things they think they need in order to be happy. I start the long walk across the natural sandy causeway that joins Seaglass's tidal island to the mainland. The house is only accessible when the tide is out, and is completely cut off from the rest of the world at all other times. Nana always preferred books to people, and her wish to be left alone with them was mostly granted, and almost guaranteed, by living in such an inaccessible place.

The invisible shipwrecks of my life are scattered all over this secluded bay with its infamous black sand. They are a sad reminder of all the journeys I was too scared to make. Everyone's lives have uncharted waters – the places and people we didn't quite manage to find – but when you feel as though you never will it's a special kind of sorrow. The unexplored oceans of our hearts and minds are normally the result of a lack of time and trust in the dreams we dreamt as children. But adults forget how to believe that their dreams might still come true.

I want to stop and savour the smell of the ocean, enjoy the feel of the warm afternoon sun on my face and the westerly wind in my hair, but time is a luxury I can no longer afford. I didn't have very much of it to spend in the first place. So I hurry on, despite the damp sand clinging to the soles of my feet as though trying to stop me in my tracks, and the seagulls that soar and squawk above my head as if trying to warn me away. The sound of their cries translates into words I don't want to hear inside my head:

*Go back. Go back. Go back.*

I ignore all these signs that seem to suggest that this visit is a bad idea, and walk a little faster. I want to arrive earlier than the rest of them to see the place as it exists in my memories, before they spoil things. I wonder if other people look forward to seeing their families, but dread it at the same time, the way I always seem to. It will be fine once I'm there. That's what I tell myself. Though even the thought feels like a lie.

The wind chimes that hang in the decrepit porch try to welcome me home, with a melancholy melody conducted by the breeze. I made them for my nana one Christmas when I was a child – having collected all the smooth, round pieces of blue and green glass I could find on the beach. She pretended to like the gift and the sea glass wind chimes have been here ever since. The lies we tell for love are the lightest shade of white. There is a giant pumpkin on the doorstep, with an elaborate scary face carved into it for Halloween; Nana does always like to decorate the house at this time of year. Before I can reach the large weathered wooden door, it bursts open with the usual welcoming party.

Poppins, an elderly Old English Sheepdog, is my nana's most trusted companion and best friend. The dog bounds in my direction, a giant bouncing ball of grey and white fur, panting as if she is smiling, and wagging her tail. I say hello, make a fuss of her, and admire the two little plaits and pink bows keeping her long hair out of her big brown eyes. I follow the dog's stare as she turns back to look at the house. In the doorway stands Nana; five foot nothing and radiating glee. Her halo of wild white curls frames her pretty, petite face, which has been weathered by age and wine. She's dressed from head to toe in pink and purple – her favourite colours – including pink shoes with purple laces. Some people might see an eccentric old lady, or the famous children's author: Beatrice Darker. But I just see my nana.

She smiles. 'Come on inside, before it starts to rain.'

I'm about to correct her about the weather – I *remember* feeling the sun on my face only a moment ago – but when I look up, I see that the picture-perfect blue sky above Seaglass has now darkened to a palette of muddy grey. I shiver and realize that it's much colder than I'd noticed before too. It does seem as though a storm is on the way. Nana has a habit of knowing what is coming before everybody else. So I do as she says – like always – and follow her and Poppins inside.

'Why don't you just relax for a while, before the rest of the family joins us?' Nana says, disappearing into the kitchen, leaving me – and the dog – in the hallway. Something smells delicious. 'Are you hungry?' she calls. 'Do you want a snack while we wait?' I can hear the clattering of ancient pots and pans, but I know Nana hates people bothering her when she's cooking.

'I'm fine, thanks,' I reply. Poppins gives me a disapproving look – she is never one to turn down food – and trots out to the kitchen, no doubt hoping to find a snack of her own.

I confess that a hug might have been nice, but Nana and I are both a little out of practice when it comes to affection.

I expect she is feeling just as anxious as I am about this family reunion, and we all deal with anxiety in different ways. You can see fear on the surface of some people, while others learn to hide their worries inside themselves, out of sight but not out of mind.

The first thing I notice – as always – are the clocks. It's impossible not to. The hallway is full of eighty of them, all different colours, shapes and sizes, and all ticking. A wall full of time. There is one for every year of Nana's life, and each one was carefully chosen by her, as a reminder to herself and the world that her time is her own. The clocks scared me as a child. I could hear them from my bedroom – *tick tock, tick tock, tick tock* – as though relentlessly whispering that my own time was running out.

The bad feeling I have about this weekend returns, but I don't know why.

I follow my unanswered questions further into Seaglass, hoping to find answers inside, and I'm instantly filled with a curious collection of memories and regrets. Transported back in time by the familiar sights and smells of the place, a delicious mix of nostalgia and salty air. The diffused scent of the ocean loiters in every corner of the old house, as though each brick and beam has been saturated by the sea.

Nothing has changed in the years I have known this place. The whitewashed walls and wooden floors look just as they did when my sisters and I were children – a little worn out maybe by the left-over love and loss they have housed. As I breathe it all in, I can still picture us as the people we used to be, before life changed us into the people we are now, just like the sea effortlessly reshapes the sand. I can understand why Nana never wanted to live anywhere else. If this place were mine, I'd never leave it behind either.

I wonder again why she has really invited the whole family here for her birthday, when I know she doesn't love or even like them all. Tying up loose ends perhaps? Sometimes love and hate get tangled, and there is no way to unpick the knot of feelings we feel. Asking questions of others often makes me ask questions of myself. If I had the chance to iron out the creases in my life before it ended, which ones would I choose to smooth over? Which points and pleats would I most want to unfold, so they could no longer dent the picture of the person I wished to be remembered as? Personally, I think that some wrinkles and stains on the fabric of our lives are there for a reason. A blank canvas might sound appealing, but it isn't very interesting to look at.

I head up the creaky stairs, leaving the ticking clocks behind me. Each room I pass contains the ghosts of memories from all the days and weeks and years I have walked along this hallway. Voices from my past trespass in my present, whispering through the cracks in the windows and floorboards, disguised as the sound of the sea. I can picture us running through here as children, giddy on ocean air, playing, hiding, hurting one another. That's what my sisters and I were best at. We learned young. Childhood is a race to find out who you really are, before you become the person you are going to be. Not everybody wins.

I step inside the bedroom that was always mine – the smallest in the house. It is still decorated the way it was when I was a girl, with white bedroom furniture – more shabby than chic – and old, peeling wallpaper, covered in a fading pattern of daisies. Nana is a woman who only says and does things once, and she never replaces something unless it is broken. She always used to put flowers in our bedrooms when we came to stay as children, but I notice that the vase in my room is empty. There is a silver dish filled with potpourri instead, a pretty mix of pine cones, dried petals and tiny seashells. I spot a copy of *Daisy Darker's Little Secret* on the bookshelf. Seeing it reminds me of my own secret. The one I never wanted to share. I lock it away again for now, back inside the box in my head where I have been keeping it.

The ocean continues to serenade my unsettled thoughts, as though trying to silence them with the relentless *shh* of the sea. I find the sound soothing. I can hear the waves crashing on the rocks below, and my bedroom window is stained with the resulting spray, droplets running down the glass like tears, as if the house itself were crying. I peer out and the sea stares back: cold, infinite and unforgiving. Darker than before.

Part of me still worries that I was wrong to come, but it didn't feel right to stay away.

The rest of my family will be here soon. I'll be able to watch them walk across the sandy causeway one by one as they arrive. It's been such a long time since we've all been together. I wonder whether all families have as many secrets as we do? When the tide comes in, we'll be cut off from the rest of the world for eight hours. When the tide goes back out, I doubt we'll ever all be together again.

# Three

*30 October 2004 – 5 p.m.*

My father is the first to arrive.

Being punctual is his only way of saying, *I love you*. For as long as I can remember he has expressed emotions through timekeeping, unable to demonstrate affection in the ways most other fathers do. But when I think about him growing up here as an only child, in a house full of clocks, on a tiny tidal island, I suppose time was always going to be on his mind. As a boy, I suspect he was often counting down the minutes until he could leave. I watch him from my bedroom window as he trudges across the damp sand. The sun is still setting, melting the sky into a palette of pinks and purples that do not look real. Dad glances up in my direction, but if he sees me, he doesn't smile or wave.

Frank Darker is a frustrated composer who mostly conducts. He still travels the world with his orchestra, but while that might *sound* glamorous, it isn't. He works harder than anyone I know, but doesn't earn as much as you might think. Once he has paid the salaries, hotel bills and expenses of an entire ensemble, he doesn't have a lot of spare change. But he loves his job and the people he works with. Perhaps a little too much: his orchestra is more like family to him than we ever were.

My father looks in pretty good shape for his fifty-something years. He still has a full head of black hair, and carries his suitcase with ease, despite it looking rather large for an overnight stay. I notice he chose not to use the wheelbarrow left on the other side of the causeway to help with luggage. I suspect it's a different kind of handout he's after from Nana. Dad's back is a bit hunched from years of sitting at a piano, and his suit seems to be hanging off him a little, as though life has made him shrink. I notice that he's dressed as if he were attending a funeral, not a family birthday, and I watch as he stops before reaching the front door, trying to compose himself like a piece of music that doesn't wish to be written.

He knows – just as we all do – that Nana intends to leave this house to a female relative. She inherited it from her mother, whose dying wish was that Seaglass would always belong to women in the Darker family. The decision to skip a generation caused my father great upset from the moment he knew about it. Dad never *wanted* Seaglass, he just *needed* money to keep his orchestra together. He would have sold this place years ago were it up to him. Nana has been bankrolling my father's ambitions since he was a child, but no matter how much she gives him, it is never enough. I head downstairs to see him, even though I know he'd rather not see me. I never leave me alone with myself for too long; I can't be trusted.

Poppins is already at the door, and Nana opens it before my dad has the opportunity to knock. Nana's face lights up when she sees who it is, a genuine smile revealing neat white teeth, still sharp enough to bite.

'Hello, Frank.'

'Mother,' he says, with an odd little nod. 'It's good to see you.'

'Is it? Perhaps you should try visiting more often?' There is a twinkle in her eye but we all know that she means it. Being alone never used to make Nana feel lonely, but the things and people we miss can change with age.

Dad doesn't reply. Subjects that sting are best avoided when you've already been stung too often. Instead, he glances at the wall of clocks, puts down his case, and hangs his coat on the stand. He's worn the same thick, black woollen coat for years, not because he can't afford a new one, but because my father has always been a creature of habit.

'Don't forget to punch in,' Nana says, blocking his path as he attempts to head into the lounge. This house used to be his home, and childhood homes are haunted by all variety of ghosts for people like my dad. The big man soon behaves like a small boy.

The clocks covering the walls in the hall are all different sizes, colours and designs. There are big clocks, small clocks, round clocks, square clocks, digital clocks, cuckoo clocks, musical clocks, pendulum clocks, novelty clocks, and even a vintage wall-mounted hourglass, containing sand from Blacksand Bay. The clock nearest the front door is one of Nana's favourites. It's an antique wooden punch clock from an old Cornish factory, originally used by staff to clock on and off. My dad sighs. He is a man who pre-empts most challenges with defeat. He takes a card with his name on from the tiny ancient cubbyhole, slots it into the clock, punches the time on it, then puts it back.

'Happy now?' he says.

'Ecstatic,' Nana replies with another smile. 'Family traditions become increasingly important the older you get; they hold us together when we've spent too long apart. If you check your card, you'll see it's been a while since my only child paid me a visit.'

This is a familiar family dance and we all know the steps.

Nana doesn't need to nag me to punch in. I *love* all of her little quirks and traditions, even the unconventional ones. But I'm used to her eccentric behaviour; unlike the rest of the family, I visit Nana all the time. When we're done with the unusual arrival rituals, we head into the lounge.

If you can imagine a room filled with mismatching retro furniture, a 1950s jukebox, pastel-coloured sofas, comfy arm-chairs, shelves filled with so many books they have started to bend in the middle from the weight of them all, enormous windows with sea views, a huge open fireplace, and turquoise wallpaper covered in hand-painted birds and elderflower blos-soms, then you can picture the lounge at Seaglass. I've never seen anything quite like it.

Nana holds up a bottle of Scotch from the brass drinks trolley in the corner. I shake my head – it's a bit early for me – but Dad nods, then makes a fuss of Poppins while the whisky is being poured. He is the only whisky drinker in our family, everyone else hates the stuff. Nana mixes herself a mojito, plucking some mint leaves, then bashing the ice with an ancient-looking rolling pin before adding a generous glug of rum. I marvel at the Darker family's version of casual drinks. There is no humble sherry in this house, not even in a trifle.

Thanks to a smidgen of subsidence – barely noticeable unless you know to look, and our family has always been very good at papering over the cracks – drinks placed on tables in this room tend to slide right off. My mother used to say it was why the whole family drank too much – always having to hold their glasses for fear of breaking them – but I don't think that's the reason. Some people drink to drown their sorrows; others drink so they can swim in them.

We sit in an awkward but well-practised silence, and I notice they both take a few sips of their drinks before attempting any further conversation. The branches of our family tree all grew in different directions, and it's best to avoid the stormy subjects that might make them bend or break. I smile politely and try to forget all the years when my dad didn't speak to me, didn't visit me in hospital as a child, or behaved as though I was already dead. I pretend not to remember the birthdays he forgot, or the Christmases when he chose to work instead of coming home, the countless times he made my mother cry, or the night I heard him blame their divorce on me and my broken heart. Just for now, while we wait for the others to get here, I pretend that he is a good father and that I am the daughter he wanted me to be.

I don't have to pretend for long.

My eldest sister is the next to arrive, the clever one, who saved me from drowning when she was ten. Rose is beautiful, intelligent, and damaged. She is five years older and almost a foot taller than I am. We have never been close. It isn't just her height that makes it difficult to see eye to eye with my sister, and it isn't the age gap either. Other than the same blood running through our veins, we simply don't have very much in common.

Rose is a vet and has always preferred the company of animals to people. Her clothes are as sensible as the woman wearing them: a striped Breton top beneath a tailored jacket teamed with smart (extra-long) jeans. She looks older than her thirty-four years. Her long chestnut hair is tied off her face in a neat ponytail, and her fringe is too long – as though she is trying to hide behind it. We haven't spoken since before she got married. We both know why.

Families are like snowflakes: each and every one is unique.

Rose is happier to see the dog than she would ever be to see me or Dad, so once again, Poppins gets all the attention. My eldest sister came here alone this weekend; I suppose we all did. Rose's marriage lasted less than a year, and she threw herself into her work and opening her own veterinary practice after that. Even as a child she was determinedly conscientious; the straight-A student who put the rest of us to shame. Rose has always had a thirst for knowledge that no amount of learning could quench. Dad calls her Dr Doolittle, because he thinks she only talks to animals these days. He might be right. Rose fetches herself a large glass of water from the kitchen, then perches on the edge of the pink sofa, next to my father, still wearing her jacket, as though she hasn't made up her mind whether to stay.

The sea is already starting to restitch itself across the causeway by the time the others arrive. While my father uses punctuality as kindness, my mother uses lateness to offend. Nancy Darker divorced our dad over twenty years ago, but she kept his name, and kept in close contact with his mother. She has travelled down from London with my fifteen-year-old niece, and Lily – her favourite daughter. They have always been close and still spend a lot of time together. Lily is the only one of us to furnish our parents with an elusive grandchild; I don't imagine there will be any more.

When my mother looks in my direction, I feel cold. She is a woman who never hides her seasons; she is winter all year round. Nancy looked so much like Audrey Hepburn when we were growing up that I sometimes thought it *was* her on TV, when she made us watch those black-and-white films over and over. She is still a very beautiful and graceful woman, and looks considerably younger than her fifty-four years. She wears her hair in the same black bob as always, and still looks, walks and talks like an out-of-work film star. The fur coat and costume jewellery aren't the only things about my mother that are fake.

The fact that she could have been an actress – if she hadn't accidentally become a parent – is something she frequently reminds us all of, as though her failed ambitions are our fault. But in many ways, I suspect some level of parental resentment is normal, even if rarely spoken about. Doesn't everyone wonder who they might have been if they weren't who they were?

The divorce settlement was generous, but dried up once we had all fled the nest. I don't understand where my mother gets her money from now, and I know better than to ask. She has made a part-time career out of competitions – entering every one she sees on daytime TV. Perhaps because of the sheer number she enters, she sometimes wins, but it can be dangerous to celebrate luck as success. Nancy has always been the puppeteer of our family, pulling all our strings in such a subtle fashion, we didn't notice when our thoughts were not our own.

When Nana heaves open the old wooden door to greet the late arrivals, the causeway is already slippery with seawater. I can see that their shoes are all soaking wet, forming little puddles around their feet. Lily is too busy blaming everything and everyone but herself for being late – the traffic, the satnav, the car Nana paid for – to notice the way we are all staring at her. It's as though she thinks the tide should have waited for her to arrive. Complaining is my sister's not-so-secret super-power. She is a walking frown. The soundtrack of her life is little more than a series of moans stitched together into a symphony of negativity, which I find exhausting to listen to. I feel the chill of the cold shoulder she gives us all, and take a step back.

Lily is a smaller version of Rose, but without the brains or cheekbones. Like my mother, she has never had a full-time job, and yet is still a part-time mum, who got pregnant when she was seventeen. My sister stinks of perfume and entitlement. I get an unpleasant waft of Poison – her favourite eau de toilette – which she's been drowning herself and our nostrils in since we were teenagers. That's not the only thing about her that has never changed. Lily still dresses in skimpy clothes from Topshop and I think she must sleep in her make-up, because I can't remember what her face looks like without it. She twists a strand of highlighted hair around her finger like a child, and I notice that her roots are showing. She is not a natural blonde. We are all dark in my family, including my wonderful niece.

Trixie is fifteen. Like most children, she was a walking, talking question mark for years, filled to overflowing with endless whys, whats, whens, wheres and hows. Finding the answers fast enough – or sometimes at all – was a constant challenge. These days, I think the bookish teenager she's become knows more than the rest of us put together. She looks like a miniature librarian, and I think that's a good thing, because I love librarians. Unlike her mother, or mine, Trixie is well read, very polite and exceptionally kind. A little precocious at times perhaps, but that's no bad thing if you ask me. Not that anyone does.

Like me, she dresses in a way that her mother does not approve of. As soon as Trixie was old enough to have a say in what she wore, she insisted on only wearing pink. She would literally cry and hold her breath if Lily tried to dress her in any other colour. The tantrums stopped years ago, but Trixie doesn't dress like a typical teenager. She wouldn't be caught dead in denim, or the cheap, trashy clothes her mother favours. I see that today's carefully curated outfit consists of a fluffy pink jumper with a white lace collar, a pink corduroy skirt, white tights, and shiny pink shoes. Even her glasses are pink, and she's carrying a small, vintage pink suitcase, which I imagine contains several books. Her shoulder-length hair is a mess of dark brown curls, and her reluctance to straighten it is yet another way she inadvertently irritates her mother. But all teenagers find ways to test their parents; it's a rite of passage.

Trixie instinctively knows how to warm the coldest of hearts, and her presence instantly defrosts the chilly atmosphere at Seaglass. She might be a little immature at times and lacking in street cred, but she's a kind and happy child, a rare breed of teenager. Her hopeful outlook on life seems to bring out the best in all of us.

'Nana!' she shrieks, with genuine excitement. 'Happy birthday!'

'It isn't my birthday until tomorrow, but thank you, darling girl,' Nana replies, beaming back at her namesake and great-granddaughter.

Hugs and hellos are exchanged between the women in the family, and I notice that we are all smiling at the same time. It's a rare sight to see, like an eclipse.

'I'm so happy to see you, Aunty Daisy,' Trixie says while the others dump their bags, take off their coats, and remove their wet shoes, tights and socks.

'I'm very happy to see you too,' I reply.

'Now, don't forget to punch in,' Nana says to everyone. 'All your cards are in their cubbyholes next to the old factory clock. You know I like to keep track of who is here and who isn't.'

Nancy sighs. 'You do know this isn't a normal thing to ask guests to do, don't you?'

Nana grins. 'My dear, I'd rather be dead than normal.'

Amused glances are exchanged, but the smiles all fade when my father steps into the hall. I watch him proceed with caution towards the late arrivals.

'Grandad!' Trixie says, smashing the silence. She hasn't inherited the family grudges yet, and rushes to hug him.

'Hello, pipsqueak!' he says. 'Gosh, you've grown!' It's been a long time since he saw her. Or any of us.

'Pipsqueak' used to be my dad's pet nickname for me when I was a little girl. My eldest sister Rose was his 'clever girl' and Lily was his 'princess'. It feels like I've been replaced somehow, as though he has transferred the affection he once felt for me to my niece, but I know it is ridiculous to be jealous of a child.

Dad can't seem to look at his ex-wife, but I catch her staring at the expensive tie around his neck as if it were a noose she'd like to tighten. Things were amicable enough between them in the first few years after my parents' divorce, but then something caused their remaining bond to break. They haven't been in the same room together since Rose's wedding, and even then, they sat at opposite ends of the table and didn't speak. My mother used to button up her resentment, but it has grown over the years, and no matter how much she tries to hide it, a little is always left on show. Life has sharpened her tongue and she is no longer afraid to use it.

'The prodigal father and son returns. You're looking well, Frank. How thoughtful of you to drag yourself away from the orchestra for your mother's birthday.'

And so it begins. We always lose when we try to play happy families.

I stare out at the causeway one last time before the sea swallows it up completely and we are cut off from the outside world. The cast of my family have all arrived, and once the tide is fully in, it will be eight hours until anyone will be able to leave.

# Four

*30 October 2004 – 6 p.m.*

Nana gathers us all together in the lounge – despite various protests – and the large room suddenly feels rather small. Without another word, we resume the seats we sat in when I was a child. I guess knowing your place in your family is like some sort of muscle memory, and not something you forget. It's so quiet now that I can hear the clocks ticking in the hallway. All eighty of them. And it already feels as though this is going to be a very long night.

'I know you all want to get unpacked and freshen up, and we have so much catching up to do,' Nana says with an ironic smile, 'but I found some old home movies that I wanted to share with you this weekend. I thought this one might help break the ice. Or perhaps just melt it a little? Rose, will you pop this in the player? You know I'm allergic to technology.'

Rose takes a battered-looking VHS tape from Nana's hands. I think the two women wink at each other, but maybe I imagined it. I can see that there is a whole row of old videos on the shelf behind them, which I'm quite certain I've never seen before. It used to be filled with books like all the other shelves in this room. Each of the VHS tapes has a white sticky label, and dates written in swirly hand-writing: 1975 to 1988.

When the TV set – which I suspect might be older than me – comes to life, the whole room stares at my mother, because it's her face on the screen and she's wearing a wedding dress. The footage must be over thirty years old. The picture is a little grainy and there's no sound, but she is breathtakingly beautiful. I watch, transfixed like the others, as a grandfather I never met walks her down a church aisle I've never seen, to stand side by side with my dad. He's wearing a flared suit and has 1970s hair. He looks so young and happy. They both do.

'This was originally filmed on my old Super 8,' Dad says, with a smile that is so unfamiliar he looks like a different man. 'I remember transferring it to VHS and thinking *that* would be the last advance in home entertainment. I suppose nothing lasts forever,' he says, leaning forward in his chair, and sounding whimsical. He glances at my mother, but she is too busy staring at herself on the screen to notice.

My parents, Frank and Nancy, met at university. She was in her first year, he was in his last. Their friends nicknamed them 'The Sinatras', and like their famous counterparts, they were doomed almost from the start. Frank and Nancy were both in the amateur dramatics society. My father arranged the music, and my mother arranged the rest of their lives by getting pregnant when she was nineteen. You'd never know it, but Rose is in this home movie too, disguised as a tiny bump and hidden by a cleverly designed wedding dress. Nancy never graduated. They got married as soon as they found out she was pregnant – because apparently that's what people did back then – and moved in with Nana here at Seaglass, until Dad had saved enough money for a place of their own. I think my parents thought they were happy for a while. She stole his joy and he stole her sorrow, and they balanced each other's emotional books that way for years. London dragged them away from the sea, music dragged him away from her, and by the time I arrived on the scene, they were strangers who just happened to be married.

'I found a whole box of home movies like this up in the attic. Family Christmases at Seaglass, birthdays, summer holidays . . . I haven't had time to watch them all yet, and thought it might be something nice for us to do together,' says Nana. 'The world we live in today is a little too careless with its memories. I hoped seeing ourselves as we were might remind us who we are.'

The wedding video doesn't last any more than three or four minutes – I guess film was expensive in those days, and people had to be a bit more picky about which moments of their lives they wanted to remember. It ends with a shot of my parents on the church steps. I recognize Nana in the background, but none of the other smiling faces. The friends throwing confetti seem to have morphed into strangers too over the years, fading from their lives like their love. The screen stops on a freeze-frame of my parents smiling at each other over thirty years ago. I look at them now and wonder where the love went.

'I'm going to go and unpack,' Dad announces, standing up.

'Where? There aren't enough bedrooms,' Nancy says, without looking at him.

'I'll sleep in the music room down here.'

'Good.'

He leaves the lounge and none of us know what to say. My father has always held his feelings hostage. His inability – or unwillingness – to express himself seemed to make my mother voice her own feelings on any subject twice as loud and twice as often. It was as though Dad could only communicate through his music, which is why the soundtrack of our childhood was filled with endless angry and melancholy compositions being played on his piano.

'You looked beautiful in the video, Nancy,' says Trixie. Nobody would dare call my mother grandma. We weren't even allowed to call her mum. Only Nancy. My niece meant it as a compliment, but the rest of us know my mother well enough to realize that the past tense will be taken as an insult.

'I think I might get a little fresh air. Check on my garden,' Nancy says.

None of us mention that it is technically Nana's garden, or that the sky has already swallowed the last of the sun. It's dark outside and has been for some time. But Nancy is like a black-and-white movie actress, making a dramatic exit from a scene she never wanted to star in as she leaves the room. The rest of us sit in an awkward silence we are well acquainted with for a little while longer. Rose looks the most uncomfortable. She can sense our parents are gearing up for a fight. She was old enough when they got divorced to remember how bad things can get between them. Pride rewrites the story of who left who in my parents' heads, and blame is something they've always refused to share. It isn't long before we all quietly retreat to our own corners of Seaglass. Not because the show is over, but because we fear it is about to begin, and maybe we all need to rehearse our lines.

I linger on the landing upstairs, peering out of the window that overlooks the back of the house, and the vast Atlantic Ocean. I see my mother walking between patches of moonlight and shadow. Nancy doesn't have much of a garden in London, so she treats Nana's as though it were her own. Her obsession with plants and flowers started when she was first living here at Seaglass, when she was pregnant with Rose. It was her choice to live with her new mother-in-law while Dad was away finishing his university degree. Nancy never talks about her own family. We knew she had one, but not much else about them. I've never met my grandparents on my mother's side, none of us did; she wouldn't even tell us their names. By all accounts, Nana was happy for my mother to stay here, but she was too busy creating children's books to have time for company, or gardening, so that became Nancy's hobby. Transforming the unloved land at the back of the house became a bit of an obsession over the years that followed. Sometimes I think it's the garden she still comes to see, not Nana.

Dad gave Nancy a copy of *The Observer's Book of Wild Flowers* when she was pregnant with Rose, and I suspect that might have inspired the names my mother gave us. It's a tiny old green book which she still carries around wherever she goes, like a little Bible. We were never allowed to help Nancy when she disappeared outside for hours; the garden was *her* space. Rose said it was because our mother was secretly growing poisonous plants. Lily thought it might be because she was making marijuana. I always thought she just wanted to be left alone.

Nancy was very good at growing most things except for children. We never grew fast enough, or tall enough, or pretty enough in her opinion. So she planted seeds of fear as well as doubt all around this house and throughout our childhoods, little saplings rising up through the floorboards, creeping in through the cracks, to remind us what a disappointing crop we were.

The world outside the window is cold and dark now. The sea looks black at night, like a liquid sky reflecting the moon and stars. I can still make out the shape of my mother, alone in her garden, even though it must be freezing out there. She appears to be picking something, small flowers perhaps – I can't tell from here. She looks up at the window then, as though sensing she is being watched, and I hurry back to my bedroom, unsure why I am so afraid of being seen.

# Five

*30 October 2004 – 8 p.m.*

Once the bags and grudges are unpacked, the whole family settles into a familiar rhythm. Whenever I see my sisters, no matter how long it has been or how old they get, we always seem to regress to the versions of ourselves we were as children. I suspect everybody time travels when reunited with their family. We think we are old when we are still young, and we think we are still young when we have grown old. None of us are acting the way we normally do. Even my parents are doing their best version of best behaviour. Nobody wants to upset Nana on her birthday.

Trixie and I are playing Scrabble alone in the lounge when Lily comes to fetch us for dinner.

'Stop that and let's eat,' my sister barks from the doorway.

'But we haven't finished playing,' Trixie argues.

Lily crosses the room in three strides, then tips all the letters off the board and onto the floor.

'You have now,' she says, before briefly checking her reflection in the mirror above the fireplace, then leaving the room.

I spend a lot of time with Trixie. Being a parent did not come naturally to my sister, but becoming an aunt was one of the best things that ever happened to me. Lily was eighteen when her daughter was born. She likes gadgets and gizmos more than babies, and soon discovered that motherhood did not come with a manual, and children don't come with an off switch. As a result, I spend a couple of nights at their house every week, looking after Trixie to give Lily a break. Though I'm not sure what from, and she never thanks me for my time. Lily and I don't really talk at all anymore. My sister still thinks of me as a child. She thinks I never grew up. I find that ironic given the way *she* behaves. Some people can't see things how they are; they only see how they used to be. I don't mind; I love spending time with my niece, and I find it rewarding. Watching her grow up to become such a wonderful human being has brought me more joy than anything else I have known.

Trixie and I find the rest of the family already in the large eclectic kitchen at the back of the house. The cupboards are all pale blue, and some of the white wall tiles have been hand-painted with animals or flowers. Nana always liked to illustrate her life as well as her children's books. The entire back wall is a giant chalkboard, which she scribbles ideas and sketches on. Sometimes, if the thoughts inside her own head are not forthcoming, she'll scribble an inspirational quote from a dead author on there. The dead often seem to know more about living than those still alive. Today, all I can spot is a recipe for chocolate brownies, a poem about falling, and an intricately drawn chalk bird. It looks like a robin. Nana has decorated the room for Halloween just like she does every year. There are black and orange paper chains hanging from the ceiling, a lot of candles and pumpkins, and what looks like a witch's broom in the corner, but I think that might be here all the time.

The space doubles as a dining room, with a long, sturdy wooden table. It's made of a single enormous piece of beech that is over five hundred years old and a real thing of beauty. The table is surrounded by eight different chairs, which Nana chose for each of us. My mother's is white, tall and thin. It looks good, but makes people feel uncomfortable, not unlike the woman it was chosen for. Dad's chair is older, wider, rounder, and black. Rose's is elegant and red, while Lily's is green and, I think, looks rather unpleasant. Mine is quite plain at first glance, but has daisies painted on the seat. Nana's is pink and purple – her favourite colours – while Trixie's seat is the newest, and smallest, and covered in silver stars. There is one spare chair, painted sky blue with little white clouds. Nana said she painted the chairs so that we would all know that we always had a home here. My mother said she did it so that we would all remember our place.

Dinner is a feast – roast chicken, potatoes, Yorkshire puddings and lashings of gravy. But the gravy is hot chocolate sauce, because Nana thinks everything should be a sweet treat at Halloween. The carrots are coated in sugar, the puddings are really marshmallows, there are Smarties mixed in with the peas, and popping candy on the potatoes. What looks like bread sauce is actually melted vanilla ice cream. The food is both surprising and surprisingly good.

The pumpkins on the table are all different sizes, and each one has a scary hand-carved face. There are also pine cones, seashells and sweets scattered on the tablecloth. With the whole room bathed in candlelight, it looks beautiful but fun, just like our host. I feel guilty about my lack of appetite, but everyone else tucks in, until the last of the crispy roast popping potatoes have been eaten. Even Lily – who complains about everything and has never cooked anyone in this family a meal

– seems satisfied. If my sister ever did invite us all for food, I suspect we'd be served a Pot Noodle for dinner and a Pop-Tart for dessert.

There are a lot of empty bottles as well as plates by the end of the bizarre banquet, and my divorced parents have definitely drunk more than their fair share of alcohol. My mother has always tried to dissolve my father's words with wine. At one end of the table, Nancy looks like she can barely keep her eyes open, while at the other end, Dad is struggling to take *his* eyes off her. He treated her so badly when they were married, but I believe he loves her now just as much as he did then, possibly more. He collected regrets while she gathered resentment. Sometimes people don't know they're in love until they're not.

The calm and quiet aura of Seaglass has been substituted with loud laughter, and the sort of repetitive storytelling that always occurs when tongues have been lubricated with nostalgia and wine. We've heard one another's stories too many times before, but for the sake of getting along, we act as though we haven't. The wall of clocks in the hall start to chime 9 p.m. All eighty of them – including one grandfather and five cuckoo clocks – so it's impossible to hear a thing at the top of the hour. As soon as the din stops, Trixie speaks.

'Nana, why did you only put Aunty Daisy in your books? Why not Mum, or Aunty Rose?'

Children always ask the most awkward of questions, but Trixie is old enough to know better. I feel as though the whole table turns to stare at me. My sisters and I haven't really spoken for years because of what happened. Rose has refused to see me or speak to me at all for a very long time, but now isn't the right moment to drag up the past. This is supposed to be a celebration. Unwanted thoughts clot inside my head and I can't shift them. Thankfully, Nana answers so that I don't have to.

'Well, the story isn't really about Aunty Daisy, I just borrowed her name is all. Why? Would you like me to use your name in a book one day?'

'No thank you, Nana. I'm too old to be in a children's book. I'd rather be in a murder mystery. I wish you wrote those instead.'

Nana was an artist for years, illustrating other people's books for very modest sums of money in return. The year my heart defect was diagnosed, a well-known author was rude about her drawings. Nana was deeply hurt by the resulting upset and unkindness, and refused to work with the author ever again. Taking the moral high ground can be an expensive route, and private hospitals and second opinions do not come cheap. So Nana wrote her own children's novel for the first time, filled with poems written while she was sitting in waiting rooms worrying about me. She illustrated the book with her own paintings, wrote her own words, got herself an agent, and found her own publisher, all to make a point. But after the success of *Daisy Darker's Little Secret*, there was no going back.

'I think most murder mysteries are overrated,' Nana says. 'There are much cleverer ways to end a person than killing them.'

Her words seem to make everyone around the table uncomfortable, except Rose, who has always been more at ease with death than the rest of us. Perhaps because she sees so much of it. Rose often works for free, which might be why her veterinary practice is in a spot of financial bother. She saves and rehomes as many animals as she can, working day and night to do so, but even she can't save them all. It's crazy and so very sad how many broken animals get dumped on a vet's doorstep – pets that were once loved, now past their best-before dates. Rose even persuaded Nana to adopt a couple of abandoned hens years ago, and Amy and Ada have lived in a brightly painted coop at the back of Seaglass ever since.

'There are also clever ways to kill someone without getting caught,' Rose says, taking such a tiny sip of red wine, the effort required to lift the glass to her lips seems barely worth it.

'Like how?' Trixie asks.

Rose – who has never had a child-friendly filter – stares at our niece. 'Well, my first choice would be insulin, injected between the toes, where people are unlikely to look. I have plenty of it at the practice and it's simple enough to explain missing batches away – things get lost or broken all the time. It would be almost too easy and I doubt I'd get caught.'

Trixie stares at her. We all do.

'I'd poison them with plants,' says Nancy. 'A bit of spotted hemlock or deadly nightshade. Morphine or cyanide if I was feeling fancy and had the time, both of which are derived from flowers and trees. It's easy enough to find at least one deadly plant in most gardens, if you know what to look for. And it takes less than a second to slip a little something into some-one's drink.'

Dad shakes his head. I sometimes think there is nothing my parents wouldn't disagree on. 'I'd have thought a good sharp blow to the skull would be a simpler way to do someone in,' he says.

'Or push them down the stairs,' Lily suggests with a wicked smile.

'Or over a cliff,' I add.

Nana beams and claps her hands together. 'What a murderous family we are!'

# Six

'Well, I think that's enough talk of murder for young ears for one evening,' says Lily. 'It's way past your bedtime, young lady—'

Trixie stares at her. 'Mum, I'm *fifteen*.'

'Then start dressing like a fifteen-year-old instead of a toddler with a candyfloss crush. Go on. The adults in the family need to relax.'

'You mean you want to smoke?'

'Say goodnight to everyone, then up to bed,' Lily snaps. 'You can read one of your boring books, that should send you to sleep.'

Lily has never understood the pleasure of reading. To be fair, I've never understood the pleasure of Lily. She is the kind of person who only ever borrowed library books in order to rip out their last pages then give them back.

'We haven't even had dessert,' says Trixie.

'If my waist was as big as yours, I wouldn't even *say* the word dessert. Don't you ever wonder why boys don't like you?' Trixie stares at her mother from behind her pink glasses. I can see the tears starting to form in her eyes, but she blinks them back with an air of defiance I'm rather proud of. She walks around the table, kissing each of us goodnight. It still seems miraculous to me that someone as cold and uncaring as my sister could produce such a kind and sweet child. As soon as Trixie has left the room, Lily lights a cigarette. She seems oblivious to the way we are all staring at her.

'Why couldn't I have been blessed with a *normal*, sulky teenager? No boyfriends, not one. And her female friends dress like nuns and speak like nerds. I wanted a cheerleader but all she talks about is charity. It's like living with Saffy from *Ab Fab*, but *worse*, boring me to tears with her books and opinions about global bloody warming all day long.'

'You should be grateful she isn't a handful like you were at that age,' says Nana.

'Can I quickly use your landline?' Lily asks, ignoring the comment. 'There's no signal on my phone here.'

Lily – who loved gadgets as a child, and spent a great deal of the 1980s having a close personal relationship with Pac-Man and her Atari – is the only person in our family to have a mobile in 2004. Dad had one the size of a brick when we were little, but it cost a small fortune to use so was mainly just for show. Lily picks up her dark blue little Nokia from the table, and we all stare at it as though it were a piece of rock from the moon.

'Sorry, Lily. My phone doesn't work anymore,' says Nana, clearing some of the plates.

'Why not?'

'I stopped paying the bill.'

'Why would you do that?'

'People kept calling me. I didn't like the constant interruptions.'

Lily looks furious. But I'm sure her tongue must be covered in bite marks, because she doesn't say another word about it.

Instead, she starts playing a game called *Snake* on her otherwise redundant mobile. I find myself staring at it over her shoulder, mesmerized.

Nana is as keen as always to show an interest in our lives, and hear all our news. Stories change a little each time they are told, even when they are as rehearsed as ours. Like children, they grow and evolve into something new, something with ideas of their own. Stories are also lies, and we're all storytellers in this family. Nana starts the routine questions with her son.

I don't wish to sound unkind, but my father's favourite subject is always himself. Dad is also rather fond of regurgitating things he's heard on BBC Radio 4. He is an intellectually promiscuous man who gorges on the thoughts of others, then shares them, dressed up as his own. Second-hand ideas sold as new. He seasons his sentences with the odd long word because he doesn't want people to hear his lack of knowledge or education. The piano was his first and only true love, and music is the only subject he has ever really studied. Tonight, as always, he talks with passion and pride about his orchestra: the cities they have visited recently, and the musicians he has worked with. My mother rolls her eyes and makes light work of sweeping up all the names he keeps dropping – insisting that she's never heard of any of them.

'How is your veterinary practice, Rose?' Nana asks, moving the conversation along like a verbal pass the parcel party game.

'Still standing,' Rose replies.

'It's impressive that you've built such a successful business from scratch at your age, but how are *you* holding up?'

'I'm holding up fine on the rare occasions I'm not falling down.'

Rose has always been able to keep her cool when it comes to quick-fire questions.

'And what about you, Lily?' Nana asks. 'Any luck finding work?'

My other sister has been unemployed since forever. She survives on Jobseeker's Allowance (despite never seeking a job), child benefit, and handouts from Nana. Lily takes another cigarette from her pocket, pops it between her pink lips and lights it using one of the candles on the table. She stopped smoking for a while when she was pregnant, allegedly, but has since given up giving up. She takes a long drag, then exhales smoke and boredom over the rest of us.

'It's really tough to find work at the moment,' she says, using a wine glass as an ashtray.

'It's always harder to find things if you don't look,' Dad mutters, and everyone stares at him, including Lily.

'Excuse me,' she says, getting up from the table and leaving the room, presumably to check on Trixie, but also to have a little sulk upstairs, no doubt. My sister has always had chips on both shoulders and throws more tantrums than a toddler. I'm expecting Nana to ask whether I am still volunteering at the care home – it might not be exciting *or* earn money, but being kind has its own rewards, and I am proud of what I do. But my mother launches a new attack on my father before the conversation turns to me.

'Why must you always be so hard on Lily? Bringing up children on your own isn't easy, I should know,' Nancy says, as soon as her favourite daughter is out of earshot. If looks could kill, my father would have been in the morgue some time ago. I've often wondered why my mother loves Lily the most. Perhaps because she sees herself when she looks at her – like a walking, talking mirror of youth, showing her who she used to be.

Dad tries not to take the bait, but bad habits are hard to break when you've got over thirty years of practice.

'She's not a *child* anymore, Nancy. She has a daughter of her own, though it's no wonder she forgets so often when you have taken on the role of being mother to them both.'

'Well, someone has to help our children. If we'd all gone off gallivanting around the world to follow our dreams, then—'

'Help her? You smother her, always have. It's no wonder she never learned to stand on her own two feet. She is what she is because of you.'

'And what is that exactly?'

'An entitled, spoilt, selfish, lazy, brain-dead bore of a woman, who still behaves like a child because you never stopped treating her like one. She cares more about her looks than her own daughter. And she's still completely irresponsible with money that isn't her own, because she has never lifted one of her manicured fingers to earn any.'

Lily appears in the doorway.

She clearly heard every word.

Nobody knows what to say.

The silence that follows isn't just awkward, it's painful. We all watch as Lily walks past the kitchen table towards the fridge, then opens the door as though searching inside for answers. When she can't find any, she opens another bottle of white wine instead.

All families experience conflict. Whether it is between husbands and wives, parents and children, or siblings, it's as normal as day turning into night. But unresolved conflict spreads like a cancer in human relationships, and sometimes there's no cure. Despite everything, I still have some happy memories of us all together, tucked away inside the folds and creases that forced us apart. We weren't always the us we are now. It's Nana who I feel most sorry for. She's made such an effort to create a lovely evening for everyone and, as usual, my family has found a way to ruin it. 'Who would like some early birthday cake and champagne?' she asks, with a weak smile.

'Me!' I say, raising my hand and trying to defuse the tension, for now at least.

I notice that Rose has barely said a word all night. She speaks when spoken to, but only offers short, succinct replies. I might have been the baby of the family once upon a time, but I find myself frequently worrying about my eldest sister. It's a special kind of love that holds families together, even dysfunctional ones. Our love is like an intrinsically woven net made from a million memories and shared moments. The knots in the net are tight, but there are holes, just big enough for all of us to slip through if caught the wrong way.

The weather outside has worsened, providing a soundtrack of rain tapping at the windows, and the candles sometimes flicker when the wind howls. My mother and Rose help to clear the table, before Nana reveals one of her famous home-made chocolate cakes, and takes her favourite champagne saucers out of the cupboard. They look like they're from the 1920s, because they are. Dad does the honours, expertly opening the bottle as though he does it every day, and Nana stands up, holding her glass and looking like she might make one of her speeches.

'I just want to thank you all for coming to Seaglass to help celebrate my birthday tomorrow. It means the world to me to have the whole family here together, and you've made an old woman very happy. Eighty is going to be a big birthday for me, and if the palm reader in Land's End was right, it might be my last! You are the only people I wanted to spend it with. Here's to the Darker family,' she says, raising her glass.

'The Darker family,' everyone repeats, almost in unison, before Nana continues.

'I also want to thank Amy and Ada, for providing us with a delicious dinner tonight.'

'Who the hell are Amy and Ada? I thought she cooked the meal,' Dad whispers to Rose, taking another sip of champagne.

'The chickens,' Rose whispers back. 'She named them after Amy Johnson and Ada Lovelace, two of her favourite inspirational women, remember?'

Frank almost chokes as Nana continues.

'Amy sadly passed away on Monday. And Ada died three days later. An act of widowhood if ever I saw it. That little chicken died of a broken heart . . .' I feel as though the whole room stares in my direction again when she says that, and glance down at my hands.

'Is it safe to eat a ten-year-old chicken?' my mother asks, looking nauseous.

'I suspect so,' Nana replies. 'Safer than jumping off a cliff at any rate. On a related subject, I don't want to be the richest woman in the graveyard, and I'm sure you all want to know what happens when I die. I'd like us to enjoy the time we have left together this weekend. So, rather than keep you in suspense any longer, I have decided to share my will with you tonight.'

 # Seven

*30 October 9:45 p.m.*
*less than nine hours until low tide*

If Nana didn't have everyone's attention before, she does now. Dad leans in, my mother sits up, Lily puts down her phone, and Rose stops making an origami bird with her napkin.

'This is my final will and testament,' Nana says, putting an envelope on the table, and staring at each of our faces as though committing them to memory. 'My solicitor witnessed me signing it earlier today and has a copy. I promise that I've thought about all of this, and all of you, very carefully, and I'm sure it's for the best. Before I begin, I'll remind you what I wrote at the start of my favourite book: The future is a promise we can still choose whether to keep. The past is a promise we've already broken. I meant those words, and I believe that the present is my only chance to protect this family's future.'

She turns to face my dad. 'Frank . . .'

'Yes, Mother?'

'I have left you my clocks, all eighty of them, in the hope that you might use the time you have left more wisely.'

His mouth falls open, but Nana continues without waiting for any words to spill out of it.

'Nancy, my beloved daughter-in-law, you gave me three

beautiful granddaughters, for which I will always be grateful. I am leaving you my drinks trolley. Like you, it's now an antique but still good for holding liquor.' My mother's face is a picture I wish someone would paint, a beautiful mix of shock and outrage. My sisters are both grinning like the naughty school girls they used to be until Nana turns to them. 'Rose, I am leaving you my unpublished artwork and brushes, in the hope that you might paint a happier future for yourself. Lily, when I die, all the mirrors in this house will belong to you, in the hope that you might see what you've become.'

Nobody is smiling now, including me. I'm terrified of what Nana might say next.

'Daisy is the only person in this family who never asked me for a penny,' she says, smiling in my direction. 'I plan to leave a sizeable sum to her favourite charities.'

'Thank you,' I say, and Lily pulls a face.

I am grateful, really I am, but I confess that I always secretly hoped that Seaglass might be mine one day. I don't think anyone in this family loves this place the way that I do. Nana takes a sip of her champagne before carrying on.

'My literary estate will continue to make donations to my own favourite charities, as long as there are sufficient funds for it to do so. I will be leaving Seaglass in my great-granddaughter's precious hands. I hope we can all agree that Trixie is the future of this family. My home will be held in trust for her alone, until she is older, along with any other royalties and future payments from publishers—'

'Hang on a minute,' interrupts Lily, lighting yet another cigarette. She takes a drag, then exhales a cloud of smoke. 'You're basically going to leave *everything* to my daughter, a *child*, and *nothing* to me? You've finally lost your remaining marbles.'

Rose smiles at the outburst. Unlike the rest of the family, she seems completely indifferent and unoffended.

Nana sighs. 'Not *everything*, Lily, and please stop smoking in my home. Before those tiny cogs in your small mind start trying to turn, the will prevents you from taking a penny of what will one day be Trixie's. Besides, I'm not dead yet. You need to learn to make your own way in life, the world doesn't owe you anything, and neither do I. But . . . it may or may not please you all to learn that I have started working on one final book.'

'You haven't written anything new for years,' says Dad.

'Well, I didn't have anything left to say. But now I do have one last story I'd like to tell. It's about a dysfunctional family, not unlike ours.'

'What?' says Nancy.

'You've written a book about us?' Lily asks.

'I've started sketching out a few ideas,' is all Nana says.

Dad slams his glass down on the table without meaning to. 'Well, I can't imagine *that* selling many copies. What I want to know is *why*? Why invite us here, if all along you planned to leave us out of the will? I'm your son. Your only child—'

'Please keep your voice down,' interrupts Lily. 'Trixie is already asleep upstairs.'

'Because the future of this family, and what I will leave behind when I am gone, has been on my mind for a long time,' Nana replies.

I think she's about to say something else, but she doesn't.

Instead she is silent and wide-eyed – like the rest of us – when we hear the melancholy sound of the wind chimes outside and the front door slam at the other end of the house.

It's almost ten o'clock.

The tide is in.

I can tell we're all thinking the same thing. It's not possible to walk across the causeway at this time of night, and nobody else was expected to join us at Seaglass this evening.

'Maybe Trixie woke up?' whispers my mother.

'And went for a walk outside in the rain? I don't think so,' Lily replies.

I think we all know that it isn't my niece we can hear out in the hall.

Every member of my family stares at the closed kitchen door in horror, as the sound of heavy footsteps coming down the hallway gets closer. There is a collective holding of breath when the door handle slowly starts to turn.

# Eight

*30 October 10 p.m.*
*eight hours until low tide*

Dad leans back in his chair, Nancy gasps, and Lily swears as the door bursts open. The candles on the table flicker, casting an eerie pattern over all the faces sitting around it, and only Rose keeps her wits on a tight leash as a man appears in the doorway. He is backlit from the light in the hall, and it takes a few seconds for me to recognize the shape of who is casting a new shadow over the evening.

Conor steps into the kitchen. The man I have secretly loved since he was a boy has been a stranger for too long. I've spent a lot of my life in love's waiting room, not being noticed by those I want to see me. Other people seem to find it all so easy – Lily has never had any problems attracting attention from the opposite sex – but I've always been a little awkward in that way. I never know what to say or do when I like someone, so I tend to say and do nothing at all. Still, nobody here would have approved of me having a relationship with Conor. Not then, not now, not ever. I'm about to say something, I think we all are, but Nana beats us to it.

'Conor, welcome. I didn't know whether you'd come.'

'You invited him?' asks my mother.

'Conor might not be a Darker, but he is part of this family,' says Nana.

'That depends on your point of view,' says Dad, staring down at the table.

Conor ignores the comment. 'I tried to call, to let you know that I was running late – I got stuck at work – but there seems to be a problem with your phone.'

'There is. It kept ringing, so she had it cut off,' Lily says, taking another large gulp of champagne, as though it were lemonade.

'Well, I wanted to be here,' he says.

Nana's face is lit up like a Christmas tree. She always adored Conor, just like all the women in this family have at one point or another. The man I see now in the doorway – looking a little lost – reminds me of the boy he was when we first met. There are some memories we can never outrun.

It was a hot summer's day when we all first saw nine-year-old Conor Kennedy with his bucket and spade. He was sitting alone, on what we had come to think of as our beach, just opposite Seaglass. It was as though he were trespassing. Blacksand Bay is a public part of the coastline, but nobody ever visits this particular stretch of black sand. It is too difficult to get to without scrambling down the cliff, and there are plenty of signs about the dangers of swimming in the sea. I don't believe in love at first sight, but *something* at first sight happened to the women in my family that day. All of us.

I was four, Lily was eight, and Rose was nine. We lived in a world of our own during those childhood summers at Seaglass, while my father was busy touring the real one. Nancy would drop us off in July and reappear in August, leaving us alone with Nana for the weeks in between. On the rare occasions we dared to ask where our mother went when she left us, the answer was always the same: somewhere else. My sisters missed her more than I did. But then I've always loved Seaglass, it's the only place that has ever really felt like home.

Strangers were a strange sight in Blacksand Bay. We all stopped and stared that day, including Nana, at this perfect-looking boy sitting on our beach. So out of place, he seemed to fit right in. Lily was the first one to speak, as usual. It wasn't exactly Shakespeare, but it was the question we all wanted to ask.

'Who are you?'

The boy glanced in our direction, looking unimpressed. 'What's it to you?'

Lily's hands formed fists and found their way to her hips. '*We* live here.'

Conor looked the same age as Rose but acted a lot older. He stood up, dusted the sand from his hands and copied Lily's stance. 'Yeah? Well, I live here too.'

He took a yo-yo from his pocket and started playing with it, without taking his eyes off us.

Things get a little hazy after that. Sometimes our memories reframe themselves.

Nana bridged the gap between herself and the boy, leaving us behind. She'd seen the bruises on his neck, the shadows beneath his eyes – the details only age teaches you to translate. She asked him where he lived, and he explained that he and his father had just moved into a cottage along the coast.

'What about your mother?' she asked.

Nine-year-old Conor stared at her, and the yo-yo went down and up several more times while he decided how to answer. 'I don't have a mother anymore.'

'Our parents are away all the time too,' said Lily, misunder-standing.

Nana invited Conor to come across the causeway and have lemonade with us, she wanted to call his father to tell him that the boy was safe. Things didn't used to be how they are now; children didn't know they might need to worry about an adult offering them a cold drink on a hot day. Conor said yes. Sometimes I wish he'd said no. I remember him walking across the causeway with us for the first time, still yo-yoing as though his little life depended on it. He was officially the most fascin-ating creature four-year-old me had ever seen.

Our new neighbour lived a mile away, but that isn't far at all when you are a child and in search of company. Conor didn't have any other children to play with, and sisters are rarely satisfied to be with one another when someone more interesting comes along. He became a permanent fixture in our lives, and I think I might have fallen in love with him that day. I liked the taste of his name in my mouth and on my tongue, so much so I would whisper it to myself on the days he didn't come to visit. It felt like snacking between meals. That chance meeting with Conor and his yo-yo changed the shape of my family forever.

We spend our youth building sandcastles of ambition, then watch as life blows sands of doubt over our carefully crafted turrets of wishes and dreams, until we can no longer see them at all. We learn to settle instead for flattened lives, residing inside prisons of compromise. A little relieved that the windows of the world we settled for are too small to see out of, so we don't have to stare at the castle-shaped fantasies of who we might have been.

There are two kinds of attractive people in the world: those who know that's what they are, and those who don't. Conor Kennedy knows it. His good looks gifted him an unshakeable confidence in life, the kind very few mere mortals experience, and fear of failure is a stranger he has yet to meet. He wears his stubble like a mask, always dresses in scruffy jeans teamed with smart shirts, and his blonde hair is long enough to hide his blue eyes when it falls over his face. He doesn't look like a journalist, but that's what he is. Thirty-something going on fifty, and addicted to his job.

Tonight, Conor's white cotton shirt is clinging to his chest, and a small puddle of water has already formed around his feet where he stands in the kitchen doorway. He looks like he might have swum from the mainland, but that's not possible – we all learned a long time ago that the riptides between here and there can be deadly.

My dad – seemingly sober all of a sudden – asks the question we all want to know the answer to.

'How the devil did you get here?'

'By boat,' Conor says.

'By boat?'

'Yes, they're a fantastic invention that you can use to sail across the sea,' Nana says. 'I get my post and groceries delivered by boat once a week now too. So I don't have to cycle into town, or worry about the tide—'

'I expect they don't deliver after ten p.m. in a storm though, do they?' interrupts Dad, narrowing his eyes at Conor, like a comedy villain with a sense of humour bypass. 'What kind of boat?'

'A boat with oars, Mr Darker.'

'You came here in a rowing boat, in a storm, in the dark?'

'Yes. I'm sorry to arrive so late. I got held up at work; there was a murder.' This would sound strange coming from most people, but Conor is a crime correspondent for the BBC. His press pass is still dangling from the lanyard around his neck. 'I managed to borrow a small boat from an old friend – Harry from the fish shop. The storm isn't as bad as it sounds, and it isn't as though I haven't rowed a boat across Blacksand Bay before. I feel as though I might be interrupting, and I don't want to be a party pooper, but I wonder if I might head upstairs and change into some dry clothes?'

'Of course,' says Nana. 'It isn't my birthday until tomorrow, I'm just glad you're here in time for that. Before you disappear . . . I found something belonging to you.' She shuffles over to the sideboard, opens a cupboard door and takes out an old Polaroid camera. It looks like a vintage item from a museum, but I remember when it was brand new. 'Would you mind just taking a quick snap of the family? Who knows when we'll all be together again?'

Conor takes the camera from her, we all – reluctantly – lean in, and he takes a photo, before passing the white square to Nana. She attaches it to her retro fridge with a strawberry-shaped magnet before the picture has even developed.

'Thank you, Conor. I suppose Daisy's room would be best for you to sleep in. It's the only one with a spare bed. Unless . . . that would be too—'

'I don't mind,' I say, a little too quickly. The thought of sleeping in the same room with Conor starts a little fantasy inside my head, one which I've had several times before. Lily pulls a face but I ignore her.

'That's fine with me. We're all grown-ups. It's just somewhere to sleep,' Conor says, and my fantasy deflates. You can't make someone fall in love with you. I don't know much, but I do know that. The rest of my family exchange glances which I choose to ignore.

'Do you remember where it is?' Nana asks.

'I'm sure Conor remembers everything about Daisy,' says Rose.

It's one of the few times she has spoken tonight, and her words feel like a slap.

I excuse myself and leave the kitchen. Conor does the same and follows. I don't mind sharing a room if he doesn't; he used to be like a brother to me. I don't say a word as we walk through the hallway and past the cupboard under the stairs. I was locked in there once as a child and I give it a wide berth.

The staircase itself is a rather grand affair, and unique in that the entire wall next to it is covered with a hand-painted family tree. Time-warped branches stretch across cracked plaster from the floor to the ceiling. Nana did it – of course – illustrating our lives as though they were the same as her books; another story to be told. We're all on there, dangling on fragile-looking twigs. She has painted us in the same style that she illustrates her children's books, using a pot of black ink and various sized dip pens and brushes. Sometimes – if she is in 'the mood' – she will draw the outline of her charac-ters with a reed from the garden. Then, when the ink is dry, she colours them in with palettes of watercolour paints. She likes to portray people, places and things the way *she* sees them, which rarely matches the view of those being drawn. Her characters are all as flawed as the world they live in, but children *love* them, maybe because of the honesty that shines through what they get to see and read. Other children's authors seem to sugar-coat their books in an attempt to make the world less scary. But Nana always told it like it was, and her readers loved her for it.

Miniature faces of the Darker family past and present, painted inside the tree's giant black leaves, permanently look down on the mistakes we've all made. It makes me feel an overwhelming sadness; the idea of this one day being a place I can no longer visit whenever I want to. We all have roots in this family and in this house. It isn't something I think any of us can just walk away from.

Conor and I head up the creaking steps to the first floor, and only when we reach my old childhood bedroom, and the door is firmly closed behind us, do I whisper:

'Why did you have to come here?'

There is an ivory-coloured metal daybed against the back wall of my old bedroom. Nana bought it second-hand, for all the times when she slept in here, too scared to leave me alone in case my heart stopped in the night. Sometimes I would wake up and see her staring at me in the darkness, whispering words I couldn't quite hear. Conor puts his bag on the daybed as though marking his territory, then starts to change out of his wet clothes, with his back to me. I sit down on the very edge of my bed and turn away. Maybe sharing a room wasn't such a great idea after all. It takes a lot of courage for me to ask the question.

'Could we maybe just talk about what happened?'

But Conor doesn't answer. It's been like this between us for a long time. No matter how sorry I am, he can't seem to move on, just like my sisters. I know he'd probably rather never see me again, but I'm glad that he chose to come anyway this weekend, for Nana. What happened certainly wasn't her fault.

The rest of the evening is a blur at best. I'm exhausted, but I never seem to be able to sleep these days, and the atmosphere in the house feels even more polluted than before. We heard the others decide to turn in and call it a night too, almost as soon as we left the kitchen. Nana's room is the largest bedroom at the back of the house, and she whispers goodnight as she passes my door. Lily and Trixie take the room that Lily and Rose used to share as children. My mother is the last person to come up. I only know it's her because I hear her talking to someone in a hushed voice at the top of the stairs.

'We'll get out of here as soon as it's light. I knew the old witch wouldn't leave us a penny.'

I listen at the door as she scuttles along the hall to the guest bedroom she used to share with my father. Rose stays downstairs, choosing to sleep on a sofa in the library. Dad also said he would rather stay downstairs, sealing himself in the music room that was his sanctuary as a child. He always needs to disappear inside his music when the real world gets too loud. But Seaglass is no longer noisy, it has returned to its own variety of silence.

I can hear the sea outside my window, and Conor's slow and steady breathing. I can tell he's still awake. I keep completely quiet when I hear him get up and tiptoe across the room, and I listen as he opens his laptop on the desk in the corner. There's no internet here, but it seems that Conor still can't resist doing a little work this weekend. He's become a workaholic since getting the crime correspondent job at the BBC. Perhaps because when you work that hard for something, sometimes you live in constant fear of losing it.

He creeps out of the room – presumably to use the bathroom down the hall – and while he is gone, I get up, cross the threadbare carpet to his side of the bedroom, and stare at the laptop screen. What I see is nothing to do with work, it looks more like a poem. Which is odd, because Conor has never been one to dabble with fiction or anything creative, he is a man who only likes to deal in facts. Or at least he was.

I hear footsteps in the hallway, creaking floorboards telling tales on anyone out of bed, and know I have to hurry. In a childish attempt to get Conor's attention and make things less awkward between us, I type a Halloween-inspired message with my index finger. I can't type properly and am dreadful with modern technology, but I smile to myself as the letters appear on the screen.

*Boo!*

Then I return to my side of the room, watch and wait. Conor stares at the word when he returns, then spins around, frowning in my direction. I wish he'd say something, *anything*, but as usual, he doesn't. Conor stopped speaking to me around the same time as Rose, and nothing I say or do seems to change things. Sometimes the way he stares so hard at me seems to physically hurt. I'm like a word he can't read, or a puzzle he can't solve, just like the Rubik's cube he couldn't work out as a kid, no matter which way he tries to twist me. Conor lies back down on the daybed and faces the wall. I turn my back on the disappointment I feel, wondering why he still can't see me for who I am now, or talk about what happened then. Nobody can run away from their own shadows, but he's always been determined to try.

It's cold in this part of the house, and I shiver on the other side of the room as I lie on the bed that was always mine. I blink into the darkness, listening to the sound of Conor's breathing as he pretends to sleep again. There are a galaxy of stars on the ceiling. They are the glow-in-the-dark sticker variety and almost as old as me. I expect they will continue to shine long after I am gone, just like the stars in the sky, and sometimes it feels as though nobody in this family would really notice if I just disappeared. Sometimes I think they wish I'd never been born. I close my eyes and a single tear escapes them, rolling down my cheek and dampening the pillow.

Sometime later, I hear a noise downstairs. I have never been a good sleeper, I'm not even sure whether I was asleep just now. That nightmare people sometimes have, where they feel like they are falling? I have it *all* the time. When I check the clock in my room, I see that it is almost exactly midnight. A few seconds later, the eighty clocks downstairs begin to chime their agreement. As soon as the final clock strikes twelve, I hear a terrible scream.

# Nine

*31 October, midnight*
*six hours until low tide*

The screaming stops.

'Did you hear that?' I whisper, but Conor isn't there.

I rush out of my bedroom, along the landing, down the stairs, across the hall, and into the kitchen at the back of the house. My niece is standing in the middle of the room wearing pink pyjamas that make her look much younger than she is. Trixie is crying. When I look down, I can see why.

Nana is lying on the floor in a white cotton nightdress. Her eyes are closed, her skin is grey, and there is a large gash on her head and a pool of blood beneath it. Poppins the dog is lying next to her, and neither of them are moving. A chair has toppled over as though Nana might have been standing on it and fallen. And I see that there is blood on the AGA oven, where it looks like she could have hit her head. Everything becomes silent and still inside the room, and seconds seem to stretch into minutes. Even the sea and the rain outside are suddenly quiet as I take in the scene, as though my world has experienced a freeze-frame. Then the sound of Trixie crying plays in my ears again. Tears are streaming down her face.

'Shh, it's okay. Just tell me what happened,' I say to Trixie, rushing over and getting down on the floor next to Nana, careful not to touch her or make things worse. 'Nana, can you hear me?'

She doesn't move, but Poppins looks up at me with sad eyes and starts to whimper.

'She'll be all right, old girl. We just need to stay calm—'

'What the hell is going on? Why are you out of bed and what's with all the screaming?' asks Lily, marching into the freezing-cold kitchen wearing nothing except a pink silk night-dress. Her daughter runs to her side. Most teenagers are children dressed up like adults, but my niece is still a child in so many ways.

'Oh my god,' Lily says, seeing Nana's body. 'Is she?'

'I don't know,' I whisper.

'What happened?' asks Rose, appearing from out of nowhere, and fully dressed as though she must have slept in her clothes. 'Stand back and let me see.'

'Why?' Lily asks. 'You're not a doctor.' Lily takes a step closer to Nana, and Poppins starts to growl. I have never seen or heard the dog behave this way before.

Rose steps between them. 'It's okay, Poppins, we're just trying to help Nana. Come on, old girl. Move out of the way.' Poppins does as she is told, as though she understood every word Rose just said, and watches from a short distance with her head bowed, quietly whimpering.

Rose gently feels for a pulse, but I don't need to be a doctor – or a vet – to know that this isn't good. The gash on the side of Nana's head looks deep, she's lost a lot of blood, and I have to look away when I see what might be brain matter in the red puddle on the floor. I've seen the same shade of grey skin on the faces of too many residents at the elderly care home where I volunteer, and fear I know what it means.

Conor appears in the doorway – fully dressed like Rose – and I wonder what took him so long and where he has been. Lily turns her back on him and tries to comfort Trixie. That's when I notice Nana's hands. One is holding a copy of *Daisy Darker's Little Secret*. The other is holding what appears to be a cigarette, but when I take a closer look, I see that it is a piece of chalk. I stare at the black wall at the end of the kitchen. The recipes and sketches that were there earlier have all been wiped off. Instead there is a poem, just like the ones in Nana's bestselling book about me. But the words have been changed. The *book* begins with the line *Daisy Darker's family were as lovely as can be*. But the chalk poem on the wall is very different.

'Look,' I say, and one by one, everyone in the room turns to read it.

*Daisy Darker's family were as dark as dark can be.*
*When one of them died, all of them lied, and pretended not to see.*
*Daisy Darker's nana was the oldest but least wise.*
*The woman's will made them all feel ill, which was why she had to die.*
*Daisy Darker's father lived life dancing to his own tune.*
*His self-centred ways, and the pianos he played, danced him to his doom.*
*Daisy Darker's mother was an actress with the coldest heart.*
*She didn't love all her children, and deserved to lose her part.*
*Daisy Darker's sister Rose was the eldest of the three.*
*She was clever and quiet and beautiful, but destined to die lonely.*
*Daisy Darker's sister Lily was the vainest of the lot.*
*She was a selfish, spoilt, entitled witch, one who deserved to get shot.*
*Daisy Darker's niece was a precocious little child.*
*Like all abandoned ducklings, she would not fare well in the wild.*
*Daisy Darker's secret story was one someone sadly had to tell.*
*But her broken heart was just the start of what will be her last farewell.*

*Daisy Darker's family wasted far too many years lying.*
*They spent their final hours together learning lessons before dying.*

Nana must have been writing it when she fell.

'Why would she write such horrible things about all of us?' Lily asks. I watch Rose and Conor staring at the chalk poem, but they don't have an answer to the question. None of us seem to know what to say or do. Lily, who always finds silence too uncomfortable to wear, dresses it with the sound of her own voice again.

'I've just realized that it's Halloween,' she says, with a weak smile. 'Maybe this is some kind of trick-or-treat prank?'

It's true, Nana did always like playing tricks on us at Halloween. It was her favourite night of the year for lots of reasons. She believed in the ancient Celtic origins of the festival, and would remind us of them each and every year when we celebrated her birthday. The Celts living in England, Ireland, Scotland and Wales over two thousand years ago believed that on the 31st October a portal between the living and the dead opened, allowing lost souls to return to earth. Nana was always willing to believe that ghosts were real, but it was the only time of year she believed they walked among us.

'Do you remember when Nana taught us to play trick-or-treat when we were children? Lighting lots of candles and scaring us with her ghost stories?' Lily says, as though expecting Nana to sit up and laugh at us all for being so gullible.

'This is no trick-or-treat,' says Rose, wiping a rare tear from her cheek. 'She's dead.'

# Nana

Daisy Darker's nana was the oldest but least wise.
The woman's will made them all feel ill, which was why she had to die.

Nana said she loved her family, but it wasn't always true.
The old bat was more bitter and angry with them than any of them knew.

She wished her son had been born a girl, or not been born at all,
The granddaughters were a blessing at first, but her hopes soon hit a wall.

The first was too clever, the second too daft, so the third was her only hope.
But the child was born with a broken heart, and Nana knew she'd
never cope.

Nana led a rather lonely life with a dog for a best friend,
She started to fear that death was near, thanks to a palm reader in
Land's End.

When the time came, no one knew who to blame, when she was found
with a blow to the head.
It was hard to grieve, for a woman so peeved; at least one of them was
glad she was dead.

# Ten

31 October 12:15 a.m.
*less than six hours until low tide*

'Who found her?' Rose asks, looking at everyone until her eyes come to rest on Trixie. 'Was it you?' Rose is better with animals than she is with children, and Trixie starts to cry again. She looks so small and vulnerable in her pink pyjamas. I have an overwhelming urge to hug her when she takes off her glasses with one hand, and uses the other to wipe away her tears. Rose adjusts her tone. 'Can you tell us what happened?' Trixie does her best to answer between sobs.

'I just came down to get a glass of water. Nana was . . . on the floor. When I touched her . . . she was cold. When I said her name . . . she didn't answer.' She starts to cry again.

'We need to call the police,' says Conor.

'What on earth for?' asks Lily. 'It's obvious what happened here.'

'Is it?' he asks.

'Yes. A chair is turned on its side. Nana was obviously using it to stand on while writing one of her bonkers poems on the chalk wall, and she must have slipped.'

'I don't think we can know that for sure,' Conor replies.

'Well, what *I* know is that you're a crime reporter, not a

detective, and nobody asked your opinion anyway,' says Lily. 'This is a family matter. You are not family and I don't even understand what you're doing here.' Even for Lily, this is rude.

'What I'm doing right now is wondering why an elderly woman I cared very much about is lying on the floor, looking as though someone has bashed her head in with a blunt instrument.' He turns to Rose. 'What do *you* think happened?'

She stares down at the kitchen tiles, as if she can't look him in the eye. 'I think Nana just died and I'm very upset. I'm sure we all are. Like Lily said, I'm a vet, not a doctor.' She glares at him, and I'm glad I'm not Conor. 'This is not the time for any of your conspiracy theories or wild accusations. Nana was never anything but kind to you; welcoming you into her home and our family. Try to show a little respect and compassion if you haven't completely forgotten how.'

Rose turns away from him and hugs Lily and Trixie, both of whom are now crying. I go to stand next to them, as though silently choosing sides.

'I'm going to miss her so much,' I say, unable to imagine life without Nana in it.

'I just can't believe she's gone,' says Lily.

Rose holds her closer. 'I know. Neither can I, but she lived a long and happy life and we will get through this. Someone needs to tell Dad what has happened.' Rose has always looked at the rest of the family as a problem with no obvious solution, a problem she doesn't quite know how to solve. When nobody else replies or makes a move, she sighs. 'I guess that'll be me then.'

We all watch as she leaves the kitchen and pauses in the hallway, outside the door to the music room, where our father chose to sleep. Rose's head is as tightly tucked in as her shirt. She stares down at the floor and I can almost hear her mind whirring. The music room was one of the few places we were never allowed to play when we were young. Rose hesitates before knocking, like the little girl she used to be, the one who was afraid of getting shouted at for interrupting her father's work.

She knocks and we all wait, but there is no answer.

Rose knocks again, before gently turning the handle and pushing the door open.

'The room is empty,' she says, looking back at us all. 'The camp bed hasn't been slept in. Dad isn't here and neither are his things.'

Lily rushes forward and grabs Rose's hand, just like she did when we were children. 'I know he was upset about Nana and the will, but you don't think that—'

'Let's try not to jump to conclusions,' says Rose, even though I'm sure we've all hurdled over several. 'I'm going to find a sheet to cover Nana's body, I'd rather remember her the way she was. Can someone else go upstairs and wake Nancy?'

I volunteer and Conor comes with me. I expect he just doesn't want to be left alone with my sisters, but I'm glad of the company. The house doesn't feel the same to me now, as though it too is grieving. Seaglass is colder, and stiller, and quieter than before. All I can hear is the sound of ticking clocks in the hallway, and the gentle lapping of waves against the rocks outside. When I was a little girl, I used to imagine the sea coming in through the cracks in the walls, and the doors, and the windows, and rushing down the chimney while we slept in our beds, until Seaglass was full to the ceiling with seawater, and we were all floating and trapped inside. I used to imagine a lot of bad things happening to my family in this house, but only at night. I might not be a child anymore, but I am still afraid of the dark.

Conor stops on the landing and I notice that there is some chalk on his jeans. He sees it too and tries to brush it away. I don't say anything. The door to my mother's bedroom at the other end of the hall is slightly ajar. I freeze, and realize that I simply don't have the right words for this situation. Conor, as though sensing my apprehension, steps forward and clears his throat. He knocks ever so gently, but the door swings open a little further, and despite the gloom, we can both see the shape of someone in bed. I don't understand how anyone could have slept through Trixie's screaming, but my mother has always been a deep sleeper. Never less than eight hours a night, or she thinks it will be bad for her skin. A good night's sleep is something pills and alcohol have often helped her to achieve.

'Nancy? I'm sorry to disturb you . . .' Conor says.

'What? Who is that?' says a voice in the darkness. But it isn't my mother sitting up in the bed. It's my father, and he looks just as surprised as we are to find him there. Nancy sits up seconds later, lifting her eye mask and removing her earplugs before squinting in our direction. When she sees Dad in the bed next to her, she practically leaps out of it.

'This isn't what it looks like,' she whispers in our direction.

'Yes, it is,' Dad says with a sigh, before holding his head in his hands.

The idea of my divorced parents sharing a bed leaves me speechless.

Conor clears his throat again. 'There's been an incident . . . and I think it might be best if you both come downstairs to the kitchen when you are . . .' I fear he is about to say *decent*. 'Ready' is the word he settles on, and we leave them to it.

Back downstairs in the kitchen, the mood has changed from disbelief to fear. Nana has been covered with what looks like a red-and-white tablecloth, and my sisters are staring up at the chalk poem about our family.

'The chalk was in her hand,' Rose says.

Nana's handwriting is beautiful and very distinctive, the poems in her children's storybooks were all handwritten with ink. I used to try and write the same way, with sloping joined-up letters, but it never looked as good. Nana had an explanation for that, just like she did for everything else: 'Of course we all have different handwriting. Just like fingerprints or DNA, it's to remind us that we are individual beings. Our thoughts and feelings are there to be expressed and they are our own: unique. I don't feel the same way as you about the world, and that's fine, we're not designed to always think and feel the same. We are not sheep. Agreeing with someone about something is a choice, try to remember that. Don't waste your life wishing to be like someone else, decide who you are and be you.'

'I'm not convinced that the poem was written by Nana . . .' I say. 'I don't think this looks like her handwriting. Maybe someone just wanted it to look like—'

'It's impossible to know who wrote this for sure,' Rose interrupts.

'But why would Nana write *that*?' asks Lily. 'And if she hated us all so much, why invite us here?'

'I'm not precocious,' says Trixie, my precocious but wonderful niece, staring up at the words written about her. It's almost a relief when my parents enter the room, looking like a couple of teenagers who've been caught behind the bike shed.

'Oh no,' Dad says, rushing to Nana and pulling back the cloth that was covering her. His reaction seems staged, and I notice that the dog starts to growl again.

'It's going to be okay, Frank,' says my mother, coming to stand by his side, still wearing her black silk pyjamas. Her matching black eye mask that she can't sleep without is still on her head too. 'We'll get through this, together.' It feels like an odd thing for her to say, given they've spent most of the last twenty years apart. I wonder whether she might still be drunk.

We watch as my parents embrace in front of us for the first time since 1988. People hold on tighter when they think they are losing their grip. The moment is punctuated by a full stop in the shape of a crying teenager.

'I want to go *home*,' Trixie sobs.

'Why don't you go and watch TV in the lounge?' Lily suggests. Television has always been a surrogate parent in my sister's house, but she looks cross when Trixie turns to me for reassurance.

'Everything is going to be okay, I promise,' I say, wondering if it's a lie. 'It's very sad that Nana has passed away and we're all going to miss her. You go and turn the TV on, and I'll come and join you in a minute.' People tend to see what they need to see and hear what they want to hear, in my experience. Trixie nods, wiping away yet more tears with the sleeve of her pink pyjamas before leaving the room.

As soon as she is gone, the discussion about the chalk poem on the wall continues. I listen while they all bicker about what it means and what we should do, unsurprised that nobody asks my opinion. As the youngest in the family, I'm quite used to nobody really caring what I think. I zone out a little, and notice the eight jack-o'-lanterns still sitting on the kitchen table. They all have such scary faces, which Nana must have spent a long time carving. There are pumpkins, squashes and turnips because, like always, Nana liked the tradition and folklore of Halloween more than the commercial version of her favourite day.

Every year when we were children, she would help us to carve jack-o'-lanterns of our own, while telling us the story of their origin, the myth of Stingy Jack. The Irish legend claims that a man called Stingy invited the devil for a drink, but then refused to pay for it. It was a trick, one of many that Jack played on the devil until the day he died. But then God wouldn't let Jack into heaven, and the devil – rather tired of a lifetime of tricks – refused to let him into hell either. So Jack was doomed to purgatory, with nothing but a burning coal inside an old turnip to light his way in the darkness. I guess turnips morphed into pumpkins at some point in history, but then all stories told often enough bend and twist out of shape over time. Stingy Jack is the reason why we carve pumpkins and put candles inside them to make lanterns at Halloween. One of my greatest gifts is knowing a little about a lot of things, and Nana taught me about most of them. She said the lesson of the legend was to pay your way in life, or be doomed to be forever lost and lonely in the dark.

'She was obviously very upset with us all,' says my mother, snapping me out of my trance. 'I think that was clear last night too. I've been wondering for a while whether Nana might have been suffering from some form of *dementia*. This . . .' she points at the chalk poem without looking at it '. . . unpleasantness is completely out of character. Perhaps she just worked herself up and then . . .'

'What? Worked herself up, wrote a poem and died?' asks Lily.

'This might turn out to be a blessing in disguise,' says Nancy.

'How can you say that?' I ask, trembling with anger.

My mother ignores me. 'And this display of . . . *dementia*, along with her odd behaviour last night . . . might mean that her will simply can't be taken seriously. If she was out of her mind when she wrote it . . .'

'She wasn't out of her mind, she was just speaking it,' says Rose.

Nancy glares in her direction.

Before they can start to argue, we all freeze when we hear the sound of Nana's voice in the distance.

'It's time for you to meet the rest of the Darker family, my darling girl.'

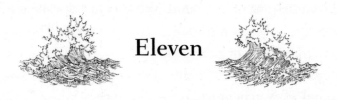

# Eleven

*31 October 12:30 a.m.*
*five and a half hours until low tide*

'Don't be cross,' Trixie says to Lily, as we all crowd into the lounge. 'I *tried* to watch television, but this started playing instead.' She points at the ancient wooden TV cabinet, and I spot Nana's old VCR player. She never upgraded to DVDs, in the same way she refused to listen to music on anything other than vinyl records on her 1950s jukebox. The retro TV set rarely worked anyway – especially in a storm – so our only screen-shaped entertainment as kids when we were here was Nana's VHS collection. It's probably why we all spent so much time outside. I remember the home movies lined up on the shelf last night, and see that they are gone. The shelf is empty. All I can see on the TV is a flickering image of a baby, until Lily snatches the remote from her daughter and hits the play button.

The screen is filled with a close-up of Nana's face, but she looks thirty years younger. She's carrying a baby into this room – which looks *exactly* the same – and it takes a while for me to realize that the child is me. My dad was a bit obsessed with making home movies when we were little kids, but I don't think I've ever seen this one before. And I'm not sure any of us really want to watch it now.

'And the rest of the Darker family can't wait to meet you,' says Nana. She carefully passes baby me to my mother, who looks so much younger. Nancy looks tired, but very beautiful, and still has a hospital ID tag around her wrist. This must be the day they brought me home to Seaglass. I always knew I was born when we were here. 'Shall I go and fetch Rose and Lily now?' says Nana's voice, out of shot. 'They've both been very patient waiting to meet their new baby sister.' The camera seems to nod, and I realize that my dad must have been holding it. I want to switch off the home movie, but Nancy takes the remote from Lily and sits on the very edge of the sofa closest to the television. I'm touched at first – that she wants to remember this moment – but then I see that she is staring at herself on the screen, not me.

The image of my past wobbles as my father puts the camera down on the table, so that he can be in shot. He comes to stand next to my mother as she lays me in an old-fashioned baby crib, before rocking me back and forth. Dad has long, slightly shocking 1970s hair, and is wearing what looks like a comedy moustache and flared jeans. The other thing that is noticeably different from the man we know today is that he looks . . . happy. They both do.

I watch, transfixed, just like everyone else, as five-year-old Rose and four-year-old Lily are led into the room, each holding one of Nana's hands. They are wearing matching yellow dresses covered in a pretty lemon print. I remember wearing the same dress myself a few years later, when it had faded from being washed so many times. My clothes were rarely new when I was a little girl; I only ever got to wear what Rose and Lily had grown out of. Rose's hair is tied back in a high ponytail on the TV screen – almost exactly like the one she has now, with the same chunky fringe – while Lily has pigtails tied with yellow ribbons. My mother often dressed them like twins; there was only a ten-month age gap, so it wasn't surprising. My sisters take it in turns to peer inside the crib and – unlike now – we really do look like a happy family.

'This is all very sweet. But what are we going to do about *the situation* in the kitchen?' asks Conor, interrupting the moment.

My father stares at him, as though he had forgotten Conor was here, then helps himself to a glass of whisky from the drinks trolley in the corner of the room. 'What do *you* suggest we do about *the situation*?' he asks Conor, before taking a large gulp.

'Call the police.'

'Here we go again,' says Lily.

'Why would we call the police? She was eighty,' says Nancy.

Conor folds his arms. 'Because I'm not convinced she died of natural causes.'

Dad laughs. 'You think one of us did her in?'

'Would you mind not suggesting such hateful things in front of Trixie,' says Lily, opening a packet of cigarettes and lighting one. The things she says and does to protect her child are almost always outweighed by the things she says and does to hurt her. I notice that Lily's fingers are trembling and wonder if it is the cold, or the need for nicotine, or something else causing it. Trixie seems not to have heard a thing, and is still staring at the home movie on the TV screen. 'Besides, the landline doesn't work and neither does my mobile. The tide won't go back out for a few hours yet. So calling the coroner, the police, or anyone else will have to wait a while.'

'I could take the boat, go and get help?' Conor suggests.

'No,' says my father. 'This is a family matter, and needs to be dealt with in a sensitive, private way.'

'Conor might be right,' says Rose, and everyone turns to stare at her. 'It's at least five hours until the tide goes out. We ought to report what has happened here tonight. I could go with him,' she suggests, before turning to Conor. 'If you don't mind.'

'I don't think that's a good idea,' says Frank, playing the protective father card I never knew he'd been dealt. Nobody asks why.

'Then maybe I could go alone?' Rose suggests. 'It might look a little bit strange if we don't *try* to get help. It shouldn't take me too long. If you don't mind me borrowing the boat, Conor?' He shrugs in agreement. My father nods at Rose and the matter is settled surprisingly quickly . . . almost as if they had rehearsed this whole exchange.

'Why do *you* get to leave?' Lily asks, taking another drag on her cigarette.

'Because she's barely touched a drink all night – unlike the rest of us – and Rose has always been the most sensible one in the family,' Dad replies, without a second or third thought for anyone else in the room.

Lily rolls her eyes. 'Thanks!'

'Besides, you can't row to save your life,' adds Rose, looking at our sulking sister. 'I'll be back as soon as I can,' she says before leaving the room.

'She barely touched her food earlier,' says my mother, when Rose is gone. 'Has anyone else noticed how thin she has got? She hardly said anything to anyone all night, and she keeps looking at her watch—'

'I expect she can't wait to leave,' Dad interrupts.

'I know the feeling,' says Nancy, as I sit down beside her on the sofa. She's still watching the TV, hasn't taken her eyes off it the entire time, and I see that my 1970s family are no longer on the screen. It's just baby me, alone in my crib. My

father must have forgotten to turn off the camera when this
was filmed all those years ago.

'Shall we stop watching this?' asks Lily, reaching for the
remote.

'No, wait,' I whisper as five-year-old Rose reappears in shot.

She looks over her shoulder, then creeps nearer to the crib.
We all seem to lean closer to the TV, as little Rose leans down
over the baby, before checking over her shoulder one last time.
We hang off her every word as she sings a sweet-sounding
lullaby.

*'Hush, little baby, don't say a word,*
*Mama's gonna buy you a mockingbird.*
*And if that mockingbird don't sing,*
*Mama's gonna buy you a diamond ring.*
*And if that diamond ring turns brass,*
*Mama's gonna buy you a looking glass.*
*Hush, little baby, don't you cry,*
*Sometimes we live, sometimes we die.'*

Five-year-old Rose reaches into her pocket and takes out
what looks like a baby mouse. Baby mice are born hairless and
pink. They are born blind and deaf and helpless. The creature
squirms as Rose holds its tail between her fingers and dangles
it over the crib, before dropping it. The child inside – which
I remember is me – starts to cry.

My sister rocks the crib and smiles, before raising a finger
to her lips. '*Shh.*' Then Rose walks out of shot.

I feel as though everyone is staring at me, but I don't know
what to say. I'd just been born. It isn't as though I can remember
the incident, or what happened next.

The tape ends abruptly, ejecting itself from the VCR player, and the TV screen displays nothing except white noise. We all exchange glances and unspoken thoughts about what we just saw, but before anyone can say anything, we hear footsteps in the hall. The door to the lounge bursts open, and thirty-four-year-old Rose reappears in the doorway, as though we have just witnessed some twisted form of time travel. She looks wet and wild and angry, and we all stare at her.

'The boat has gone,' she says, sounding breathless. 'The rope attaching it to the jetty looked like it had been deliberately cut. We're all stuck here until the tide goes back out.'

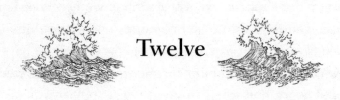

# Twelve

*31 October 12:45 a.m.*
*less than six hours until low tide*

Everyone stares at Rose.

'Why are you all looking at me like that?'

Lily smiles. 'You just got caught.'

Rose takes a step back towards the door. 'What?'

'Putting a baby mouse in Daisy's crib the first day they brought her home!'

Rose exhales, shakes her head as though relieved.

'Rose was just a child. Children do strange things sometimes. There's no need to drag up the past or upset anyone now. We have enough to deal with,' says Nancy.

'Yes, like a missing bloody boat,' says Conor, storming out.

I glance around the lounge and can see that everyone looks just as upset and exhausted as I feel. The fear and sadness in the room is like something solid and real, binding us together even though we might rather be apart. Our grief gives us something in common. They all had reasons to be upset with Nana, and not just because of the will – she could be a difficult woman to love sometimes. But I'm sure nobody in this family would have wished her dead.

'Rose is right, the boat is gone. It wasn't even mine,' Conor says, reappearing in the doorway.

'Maybe you didn't tie it to the jetty properly,' my dad says.

Conor glares at him. 'I tied it just fine. You heard Rose, the rope looks as though it has been cut.'

Dad nods. 'Well, looks can be deceiving. It's been a terrible night for us all, everyone is tired. I don't think we should let our imaginations scare us into thinking what happened here tonight is anything more than it is: a tragic accident and a missing boat.' He stands, a little wobbly on his feet I notice. Then he walks back over to the drinks trolley and pours himself another glass of whisky. Liquid anaesthetic to numb the pain.

'And you wonder why we got divorced?' mutters my mother beneath her breath, before tutting, which is one of her most favourite things to do.

'Because I like whisky?' he asks.

'No, because you're selfish. It doesn't even occur to you that someone else might like a drink.'

Dad holds up the decanter. 'There's plenty for everyone.'

'They don't want *whisky*. Why don't I make us all some tea? Including you. Clear heads are what is required.'

She leaves the room without asking who wants what. My mother has always been of the belief that a cup of tea can solve almost anything. Bad day at the office? Have a cup of tea. Struggling to pay the bills? Have a cup of tea. Find out that your husband is cheating on you with a twenty-year-old harpist? Cup. Of. Tea. She forgot my birthday once, but my mother *never* forgets how a person takes their tea. It's oddly important to her. Although in our family it is pretty easy to remember – she is the only one of us who takes sugar. As soon as she leaves the room, my dad takes another large gulp of his Scotch.

'What?' he says, to nobody in particular. 'My mother just died. I'm supposed to be upset and I'm allowed to have a bloody drink if I want to.'

No one argues with my father; it's never been a good use of time. Arrogance always translates his opinions into facts inside his head.

Nancy returns with a tray, after being gone longer than expected. I see that she's swapped her black silk pyjamas for a black roll-neck, cropped trousers and ballet pumps, one of her classic Hepburn ensembles. She's put on some make-up too – thick black eyeliner and a little blusher. I suppose everyone deals with grief differently. Her blue-veined hands are visibly trembling, and the tray rattles as she sets it down on the coffee table. Everyone takes their own cup. They have our names on them – hand-painted by Nana – even Conor has his own.

'*Mum*,' Trixie whispers, ignoring the cup of tea placed in front of her. My niece has been quieter than normal, and I wish I could have protected her from all of this.

'Mmm hmm,' Lily says, without looking up.

'I need the bathroom.'

'So why are you telling me about it?'

Trixie frowns. 'Because I'm scared.'

I jump to my niece's defence before her mother can reply. I can't stand it when Lily bullies her own daughter. 'I'll go with her, I don't mind—'

'*Nobody* is going to go with you or hold your hand,' Lily snaps, ignoring me. No one says anything, but their eyes speak the words that their mouths don't. 'There is no reason for you to be scared of going to the bathroom. You're fifteen, not five. All those bloody books you read are putting silly ideas in your head. And there's no need to be scared of Nana anymore, darling. The old bat is dead.'

Dad takes another sip of whisky, and Nancy tuts again, louder this time. Neither of them was ever any good at telling my sister off when she was out of line, which is why she's never been in step with the rest of the world. It's almost as if they're scared of her.

'You shouldn't speak ill of the dead,' Nancy says.

'Why?' Lily asks. 'You always speak ill of the living. Go to the bathroom, Trixie. There's no need to be scared, it's just across the hall. Go on, and grow up while you're at it,' she says to her fifteen-year-old daughter who has just seen a dead body for the first time. Trixie glares at her mother, pushes her pink glasses a little further up her nose, and leaves the room.

'I think we ought to come up with a plan,' says Conor.

'I don't remember anyone asking what you thought,' slurs my dad.

'Surely we all just stay together until the tide goes out?' says Rose.

The rain outside lashes against the elderly glass in the windows, making it rattle inside its frame. Lily's teeth start to chatter as though it's contagious.

'If we're staying down here until the sun comes up, then we'll need to keep warm,' she says. 'This house is freezing.' My sister can always find something to complain about, but to be fair, she is only wearing a nightdress. 'I'll get some jumpers from upstairs. Does anyone else want anything?'

Looks are exchanged like unwanted gifts, heads are shaken, and shoulders are shrugged.

Trixie returns, Lily leaves, my dad pours *another* drink, and my mother tuts again.

'Is that really a good idea, Frank?' she asks.

'No, it's an excellent idea.'

'Do *you* really think it was an accident?' Conor asks him.

'Enough!' Dad snaps. 'This isn't a crime scene for a BBC correspondent to report on or a murder mystery story for someone to solve. She was my *mother*. She slipped and fell. Simple as that. There was no murder, there is no mystery. She was eighty, had already lost most of her marbles, and now she's dead. That's the end of it.' His face closes like a door. The conversation is over. Then Dad frowns and stares out of the window at the sea lit by moonlight, almost as though he has forgotten the rest of us are here. 'Forgive me, I think I need to be alone for a while,' he says quietly.

Lily returns with some jumpers and blankets, and has dressed herself in jogging bottoms teamed with a tight top. Dad leaves the room as she enters it, taking his whisky with him and closing the door. We hear him go into the music room, and a few minutes later, we all hear the familiar sound of him playing the piano. Even though he is drunk, he plays perfectly.

'I'm still cold,' whispers Trixie, despite the jumper Lily has given her. It's the pink jumper from last night, and matches her pyjamas.

'I brought one of your books down for you,' Lily says.

'I'm too upset to read.'

'Suit yourself. Here, play with this, see if you can beat my highest score,' Lily says. Trixie takes her mother's mobile phone and plays *Snake*, the glow of the screen reflected in her glasses and illuminating her sad little tear-stained face.

'I'll go and fetch some firewood,' offers Conor. 'I think we're in for a long night.'

'Thank you, Conor,' says Nancy with uncharacteristic sincerity.

He's gone a very long time. I think maybe I'm the only one to notice until my mother speaks again.

'You don't think Conor is doing a runner, do you?'

I think she was trying to make a joke, but it doesn't quite land, and her face suggests she regrets it. Nana and Conor had a very special relationship, I don't believe he could be capable of hurting her. At least, not like that. She was the grandmother he never had, and we all knew how much she adored him. There was a time when Nana didn't just treat Conor like family, she treated him better.

A year after appearing in Blacksand Bay, Conor would regularly turn up at Seaglass, with or without an invitation. So did I. My mother often felt the need to 'run away' without much notice – sometimes visiting my father while he toured abroad, sometimes none of us knew where she went – but I was always sent to Seaglass when my existence wasn't convenient for my parents' lifestyle. Not that I minded. I loved spending time here with Nana. So did Conor.

I was a bit too young to hold his attention back then, so if my sisters were away at boarding school, he would amuse himself looking for crabs in the rock pool at the rear of the house. It was carved out, courtesy of the sea, from the natural stone Seaglass was built on – a private treasure trove of watery magic, starfish and crabs. Nana told us it was where fairies went to swim at night, while the rest of the world was sleeping. If the weather was bad, Conor could often be found indoors helping Nana mix her paints – he and I were the only ones allowed in her studio – or playing with his yo-yo and staring out to sea. But one morning, Nana and I found him outside the back door, curled up asleep in the log store.

'Conor, it's seven a.m. and it's freezing, what *are* you doing out here?' Nana asked, squinting at the boy in the shadows. His only blanket was the night sky, sequinned with stars. There are no views of the bay or the mainland from the back of the house. All that can be seen or heard is the Atlantic Ocean. As soon as the sun goes down, the world outside of Seaglass's walls is cold and dark. The sea looked black, and the tide was in that morning. Which meant that Conor must have been out there for hours. He knew better than to risk the rips and tides hiding beneath the surface of an unforgiving ocean.

'I didn't want to wake anyone,' Conor said, staring at Nana. They had a silent exchange, which five-year-old me was too young to understand.

'Come on, let's get you inside. I'll run you a hot bath so you can warm up.'

'Why are you limping?' I asked Conor as he followed Nana up the stairs. He smelled pretty bad too, and his blonde hair looked shiny and wet with grease.

'Go to your room, Daisy,' Nana said. She could see that I was about to protest; being sent to my room was one of my mother's favourite forms of punishment, not Nana's, and I hadn't done anything wrong. Nana's face softened. 'We can have jelly and ice cream with chocolate sauce for breakfast, but only if you go to your room,' she said with a wink. So I did as I was told. But I couldn't resist creeping out onto the landing a little while later, and peeking through the crack where the bathroom door was open just enough to see.

Nana used my bubble bath for Conor, not that I minded. The bottle looked like a smiley sailor called Matey, and it turned the water blue. I loved bubble baths, but Conor didn't smile or look happy at all. I watched as Nana helped him out of his jumper and shirt – he dressed like a middle-aged man when he was ten – and I saw the cuts and bruises all over his back. Conor looked ashamed, as though it was his fault.

'Who did this to you?' Nana asked, already knowing the answer that Conor wouldn't give.

She held his face in her hands. 'You're going to be okay, I promise. You take the rest of your clothes off and pop them in this bin liner. I'm going to find you some clean, dry clothes and start making us all some breakfast. Call me if you need anything.'

'Mrs Darker—' he said.

'Yes?'

'Please don't tell anyone. He didn't mean to do it.'

Nana had her back to him, and I could see she had tears in her eyes. 'I had a dad who didn't mean to hurt me too, once upon a time. I promise you can trust me. For now, just have your bath. There's a clean towel and flannel on the side. Don't forget to wash behind your ears.'

I ran back to my bedroom before Nana came out onto the landing, and listened to her march down the stairs. She was still wearing her fluffy purple dressing gown and pink slippers, but she looked really mad, and her face looking all cross like that made me feel a bit afraid. Nana was rarely angry about anything, but boy did everyone know about it when she was.

The only telephone at Seaglass in those days – or ever – was in the hallway. It was on a little round table along with a fancy notebook full of handwritten numbers. I watched from behind the banister at the top of the staircase, as Nana flicked through the book, found Conor's dad's number, and dialled. It was a rotary phone, so took forever. Her foot was tapping the way it did when she was proper cross, while she waited for someone to answer the call. Patience was never one of Nana's virtues.

'Hello, Mr Kennedy, how are you today? Oh, a little under the weather? I'm sorry to hear that. Is that why you beat your ten-year-old son with your belt last night?'

There was silence, in which I'm sure Conor's dad and I were both busy putting together pieces of a puzzle we weren't sure how to solve. Wondering if those pieces were in the right order. Not really liking the picture that they made. Nana went on.

'I suspect you didn't even know where he was overnight. Let me put your mind at rest and tell you that he's here at Seaglass with me. Which is where he is going to stay, until I can reach social services and have him taken away from you forever.'

She was quiet again. I wished I could hear what was being said on the other end of the line.

'He's a child. It's not his fault your wife died. You are supposed to be his father. You're supposed to protect him from all that is bad and wrong about the world, not constantly hurt him and let him down. Doing your best? Well, your best isn't good enough. You're depressed? Aren't we all. It doesn't give you the right to do what you did. You are a disgrace to depression, and you don't deserve to call yourself that child's father. Either you get yourself some help or you will lose your son. I never met your wife, but I can only imagine that if she could see what you have become, she would be deeply ashamed and wish she'd never met you. He's her son, all that is left of her; think of that next time you take your shitty existence out on your child.'

Then she hung up, and I was both scared and in awe of her all at once.

Nana never stopped looking out for Conor from that day on. His father went to AA, was in rehab for a while, and although there were months, sometimes years, when things would be okay, she always kept a close eye on Conor back then, trying to protect him.

Back in the present, I get up and leave the lounge to find out where he has disappeared to. I immediately feel the slap of cold air, and the sound of the sea is louder than before. Almost as though it is inside the house. When I step out into the hallway, I can hear the back door banging in the wind. Conor must have left it open when he went in search of wood. The quickest way to get to the log store is via the kitchen, but I don't really want to go in there. I don't want to see Nana's body on the floor again, or the unkind chalk poem on the wall, so I avert my eyes as I hurry to the back door.

Conor walks through it before I get there, carrying a basket full of logs. He looks completely drenched, and I don't understand what took him so long. I'm about to ask when I notice him staring at something behind me. I think I know what it is – Nana – but when I turn to look for myself, I see that her body has gone. Conor puts the logs down and stares at the kitchen table. There is a VHS tape on it. One of the ones I'm sure I saw on the shelf in the lounge last night. Someone has stuck Scrabble letters to the front of its white cardboard case, spelling out the words: **WATCH ME**. Next to the tape, there is a torn piece of paper. When I read the words that have been written on it, in handwriting I do not recognize, my whole body turns icy cold.

*TRICK-OR-TREAT THE CHILDREN HEAR,*
*BEFORE THEY SCREAM AND DISAPPEAR.*

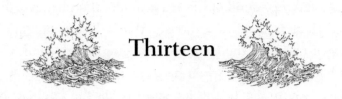

# Thirteen

*31 October 1 a.m.*
*five hours until low tide*

The clocks in the hallway all start to chime. Thankfully just once as it's one a.m., but they are a little out of sync as usual. Conor stares at the space on the floor where Nana used to be, but there's no body, and no blood, as though what we saw before might just have been a bad dream. Then he looks at the VHS tape and note on the kitchen table. He turns to look in my direction, but doesn't say anything, almost as if he suspects *me* of putting them there. I can still hear my dad's piano in the music room, he hasn't stopped playing since he locked himself away from the rest of us. The men in my life have never been good at using their words, so I find a few of my own.

'I understand why you've refused to see me for years, and why you still don't want to talk to me now, and that's fine, but can we please put what happened with *us* to one side, just for tonight? I'd really like to know what you think is going on here, because I'm scared,' I say, quietly enough so that the others won't hear. I used to think of Conor like a big brother, and I miss him playing that role in my life.

The look on his face is opaque; there is no reflection or

even an acknowledgement of what I just said. I hate that things have become so awkward between us, but I have never managed to find the right words to fix things. I don't understand why we can't move on. Especially now. Everything we've just seen confirms that Nana's death was not an accident.

I'm not naive. I know that everyone was upset about Nana's will last night, and I do have a hunch about what might be going on here. But hunches aren't just there to be had, they're there to be thought about, analysed, agonized over and – most importantly – should rarely be shared. Conor stares at the words written on the piece of paper on the kitchen table, then at the VHS tape, then again at the place on the floor where Nana's body was earlier. I just stare at Conor.

He grabs a red chequered tea towel from the kitchen worktop and does his best to dry himself off from the rain, then he reaches inside his pocket and takes out a mobile phone. It's a dark blue Nokia, the best that 2004 has to offer, just like Lily's, but Conor seems to have forgotten that there is no signal here. He holds it high up in the air, as though that will make it work, but of course it doesn't. I watch as he strides out to the little table in the hallway where the landline used to live. The old pink rotary phone is still there, on a doily, but Nana wasn't joking when she said she stopped paying the bill. She wanted peace and quiet and I guess she got her wish, because the phone is dead. I find the fact that Conor so clearly wants to call the police reassuring, despite knowing that he can't.

There is a picture of me and my sisters by the phone. When they were here it used to ring all the time. Most calls were for them – friends from school wanting to catch up in the holidays, study partners for Rose, boyfriends for Lily – but occasionally it was my dad, calling from one city or another, between rehearsals and performances. He could never talk for

more than a few minutes – long-distance calls cost a small
fortune in those days – and it never took him too much time
to ask Nana for more money. Sometimes publishers called for
Nana, and her agent always called to wish her a happy birthday.
But I can remember one Halloween when I was the only person
here to help her celebrate, and the phone rang. The person
calling was Conor. I suppose I must have been five or six.
Nana had just blown out all of her candles – there were a lot,
even back then – and we were about to eat pineapple upside-
down cake with Angel Delight. The memory of that phone call
is as clear now as if it had happened yesterday, not over twenty
years ago.

'Hello,' Nana said, answering the phone with a big smile,
expecting it to be someone calling to wish her a happy birthday.
The smile slid straight off her face. 'It's going to be okay. You
did the right thing calling me. Stay exactly where you are and
I'll be there soon.'

'Who was it?' I asked.

'Conor. Something's wrong, I need to go over there,' Nana
said, looking for her handbag. She could never seem to find
it, even though it was both brightly coloured and enormous.
The bag was made from pink and purple patches and was older
than me. Nana shook her head while searching for it, and her
curly white hair seemed to dance. I wondered if mine would
look like that when I was older. Then I remembered that I
would never be old enough to have white hair, and it made
me feel so sad. It's odd, the little things that used to upset
me. Most people don't want grey or white hair, but in that
moment, I did. Maybe people wouldn't complain about getting
old all the time if they were scared that they never would.

When Nana found her handbag, she slipped a wooden rolling pin inside it.

'What should *I* do?' I asked, a little scared of being left on my own at Seaglass.

Nana stared at me as though I had said something wrong. 'Daisy Darker, do you care about Conor?' I nodded. 'Good, I'm glad to hear it. Caring about other people is more important than being curious about them. When someone you care about is in trouble, you do everything you can to help. Which means you are coming with me. Now find your shoes and let's skedaddle.'

'What about your birthday cake?' I asked.

'We'll take it with us. Conor sounds like he needs cheering up.'

Ten minutes later, having crossed the causeway when the tide was already fast coming in, the two of us climbed the rocky path with wet shoes and socks. At the top of the cliff, behind the sand dunes, there was an old shed where Nana kept her only form of transport. It was an ancient bicycle with a large wicker trailer attached to the back, which, now that I think about it, can't have been legal. I climbed into the wicker trailer and Nana climbed onto the saddle, dangling her handbag on the handlebars.

Nana pedalled faster than I knew she could along the coastal road, until we reached Conor's cottage, a mile or so away on the other side of Blacksand Bay. The place was really nothing more than a dilapidated two-bedroom bungalow on a rocky stretch of the coast. One of the windows was cracked, and the blue paint on the front door was peeling right off. They'd moved there when Conor's mum died, and the building was as abandoned and unloved as the two people who lived in it.

We didn't knock. There was no need; the door was open.

I'd never been inside before – Conor always came to visit

us, never the other way round – and I was shocked by what I saw. I think we both were. The front door opened straight into a little lounge and there was mess everywhere. The previously white net curtains were a grubby grey, and when Nana switched on the light, the place looked even worse than it had in the gloom. The old green sofa in the middle of the room had sunken seats, and holes in some of the cushions. There were dirty cups and plates stacked on the coffee table, and chip shop wrappers and crushed beer cans all over the stained carpet. Picture frames – which presumably used to hang on the rusty hooks on the walls – were smashed on the floor. They were all of Conor with his parents, before his mum died. A broken happy family. There were bits of glass and rubbish almost everywhere I looked. Conor was sitting in the corner of the room, hugging his knees to his chest.

'Where is he?' Nana asked.

'In the bedroom,' Conor whispered without looking up.

'You stay with Conor,' Nana said to me. 'Be as kind to him as you would want someone to be to you if you felt broken.' Then she took her rolling pin out of her pink and purple patchwork bag, and the way she held it made me think it wasn't so she could do some baking. I wanted to be kind to Conor, and I knew what it was like to feel broken, but I followed Nana, even though I knew I wasn't meant to. Curiosity doesn't only kill cats.

The bedroom was dark and smelled bad. There were piles of clothes all over the floor, and a filthy-looking man lying on the bed with his eyes closed. Empty bottles of pills were on the stained bed sheets beside him. Nana dropped the rolling pin and used the phone on the nightstand to call for an ambulance.

He wasn't dead, he just wished that he was. Even though I was very young, the thought of anyone feeling that unhappy made me feel overwhelmingly sad. When the nice paramedics had taken Conor's dad to hospital, the three of us ate Nana's birthday cake. It seems like a strange thing to have done, looking back. But then my childhood was rarely normal.

Mr Kennedy lived to tell the tale, and Nana paid for him to go to rehab. 'We all get broken sometimes and if you can help fix someone, you should always try,' she said. I think Conor's dad was a bit like me in that way. But he wasn't born with a broken heart; his heart broke when his wife died. Conor said he rarely drank at all before then and that he used to be happy. They all were.

Conor stayed at Seaglass for a little while, and the three of us – him, Nana and me – spent a week straightening out the cottage where he and his father lived. We cleared out all the rubbish and washed everything that could be cleaned. Nana pulled up the old carpet, sanded the floors, painted the walls – inside and out – and bought some new cushions and bed linen. Nana was always of the opinion that if you could help change a life, you could help change the person who leads it. She put fresh flowers in every room, and filled up the fridge and freezer with food before Conor's dad returned. She even paid for us all to take a taxi to collect him from rehab. He looked like a different man to me, so much so I thought we'd picked up the wrong person. He'd put on some weight, his clothes were clean, he'd shaved off his horrible beard, and he didn't stink of booze or cigarettes.

'Are you sure you're Conor's dad?' I asked in the car, and everyone laughed even though I hadn't been joking.

'Thank you,' he said when he stepped inside the bungalow and saw how much work we had all done to make their house a home. 'For everything. How can I ever repay you?'

'Just stay well,' Nana replied.

Then she shook hands with him, kissed Conor on the cheek, and we left them to try again.

'Everyone deserves a second chance,' Nana said when we were alone.

'Even bad people?' I asked.

'Everyone you know is both good and bad, it's part of being human.'

I think I was too young to understand at the time.

'Can you bring some matches as well as logs?' Lily calls, sticking her head out of the lounge door, snapping me out of the past and back to a present that is no less upsetting.

'I think you should come and see this. All of you,' Conor replies.

Lily tuts – one of many bad habits she inherited from our mother – then tells Trixie to stay behind while the rest of the women in the family join us in the kitchen.

'Where's Nana?' asks my mother, staring at the floor where Nana's body used to be.

'Exactly,' says Conor, and we all look at one another. 'Did somebody move her?'

Everyone shakes their heads.

'Well, someone left this VHS tape and this note on the kitchen table,' he says. 'The words didn't write themselves.'

Nancy picks up the scrap of paper and reads out loud.

'*Trick-or-treat the children hear, before they scream and disappear*. What does that mean?'

'WATCH ME?' says Lily, picking up the tape and reading the Scrabble letters stuck to its cover. She puts it straight back down, as though it might hurt her. 'What is this? A sick version of *Alice in Wonderland*?'

'Nana disappearing isn't the only thing that's changed in here,' says Rose, and we turn to see what she is staring at on the kitchen wall. The poem written in chalk is still there, but four of the lines have been crossed out.

~~Daisy Darker's nana was the oldest but least wise.~~
~~The woman's will made them all feel ill, which was why she had to die.~~
~~Daisy Darker's father lived life dancing to his own tune.~~
~~His self-centred ways, and the pianos he played, danced him to his doom.~~

'What is *that* supposed to mean?' Lily says, looking at our mother.

'Why are you asking me?'

'You came out here, alone, to make tea. Who else had time to do all of this?'

Nancy looks flustered for a second, but soon recovers. 'I think you'll find we all left the lounge alone at one stage or another. Rose went to the jetty – only to find that the boat was gone. You went to get jumpers from upstairs. Conor just went outside to fetch logs – maybe *he* moved the body . . .' she says.

'Or maybe it was Frank,' Conor says in a hushed voice. 'He's very upset, and he's had a lot to drink. Maybe he crossed out his own name so that—'

'So that we'd all think *he* killed Nana?' interrupts Lily. 'Why would the murderer implicate themselves?'

'So you admit that a crime might have taken place here tonight and that your nana may have been murdered?' Conor replies. 'From what I can tell, you all had a motive to kill her because you all needed her money and would have been furious about not getting a penny more of it. Money is why you're all here. Rose's veterinary practice is in financial trouble, Frank's orchestra costs more than it makes these days, Nancy's divorce settlement has dried up, and Lily has always sponged off the rest of the family—'

'You arrived *after* Nana read us her will,' interrupts Rose. 'So how did you know none of us were going to get the money?'

'And why are *you* here?' Lily asks.

Conor glares at her. 'I have my reasons.'

*Having your reasons is fine unless they are someone else's.* I wish I could say it out loud, but I've never been as brave as people who say what they really think.

'That's enough, Conor. You can't go around accusing people of things you know nothing about. You don't know Frank the way the rest of us do. He was my husband and is still their father. But I do think we need to talk to him,' Nancy says. She starts walking towards the music room. *'Together,'* she adds, when none of us follow.

The piano music gets louder with every step we take towards the door.

My mother gently knocks on it. 'Frank?'

There is no answer, so she knocks again, but the piano music continues to play. Nancy tries the door handle, but it's locked.

'Stand back,' says Conor, so we do. Only Lily laughs when he tries and fails to force the door open by running at it. Rose surprises us all then, with a well-aimed kick that causes the door to fly open. But nothing is as shocking as what we see next.

The piano is still playing, because it's one of those pianos that can play itself.

My father is lying on the floor beneath it, with an empty whisky glass in his left hand. His conductor's baton has been snapped in two, and tied to his right hand with a red ribbon. His eyes are wide open and he appears to have vomited blood.

I feel numb, and sick, and confused.

But I am certain of one thing: my dad is dead.

# Frank

*Daisy Darker's father lived life dancing to his own tune.*
*His self-centred ways, and the pianos he played, danced him to his doom.*

*An unexpected pregnancy resulted in marriage and three girls,*
*But instead of seeing his family, Frank chose to see the world.*

*His orchestra was his one true love, and he thought they loved him too,*
*But those out-of-work musicians just needed cash and something to do.*

*Frustrated as Frank became about his own music not being performed,*
*He carried on touring, though failure was boring, still hoping to be adored.*

*While the family who truly loved him was abandoned and alone,*
*It was all too late, when he accepted his fate: he might have been*
*happiest at home.*

*When the time came, no one knew who to blame when he was*
*found poisoned by his drink.*
*It was hard to feel sad for an absent dad. His grieving girls didn't*
*know what to think.*

# Fourteen

Rose switches off the piano and I'm glad. The sight of it playing all by itself with my father lying dead beneath it is an image I wish I could wipe from my memory forever. I notice that one of the piano keys has gone, like a missing tooth in a musical smile, almost as though the piano itself is laughing at us. The rain outside lashing against the glass windows serves as white noise while we stand and stare in silence.

'He must have done it,' Lily says quietly, as if scared he might hear her accusing him. 'He must have killed Nana because he was so upset about her will. Then he drank himself to death because of the guilt. Didn't he even joke last night that his preferred form of murder would be a sharp blow to the head? That's exactly how she died!'

My dad is many things, but I'm certain that a murderer isn't one of them.

'Why would he move Nana's body?' I say. 'And where is she now? And what do the note and the VHS tape in the kitchen mean?'

Conor steps forward. 'This doesn't look like suicide if you ask me.'

'Nobody did,' Lily replies. 'Are you sure he's . . .'

'Dead? Yes,' says Rose, closing my father's eyes. She takes the empty whisky glass from his hand and sniffs it, before doing the same with the empty decanter on top of the piano. It seems like an odd thing to do.

'Why would he tie his conducting baton to his own hand?' Conor asks, looking at the rest of us as though we might be dangerously stupid.

'Why did he do *any* of the daft things he did?' Nancy snaps, wiping a trickle of tears from her face with a pretty embroidered handkerchief from her sleeve. It has a letter B on it, and I presume it must be Nana's, or Trixie's, though nobody ever calls my niece Beatrice. 'This all feels like a bad dream . . . it *can't* be real,' my mother says, in a voice that sounds too small for her. 'What are we going to do?'

'Why are you so upset?' Lily asks. 'Just because you chose to share your bed with him last night – which is disgusting, by the way – have you forgotten everything else that Dad did? He abandoned you years ago. He abandoned us all.'

'How can you speak like that when the man is lying dead on the floor? He was your father and I loved him . . . even when I didn't *like* him, I still—'

'I'm not going to pretend he was ever dad of the year just because he is dead.'

'I didn't raise you to behave like this, Lily.'

'You barely raised me at all, and he certainly didn't have much to do with it. I was mostly brought up by strangers at boarding school. *You* dumped us here on Nana most holidays, while my so-called father spent his time with "musicians" half his age.'

'The man is dead, show some respect.'

'For him?'

'For *yourself*,' Nancy says. My mother always has an argument under construction – sometimes several at once – and if I had a hard hat, I'd wear one. Lily wouldn't dare answer back if she hadn't had so much to drink tonight. Just when I think it might be over, Nancy throws another verbal brick. 'He stayed as long as he was able.'

'Ha! That's a good one. He didn't *have* to have kids. We didn't *ask* to be born. Plenty of people get pregnant by accident . . . I did!' Lily says.

'Well, I didn't,' Nancy replies, and the room is even quieter than before. 'I knew your father was going to choose music over me, even when we were students. I got pregnant on purpose so that he'd marry me. So that he'd have to stay.'

My sisters and I try to process this latest bombshell, but it's all a bit much to take in: finding Nana dead in the kitchen earlier, now Dad in the music room. It's like a messed-up-family edition of Cluedo. But this isn't a game; two people have died here tonight. I think part of me always suspected that Nancy deliberately got pregnant and tricked Dad into marrying her, but hearing her say it out loud is surreal. Half of me hates her for it, while the other half knows I never would have been born if she hadn't.

'So he didn't really want *any* of us?' asks Rose. 'That explains a lot.'

'He loved all of you in his own way,' Nancy says. 'I just can't believe he would do this.'

'Maybe he didn't,' Conor says.

Nancy stares at him. 'The door was locked, there was nobody else in the room . . .'

'The door could have been locked from the outside,' he replies calmly. 'Either way, the police will have to be called now.'

Everyone looks scared for the first time, and I can't help wondering why it took so long.

'Conor is right,' says Rose, always in control of her emotions. 'We will have to involve the police when we can. It's only five hours until low tide now. We'll leave together in the morning and call for help. In the meantime, maybe we could all just try to be kind to each other? We should go back to the lounge. Trixie is on her own in there,' she adds, taking charge like before. 'After everything that has happened here tonight, I'd feel a lot better knowing that we were all safe and together in one room.'

My eldest sister often took charge of situations when we were children, and the fact that she is doing so now feels like a relief. I pretend not to notice, but I see her tap Conor on the arm as we are all leaving the music room, and feel a stab of inexplicable hurt when he hangs back. They don't speak until they think the rest of us have returned to the lounge, but unknown to them, I'm waiting quietly out in the hall. I have to strain to listen, and cover my mouth with my hand to stop myself making a sound when I hear what they say.

'You are right, we do need to call the police,' Rose whispers.

'Why do you agree with me all of a sudden?' Conor asks.

'No animal I know shares the human capacity for self-harm, but this wasn't suicide.'

'Why do you say that?'

'Sadly, I often see poisoned pets in my line of work. People can be monsters. It's one of the many reasons why I prefer animals. Dad is the only person in the family who drinks whisky. When I smelled his glass, it didn't just smell of alcohol. My father was poisoned. It was murder, I'm sure of it.'

I don't say a word, but I do wonder why Rose would choose to confide in Conor and not the rest of us. And why neither of them wanted to share that information with me. The shadow of a thought lingers in my mind, and I can't seem to shake it. Not that I'll ever say anything to either of them about it. I only self-destruct in private.

Back in the lounge, Trixie has fallen asleep on the large window seat at the far end of the room. It's one of my niece's favourite spots in the house, and she can often be found curled up there with a blanket and a book. Poppins the dog is stretched out on the floor beside her, gently snoring. It breaks my heart that such a kind child could have been born into such a cruel family. I'm glad she's sleeping now. Hopefully she'll stay that way until we can all leave.

I think that Rose is looking at her too, but it turns out she was looking at the dog.

'Poppins is taking all of this very well, poor old girl,' she says, to nobody in particular.

On hearing her name, Poppins comes to sit next to Rose.

'That's a good point. What will happen to the dog now that Nana is dead?' Lily asks.

'I'll take her with me,' Rose replies without hesitation.

'You said that as if you'd already thought it through.'

We sit in silence for a while. I don't think any of us know what to say. I look at each of their faces and see a mix of fear, shock and sorrow on every one. Rose strokes the dog and stares at the flames in the fire, with an expression I've never seen her face wear. Conor stares at Rose. Despite throwing another log on the fire, Nancy can't seem to stop shivering. Lily goes to sit next to her and they hold hands. They have one of those mother–daughter relationships where they squabble all the time but never stay cross with each other for long. It's another thing that I've always been jealous of.

'Are you all right?' Nancy asks her favourite daughter.

Lily shakes her head. 'No, of course not. It's just so awful. I think I'm in shock, we all must be.'

'I meant you look pale. Are you feeling okay?'

'I can't find my diabetic kit, but don't worry. Missing one shot of insulin won't kill me.'

Lily wasn't diagnosed as diabetic until her early twenties. She injects twice a day now and makes sure that everyone knows it. I've spent a lot of time with diabetics at the care home where I volunteer, and I feel for them, I really do. It isn't an easy disease to live with at any age. But Lily doesn't take her condition as seriously as she should, and her sweet tooth and habit of overindulgence was demonstrated again at dinner. My sister rarely worries about the things that she should.

'Look how peaceful Trixie looks,' Lily says, staring at her daughter. 'I don't know how I'm going to tell her what has happened. First Nana, then Dad . . .'

'Maybe you don't have to tell her? Let her sleep for now?' Nancy suggests.

Lily nods, and I watch her quietly place a blanket over Trixie with unusual care and compassion. For a moment, I feel guilty about the bad thoughts I so often have about my sister. Maybe she *is* capable of loving someone more than she loves herself. Lily gently kisses her daughter on the forehead and strokes her hair, in a rare display of maternal affection.

'What do we do with this?' asks Conor.

He's holding the VHS tape from the kitchen with the words WATCH ME on the front. We all stare at it and him as though he's holding a grenade and has suggested pulling out the pin.

'Throw it on the fire?' suggests Lily.

'Why would someone leave that there for us to find?' I ask.

'*Who* put it there is the question we should all be asking,' says Conor. 'And what if it explains what is happening here tonight?'

'It just looks like another Darker family home movie,' Rose replies, as Conor removes the tape from its cover. We can all see the white sticky label on the side of it. '*SEAGLASS ~ 1980*' written in Nana's swirly handwriting. Rose takes the tape from Conor's hands.

'Should we watch it?' asks my mother. The rest of us exchange glances. 'What else are we going to do for five hours? Sitting here in silence while we wait for the tide to go out will only make the hours pass more slowly, and things surely can't get any worse. Personally, I'd welcome any distraction to take my mind off what has happened here tonight, and it might be nice for all of us to remember happier times?'

'What about Trixie?' Conor asks, looking at the sleeping teenager in the corner of the room. 'Shall I turn the volume down?'

'Don't worry, nothing wakes her when she's like this. She'll be out for the count until morning,' Lily replies.

'Is that normal for a teenager?'

'It is when I've given her a strong sedative.'

'You did what?'

Conor looks genuinely shocked but the rest of us barely react. All families have their own version of normal, and I confess that ours is a little different from most.

Lily shrugs. 'I asked Nancy to crush one of her pills and put it in Trixie's tea earlier—'

'I used to secretly give *my* daughters sleeping pills all the time when they were kids,' Nancy interrupts, as though proud of the fact.

'And *we* turned out just fine!' says Lily, with a large dose of irony. She smiles, before turning to our mother. 'I remember catching you putting the pills inside gummy bears, so we thought it was a bedtime treat before brushing our teeth. Mine were hidden inside green bears, Rose got the red ones, Daisy's were always gold. We never questioned it, just did as we were told. Trixie wouldn't stop crying after finding Nana. Hopefully she'll just sleep now until the tide goes out and we can leave. I wish I could do the same.'

Lily opens a new packet of cigarettes, her fingers shaking with impatience while she lights one. Any guilt I felt regarding my feelings about her evaporates. Nobody says anything about Lily smoking, or the fact that she drugged her own daughter to stop her from crying. We all have bad habits, some we let the world see, some we only reveal with family, and some we're too ashamed to share with anyone except ourselves. She lights up and instantly looks calmer, appearing to breathe out her unease with a puff of smoke.

Conor shakes his head, but Lily ignores him. Rose – I think sensing that a distraction might be good for the whole family – switches on Nana's old TV set. It slowly comes to life, displaying fuzzy grey and white pixels.

'The tape says WATCH ME, so let's see what happens when we do,' she says, sliding the video into the VHS machine, which swallows the tape whole. An image fills the screen, and it feels like the past is coming back to haunt us all.

# Fifteen

*SEAGLASS – 1980*

The face of my nine-year-old sister fills the screen. It appears to be Lily's turn to be the star of the family home movie. Some people are born to be the stars of their own show, and she was never interested in learning life's lines unless they were from her own script. Other people are viewed as little more than extras in Lily's rather narrow field of vision. If you don't have a scene in her story, you don't exist in her world.

Our summers at Seaglass were always my favourite time of year as a young child. As soon as school was over for my sisters, my mother would load up the car with suitcases, food, wine, and us, then we'd make the journey from London to Cornwall and escape the city for six weeks. Inevitably we would always time it wrong, arriving when the tide was in so we couldn't cross the causeway, but that didn't matter. As soon as I could see the old house, with its turquoise turrets, it always felt like I was home. We would play on the thin strip of remaining black sand while we waited for the sea to retreat. Sometimes having to wait for something just makes you want it more.

Nana was always so happy to see us. She would cross the sandy causeway as soon as it was safe to do so, always with the rusty old wheelbarrow in front of her and a dog close behind. I remember a black Labrador called Bob before Poppins came along. Nana would hug and kiss us all, then load our bags onto the wheelbarrow, to make it easier to transport everything to the house. It took a few trips back and forth, and we'd take it in turns to ride on top. Our bedrooms were always as we'd left them, but with clean sheets, fresh flowers, and a chocolate coin beneath the pillow of each bed. Nana always knew how to make us feel welcome and loved when we were children.

Dad was rarely there even before the divorce. My father would normally join us for at least a couple of weeks, but I don't remember him being there at all during the summer of 1980, until after it happened. Which makes me wonder if my parents' marriage was already in trouble, way back then. It was also around that time that our mother insisted we call her Nancy – she said that to keep calling her anything else made her feel old.

The room is completely quiet as the video begins. Nine-year-old Lily is standing in the hallway full of clocks at Seaglass . . . there are still spaces on the wall for the extra twenty or so clocks Nana has collected since. I remember this as Lily's *Fame* phase. I think we all do, and Nancy smiles in the present when her favourite daughter smiles in the past. Lily takes a few steps back from the camera, to reveal a 1980s outfit that these days would be mistaken for fancy dress. The neon-pink T-shirt, purple leggings, tutu, headband and pink leg warmers bring it all back. I notice the others smiling as the child on the screen dances to the music and sings along, knowing every word of the *Fame* theme tune. Her endless singing about living forever seems to bother me the most, along with the other lyric she repeats a few seconds later, staring straight at the camera.

'Remember. Remember. Remember. Remember.'

I do remember that summer at Seaglass. I wish that I didn't.

If you were to walk into Nana's house, there are three doors on the left of the hallway, two at the end, and one on the right. On the left you'd find a lounge, then a small library, then the music room. At the far end of the clock-filled hall is a door to the enormous kitchen, and a door to a tiny bathroom. An elaborate staircase is on the right of the hallway, but just before that there is one other door. Which was almost always locked. Nana's studio, or 'the West Wing', as she sometimes liked to call it, was very much out of bounds when my sisters came to stay. It runs the full length of the house, with a door at each end, and is where she liked to write and illustrate her children's books. These days there are giant framed book covers on the walls, including *Daisy Darker's Little Secret* and some of Nana's other favourites: *Suzy Smith's Best Birthday*, *Danny Delaney's Lost Dog*, *Poppy Patel's First Fib* and *Charlie Cho's Worst Weekend*. But back in 1980, Nana was still illustrating other people's books and had yet to write one of her own.

Inside the studio, there were three large desks permanently covered in sketch books and drawings, four windows letting in lots of light, endless rows of different watercolour paints, pots full of ink, pens, pencils and brushes, and enormous drawers filled with different coloured paper. There were shelves crammed full of all sorts of paraphernalia that Nana once described as 'a few of my favourite things', and there was a huge easel with a white sheet over the top on the day this home movie was filmed. The sheet was hiding Nana's latest work in progress – she didn't like anyone to see her work until it was finished. A newspaper once described Nana as the female Quentin Blake. She was furious, and said that they should have called *him* the male Beatrice Darker.

Nana's studio was the only room in Seaglass where my sisters were not allowed to look at anything, touch anything, or even venture inside. *I* was allowed, when it was just Nana and I, and so was Conor, but she never trusted my sisters. Even back then. They both knew and understood the rules, but Lily was never very good at following them. When she got a pair of roller skates for her ninth birthday, all she wanted to do was skate around the house. With all the internal doors open, it was possible to skate from the hall to the lounge, through to the library, then the music room, the kitchen and Nana's studio in a giant loop, and there was nothing Rose or I could say to persuade her that this was a very bad idea.

As soon as Nana had left that morning to cycle into town for supplies, Lily put on her skates. She insisted that Rose time her skating laps, and film her doing them. It was my job to watch the causeway from my bedroom window upstairs and warn my sisters when Nana returned. Which I fully intended to do. But the sky was extremely blue that day, and the clouds drifting across it made very interesting shapes.

I spotted a cloud pony and a cloud castle, both of which were distracting for a four-year-old with a big imagination. I'd been taught to name a few clouds by Rose, the walking, talking encyclopaedia of the family. There is nothing more calming than a good fluffy white cumulus in a bright blue sky, or the birdlike beauty of cirrus clouds made from tiny ice crystals, *or* a sky full of thick stratocumulus, because in real life we all contain shades of light and dark. There are as many different kinds of clouds as there are different kinds of people and, like people, they all float and drift as they please, being one thing one minute, transforming into something quite different the next. Unrecognizable in the blink of an eye. The circle of life exists in every aspect of nature, and we all just play our part for as long as the universe decides.

The home movie begins with Rose filming from the hallway as Lily shoots past, skating through every room and singing along to the *Fame* theme tune at the same time.

'Is this my best side?' Lily asked, whooshing by.

'They're both as bad as each other,' ten-year-old Rose replied from behind the camera, and I imagine her smiling to herself.

The video is surprisingly good. Then the star of the show got a little more ambitious and decided to film herself, while skating and singing. Sometimes she aimed the camera down at her feet, and I could see the red-and-white roller skates I remember so well, zooming across the wooden floors. It took her forever to lace up those skates, and Lily was almost as tall as Rose when wearing them. Perhaps that was another reason why she loved them.

The music was so loud that neither of my sisters heard Nana return. The home movie shows Lily's point of view as she is filming and skating into one end of the studio. The camerawork wobbles when she spots Nana standing at the other end of the room, with her arms and face folded into cross shapes. Then Lily collides with an enormous easel, sending a giant painting crashing to the floor. The film ends on a sideways, ground-level shot, showing puddles of red and blue paint.

Nana marched over and peered down at my sister where she had fallen.

'Lily Darker, you have a lot to learn. If you must always break the rules in life, you need to understand how to do so without getting caught. *Look like the innocent flower, but be the serpent under it.*'

'What?' Lily said, rubbing a bruised knee.

'Pardon, not what. It's Shakespeare.' Nana may as well have

said it was Swahili. 'Look, Lily, I admire your spirit and your ambition to always get your own way in life, but I fear others might find your personality tiresome and petulant when you are older. If you want to be bad and get away with it, you need to be better at pretending to be good. Like the innocent flower they all wish you were. Understand?'

Upstairs, I had just spotted a cloud dragon in the sky outside my bedroom window, and when Lily appeared in the doorway, red-faced and with flaring nostrils, she looked a lot like a dragon and nothing like an innocent flower.

'You were supposed to be on lookout,' she hissed. 'Why must you be such a baby, and when are you going to grow up?'

I reached inside myself for a suitable response but, despite a frantic search, could not find one until the moment had passed and she was no longer there to hear it. There are a lot of things I wish I'd said to my older siblings when I was a child, if only I had been clever enough to think of them at the time. But I just said sorry, like always. Apologies were a bit like Get Out of Jail Free cards in our house.

Lily was banned from roller-skating inside or outside Seaglass for a week, and I got the blame. She didn't speak to me at all for three days – which was a blessing in some ways – but then Lily did something I have never known her to do before or since: *she* apologized.

'I'm sorry I shouted at you, Daisy,' she said, wearing another one of her neon-coloured 1980s costumes. 'It wasn't fair of me to blame you for what happened. And I've got you a little surprise to make up for it. It's in the cupboard under the stairs.'

'I don't believe you,' I said, because I didn't – Lily was always telling fibs, and we were all a bit scared of the cupboard under the stairs. The reason why someone is lying is almost always more interesting than the lie itself.

'Don't then,' she replied with a custom shrug of her shoulders. 'Rose! Isn't there a surprise for Daisy downstairs?'

Nana was out walking the dog, and had left Rose in charge because our mother was taking a nap. Rose was passing my bedroom with her nose in an *Encyclopaedia Britannica* that looked heavier than me, and she was clearly only half listening. Rose knew that she wanted to be a vet from a very young age, just like Lily knew that she didn't want to be or do anything. Neither of them changed their minds over the years. It was different for me. My dreams changed shape as often as the clouds I liked staring at. One year I wanted to be a musician like my father, another I dreamt of writing books like Nana, but I never thought I'd live long enough to do either. Which might be why I stopped aiming for a life that felt too out of reach.

Rose was often left in charge because she was the oldest. It was a responsibility that she, like a lot of eldest siblings, came to resent. 'Oh, yes, the *surprise*,' she said. 'We all know about it . . . the one downstairs?'

Looking back now, I don't think she knew what was going on. But I trusted Rose, so I went down the creaky steps sideways and one at a time – they were steep, and my little legs were still rather short – completely oblivious to the fact that Lily was filming the whole thing.

'That's right, step inside the cupboard,' she said. 'There's a secret fairy door in the wall, right at the back there, do you see it? You'll have to go all the way in to find it.' The idea of a secret fairy door in the skirting board was very exciting to four-year-old me. I soon overcame my fear and went inside. 'Knock on the wood,' said Lily. 'The fairies might come out and say hello.'

I did as she said, but what appeared wasn't a fairy. The tiny door shape in the skirting board was in fact a mouse hole, but the mouse that ran out looked enormous, more like a rat. As soon as I screamed, Lily closed the cupboard door, locking me inside.

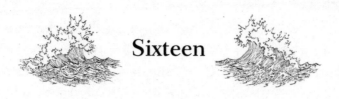

# Sixteen

## SEAGLASS – 1980

I cried in the dark for what felt like hours, and I banged on that door until my knuckles bled. I was never afraid of the dark before then, but I have been ever since. I don't think that's childish or silly. I think it's completely logical to fear what you cannot see. Our mother was sleeping off a vat of cheap wine she'd drunk alone at lunchtime, while I was locked inside the cupboard under the stairs. She'd taken a pill *and* put in earplugs to drown out the sound of her children – so it was only when Nana came back from walking the dog that anyone heard me crying. Her face was one of horror when she finally found the keys and unlocked the cupboard door. Lily was banned from roller-skating for two more weeks, and it was Nana's idea that Rose and Lily should be further punished by having to take me to the beach on my fifth birthday.

The following week, after a breakfast of pancakes with hot chocolate sauce, that's what they begrudgingly did, both holding one of my hands so that I could swing between them.

'And do *not* take your father's camcorder. I've told you

before, it's not a toy. If you get sand in it and it stops working, I'll never hear the end of it,' said Nancy, waving us off at the door.

'Okay!' yelled Lily, already marching down the causeway with the camcorder tucked inside her backpack. She held my hand as we headed for the beach, until she thought Nana and our mother could no longer see. I remember her grinning in my direction. Her smile had holes where the tooth fairy had stolen her teeth, a bit like the piano with its missing key.

'You're five now, Daisy. And I think you're old enough to play with Rose and me more often,' Lily said. Rose frowned as though hearing this for the first time. 'Would you like that?'

I nodded. I would have done almost anything to get them to like me more. The age gap between them at nine and ten was minimal, but the years between them and me always seemed vast. I would often watch them playing clapping games, tapping their hands together, faster and faster, while chanting strange rhymes. There was one about going to a Chinese restaurant, to buy a loaf of *bread bread bread*. It made no sense to me, but I longed to be a part of it anyway. I had tried several times before to keep up with their big-girl games, and it rarely ended well. I was permanently covered in scratches and bruises, and my nostrils were frequently overcome by the smell of Savlon and TCP.

We played with an old skipping rope until Lily got bored, chanting the rhymes their friends had taught them, and they had taught me. I didn't know what half of them meant, but I learned the words through repetition and a desire to join in, just like all children do. I remember my favourite rhyme we used to chant and skip to:

*Lizzie Borden took an axe,*
*She gave her mother forty whacks.*
*After she saw what she had done,*
*She gave her father forty-one.*
*Lizzie Borden got away.*
*For her crime she did not pay.*

Rose *loved* that rhyme. Those skipping games on the beach were one of the few childhood activities at Seaglass that required all three of us: two to swing the rope, one to jump.

'Let's play the mermaid game instead. Do you want to go first?' Lily said, with her hole-filled smile.

They buried me in the black sand until my face was all they could see. Then they made a sand-shaped mermaid's tail and decorated it with seashells. They left me there for over an hour while they built sandcastles nearby. Our family seems like a sandcastle to me now, quick and relatively effortless to build, and even faster to wash away, as though it never existed. I can remember nothing solid about the relationships we had with one another, nothing substantial that couldn't be obliterated in a mere moment by a cross word or the crash of a wave none of us saw coming. I remember hating both of my sisters for the first time that day. *Really* hating them. I couldn't move – the sand was too heavy where they had buried me beneath it. My face was burning in the hot sun and I was crying, until Conor came along. He had two yo-yos that year, and could do all kinds of clever tricks with them, both at once. I heard him talking to Rose before I saw him.

'Did you know that Seaglass was one of the properties used in the Second World War to look after evacuated children?' he said.

'No, how do you know that?' ten-year-old Rose asked, sounding genuinely interested.

'I read about it at the library, and now I'm writing about it for my school newspaper. I'm going to be a journalist one day. Children would walk here to this stretch of coast, all the way from Plymouth. A long line of them carrying their little suitcases over the hills and sand dunes, to escape the bombings in the city, leaving their parents behind.'

'Conor, help me!' I yelled.

He looked amused at first when he spotted me stuck in the sand with my mermaid's tail of shells. But when he saw that I'd been crying, he dug me out at once and pulled me up.

'It was just a joke,' said Rose, looking at Conor, not wanting him to think badly of her.

'Yeah, don't be such a crybaby all the time,' said Lily.

'I *hate* you both!' I said, then stormed off to get my armbands. 'I'm going to swim to America and I never want to see either of you ever again.' When Lily laughed it only made me more determined. The tide was coming in, and I think deep down I knew I'd probably only make it to the little rock island half a mile out, but I thought I was a good swimmer. And with my orange armbands, I felt invincible. I looked at Rose, who was the eldest after all, but she just stared down at the sand.

That was when Lily picked up the camcorder again.

I watch now in horror, along with the rest of the family in the present, as five-year-old me starts to swim out to sea. It reminds me of when we watched *Titanic* together, knowing that the film couldn't possibly end well. I see myself getting smaller and smaller, doing my own variation of backstroke, which involved rolling over for a bit of doggy paddle now and then to see where I was going. Only Lily and Rose had been sent for swimming lessons.

When I was halfway to the rock island, I got scared and turned around. Rose was at the water's edge, yelling something

I could not hear. Conor was waving his arms, and even Lily appeared to be a little worried, beckoning me to come back. They all looked very small and far away, and I decided maybe it wasn't a good idea to swim to America that day after all. I tried to head back towards Blacksand Bay, but the sea had other plans.

I was dragged sideways first. Then backwards. Then one of my armbands came off when a wave crashed over me. We'd been warned about the dangerous undercurrents in the bay when the tide was this distance from the shoreline, but I was too little to understand the consequences of ignoring them. Fear is something we have to feel to learn, and learn to feel.

The harder I tried to swim towards my sisters, the further away they seemed to get. The ocean was suddenly very loud inside my little ears. It dragged me under. I remember the panic and the pain. I felt as though the cold water had stolen the air from my lungs and I couldn't breathe, then the sea and sky folded in on each other and on me. I was drowning in blue. Then life turned black.

Rose pulled off her clothes, dumped them on the sand, and ran into the ocean wearing a red swimsuit. She was only ten, and she knowingly risked her own life to save mine that day. Things were different after that. Once Rose knew I was broken, I became something she wanted to fix. An injured bird in her imaginary cage. She dragged me back to shore, then performed the CPR that cracked two of my ribs. And Lily filmed the whole thing.

It feels like an out-of-body experience as I watch myself coughing up water, and see Nana and my mother running onto the beach. The film stops then, but I remember the paramedics doing their best to cross the causeway, and I remember seeing Conor and Rose holding hands as I was carried away from them all. He wrote a story about her for his school newspaper after that, the headline read: *Local Hero Saves Her Sister's Life*. It was the first time that I understood that friendships can change a person. True best friends bring out the best in you.

I was in hospital for two weeks while the doctors prodded and poked me. Routine tests revealed my broken heart, and things were never the same again. The first night, when my family had all left and I was alone on a scary ward, I was grateful that my bed was next to the window. The moon was bright that evening, and it meant that I could see cloud creatures, even though the sky was black. They danced across the shy moon, but the shapes they made no longer resembled ponies or dragons. Only monsters. Monsters don't always hide in the dark. Some walk around in broad daylight, happy to be seen by anyone foolish enough to look in their direction.

My mother blamed herself for my broken heart. I have always known that deep down, but never quite understood why. Something she did while pregnant with me perhaps? The doctors said my condition was so rare they still didn't know what caused it. Nancy spent days sitting by my bedside or in waiting rooms. She tutted and sighed and flicked through the free magazines, looking for competitions to enter. Nancy rarely *read* anything except a TV guide.

I remember when the doctors said that I was well enough for the whole family to visit. My sisters gave me home-made get-well cards, Nana brought me a bottle of Lucozade, and a box of Quality Street filled with only toffee pennies because they were my favourites. Dad sent 'all his love' from a concert hall in Vienna. Apparently there were no flights back to the UK that week. Lily wore a new dress and her very best smile for the occasion. She was the last one to leave my hospital bed, and rushed back over when they were all about to go. Everyone waited in the entrance to the ward while she whispered something in my ear before kissing me on the cheek.

'Good girl,' said Nancy, happy that her favourite daughter was trying to make up for what had happened. She has always been a firm believer in fraudulent feelings. She presumed Lily had apologized and didn't hear what my sister had really said. None of them did, but I've never forgotten it:

'I wish you had drowned.'

 # Seventeen

*31 October 1:45 a.m.*
*less than five hours until low tide*

I was never allowed to go to school once my hidden heart problem was exposed, and life was never allowed to return to normal. For any of us. My parents divorced less than a year later. Some marriages are held hostage by memories of happier times, others are imprisoned by the idea that parenthood can only be performed well in pairs. A dying child seemed to set my parents free from each other. My two older sisters were sent to boarding school; I was more than enough for my mother to look after and they were too much. A groundless guilt consumed her and she wrapped the rest of my childhood in cotton wool, which in turn led to me wrapping myself inside books. Hundreds of them. Reading was one of the few things I was still allowed to do.

Books saved me, and I ran away inside the stories I read as a child. They were the only place where I could run, and swim, and dance without fear of falling and not being able to get back up. Books were full of friends and adventures, whereas my real childhood was cold, and dark, and horribly lonely. I've never spoken honestly about it with anybody. Until now. And the only place that felt like home when I was a child was Seaglass. I think that's why the idea of never coming back here hurts too much. Nana's little library was my Disneyland, and the books inside it were the paper-shaped rides that let me live, while everyone else was waiting for me to die.

Sometimes people get impatient when they have to wait too long for something.

'I've always felt terrible about what happened that day on the beach, and all the other days when I wasn't as kind as I could have been,' says Lily, back in the present, where she can no longer bully me the way she used to. She doesn't look me in the eye when she says it. I don't think she can, and I don't really believe that Lily is sorry at all.

Her words do nothing to blunt my anger, instead they sharpen it into a more dangerous shape, one which will leave a mark. But I bite my tongue, as always, keen to keep the peace. My sisters won't talk to me because of what happened with Conor a few years ago. It seems so unfair, given all the things *they* did when I was a child. But saying how I really feel about it all now isn't going to help fix what got broken then, and there are bigger things to worry about.

Why would someone want us to watch that home movie?

I look at my sisters tonight and see us all exactly the same way we were then. They might be taller, older, have a few more wrinkles, but we are all just children masquerading as the adults we thought we should become. My personality is very similar now to what it was when I was a child. I'm still shy, and quiet, and happiest at home. Rose and Lily haven't changed very much either; none of us have, not really. There are pockets of sadness in all of our lives, and mine are deep. The diagnosis of my broken heart felt like a death sentence, and five is awfully young to find out that you won't live forever.

They say that your life flashes before your eyes when you die, so you should make it a life worth watching. But, as someone who has died several times, I don't think that is true. For me, every time my heart stopped beating, it felt like a delayed train journey through the cruellest moments of my life. The memories didn't flash, they were slow and painful. It was like travelling through time and space to somewhere dark and cold, to relive my worst mistakes in technicolour misery. Sometimes I could still hear people around me, when my heart stopped. I swear I heard doctors or nurses saying that I was dead on more than one occasion. My parents didn't believe me back then, but neurologists have since confirmed that the human brain is still active for a period of time after death, and I promise you that it is true. Dead people can hear you, so be careful what you say. I hope it wasn't too awful for Nana. Or my dad. I hope neither of them heard something they shouldn't have.

We take death almost as for granted as life. We think we know what to expect because we've read a chapter of a book or watched a scene in a film. We no longer seem capable of separating fiction from facts. There is so much that we don't know we don't know. It scares me. When you've died as often as I have, it's hard not to become a little preoccupied with it all, and seeing other people take their good health for granted makes me so angry. None of them understand what it's like for me. How could they? I'm grateful to still be here, but death has been part of my life for so long, I worry about it all of the time. Our future is just our past in the making.

'I don't get it,' says Conor. 'Who left this tape on the kitchen table with the words WATCH ME stuck to the front? It must have been one of us, so who was it?'

Nobody answers him.

Lily lights another cigarette before tossing the match and a log on the fire, which crackles, and spits and choreographs a hundred eerie shadows to dance across the room. Then she takes a long drag before slowly blowing smoke from her pink lips.

'Do you *ever* think about anyone except yourself?' Rose says, staring at her.

'What does *that* mean?' Lily asks, sitting up and staring back.

'Rose,' says Nancy, trying to prevent storm damage when the rest of us can see that the roof has already blown right off. The home movie has brought back some unhappy memories for everyone. Maybe *that's* why someone thought we should watch it. When Lily loses her temper, she's the only one who can find it again, but it's unlike Rose to lose control of her emotions.

'Honestly, you are the most selfish and spoilt person I've ever had the misfortune to know. I'd actually forgotten how cruel you used to be to Daisy when we were kids. The poem in the kitchen, and everything Dad said about you last night is true,' Rose continues, while we all wait for Lily to react. I fully expect her next words to be soaked in sarcasm, her preferred form of self-defence. I confess I do enjoy it more than I should when my older sisters squabble. It always felt like them against me when we were younger, and them against one another is much more fun. All families have their own private routines and secret language, and all families know how to hurt each other.

'I don't care what Dad thought about me, and I don't care what you think either. Why don't you get a life and stop judging mine,' Lily says.

'I'd gladly not watch the car crash that is your life any longer, it's embarrassing. Maybe with Nana and Dad gone, we don't need to keep playing happy families. Perhaps we can all just go our own separate ways for good when the tide goes out?'

'Rose, you don't mean that,' says Nancy.

'Don't I?' As soon as she sees the look on our mother's face, my eldest sister softens again, retreating inside the version of herself she thinks we all want her to be. 'I'm . . . sorry. I already had a terrible day before I got here and, like everyone else, I just can't believe what has happened. Or that Nana and Dad are gone.'

Rose's unexpected Jekyll and Hyde routine catches us all off guard. When I try to translate the look on her face, I think it is fear. Rose is terrified, and maybe she is right to be. Maybe finally, and for the first time, my family *does* know what it is like to be me; to live with the constant fear that today might be their last. I see the same fear on the faces of the residents at the care home where I volunteer; because they know their time is almost up. I do my best to comfort them, listen to their regrets and ease their anxiety, but they know it's inevitable. Life kills us all in the end. I stare at my family as we sit in yet another awkward silence, wondering how it came to this. In contrast, the storm outside continues to make itself heard, the sound of rain constantly tapping on the windows like a thousand tiny fingernails.

'Why was yesterday a bad day?' Conor asks Rose, sounding genuinely interested.

She makes eye contact with him very briefly, then stares into the distance as though reliving another memory she would rather forget.

'I got a call from the RSPCA yesterday afternoon. I had to stop off at a disused barn on the way here and there were six ponies locked inside. They hadn't had food or water for days.'

Even Lily looks moved. 'That's so sad. What did you do? Will they get rehomed?'

'I shot every one of them. Between the eyes.' Rose looks up, but nobody says anything. I look around the room and see that everyone is as shocked as I feel. 'I had to,' she says. 'It was too late to save them, there was nothing I could do. They were in agony. I had to do something to end their pain, but I didn't have enough anaesthetic to inject them all. My gun was the only option. It was awful. I can still hear them. Did you know that horses cry when they are scared? Like children.' Her hands tremble a little and she balls them into fists. 'I wish I could have shot those responsible instead. Sometimes I *loathe* people, I really do. I don't understand how human beings are capable of such horrific things, or why they inflict so much pain on others.'

The silence seems to swallow us all this time.

'I didn't even know you had a gun,' says Lily.

Rose sighs. 'It's just a small handgun. A lot of vets have guns and are licensed to use them. It's normally locked in the safe at the practice.'

Nancy frowns. 'But if you did . . . *that* on the way here, does that mean there is a loaded gun in the house? With real bullets?'

'Don't worry. I hid it somewhere safe when I arrived.'

The silence resumes and I study my eldest sister for a while. I know that her vet practice is having a little money trouble, but I also know she has always been too proud to ask for any financial help from anyone, unlike Lily. Rose would have really benefited from Nana's money had she been left any, and would have put it to good use. I notice how she keeps checking her watch, and wonder whether she is just counting down the hours before we can leave. Just over four now, I think. Rose looks so sad. She has always found human company unsatisfying. She says she finds it exhausting to listen to the manufactured feelings of people too stupid to know when their thoughts are not their own. I wonder what her thoughts are now as she checks her watch again, for the second time in less than a minute. I'm not the only one studying Rose, and it's as though the weight of our stares are too heavy for her to bear.

'Why are you all looking at me like that?' she asks.

'I think, given everything that has happened tonight, we all might feel a bit anxious about there being a gun in the house,' says Nancy.

'Fine. My gun didn't kill anyone, but if it will make everyone feel better, I'll go and check that it's still safe where I left it,' Rose says, standing to leave the room.

Vets are more likely to commit suicide than almost any other profession. That statistic used to make me worry about my eldest sister – vets work long hours, often alone – and when I think of all the horrific things she has seen, it scares me. Rose knows how to end lives as well as save them; sadly, it's part of her job.

'I might see if I can get a signal on my phone upstairs . . . maybe it will work up there,' says Conor.

'It won't,' says Lily. 'I don't feel quite right. I'm going to my room to try to find my diabetic kit.'

Nancy nods. 'I can feel one of my migraines coming. I'm going to get a glass of water and some pills from the kitchen,' she says, heading for the door like the rest of them. My mother thinks there is a pill for any and all situations.

'Well, I might just get a bit of air,' I say, not wanting to be left behind. I think we're all feeling a little claustrophobic trapped in this house together, but also all scared of being alone. I stand in the hallway and can hear different corners of the house creaking with quiet activity. The noise does nothing to calm my nerves. I have always preferred the sound of silence.

I notice that the front door is slightly ajar and step out onto the porch, but there is nobody there. The roar of the sea and the melody of the wind chimes remind me how isolated we are out here, cut off from the mainland for several hours every day. And night. When you've spent as much time alone as I have, it can be hard to be around people for too long. Even family. Especially one like ours.

I was the last to leave the room, but think I'm the first to return to the lounge a short while later, and I spot something unfamiliar on the coffee table. The rest of the family come back before I can take a closer look. Conor is the last to return, but he's the first to see what I saw, and from the tone of his voice, it's as though he's accusing me of putting it there.

'What's that on the table?' he asks.

'It's the tape we just watched,' Lily replies.

'I don't think it is,' I say, taking a step back.

'No. It isn't,' Rose confirms.

We're all looking at the tape now. It wasn't there before, and the Scrabble letters stuck to the case of this home movie spell a different message:

**HEAR ME**

'What the hell?' says Conor. 'Who did this?' He looks around the room at each of us.

'*You're* the one who noticed it, maybe it was you,' says Lily.

Rose picks it up carefully. 'The last tape said WATCH ME. This one says HEAR ME. This is super messed up. Who would do this, and why?'

We are all staring at one another, silent accusations exchanged in the form of wary glances.

'We should watch it,' I say, and then everyone starts arguing about the pros and cons of doing so.

'Enough!' Nancy says, and the rest of us are quiet. 'No more games. Nana and your dad are dead. There's nobody else here at Seaglass and I don't believe in ghosts. Who left that tape on the table?'

Nobody answers.

'Maybe the only way to find out is to watch it,' Rose says, and when nobody argues, she slides the video out of its case and into the machine, then presses play.

 # Eighteen

## SEAGLASS – 1982

Christmases at Seaglass were always magical, until my parents got divorced. Nana made a bigger effort than ever to welcome my mother, my sisters and me, but it didn't feel quite the same without Dad there. I'll never forget the Christmas of 1982. I was seven, Lily was eleven, and Rose was twelve. We had a huge tree that year – delivered by boat – which we all helped to decorate. We made paper chains, and a wonky chocolate yule log, then on Christmas Eve, the Darker family women watched *ET*. It was my first ever trip to the cinema, and I loved every minute of it. But the home movie I can see on Nana's old TV now didn't capture any of that. It starts on Christmas Day 1982 and, as usual, begins with Lily.

If Father Christmas really did make a naughty list every year, then my sister would have been at the top. But she still got all the gifts and toys she wanted as a child, even when money was tight. I think Nancy thought that the tantrums would cost her more in the long run. High on Lily's wish list that year was a Walkman. As soon as she had unwrapped it, Lily listened to it *everywhere*, even when she was eating, or roller-skating, or watching TV, which made little sense to me.

And she was always singing along to something, normally very badly. The song I most remember her murdering that year was 'Physical' by Olivia Newton-John.

'I'm bored of filming this now,' says twelve-year-old Rose from behind the camera.

'One more lap, I'm getting faster every time!' says Lily, whooshing past the outside walls of Seaglass on a newer, bigger pair of roller skates.

'The slush puppies are nearly ready!' I hear seven-year-old me say, and it's a shock when the camera turns in my direction. We're in the garden that my mother loved so much, and it looks freezing cold. I'm wearing a fluffy bobble hat and one of Lily's hand-me-down coats. I remember the wooden toggles that I found inexplicably difficult to fasten. I'd had two oper-ations on my heart that year, and I do not look well. I'm far too skinny and there are dark circles beneath my eyes. But I do look happy, playing with my Mr Frosty toy and making syrupy crushed ice drinks for the Care Bears my sisters were too old to play with. The bears had been gifts from Nana. Mine was pink with a rainbow on its tummy. Lily's was blue with a raincloud, and Rose's bear was turquoise with a shooting star – she was obsessed with the solar system that year.

'Stick out your tongue!' says Rose from behind the camera, and when I do, it is stained red from slush puppie syrup.

The camera turns a little further and I see Conor. He's sitting at Nana's ramshackle old garden table, wearing two jumpers, a paper cracker hat and a frown. He appears to be deep in concentration while writing something.

'Hey, Conor! What are you doing? Working on another article for the school newspaper?' asks Rose.

'No,' says the lanky but handsome boy.

'What is it then?'

'It's the Darker family tree. I'm making it for your nana, to say thank you for having me.'

I don't remember him being with us that Christmas, but I suppose he often was at Seaglass whenever his dad wasn't well enough to look after him. I do remember the family tree, though. It inspired Nana to paint her own version of it on the wall next to the staircase, with all our hand-painted faces and dates of birth. The shot seems to linger on Conor's face for a long time.

'Who is that?' Lily says, skating past the camera again, which turns 180 degrees to reveal the sandy causeway.

The tide was out, and Nancy came to stand beside us. We all stopped and stared at the silhouette of a Dad-shaped figure in the distance. I looked up at Nancy's face, and the strained smile stretched across it confirmed that it was him. I dropped my slush puppie, Lily pulled off her roller skates, and I think Nancy must have taken the camera from Rose, because the next thing I see is the three of us running towards our father who we hadn't seen for six months. He was dressed as Father Christmas, but barefoot, with his red trousers rolled up to his knees to avoid getting the costume covered in seawater and sand.

We ran across the causeway to greet him as though he were a brave knight returning from battle, which I know must have hurt my mother at the time. She was the one who stuck around to take care of us when he took off – sort of, when my sisters weren't at school, or we weren't all dumped on Nana – but we were just children, and didn't understand the politics of parenthood when people got divorced. Nancy waited where she was on the stone steps that lead up to the house, filming the moment. When my dad went to kiss her on the lips, she turned her head so that he kissed her cheek instead.

One of the best things about Dad coming back from touring around the world with his orchestra were the guilt-induced gifts he brought with him. Don't get me wrong, we were very happy to see the man, but we were also eager to see what he had bought us. My sisters and I followed him inside and stood in the doorway of the music room, watching Dad as he opened his giant suitcase, instead of unpacking in the bedroom he used to share with our mother.

Lily was never backward in coming forward, and blurted out the question we were all wondering about the most.

'Did you bring us presents?'

'Maybe,' Dad said and we cheered. When my mother said 'maybe' it meant no, but when my father said 'maybe' it meant yes. One word, two meanings. We might have only been children, but we were more aware than anyone that our parents spoke different languages.

Lily's smile slid right off her face when she opened her gift, tearing the wrapping paper without even bothering to read the neatly written tag.

'I've already got a Walkman! I unwrapped one this morning!' she whined.

Our father looked genuinely sad. 'Oh, I'm sorry, princess. Mummy said that was what you wanted this year . . .'

'The *real* Father Christmas bought it for her,' said seven-year-old me.

'There is no real Father Christmas. Why are you such a baby?' snapped my sister, glaring at me as though it were my fault that she received the same gift twice. I knew she was telling the truth about Santa, and suddenly my whole world – not just Christmas – felt like a lie. I started to cry.

'Lily, that's enough. *I* mentioned the Walkman to your father a few weeks ago, but he forgot to tell me *and* Father Christmas that he was going to get you one. Don't worry, darling. I'm sure we can change it for something else. Why don't we do this properly? Conor, can you take the camera for me? We don't all need to be huddled in the doorway. Girls, give your dad some space and we'll open the rest in the lounge.'

Lily folded her arms and went into full sulk mode as my dad gathered up all of the presents.

'I got you another gift, Lily. Just a small one,' he said, trying to redeem himself. We shuffled into the other room, all with one eye on the gifts my father was carrying, while my mother wrestled us out of our hats and coats.

'For god's sake, Frank. We said one present each.' Nancy's words sounded like they got stuck behind her teeth. Her gifts were like her love for us and always came with a sense of economy. We sat impatiently in our familiar seats in the lounge. I sat closest to the Christmas tree and the fireplace, and instantly went from being too cold to too hot, so I took off my jumper. I was wearing a red woollen V-neck dress underneath, covered in white lace snowflakes. It was a gift from Nana, and I wanted to wear it every day.

'I know we said one present each, but I couldn't resist. I found this in a little shop in Vienna and thought of you,' Dad said, giving Lily a small pink parcel.

'Good to know they weren't *all* last-minute duty-free purchases from the airport,' mumbled my mother beneath her breath. She tutted for good measure.

Lily ripped off the paper and beamed when she found a tiara inside. It was covered in fake jewels.

'Because I'm a princess!' she said.

'Yes, you are,' said Nana, walking into the lounge wearing a pink and purple apron, and speaking in an ironic tone I was too young to appreciate at the time. She gave Lily a withering look before putting a tray of warm mince pies on the table. Nana – always preferring to do things her own way – made savoury mince pies at Christmas. They contained minced beef, onions, and a secret splash of Tabasco, and were served with tiny jugs of gravy.

Lily pouted. 'Why can't we have *normal* mince pies?'

'Because normal is boring,' Nana replied. Then she hugged her son, my father, and sat down next to Nancy. I think she always wished that our parents would get back together just as much as we did, forever orchestrating family reunions that she hoped might actually reunite us.

The camera turns to Rose, and zooms in on her face. She was holding a box wrapped in tissue paper that was turquoise – her favourite colour. Unlike Lily, she opened her gift slowly, without tearing the paper at all, while we waited to see what was inside.

'Wow! Thank you, Dad,' she said, holding up a telescope.

'You're very welcome, and just in case the stars don't always shine for you . . .'

Rose opened a second gift, and I remember what it was before seeing it on the TV screen: a box of glow-in-the-dark stars.

'Thank you!' she said again, giving him a huge hug. It made me realize that Lily never thanked him once.

'I want stars!' Lily whined, folding her arms.

Dad ignored her. 'And this gift is for Daisy, my little pipsqueak,' he said, passing me a box.

Inside, there were five new books. They were all beautiful hardbacks, and I couldn't wait to start reading them. 'It's always important to have adventures, even if only in your imagination. Sometimes those are the best adventures of all,' he said, sounding more like Nana than himself. Then he gave me a second gift, and I didn't understand what it was when I first saw it.

'It's a View-Master,' explained my father, leaving me none the wiser as I stared at what looked like a red plastic pair of binoculars. 'I know it must make you sad, that your sisters get to go away to school, and I get to travel with my orchestra, and you have to stay behind . . . but now you can look inside this and pretend to be anywhere.'

Dad put a strange-looking reel inside the contraption, then held it up to my face. I remember being scared at first, but then I saw a picture of a forest, so real I thought I might be able to touch it. He showed me how to click the side of the gadget. The reel moved, and I saw a picture of a waterfall. It was like magic. I laughed, and my dad grinned, but his smile faded a little when he noticed the pink scar down the middle of my chest. I watched his reaction as he remembered that I was broken, and felt guilty that it made him so sad.

'I've missed you all so much,' he said. His words were like a hug, and I wanted to believe them. The camera catches him looking at my mother, and her looking away. I was too young to understand any of what was going on between them back then. When you hold on too tight to something, it can start to hurt.

'Conor, I was hoping you would be here,' Dad said, holding out a small gift. 'Let me take the camcorder while you open it. I hope you like it.' The camera turns to reveal a ridiculously happy-looking Conor, as though he had never been given a Christmas present before, and it made me wonder if maybe he hadn't. Nana said there were people who didn't believe in Christmas, or celebrate it, and just the idea of that made me feel sad.

'Different people believe in different things,' she said, when I didn't understand.

'What do you believe in?' I asked.

Nana smiled. 'I believe in kindness and hard work.'

'What about God?'

She smiled again. 'I believe that God believes in hard work too.'

'What should I believe in?' I asked.

'You should only believe in what *you* want to believe, and you should always believe in yourself.' It was a good piece of advice that I've never forgotten.

Conor carefully unwrapped a yo-yo unlike any I'd seen before.

'I found this in Shanghai when I was performing there,' Dad said, and my mother rolled her eyes. 'I'm told they're the best yo-yos in the world, but you're the expert!'

'It's perfect. Amazing. Thank you,' said Conor, with actual tears in his eyes, as though our father had given him a yo-yo made of gold.

'And . . . I'm told you've been writing for the school newspaper. I thought this might come in handy if you don't have a photographer,' Dad said, giving him another, slightly bigger parcel.

It was a Polaroid camera, and Conor's face lit up like the Christmas tree he was sitting next to. I remember him taking pictures of us all for his Darker family tree that afternoon. He took more of Rose than of anyone else. Nana used those pictures to paint our faces on the wall at Seaglass a few weeks later, so that who we were that day was captured in time forever.

Dad's gift for Nana was a cuckoo clock from Germany. It's one of the most eccentric clocks in the hall. Every hour, on the hour, a little wooden man and a little wooden woman come out of two tiny doors, and meet in the middle before she chops off his head with an axe. They do this all day, every day. My father's gift for his ex-wife was less disturbing. He gave my mother a small red velvet box, and Nancy smiled her real smile when she opened it. We all admired the beautiful silver heart-shaped locket. There was room for two tiny pictures, and when my mother smiled at my sisters, I was sure it was their faces she wanted to keep inside.

Memories are shapeshifters, especially the childhood variety, but that was a good Christmas. I don't think any of us appreciated our parents spending it together for us, despite being recently divorced. Looking back, I think they might have done more to make life better for us than we sometimes remember. My collection of happy childhood memories is a little threadbare.

We make moments with our families. Sometimes we stitch them together over time, to make more of them than they were. We share them and hold onto them together as if they were treasure, even when they start to rust. Sometimes those moments change shape in our memories, sometimes we stop being able to see them how they really were. Sometimes we have different recollections of the same moments, as though they were never really shared at all.

I remember the food we ate, the games we played, and the music we listened to. I remember John Lennon singing about Christmas on the radio, and my mother saying how sad she still was that he was dead. I asked if he was a friend of hers; I was too young to understand people grieving for someone they'd never met. I remember me and my sisters singing along to 'I Wish It Could Be Christmas Everyday', and the whole family singing carols with Dad playing the piano.

I overheard my parents briefly squabble in the kitchen, but not for long.

'You can't *buy* their love,' Nancy hissed, and Dad mumbled some inaudible reply. Now that I'm older, I realize that the problem was that he could. He'd show up once or twice a year with gifts wrapped in shiny paper tied with pretty bows, and we treated him like a king. Meanwhile we took her, and Nana, a bit for granted. There are things we all should know better, but being human means you can never know it all.

Alcohol always seemed to help my parents to tolerate being in each other's company, so they drank more and more of it over the years, and the squabbles were replaced with quiet stares, and the variety of silent conversations all parents have when their children are in earshot.

That night, when my parents put me to bed – together but apart – and turned out the light, I saw a galaxy of luminous stars on my bedroom ceiling. Rose had used her precious glow-in-the-dark stickers to decorate my room instead of her own.

'Night, night, pipsqueak,' she whispered, standing in my doorway.

'Why?' I whispered.

'Because you deserve to see the stars just as much as the rest of us.'

 # Nineteen

*31 October 2 a.m.*
*four hours until low tide*

'Why were you with us that Christmas?' Lily asks Conor when the film comes to an end.

He answers without looking at her. 'My father was in rehab, again, and Nana offered to look after me.'

The silence that follows is smashed by the sound of the clocks in the hallway. It's two o'clock in the morning, and we all look exhausted, especially my mother. She takes a sip of cold tea.

'Is there a way to turn off the clocks? I don't want them to wake Trixie,' Lily says.

My niece has been so quiet, sleeping on the window seat at the back of the room, I'd almost forgotten that she was here. I'm surprised that the sound of the TV didn't wake her, never mind the clocks, but then I remember the sedative they put in Trixie's drink earlier. My mother's sleeping pills are strong enough to take out an elephant. Lily gets up from the sofa to check on her daughter.

'Where is she?' Lily asks.

We're all up and out of our chairs within a matter of seconds. We stand and stare at the empty window seat and the blanket on the floor.

'Where is Trixie?' Lily shrieks, asking the question a second time, but still nobody replies. She stares at each of our faces, looking for an answer. In the absence of one, we start searching the room – checking behind the sofas and curtains – but Trixie isn't here.

'She's gone,' Lily says. 'I don't understand.'

Rose comes to her side, the protective-older-sister autopilot kicking in, their earlier squabble forgotten. 'Try to stay calm. She can't have gone far. You know what teenagers are like, you used to be one.'

'I thought we put a sleeping pill in Trixie's tea?' Nancy says. Lily turns on her. 'We *did*.'

'But that would have knocked her out for hours. Unless . . .'

'Unless what?' Lily snaps.

'Someone moved her . . .' Nancy whispers.

I don't understand how anyone could have moved Trixie without one of us seeing. But the window seat is in the far corner of the room, and we were all staring in the opposite direction at the TV. Plus, it's the middle of the night now, and we are exhausted with grief and tiredness. We all left the room earlier. Was Trixie here when we came back? Did anyone check? Despite her mother's constant digs about her dress size, Trixie is a normal weight for a girl her age. If anything, I'd describe her as petite. Easy enough for an adult to lift. I think it *is* possible that someone could have taken her, and knowing that makes me feel even worse, because at least one of us should have been keeping an eye on her.

The clocks stop ringing in the hallway. Nobody speaks, but we all follow Lily as she rushes out of the lounge, through the hall and into the kitchen. She stands in front of the chalk wall, and when I see Nana's poem, I understand why.

*Daisy Darker's family were as dark as dark can be.*
*When one of them died, all of them lied, and pretended not to see.*
~~*Daisy Darker's nana was the oldest but least wise.*~~
~~*The woman's will made them all feel ill, which was why she had to die.*~~
~~*Daisy Darker's father lived life dancing to his own tune.*~~
~~*His self-centred ways, and the pianos he played, danced him to his doom.*~~
*Daisy Darker's mother was an actress with the coldest heart.*
*She didn't love all her children, and deserved to lose her part.*
*Daisy Darker's sister Rose was the eldest of the three.*
*She was clever and quiet and beautiful, but destined to die lonely.*
*Daisy Darker's sister Lily was the vainest of the lot.*
*She was a selfish, spoilt, entitled witch, one who deserved to get shot.*
~~*Daisy Darker's niece was a precocious little child.*~~
~~*Like all abandoned ducklings, she would not fare well in the wild.*~~
*Daisy Darker's secret story was one someone sadly had to tell.*
*But her broken heart was just the start of what will be her last farewell.*
*Daisy Darker's family wasted far too many years lying.*
*They spent their final hours together learning lessons before dying.*

The part about Trixie has been crossed out.

'Oh my god,' Lily whispers, staring at the chalk words and covering her nose and mouth with her hands, as though praying to a God I know she does not believe in. 'It's coming true,' she says quietly, then turns to look at us all. 'It's. Coming. True.'

'What's coming true?' my mother asks.

Lily is shaking now. She points up at the poem, searches the faces of our family for any sign of understanding and finds none. But I know exactly what she means, even if I'm too scared to say it out loud. There is a low rumble of thunder in the distance outside. I hadn't noticed how hard it was raining. The storm is getting closer, and the house feels bitterly cold.

Lily's words tumble too quickly out of her mouth for the rest
of the family to keep up.

'Nana's poem on the wall. Can you not read it? Am I not
making sense? It's a poem about *us*. Dying. One by one. Nana
is *dead*, Dad is *dead*, and now Trixie is—'

'Missing. She's just missing. We'll find her,' says Rose.

'It's just one of Nana's silly poems,' says my mother.

'How do you know that she wrote it? I don't think it looks
like her handwriting. Anyone could have sneaked down here
in the night and written a poem on the wall,' Conor says
unhelpfully, as though thinking out loud. I remember the chalk
I saw on his jeans earlier, and the way he quickly dusted it
off. He's been quiet for a long time, and everyone turns to
stare at him.

'You're right,' says Lily. '*Your* name isn't up there. Maybe *you*
wrote it.'

'Maybe we should stop wasting time and look for Trixie,' I
say.

Before anyone can answer, there is another rumble of
thunder, but this one is so much louder than the last. Nancy
sways a little and grabs the side of the kitchen table to steady
herself.

'Are you okay?' Rose asks.

'I'm fine. Honestly,' Nancy says. 'It's a headache and I'm just
tired, like all of us. We need to find Trixie. Why don't you lot
check upstairs, and I'll carry on looking down here?'

'Good idea,' says Lily. She never listens to anyone except
our mother.

Rose, Lily, Conor and I run upstairs, calling Trixie's name,
before each disappearing into a different bedroom to search.
I start in the one Lily and Trixie shared last night.

This used to be my sisters' bedroom whenever they stayed

at Seaglass when we were children. It's bigger than mine, but I suppose there were two of them. Everything is very much the same as it was then, with ghastly pink carpet, pink curtains and floral wallpaper. My sisters were girly girls. I can still see the dark rectangles where they used to stick their posters when we were here for the summer holidays – always boy bands for Lily, cute animals for Rose. There are two beds on opposite sides of the room, two little tables, two windows, and a wall of built-in wardrobes.

'Trixie?' I whisper, but there's no reply. All I can hear is the rain lashing the window, and the sea crashing against the rocks outside. This is still a room of two sides. Lily's bed is unmade, with clothes on the floor around it, and her bedside table is a mess of magazines and make-up, even though she's only been here for a few hours. On the other side of the room, and in stark contrast, Trixie's bed is neatly made. All I can see on her bedside table is an old book she must have borrowed from Nana's library, and a glass of water.

I get down on the floor and look beneath the beds, but there is nothing there. I hear another deep rumble of thunder in the distance and have an overwhelming urge to hide. Storms at Seaglass seemed to be a regular occurrence when we were little girls, both the emotional and literal varieties. I remember being so scared by the sound of thunder outside – or shouting downstairs – that I would often run in here at night. Fear was one of the few things that seemed to unite me and my sisters when we were children.

A storm at Seaglass is not the same as a storm in London, or anywhere else that I have lived. Being in a storm here, on this tiny island, feels like being on a rickety old ship in the middle of the sea, one that will surely sink if the waves get too high. We used to hide together under the beds in this room when life got too loud – Lily under one, Rose and I huddled under the other. Then we would count the number of seconds between the lightning and the inevitable thunder that followed, to know how many miles away it would strike. I find myself counting again now.

*One Mississippi . . . Two Mississippi . . . Three Mississippi . . .*

There were other times, when a storm sneaked up on us in the night, when I would have to hide alone, under my own bed in my room. But we could always hear one another counting through the walls in the darkness. The closer the storm got, the more frightened we became, as a flash of light lit up whichever room we were hiding in. I'm sure my sisters are probably sharing the same silent memories now.

*One Mississippi . . . Two Mississippi . . .*

The doors on the built-in wardrobes that line one wall of the room all have wooden slats. As I take one last look around, I'm convinced I see one of them move out of the corner of my eye. I stop and stand perfectly still, listening.

'Trixie?' I whisper.

I hear something.

'Trixie, are you in there?'

The silence that follows suggests I must have imagined it. But then I hear what sounds like someone breathing very quietly.

I want to fling the doors open, but I'm scared of what I might find.

A flash of lightning lights up the sky outside the window for a second time, and I think I hear something move behind the wardrobe doors again. It's impossible to ignore now, and I force my feet to take a step closer. I pretend that there is nothing to be afraid of, even though events so far tonight suggest otherwise. The wardrobe is within touching distance,

and I slowly reach for the handle. Then there is another flash
of lightning.

*One Mississippi . . .*

I don't get to two.

The thunder claps as though eagerly applauding the show
before it is over. The noise is almost instant and so loud that
it seems to shake the house. The lights go out and I am a child
again, terrified in the darkness, too scared to move or make a
sound. I tell myself it's just a power cut and try to stay calm.

But then lightning strikes again.

It illuminates everything, including the wardrobe doors, and
I see two eyes between the slats staring right at me before the
room goes black.

Then the doors start to shake and rattle.

Someone is trapped inside, and they want to get out.

# Twenty

*31 October 2:15 a.m.*
*less than four hours until low tide*

It all happens so fast: the lightning, the eyes behind the wardrobe door, the darkness, and then the sound of Rose's voice right behind me in the room.

'What are *you* doing in here?' she asks, and at first I think she means me.

She has a torch – as though she knew the lights were going to go out – which she aims at the wardrobe before flinging the doors open.

Poppins the dog jumps out, rushing towards us. She barks and wags her tail before licking Rose's hand.

'Who put you in there?' Rose asks, and when the dog doesn't answer, they both turn to stare in my direction.

'It wasn't *me*,' I say.

'There's no sign of Trixie in the other bedrooms,' Conor says, appearing in the gloomy doorway. He holds up his hand to shield his eyes from the light when Rose points her torch at his face. 'Where did you get that?' he asks.

'When I checked Nancy's room it was under the bed,' says Rose. 'I thought it might come in handy if the lights went out

– they often do when there is a storm – and that wasn't all I found there.'

'Trixie?'

Rose lowers her voice to a whisper. 'No. This.'

Conor steps further into the room, and Rose produces a small floral bag.

Conor shakes his head. 'What is it?'

'It's Lily's missing diabetic kit.'

'I thought she couldn't find it. What's it doing under your mother's bed?'

'I don't know.'

The bedroom door squeaks, telling tales on the person behind it. We all turn and take a step back – I'm not the only one who is afraid now – and Rose's torch reveals Lily standing on the landing. She has used her lighter to find her way in the dark, and is still holding it up, like someone at a pop concert. Her face looks strange, as though she can't quite see us.

'There's no sign of Trixie in Nana's bedroom. Did you find anything?'

'No,' answers Rose before anyone else can. 'Let's head back downstairs, maybe Nancy might have had more luck. Try not to worry, we will find Trixie.'

'Okay,' Lily says, nodding, as though desperate for someone else to take charge. The habitual fight has gone out of her, and she seems broken. It's as though Lily's lights switched off when Seaglass's did.

Rose leads the way with her torch as we creep downstairs in the darkness. Our silent fear seems as loud as the storm outside. It's even colder down here now that the fire has almost burned itself out, but that isn't why we are huddled together in the lounge. Conor takes a candle from the mantelpiece and lights it, and we return to the window seat – the last place we all saw Trixie.

'I don't understand, she was *right* here,' Lily says, picking up the blanket and holding it to her nose, like a dog checking for scent.

'We'll find her,' says Rose, but from the tone of her voice I'm not convinced she believes it. 'You look pale. I found this upstairs. When did you last inject?'

Lily takes the diabetic kit from her and unzips it straight away 'Hours ago. Where did you find it?'

Rose stares at the floor. 'Nancy's room.' For some reason, her answer sounds like a lie.

'My insulin pen is missing,' Lily says.

Time seems to stop again while we all catch up with life's latest plot twist.

'Nancy?' Lily calls, but there is no answer. Our mother is now also nowhere to be found.

We search the rest of the rooms downstairs together, with Poppins following us. I think she thought it was a game before, but now she walks with her tail between her legs and her ears back. I can't help wondering whether she might be able to hear something we can't. The thunder and lightning continue as we move through the house with just a torch and a candle, though the storm does at least seem to be moving further away.

'Trixie!' Lily calls her daughter's name repeatedly – we all do – but there is no answer.

We step inside the library. It is filled with Nana's books, crammed in no particular order into every available space on the shelves that line the room. The sofa shows no sign of where Rose slept on it earlier, but her overnight bag is in the corner. The room is cold, and dark and empty.

Rose leads the way to the kitchen next. It's obvious that the huge room at the back of the house is uninhabited too, but we take it in turns to look under the table, inside cupboards and behind curtains. Conor is taller than the rest of us, and accidentally walks into the black and orange paper chains Nana had decorated the ceiling with for Halloween. I feel as though we are going through the motions, scared of running out of places to search. And we are all trying *not* to look at the chalk poem written on the wall.

'We should check Nana's studio,' Rose says. She and Lily exchange uncomfortable glances, I think because it is somewhere they were not allowed to go as children.

'It's probably locked, always used to be,' says Lily, walking towards the door. But when she tries the handle, it swings open with an eerie creak. Even in the dim light, we can all see that the studio has been ransacked.

Conor steps inside first. 'What the—?'

'Maybe someone was looking for the book Nana said she was working on?' Rose suggests, offering an answer before anyone had time to ask a question.

'Or looking for Beatrice Darker author memorabilia they can flog on eBay,' Conor says.

Rose ignores him. 'Nana said she was going to write one last book about all of *us* . . . maybe that was something someone didn't want people to read.'

The studio, which always had an air of organized chaos, has been trashed. There are drawings and paper strewn all over the floor, drawers pulled out, pencils snapped in two, and paints knocked over. We walk through the mess, from one end of the room to the other, and I notice some of the newer illustrations and poems on the wall. They are all very different, but all very Nana.

*This is where the story ends,*
*Of fractured families and forgotten friends,*
*And people too blind to make amends.*

One of my favourite Nana sayings is painted in silver writing over a blue and black background of the sea. It always makes me think of Seaglass, and of coming back here year after year.

*If you can't find your way back to Happy,*
*Navigate to the place you know as Less Sad.*

'I think Rose might be right. What if someone in the family wanted to find Nana's last book, to stop anyone from publishing it?' says Conor.

'I think someone should stop playing detective,' Lily says, but he carries on regardless.

'Nana was always hiding secret meanings in the poems she wrote . . . they were never really just for children . . .'

'What if someone had secrets they didn't want shared?' I say, agreeing with him.

'Secrets worth killing to keep,' Conor adds. 'And that's why they killed her—'

One of the windows is open, and a gust of wind blows out the candle Conor is carrying.

'Can we please concentrate on trying to find my daughter?' Lily says.

'Where is Nancy?' I ask, but nobody replies. I think we're too scared of the answers silently auditioning inside our heads. My mother was always a proud and private person. We all know how much she would have hated the idea of someone writing the truth about her or her children. Even disguised as fiction.

The last little poem on the wall is accompanied by an illustration in Nana's familiar style. The watercolour silhouette is
of three little girls holding hands. It was destined for her final
book, the one about us, I'm sure of it. The room feels colder
than before when I read the words. The same ones that were
on the kitchen table earlier, but this time in Nana's swirly
handwriting. Which makes me think that someone else found
the illustration in here, copied the words, and left them on a
scrap of paper in the other room for us to find.

*Trick-or-treat the children hear,*
*Before they scream and disappear.*

I was never allowed to go trick-or-treating with my sisters
when we were children. My mother said it was too risky. As a
family we always dressed up for Halloween – it was Nana's
birthday, and she insisted – but then Rose and Lily would be
allowed to go trick-or-treating with the rest of the local kids,
and I would stay behind, jealous of all the fun they had and
the sweets they brought home the next day. The tides meant
that they always stayed with friends, unable to get back to
Seaglass until the sea retreated again. That was something else
my sisters had that I didn't when we were children: friends. I
was never allowed to make any.

Nana always tried to cheer me up with some secret sweets
just for me hidden around Seaglass. While Rose and Lily were
out having fun, I'd spend the evening with her sitting by the
fire, listening to her stories. She did not approve of trick-or-
treating, and would remind me why every year. What we see
as innocent fun on Halloween originated as part of a pagan
ritual, where people dressed up in scary costumes on 31
October to frighten away the dead. They offered food or drink

to try to appease them, which is where all the free candy and sweets originated from. In the Middle Ages, the ritual was known as mumming. By the time Christianity arrived in Europe, a new practice called souling was on the Halloween scene. Poor people would visit the houses of the rich and receive pastries called soul cakes, in exchange for promises to pray for the homeowners' dead relatives. Scotland took the tradition and bent it a little more out of shape, encouraging young people to visit their neighbours' houses and sing a song, recite a poem, or perform another sort of 'trick' before receiving a treat of nuts, fruit or coins. The term trick-or-treating wasn't used until the 1920s in America, and Nana said it made a mockery of what started out as an important ritual. It bothered her a great deal that people were encouraged to fear the dead instead of honour them, and she'd always end her story with the same line:

'There's no need to be afraid of the dead; it's the living you have to watch out for.'

We leave Nana's studio together, none the wiser, and no closer to finding Trixie.

The music room is the last place left to look. I think it turned out that way because none of us want to see my dead father again. Lightning strikes just before we open the door, and I automatically start counting.

*One Mississippi . . .*

The lightning lights up the room, and the shadow of the piano casts a dancing pattern over the walls.

*Two Mississippi . . .*

There is no sign of Trixie in here either. Nothing out of place at all, apart from the missing piano key I spotted earlier. I remember middle C and see that it's a B key that has gone.

*Three Mississippi . . .*

Then I realize that's not the only thing missing. My father's dead body has disappeared, just like Nana's did before.

Conor steps forward. 'What. The. F—'

Thunder rumbles in the distance, and we all stare at one another in the darkness. Our faces are mostly in shadow but look equally scared. Lily steps closer to Rose and holds her hand, the way she did when they were children. The rain that has been lashing the windows seems to pause for thought, and there are a few brief seconds of total silence.

Until we all hear the sound of scratching – like nails on a chalkboard – out in the hall.

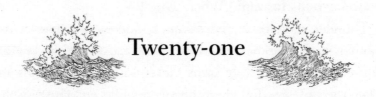

# Twenty-one

*31 October 2:25 a.m.*
*less than four hours until low tide*

Conor snatches the torch from Rose's hand and rushes out into the hallway. None of us are far behind, and when we catch up, we see the source of the sound.

Poppins is scratching at the cupboard under the stairs, and she starts to whimper.

Lily steps forward and tries to open the door, but it's locked.

'Trixie?' she calls, banging her fist against it. 'Are you in there?'

There is no answer. Lily bangs on the door again, louder this time, and the wooden door rattles on its elderly hinges. She shakes the handle in frustration.

'Let me try,' says Conor, giving the torch back to Rose. But he can't open the door either.

'Where is the key for this bloody cupboard?' Lily asks, but I suspect none of us know.

The dog barks and scratches at the door again.

'Be quiet, Poppins!' Lily shouts.

'She has the key,' Rose whispers.

'What?'

'Poppins has the key.'

'Have you lost your mind?'

'It's attached to her collar. Look!' Rose says, shining the torch down at the dog.

We seem to stare at Poppins for a long time before anyone says anything else. She blinks back in our direction, peering out from behind the two little plaits that keep her hair away from her eyes. Looking a smidgen guilty, if I'm honest. But it doesn't seem rational – even to my irrational family – that an Old English Sheepdog could be behind everything that has happened here tonight. Rose bends down to remove the key from the collar. It's hard to see anything in the dim light, and it takes her a while to untie it.

'Hurry up!' says Lily.

'I'm trying my best,' Rose replies calmly. When she finally removes the key, she slots it into the locked door and we hold our breath. We were all afraid of this cupboard as children. We knew that there were mice and cobwebs in there. I used to imagine a family of giant spiders living in the shadows, waiting to feed on anyone foolish enough to enter.

Rose turns the key, and the door creaks as she slowly pulls it open.

It's too dark to see inside. There was never a light.

The rest of us peer over her shoulder from the imagined safety of the hallway as Rose steps forward, shining the torch.

The first thing I register is the smell; bad things happen when people die. The first thing I *see* is Nana. She's sitting on the floor of the cupboard, leaning against the exposed brick wall in the gloom. She would look like someone taking a nap – in a cupboard – if it weren't for the grey colouring of her skin, the giant bloody gash on her head, and the blood that has spilled all down her cheek and onto the shoulder of her white cotton nightdress. The piece of chalk she was holding when we first found her has been replaced with a pen and paintbrush, tied to her hand with a red ribbon. My father's body has been moved in here too, with his broken conductor's baton still tied to his right hand in the same way. It hovers in mid-air, presumably thanks to rigor mortis, as if he is conducting an invisible orchestra in the cupboard under the stairs. The surreal image creates a flashback in my mind, one I would rather not picture. I think it must have been early 1983. The third time I died was the first time I lied about it.

My dad had a series of ornamental girlfriends after my parents parted company. They were almost always the same person in my memory: someone pretty and half his age who played in his orchestra. Men are infinitely more predictable than women, and the way my father behaved before and after the divorce was borderline clichéd. But there is really no telling what an angry woman will do. My mother stored up her anger until it was as much a part of her as we were.

I don't think my sisters or Nancy took any of Dad's 'relationships' with his musicians – mostly violinists, who I've always been suspicious of ever since – seriously. They never lasted more than a few months. Until Rebecca. She. Was. Beautiful. And funny, and clever, and kind. Even now I can still picture her long blonde hair, pale skin and blue eyes, perhaps because she looked so different from all of us with our Darker family features. Rebecca encouraged Dad to spend more time with his daughters, taking us on trips to Thorpe Park and Madame Tussauds in the school holidays. She took us to McDonald's for Happy Meals – which I confess *did* make us happy – and she plaited our hair in ways we'd never seen before. We adored Rebecca. My mother did not. I can only imagine how awful it must have been when we came home beaming, and full of stories about how *wonderful* Dad's new girlfriend was. Children can be so indiscreet.

I was happy with the whole arrangement, until the night my father was asked to conduct a special evening of music at the Royal Albert Hall. It was his life's ambition, and all of us – including Nana and Nancy – were invited to witness the momentous occasion. We had our own box to watch the perform- ance of a lifetime, and were allowed in early to have a tour of the concert hall before anyone else arrived. Lily hated the whole thing, she thought it was boring, and I always remember what she said that day. It was one of the only times I can recall my sister being genuinely funny, and the memory still makes me smile now:

'I'd rather he was a bus conductor, at least then we could get free rides.'

When Dad came to meet us, an hour or so before the show was due to start, he walked into the box with Rebecca. She was smiling and appeared to glow with happiness, and I noticed – despite being only seven – how her presence seemed to make my mother shrink into the shadows.

'We have some news!' My father beamed at his first family.

Rebecca held out her hand for us all to see, and I didn't understand the significance until she spoke. 'Your dad has asked me to marry him, and I've said yes.'

I stared at the ring on her hand, then I turned to my mother, who looked as though she had been punched. Her face was pinched tight, as if every muscle was working its hardest to hold her smile in place. Nana's mouth formed a perfect O. I had never seen what she looked like when surprised before. My sisters and I shuffled closer together, as though instinct told us our pack was under threat. Sometimes the thinnest of threads can tether people to one another, and that was always true in my family.

Thoughts collided inside my head, bad ones, causing a series of small explosions. Until that moment, I think I always thought that my parents would get back together one day. We had all agreed that Rebecca was wonderful, but our opinion of her changed in a heartbeat. Now she was an awful, hateful witch of a woman – who I had adored only a few minutes earlier – because she was trying to destroy my family.

I can remember my sisters spinning me round and round as a child, on the beach or in the garden, then telling me to try to walk in a straight line. It was impossible, and for some reason very funny, to be that dizzy. We would laugh as I staggered and swayed all over the place, before collapsing in a heap. But when I thought my dad was going to marry someone who wasn't my mother, I felt a very bad kind of dizzy. Then I felt sick. Then I fainted.

I'm sure that's all it was. The Albert Hall was extremely hot, the box we were in was very high up, and the idea of my father remarrying caught me off guard. I *just* fainted. But Nancy was convinced my heart had stopped again, having literally been broken by Dad's news. An ambulance was called, and I was rushed away to hospital, along with the rest of the Darker family women. My dad stayed with his orchestra and his fiancée. We never got to see him fulfil his dream on stage at the Albert Hall, and we never got to see him marry Rebecca. She broke it off two weeks later, saying that she couldn't be with someone who put his career before his child, even when they had been rushed to hospital.

It was all my fault, and my heart didn't really stop that day, not that I ever told anyone. It was the first time I understood that withholding the truth was almost, but not quite, the same as lying. And although I felt guilty about everything that happened as a result, I never confessed. You can get away with murder when everyone thinks you are dying.

'Trixie!' screams Lily, snapping me out of the memory.

I turn to see where my sister is looking at the very back of the cupboard under the stairs, and spot my niece curled up on the floor in the shadows. Her pink pyjamas are covered in dust and dirt, there are cobwebs in her hair, her eyes are closed and her skin is so white she looks like a ghost. She doesn't move, even when Lily screams her name a second time.

# Trixie

*Daisy Darker's niece was a precocious little child.*
*Like all abandoned ducklings, she would not fare well in the wild.*

*Aged fifteen (going on thirty) Trixie Darker was clever and kind,*
*But she asked too many questions, and some truths are hard to find.*

*The child was unexpectedly chosen to inherit her grandmother's estate.*
*A decision which caused much unhappiness, and jealousy, and hate.*

*Her own mother felt angry and cheated, most of the family felt the same.*
*The child's father might have been happy for her, but nobody knew*
*his name.*

*Despite her endless questions, the child most wanted an answer to one:*
*Who was her dad, did he know she existed, or would she only ever*
*have a mum?*

*When the time came, no one knew who to blame, when she was*
*found under the stairs.*
*It's hard to know who to trust, when a child is left for dead in the*
*dust, wondering if anyone really cares.*

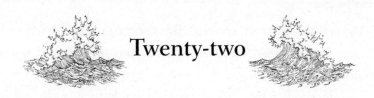

# Twenty-two

*31 October 2:30 a.m.*
*less than four hours until low tide*

Rose crawls inside the cupboard and gently pulls Trixie out. Nobody speaks, and the house is eerily silent. It seems strange to me that Lily doesn't rush to her daughter's side, but I think she must be in shock. We all are. Except for Rose, who takes charge of the situation again. She carefully lays Trixie on the parquet floor in the hall.

'Hold the torch steady,' she barks at Conor, leaning down over my niece and feeling for a pulse. It seems to take the longest time, but finally Rose nods.

'She's alive.'

'Oh, thank god!' Lily says, but the smile soon slides off her face. 'Who did this?' Nobody answers. 'Which one of you did this? She didn't lock *herself* in the bloody cupboard.'

'Wait,' says Rose. 'She's alive, but something isn't right.'

We watch as she examines Trixie from head to toe. She's unconscious, deathly pale, and I notice that one of her socks is missing. Rose sees it too, and stares down at her bare foot.

'There is a small amount of dried blood between her toes,' Rose says, almost to herself.

'What does that mean?' asks Lily.

'I . . . can't be sure. But my best guess is that someone has injected her with something.'

'What? Who?'

'I don't know,' Rose replies. 'But we can't find Nancy. Your diabetic kit was in *her* bedroom, and your insulin pen is now missing from it—'

Lily shakes her head. 'You can't seriously be suggesting that our mother did this to Trixie? She *loves* her grandchild, far more than she ever loved us.'

Rose sighs and seems to visibly deflate. 'Then where is Nancy now? We don't have time for this. I need your diabetic kit.'

Lily hands it to her, and Rose takes a small device from the bag. Nobody dares to ask what she is doing, and I feel as though we are all holding our breath. Rose pricks Trixie's finger and squeezes a tiny drop of blood onto the machine.

'I think she's been injected with insulin. If I'm right, we have to act quickly or—'

'Just do whatever you need to do,' Lily says in a quiet voice, and it is so strange to see her crying and vulnerable. She was always the indestructible sister.

Rose runs to the library where she slept and returns with a bag of her own. It looks like an old-fashioned brown leather doctor's bag. A gift from Nana when Rose got a place at Cambridge to study veterinary science. She opens it, takes out a large needle and a small vial.

'What is that?' asks Conor.

'Glucagon. There should be some in Lily's kit, but that's missing too. It's the same treatment for dogs. So if I'm right, then . . .'

'What if you're wrong?' Lily whispers.

Rose ignores her and injects the drug into Trixie's arm.

We wait for what feels like forever. Time seems impossible to tell. Then Trixie opens her eyes. They blink a few times before finding Lily.

'Mum?'

'Oh, thank god. Thank you, thank you, thank you,' Lily says, sweeping Trixie up in her arms and kissing her. I'm crying tears of joy, and relief and love. Looking around, I see that we all are. Nobody who is here now would ever have hurt this child.

A short while later we are all back in the lounge, with a chair up against the door to prevent anyone coming into – or out of – the room. We have barricaded ourselves inside, and added some logs to the fire for heat. Rose has lit some old candles for light. Even in the darkness, I can see that Lily is trembling. Trixie is by her side, wrapped in a blanket, staring at the flames. We don't have anything to eat or drink, but I doubt any of us have an appetite. It feels as though none of us want to acknowledge what is happening here tonight, as if maybe by not talking about it, we can pretend it isn't. Nana and Dad are dead, and Nancy is missing. Either she did something very bad, or I fear something very bad has happened to her.

The last thing Trixie remembers is drinking a cup of tea – which we all know contained one of my mother's sleeping pills – and Lily placing a blanket over her on the window seat.

She doesn't remember being in the cupboard.

Or how she got there.

Or who locked her inside.

Or who she was in there with.

All Trixie knows is that she went to sleep on the window seat, then woke up in the hall. I know that being completely oblivious about everything that happened in between is best for her, but it's frustrating and frightening for the rest of us. I think back to last night, when we were all sitting around Nana's kitchen table, joking about how we would murder someone if we wanted to get away with it. Rose was the one who said insulin between the toes. Seems like someone had the same idea as her, and tried using it to kill my niece.

I can't believe any of this is really happening, and can't think of anyone who would hate my family enough to do this to us. I look around the room. Everyone in it had a reason to be upset with Nana because of the will. My mother and Lily both hated my father for a long time after the divorce, but nobody here would want to hurt Trixie. Surely I must be right about that?

The power comes back on, making us all jump, and light floods the room.

'Well, that's a good sign,' says Lily.

'Is it?' replies Rose, before examining Trixie again to make sure she is really okay.

I can't help noticing the handgun in Rose's leather bag as she packs her things away, and I'm not the only one. Trixie's eyes are wide as saucers, and her face writes a question mark on itself.

'Why do you have a gun, Aunty Rose?' she asks.

'I thought you said that was somewhere safe?' Lily says.

Rose sighs at Lily. 'It was, but after everything that has happened, *I* feel safer having it with me.' She turns back to Trixie. 'Sometimes vets need guns. They probably look a lot like the guns you see on TV – because they are – but vets use them for different reasons. It's very sad, but if an animal is seriously poorly, then—'

'You *shoot* it?' Trixie asks.

'Sometimes. But only if that's the only option . . . if the animal is in lots of pain.'

'Would you shoot one of us if we were in pain?' my niece asks without a hint of irony.

'You should try to get some rest. We'll all leave as soon as the tide lets us. You're going to be okay, I promise.'

Trixie's face attempts a smile, but it doesn't take. She's old enough, and clever enough, to know that we haven't told her everything about what has happened here tonight.

Rose goes to leave the lounge.

'Where are you going?' Lily asks, sounding afraid.

'I'll be back in less than a minute. I just want to check something.'

'Do you want me to come with you?' Conor offers.

Rose stares at him for a long time, but leaves without giving a reply, which I suppose is an answer in itself. The rest of us sit in silence as the fire spits and crackles. Shadows dance around the walls and across our faces, the thoughts inside our individual heads so loud that I can almost hear them. Conor gets up to leave the room a few minutes later. I follow him, watch from the doorway, and see him standing too close to Rose out in the hall.

'Are you okay?' he asks her.

'No. Of course not,' Rose whispers back. 'I came to get the key from the cupboard door,' she says, patting the pocket of her jeans. 'I think it's a master key. If I'm right, we can lock ourselves in the lounge until the tide goes out. Someone here tried to kill Trixie, and I don't think this is over.'

'I think you're right. But who? And why?'

'I don't know. But until we figure this out, we're all in danger,' Rose says.

'It started with Nana, so it has to have been someone who was upset with her. I don't think it was just about the will either. Somebody trashed her studio looking for something, so my guess is it's someone who didn't like the idea of her writing one last novel about this family. Someone with a secret.'

'We all have secrets,' says Rose.

'Yes, but we don't all go around killing people in order to keep them.'

Rose stares at him when he says that, but Conor is too lost in thought to notice.

'Who had a motive to kill Frank?' he continues. 'And why would someone try to kill Trixie? Did she see something she shouldn't have last night when she came downstairs and discovered Nana's body? Something which might identify the killer?'

'Whoever it is, they're someone who likes to tidy things away, out of sight,' Rose says, staring at the cupboard under the stairs.

Conor opens the cupboard door a little wider. It still has all of our names and ages, and a ladder of a line with our heights written inside it. I read the top three.

Daisy, aged 13 - 5 feet, 1 inch
Rose, aged 10 - 4 feet, 7 inches
Lily, aged 9 - 4 feet, 2 inches

It's the only place in space and time where I was ever taller than them.

'At least we know where the missing bodies are,' Conor says. 'And that explains why Poppins was scratching at the cupboard door. That dog could never bear to be away from Nana for more than a minute.'

Rose closes the cupboard door and locks it. 'I don't want to see what's in there anymore. And I don't want to talk about it.'

They start walking back towards the lounge, and I retreat inside the room. I'm not sure why, but I'm glad they didn't see me. I feel like I'm missing a piece of the puzzle, and it's increasingly difficult to know who to trust.

Everyone is afraid now and they are right to be.

*Someone* is killing the Darker family one by one.

And I fear it's only a matter of time until it happens again.

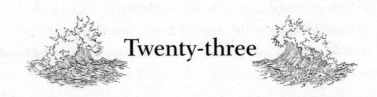

# Twenty-three

*31 October 2:40 a.m.*
*less than four hours until low tide*

Back in the lounge, Lily and Trixie are still sitting huddled together on the sofa, trying to keep warm. Rose slots the cupboard key into the lounge door, and she's right: it is a master key.

'What are you doing?' asks Lily.

'Locking us inside until the tide goes out. To keep us all safe.'

'But what about Nancy?' Lily asks. 'She isn't safe. She's out there somewhere, she didn't just vanish. Am I the only one who cares about our mother and is worried about her?' Nobody answers. 'Are we just not going to talk about it? I suppose that *is* what we normally do in this family, as though pretending something bad didn't happen will mean it never did. I know what you're all thinking, but Nancy wouldn't do this.'

'Do what?' Trixie asks. She doesn't know what really happened to her. She doesn't even know that Dad is dead. As far as she knows, Nana had an accident and we're all just waiting for the tide to go out.

'Maybe we shouldn't have this conversation in front of Trixie,' I say.

But Lily ignores me. My sister is always a stranger to any point I try to make.

'I've been thinking about everything that has happened tonight, and the only explanation is that someone else is here, at Seaglass,' Lily says. 'Someone else has been here the whole time, since before we arrived, waiting for us to go to bed and then picking us off one by one. Someone close to the family. Someone who knew about Nana's eightieth birthday, and that we'd all be here to celebrate it.'

'Everyone knew that Halloween was Nana's birthday. She made us celebrate it every year,' says Rose.

Conor nods. 'And everyone knew that she believed it would be her last, because of that premonition by the palm reader in Timbuktu—'

'Land's End,' Rose corrects.

'Whatever. They said her eightieth birthday would be her last . . . which it was. She was literally found in a puddle of her own blood just after midnight.'

My niece starts to quietly cry.

'I'm sorry, Trixie,' Conor says. 'That was very insensitive of me. This has been a terrible night for all of us, but you must be so upset about Nana and Frank.'

Trixie frowns. 'What's wrong with Grandad?'

'Nothing,' Lily lies. 'He's just very upset about Nana, so he's having a lie-down.'

'Is Nancy having a lie-down too?' Trixie asks.

Nobody knows what to say, including me, but Lily isn't the only one to think that Nancy isn't responsible for any of the things that have happened here tonight. And she's right to be worried about her. My mother can be many unpleasant things – sometimes all at once – but a killer isn't one of them. I'm certain of that.

There is a picture on the mantelpiece above the fireplace, which I often find myself staring at. It's of three generations of Darker family women: Nana, my mother, my sisters and me at Seaglass, posing like the happy family we rarely were, here in this room. I'm guessing it would have been 1983, when I was seven, because of the matching blue dresses my sisters and I are wearing. I remember the day Nancy and I went to town to buy them. I lied to my mother that day, and I don't think she ever found out the truth.

The trouble with little white lies is that they sometimes grow up to become big dark ones.

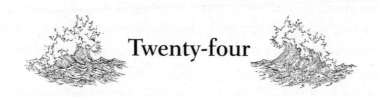

# Twenty-four

## SEAGLASS – 1983

My mother always dressed up to go shopping; for her it was like putting on a show. I remember that she was in a good mood that day – it was a rare and therefore memorable thing. Nancy sang along to the car radio as we drove along the coastal road into town – completely out of tune – to a song called 'Stayin' Alive'. She had a video of a film that had the same song in it, something about a man called John Travolta who had a fever on a Saturday night. Her favourite shop in the whole wide world was called Debenhams, and that was where we were headed.

We were at Seaglass for the Easter holidays, but Nana didn't come with us. She hated all forms of shopping. 'Material things only matter to material people,' she would say. But Nancy *loved* to shop. The only problem with her spending habits and expensive taste was that we rarely had any money in those days. The divorce settlement was generous, but after paying the mortgage on our tiny house in London, and my sisters' school fees, there was very little left over. Which was why the start of the sales was *very* important to Nancy. We had to get there on day one, as soon as the shop doors opened, even if that meant queuing. The only thing my mother loved more than shopping was believing that she had paid less for something than it was worth.

I loathed being dragged around department stores. They were too big and I was too small, and I was always afraid of getting lost. I preferred the smaller shops we used to visit on our old high street. I always loved Woolworths because of the pick 'n' mix; the memory of all those cola bottles, cherry lips and flying saucers still makes me smile. Lily's favourite shops were Our Price – where she went to buy the latest cassettes and music posters – and Tammy Girl and C&A, where she and Rose shopped for clothes. I always enjoyed our trips to Blockbuster Video – even if I was rarely allowed to choose which film we would rent – and visits to the little independent bookshop with Nana were my favourite outings. Buying books was the only form of shopping she ever enjoyed. It makes me sad to realize that none of those shops exist now. So many high streets are more like ghost towns these days.

Nancy pushed through the crowds and headed straight up the escalator to the children's department in Debenhams, where she quickly chose two new dresses for Rose and Lily. I had to run to keep up with her walk, but I remember the navy blue velvet dresses with white collars, and how much I wanted one of my own. My mother always liked to dress my sisters in matching clothes – as though they were twins – but I rarely had anything new to wear.

We went up another floor to women's fashion, so that Nancy could buy a little something for herself. My mother always walked up the escalator in her hurry to find a bargain. The moving steps were very big, and seven-year-old me found it difficult to keep up. I've been scared of escalators ever since. I always felt as though I was going to slip, or trip, or fall through the cracks. I had to jump when we reached the end, to avoid the gap and certain death.

On arrival in women's fashion, Nancy started to browse the reduced-price clothes like it was a sport. I remember the ugly sound of hangers screeching across the metal rails. If other shoppers dared to get in her way, Nancy would tut until they moved. My feet started to ache in my second-hand shoes, which were pretty but too small. So, while I waited for Nancy to find the things she thought would make her happy, I sat down and collected the coat hanger size cubes that had fallen to the floor. There were different colours for each size in those days: orange for 10, green for 12, blue for 14. Nancy has almost always been a size 10, and I wonder if that's why I hate the colour orange.

Everything was fine until we got to the changing room. My mother had taken in the maximum number of dresses to try on, but started to get upset almost right away because the first dress didn't seem to fit.

'Just pull the zip *up*,' she said, glaring at me in the mirror as I tried, and failed, to help.

'It won't budge,' I replied, tugging on the zipper, and she tutted and shook her head at me as though it was my fault.

'There must be something wrong with the sizing of this dress,' Nancy said, pulling it off over her head and dumping it on the floor. But the next dress, another size 10, didn't fit either. Nor did the next one. That's when Nancy started to cry.

'Having children *ruined* my body. Ruined it. The sacrifices I have made for you . . .'

'I think you look beautiful,' I said, shoving my hands into my pockets, not really knowing what to say or do. 'I could just go and get you a bigger size?'

I was so scared by the look my mother gave me then, I ran

out of the changing room without waiting for a reply. Some of
the size cubes I had picked up earlier were still in my pockets.
Feeling them gave me an idea. I found the dress my mother
liked the most out on the shop floor, went on tiptoe to select
it in a size 12, then changed the green size cube on the hanger
for an orange size 10. I ran back to the changing room.

'I already tried that one,' Nancy snapped, staring at the dress
as though it had offended her.

'But maybe this one will fit?' I said, holding it out in both
hands like a fabric peace offering. 'It did look very pretty on
you.'

She snatched the dress and started to pull it on. When I
helped zip it all the way up at the back, she smiled at herself
in the mirror. Then she smiled at me.

I don't know whether Nancy ever looked at the size label
sewn into the inside of the dress she bought for herself that
day. All my mother ever really cared about was what was on
the outside, what other people saw and how they viewed her.
I still think it's a very sad way to live. But we stopped off in
the children's department again before we left Debenhams that
afternoon, and my mother bought me the same dress she had
bought for my sisters. It was the first and only time she dressed
me the same way as them. Sometimes the things that make
one person sad are the same things that can make another
person happy.

Nancy sang along to the radio again as we drove home.
There were big bags full of half-price dresses in the boot of
her little red Mini. All of them with the wrong size on the
hangers. I never told her what I did because sometimes keeping
secrets is the kindest thing to do. I still remember how happy
she was, until we saw a boy walking alone along the coastal
path near Seaglass. I guess Conor would have been thirteen

at the time. That awkward stage where he still looked like a boy but was starting to think and behave like a man. He was limping. My mother pulled up beside him and gasped when she saw his face. He had a black eye and a bloody lip.

'Stay here,' she ordered, yanking the handbrake as though it were to blame.

She got out of the car and rushed over to Conor.

'Did your dad do this to you?' Nancy asked.

Our whole family knew about Conor's dad, and my parents did not approve of Nana getting involved. They viewed spending what they saw as their inheritance on Conor's father's rehab as a waste of time and money. My mother had been waiting for the moment when she would be proved right. Conor looked away and stared at Blacksand Bay down below the cliffs. Nancy tried again, softening the edges of her words.

'You don't need to say it out loud if you don't want to, but I do need to know what happened, Conor. Did your father do this to you? Nod or shake your head.'

Conor stared at her, but he didn't move his head or even blink.

'Jump in the back seat,' she said, and he did as he was told, sliding in beside me. He stank of blood and sweat.

My mother was more than capable of hurting her own children behind closed doors – albeit only with words – but she could not tolerate the thought of any other child coming to harm. The car's brakes squealed as we pulled up outside Conor's dad's cottage, the one Nana had lovingly renovated a couple of years earlier. Sadly, people can be harder to restore than places.

'Stay there, both of you,' Nancy ordered.

She got out of the spotlessly clean Mini and tutted at the state of Conor's dad's blue Volvo. It was so dirty, I couldn't read the number plate, even though we were parked right behind it.

'He's going to kill someone driving drunk along that cliff road one day,' she muttered, and I watched, with my face pressed against our car window, as Nancy marched up to Conor's house. I started whispering under my breath, waiting for my mother to strike like lightning.

*One Mississippi . . . Two Mississippi . . . Three Mississippi . . .*

I didn't have long to wait.

'Open this door,' Nancy yelled, banging her fist on it. 'My mother-in-law might have been taken in by you, but I know people like you *never* change. You are a disgrace of a man. Your son is sitting in my car looking broken, and I thought you might want to say goodbye before I take him back to Seaglass and make sure you never see him or hurt him again.'

Nancy had fallen for Conor by then, just like the rest of the women in the Darker family. We all wanted to protect him. It was instinct. Not something any of us thought to question, or knew how to explain. Like if you found an abandoned puppy: you couldn't help wanting to protect him and give him a home.

I looked at Conor but he just stared at the floor of the car, his hands forming two little fists in his lap. The cottage door opened, and I could feel my heart beating so fast I thought it might burst right out of my chest. Then a man I didn't recognize appeared in the doorway.

He looked like Conor's dad, but at the same time, he didn't. The man I had seen before was all too often a skinny, smelly, dirty man with torn clothes, a beard and long hair. This man stood tall with his head held high. His hair was neatly cut, his face was cleanly shaved. He'd put on weight, looked as though he'd been working out, and was dressed in clean clothes. I remember that his trousers and shirt seemed to have a ridiculous number of pockets and I wondered what he kept in them all. He folded his tanned arms and smiled. The world seemed topsy-turvy, as my mother – who thought she was the hero of this particular story – appeared to be in the wrong, while the baddie had become a calm, well-mannered, good-looking man.

'Hello, Mrs Darker,' he said, before inviting us all inside.

It turned out that Conor's dad hadn't started drinking again. Or hitting his son. I watched while he very slowly made some tea. He looked like a man who had never been in a hurry to do anything or get anywhere his whole life. Despite the slow motion, Mr Kennedy had very much got his life back on track, and was working as head gardener at a National Trust property a few miles away. That sounded good to me, but Conor said his dad was always careless with jobs and often lost them. Even before his mother died.

It turned out that Conor had been a little bit careless himself. He was getting into trouble at school, and was in a fight with a boy three years older than him that day. I found out later that the boy had been spreading rumours about Lily and Rose, and Conor was defending them. Lily – who loved Easter because of all the chocolate – had promised to give some of the local boys a peek inside her panties in exchange for an egg. The bigger the egg, the longer they got to look. She was eleven years old. That was just the start of my sister getting a name for herself for all the wrong reasons in Blacksand Bay. My mother, thankfully, never found out the truth.

Conor's dad opened a first-aid kit, cleaned up his son's face, then served us all tea and biscuits in the kitchen. The house was just as clean and tidy as the man who owned it, and it was a surreal experience to see my mother lost for words. Even stranger to hear her apologize.

'I'm so sorry, I just thought that—'

'It's okay, I would have thought the same thing,' Mr Kennedy said with a polite smile. 'I was broken after my wife passed away, and I'm sorry for all the things your family had to see. That wasn't me, at least not the real me. I'm still grieving, but I feel more like myself again now. I'm so grateful for everything that your mother-in-law did for me – and my son – when times were tough. I've even started writing about it.'

'A book?'

'Maybe. I haven't decided and I don't know if it's good enough yet, but writing about it – the overwhelming grief, the drink, all of it – helps me to process what I became. And if sharing that experience – as awful as it was – might help others to not take the same path, or find a way back if they already have, then maybe . . .' He turned to Conor. 'I hope you thanked Mrs Darker for bringing you home?'

'It's fine, and I've told him to call me Nancy, so you should do the same.'

'I've always liked the name Nancy. Perhaps we could start over? I'm Bradley, it's good to meet you.' He held out his hand, and my mother blushed when she shook it.

'I didn't know you were a gardener,' she said, taking a sip of tea, anything to keep her hands busy and out of reach. 'Maybe you could give me some advice for the little patch of land at the back of Seaglass?'

'I'd be happy to.'

She blushed again. 'My mother-in-law was going to invite Conor to visit us on Easter Sunday. My older girls are home from school, and it's nice for them to spend time with someone their own age. Maybe you could join us too . . . if you're free?'

'I'll check my diary,' Mr Kennedy said with a straight face. When he smiled, and my mother realized he was joking, she laughed. I noticed again what a rare sound it was to hear. It was strangely beautiful, just like her.

I might never have gone to school, but I felt like I learned a lot of valuable lessons that day, including that people aren't always what they appear to be. A middle-aged man with a drinking problem might just be a person poisoned by an all-consuming grief. While a middle-class woman with nice manners and nice things might just be a failed actress who can't handle being a dress size bigger than she wants to be. Life is a performance, and we don't all like the scripts we're given; sometimes it's best to write your own.

Conor and his dad did visit us at Seaglass that Easter. They wore suits and ties, and brought chocolate eggs for the whole family. Mr Kennedy spent a lot of time out in the garden with Nancy, and we listened to the sound of her laughing all after-noon. Bradley Kennedy never gave up drinking for good, but at that moment in time he seemed to know when to stop, and he never laid a finger on Conor again.

When I look at that picture of the Darker family women on Nana's mantelpiece now, I remember that Conor took it that Easter, using the Polaroid camera my father had given him. In the photo, Nana is wearing a pink dress and a purple Easter bonnet. Lily, Rose and I are *all* wearing matching dresses for the first and only time. They are the navy blue velvet ones from Debenhams. Nancy is dressed in one of her Audrey Hepburn ensembles, and she looks very pleased with herself indeed. She is gazing just off camera. I think she was looking at Conor's dad.

I smile too when I look at the image of her back then, because I was so proud of her for what she did that day, ready to stick up for Conor, no matter what. She was protective of those she cared about. And if she loved something, or someone, she loved them with all her heart.

I just wish she had loved me that way.

My mother might never have fulfilled her ambition of becoming an actress, but at least some of her dreams came true. She had a good life, a nice home and a beautiful family. What happened a few years later was not her fault. Neither is anything that is happening now. Sometimes we have to let go of what we had in order to hold on to what we've got.

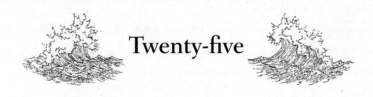

# Twenty-five

*31 October 2:45 a.m.*
*less than four hours until low tide*

'Shouldn't we at least look for Nancy?' Lily says, and the rest of us stare at her.

'It feels safer to me if we all just stay here,' Rose replies.

They both look at Conor, who is busy checking that the windows are locked. 'Is that what you think too?' Lily asks him.

'We searched the whole house when we were looking for Trixie. If Nancy had wanted to be found, we would have found her. I agree with Rose.'

Lily pulls an ugly face. 'I guess some things never change.'

I understand why the others suspect Nancy, but they're wrong.

The fourth time I died, I was here at Seaglass. It was spring 1984, and Nancy and I were sitting on her favourite bench in the garden, pressing flowers. It was something she liked to do. But not when they were perfect and pretty, only when they were dead. Ideas are sewn in our heads, just like seeds. Some are scattered and soon forgotten, others take root and grow to become something much bigger than they were in the begin-ning. Sometimes we make notes in the margins of our minds, thoughts and ideas that are just for us alone to read and ponder over. Thoughts and ideas we do not share. I've never forgotten what my mother said that day.

'We only really acknowledge the beauty and brilliance of someone or something when they die,' she said, holding her pruning shears and deadheading some roses.

*Snip.*

She handed me a ball of dark crimson petals before moving onto some white lilies. 'I've always found that strange, the way people don't appreciate what they have until it is gone.'

*Snip. Snip.*

Then she bent down and cut a few dead daisies from the lawn. Seconds later, it was as though they were never there.

*Snip. Snip. Snip.*

The silver heart-shaped locket my father had given her one Christmas dangled from her neck. She'd worn it every day since, and I imagined pretty pictures of my sisters inside. My mother used to hold it between her thumb and her index finger when she was thinking. I wondered if she thought of them when she did.

I don't remember why we were together at Seaglass without my sisters. Normally Nancy dropped me off alone when *they* were at school and *she* needed to disappear. She had joined an amateur dramatics group in London, and spent an increasing amount of time getting out of parental duties and getting into character for performances at the town hall. The local newspaper once described her as 'a hard act to follow'. They did not mean it kindly. Nancy said we weren't allowed to see her in a show until she was cast in a lead role, which meant we never saw her on stage.

I know Nana liked having the adult company when my mother came to stay at Seaglass. The two women had more in common than either of them realized or cared to admit. Acting and writing are surprisingly similar, and the wish to walk in someone else's shoes – which is what actors and writers do – is a very human desire. But if they forget to take those shoes off, or forget who they really are, it can be a dangerous obsession.

Sometimes London was a little too loud for Nancy. Whenever she was having one of what she called her 'blue days' she needed to hibernate. Those days frequently coincided with her not getting a part she had auditioned for, or finding grey hairs, or not liking how she looked in a photo. But there were often times when I couldn't tell what triggered my mother's melancholy. When she was low, she preferred silence and solitude to hustle and bustle, and Seaglass became a place of sanctuary. Nancy would disappear into a world of her own when we were by the sea. When the tide rolled in, surrounding Seaglass with salty waves, it felt like a moat, separating her from the rest of mankind and the people who had hurt her. Because *someone* hurt my mother; it's the only explanation I can think of for why she was the way she was.

We dried and pressed the dead flowers between the pages of her *Observer's Book of Wild Flowers* that afternoon, drinking home-made lemonade and enjoying the sunshine, and for a little while I think we were almost happy. But it didn't last.

'Are all the flowers in Nana's garden wild?' I asked.

'All living things are wild,' Nancy answered.

'Even children?'

'Especially children.'

As she closed the book on the flattened daisies – the least interesting or beautiful of the flowers she picked – I felt as though she'd like to flatten me between the pages of a book too. It's hard to explain, but it was the first time I truly understood that my mother didn't really love me. The sea sounded louder, and I remember feeling filled with sorrow, as though the lonely thoughts inside my young head might drown me. I was nothing but a disappointment. A broken promise. She blamed herself for my broken heart, and when she looked at me, all she saw was guilt. In that moment, I understood that my mother loved my sisters, and she loved that garden, but her love for me was not evergreen, or even perennial; it would not grow back. Sad memories hide inside us all like ghosts.

It started the way it always did, a strange sensation in my chest. Then I could hear my heartbeat in my ears, even louder than the waves crashing on the rocks around Seaglass. Nancy sensed something was wrong when she looked at my face.

'Is it happening again?' she asked, without saying what.

I nodded. 'I think so.'

She just stared at me.

'Is everything all right?' called Nana from the house.

There was only a brief hesitation, but it was there, before Nancy told her to call an ambulance. By the time she did, I was lying on the grass, my arms hugging my chest, my face pressed against the spot where the dead daisies used to be.

Nana and Nancy carried me across the causeway and up the cliff path wrapped in a blanket, to meet the paramedics on the road. The tide was already coming in, and I was running out of time. My heart stopped just before the ambulance arrived with a defibrillator. I always remember the dying part: the excruciating pain in my chest, the way it felt as though someone was squeezing the air out of my lungs, and the dizzy, light-headed moment just before blacking out. Then an infinite black.

My heart didn't beat for three minutes, and I don't remember anything about it. Nothing at all. Sometimes I feel jealous of other people's near-death stories. For me, despite having died so often, there have never been any white lights or long tunnels, or men with white beards waiting to welcome me at the pearly gates. My experiences were frightfully dull in comparison. I was there and then I wasn't. But I do remember waking up on an unfamiliar ward; I was in hospital for four weeks the fourth time I died.

Because we were in Cornwall when it happened, there wasn't time to get me to the children's hospital in London where I'd been treated so many times before. At first, I was on a ward with all kinds of people – some very old, some very young – with all kinds of problems. The one thing that they had in common was that they all seemed more interested in my health than their own.

It has always fascinated me, how people seem to know so little about how their bodies work. But maybe that's because their bodies *do* work, and it is human nature to take things that aren't broken for granted. I lost count of all the people I had to explain my heart condition to during that stay. Over and over, I had to teach grown adults how *their* hearts worked and clarify why *mine* didn't. People seem to know more about how their phones function than their own bodies. It's bizarre and makes no sense to me.

The heart is a muscle, cleverly designed to pump blood all around the body and keep you alive. It's simple and very complicated at the same time. The right side of your heart receives oxygen-poor blood from your veins and pumps it to your lungs, where it picks up oxygen and gets rid of carbon dioxide. The left side of your heart receives oxygen-rich blood from your lungs and pumps it through your arteries to the rest of your body. A septum separates the right and left sides, and the left side has thicker walls because it needs to put the blood under higher pressure. The heart is so strong that this whole process only takes about one minute, so if it stops for any reason, the person it belongs to stops pretty soon after. I find people glaze over when I start talking about atriums, or ventricles, or my problematic aorta, so it's easier to just say I've got a faulty valve.

'My radiator had one of those,' a woman on the ward said. I didn't know how to reply to that, so just nodded and smiled until she shuffled away in her back-to-front hospital gown.

Me being in hospital was like a holiday for my mother. The dark circles beneath her eyes were several shades lighter than before. Every time I almost died, she looked rejuvenated. She was happier and healthier without me in her life, and a little secret part of me hated her for it.

Nana was the only person who came to visit me regularly. She would read me stories, and make up new ones about all the hospital staff. Sometimes I'd wake up and she would be asleep in the chair next to me, holding a book in one hand and my hand in her other. I think that was the first time I knew that Nana loved me the most. More than she loved my sisters – unlike my mother. Though I didn't understand why.

'Don't you mind that I'm broken?' I asked one day when she came to visit.

She took off her pink and purple coat, sat down on the bed, and smiled. 'You're not broken in my eyes, and you shouldn't see yourself that way either. We are who we think we are, and there is much beauty in imperfection.'

'But the doctors said that—'

'Pay no attention to the Doctors of Doom. They've been taught how to fix people, but not how to feel. You can do anything. You can be anyone. You just have to believe it.' She took the tray of uneaten hospital food that was next to the bed, and tipped everything that had been on it into the bin.

Then she put a red-and-white tablecloth over the sheets, and put an elaborate-looking cake stand on top. It was covered with posh sandwiches and cakes . . . a takeaway afternoon tea from the Ritz. We started with scones, clotted cream *on top* of the jam, the Cornish way.

'The hospital food is terrible, no wonder you don't eat it. I decided to smuggle something better in. I don't want you starving, and I don't care what the doctors think,' said Nana, taking a bite of her scone and getting cream on her nose. 'You're going to be just fine. People told me I'd never be a published author, but here I am. I believe that you can be whoever you want to be too. Forget what other people say about you, and write your own story.'

I've thought a lot about what Nana said that day. Her words played on a loop inside my head and had a profound effect on me. For the first time in a long time, I felt hopeful about the future again. Her believing that I had one made me believe it too. I decided that she was right, and from that moment on, I was determined to prove those doctors wrong.

I might have been young, but I could tell that my mother came to visit me in hospital out of a sense of duty and my nana came to visit out of love. Sometimes people confuse love and duty, but they are not the same. Neither were the women in my childhood.

'Thank you for coming to visit me, Nana,' I said. I felt overwhelmingly sad as I watched her put the pink and purple coat back on, preparing to leave the hospital.

'It was my pleasure, Daisy Chain. Just you remember to come and visit *me* at Seaglass when I am old and lonely.'

'I will.'

'Hope so. Just between us, you're my favourite.'

I like to think she meant that. I wanted to be someone's

favourite something. Didn't really mind what. When I think about Nana being gone from my life forever, I feel more broken than I ever have before. She was the only one who ever really believed in me, and I don't know how to exist without her.

Secrets are like unpaid debts: they pile up, and too much interest is best avoided. I'm not as sweet and innocent as everyone thinks I am. Just because I don't spend my life complaining like one sister, or thinking I'm better than everyone else like the other, it doesn't mean I don't have occasional dark thoughts. Nana's book, *Daisy Darker's Little Secret*, was a bestseller all over the world. I know some people thought the character was based on me, but the real Daisy Darker was never quite as sweet or broken as everyone wanted to believe. I have a secret of my own. And some secrets are worth killing to keep.

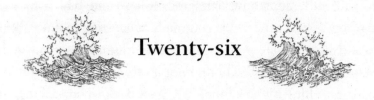

# Twenty-six

*31 October 2:50 a.m.*
*less than four hours until low tide*

'What time is it now?' Lily asks.
        'Five minutes since the last time you asked me,'
Rose replies.

'Really? It feels so much longer.'

I agree. Time moves more slowly when your heart is broken, and theirs are surely broken now too. Time stretches so that seconds seem like minutes, and minutes seem more like hours. It's starting to feel as though I've been trapped inside this house with my family forever.

Lily shakes her head. 'Is there no way we can try to leave Seaglass *now*? Waiting here like sitting ducks for another three hours seems like madness. My car is parked in the sand dunes across the causeway. We could all drive to the police station in town together? Get help? I don't want to be here anymore.'

'None of us want to be here anymore,' says Conor.

'You know we can't leave until the tide goes out,' says Rose. 'Not without a boat.'

Lily has started pacing the room. 'Can't we *make* a boat? There must be something that would float? We could take one of the doors off its hinges?'

Rose sighs. 'Can you hear the storm outside? Can you hear the waves crashing on the rocks, out there in the darkness? Do you remember how dangerous Blacksand Bay is to swim in at the best of times? Are you really suggesting that we should try and float to safety on an old door? Should we use wooden spoons for paddles?' There is something unusually unkind about my eldest sister's tone. Lily goes back to her pacing, and Rose starts biting her nails.

'I think we're all very upset and very tired, but maybe we could try to be a little bit kinder to each other? Nobody in this room is to blame for what has happened here tonight,' I say, and it seems to do the trick.

'I'm sorry,' says Rose. 'I know you're scared, Lily. We all are, but this situation must be even more terrifying after what happened to Trixie.'

'I thought you said I just fainted in the hall?' Trixie says.

'That's right,' Rose replies, realizing her mistake. 'But it gave us all a fright, especially your mum. We just have to wait a little while longer, then we can leave.'

Rose checks her watch again. She's been doing that a lot since she arrived last night. And it was Rose who said that Conor's boat was gone, that the rope tying it to the jetty looked as though it had been cut. She's the only one who left the house – as far as I know. What if she cut it herself? I try to stop thinking the worst about everyone in the room, but it's impossible to know who to trust. I'm sure they're all doing the same.

Trixie shivers. 'Why is it always so cold here?'

'I'll put another log on the fire,' says Lily, standing up and crossing the room. She stares down at the log basket, and I wonder whether she is scared of breaking one of her manicured nails. 'There's another one,' she whispers, not moving.

'Another what?' asks Conor, coming to stand by her side. He slowly bends down, reaches inside the basket and takes out a VHS tape. 'This wasn't here before, I'd have seen it,' he says, looking around the room at each of us.

'What does it say?' asks Rose.

Conor holds the tape up so we can all see the Scrabble letters stuck to its cover:

**NOTICE ME.**

'I vote we burn it—' Lily says.

'No!' Rose interrupts. 'What if this tape reveals what is really going on? What if we never find out the truth if we don't watch it?'

'You said that last time,' Lily replies. 'Don't you get it? Someone is trying to mess with our heads, and by going along with it, we're just making things worse.'

'I'd like to watch it. It's fun seeing you all when you were younger,' says Trixie.

'I said no!' Lily snaps and Trixie stares at her.

'It's not *her* fault,' I say.

'I think we should watch it too,' says Rose. 'I want to understand what is happening, and what *else* are we going to do?'

Lily looks around the room, waiting for someone to take her side, but none of us do. 'Fine,' she says. 'Do what you want, you will anyway.'

Conor slots the tape into the machine, then picks up the remote control before sitting down next to Rose at the back of the room. I sit on the floor, next to Poppins, just like I did when she was still a puppy. Dogs are much more comforting to be around than humans.

The home movie starts with a shot of Nancy's garden at the back of Seaglass. It looks like summer, and the flowers are more spectacular than I remember them being. I subtly look over my shoulder, and see that Trixie and Lily are staring at the screen. But Rose and Conor are now sitting very close together. They are whispering – for Trixie's benefit, I suppose – but I can just about make out their words.

'If this were a murder mystery, then the killer would be the least likely suspect,' Conor says.

I look back at the TV, pretend I can't hear them.

'You don't think that Daisy . . .' Rose whispers.

'No. That's crazy,' Conor replies, and I feel a strange sense of relief, followed by a rush of anger. The sound of waves crashing on the rocks outside seems to get louder in my head, along with the ticking clocks in the hallway. Having a broken heart doesn't mean I am incapable of breaking someone else's.

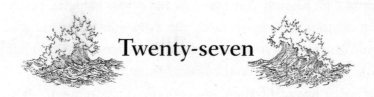

# Twenty-seven

SEAGLASS – 1984

The weather at Seaglass is always a bit hit-and-miss, especially in summer. Blacksand Bay seems to have its own microclimate, blissfully unaware of the seasons. But my family were very good at being very British, come rain or shine. If the calendar said that it was summer, we would all play outside wearing shorts and T-shirts, even if it was snowing.

The home movie on the ancient TV now proves that the sun did sometimes shine at Seaglass. The wobbly shot reveals a blue sky over a lush garden, a makeshift stage consisting of a navy upside-down rowing boat, and some chairs on the lawn. Nancy appears in the doorway at the back of the house, looking stunning in a white blouse, belted skirt and silk scarf, just like Audrey Hepburn in *Roman Holiday*. She's smiling. A lot. It's surreal to see. The camera moves closer, then ducks behind a large plant. Whoever filmed this was spying on our mother.

A man appears beside her on the terrace. He's smiling too. At first, I think it's my dad. But as the camera zooms in, I realize it isn't. It's Conor's. Mr Kennedy helped Nancy to completely redesign the garden at the back of Seaglass, landscaping what was already there, as well as planting new flowers and a pretty magnolia tree. She loved that tree and would often sit on the bench beneath it. Nana said it was a symbol of what friendship and hope can achieve, and how helping to make others happy can make you happy too. Nancy and Conor's dad sit down side by side, moving their chairs a little closer together on the lawn. I think they had been 'friends' for about a year by then.

My sisters and I were putting on a play, just like we did most summers at Seaglass, and the empty chairs for the 'audience' were filled with teddy bears and dolls. I don't remember how or when the annual Darker family plays started. Like most family traditions, it became something we always did simply because it was something we had always done.

Dad's piano had been wheeled out onto the lawn, with some considerable team effort. That would have made him cross, which is perhaps why my mother let us do it. She loved to see us singing, or dancing or acting. Nothing seemed to bring her more joy. Nancy loved all things theatrical. She always helped with the costumes and the choreography, and was our most enthusiastic member of the audience, whooping and cheering while Nana and Mr Kennedy just clapped. I remember that was the first year my sisters allowed me to have a speaking role. Rose and Conor were fourteen, Lily was thirteen, and I was nine.

The fabric of the relationship with my sisters has been repeatedly stretched, torn and restitched over the years. A patchwork quilt of antiquated love and lies, born out of duty and expectation. We are supposed to love our family. It's an unspoken rule. Whenever I see pictures of other families, their happy faces all covered in matching smiles, I find myself wondering whether it is real. Or if the happiness they're portraying is simply a mask worn for the sake of others. Surely all families have fights, and disagreements and conflict . . . maybe the way we were with one another was more normal than I thought. We all have our own version of the truth, and it is rarely whole.

As always, our play that year was a strange mix of stories from our favourite films, blended into an elaborate tale of our own. It's clear that 1984 was a year when we were all into *Star Wars*. Lily walks out onto the 'stage' dressed as Princess Leia, with her plaited hair in giant buns on either side of her head. She stands on top of the upturned blue boat and starts talking about a galaxy far, far away. Before she finishes, I see nine-year-old me hurry out of the kitchen door and sit down at the piano. I avoid eye contact with the audience or my co-stars the whole time – I was always horribly shy compared to my sisters – possibly even more than normal on that occasion, because I was dressed as Gizmo from *Gremlins*.

We were a musical family before our composition changed. Some families know all the lyrics to one another's songs and live in harmony, but not us. My sisters showed little interest in following in our father's footsteps after he divorced our mother – Rose dabbled with the recorder, and Lily could just about keep time with a tambourine – but I always enjoyed playing the piano. I used to play imaginary notes on the kitchen table when I couldn't play the real thing, my fingers silently moving to a melody that could only be heard in my imagination. Nana said that I sometimes did it while holding her hand, and that she occasionally saw my fingers twitching even when I was in bed, as though playing the piano in my sleep. My dad was so proud and pleased that I had shown an interest in what he loved most, music. And he was the real reason I played, desperate to earn his affection. I was definitely a daddy's girl when I was a child, but he could never live up to the man I turned him into inside my head.

I was still delighted when he appeared in the garden at Seaglass that afternoon. He had a frown on his face as he sat down next to Nancy in the audience. I presumed it was because his precious piano was outside, but now I think it might have been more to do with the other man sitting next to my mother. Dad smiled when I started to play, and it made all the hours of practice seem worthwhile. Rose was tone-deaf, and Lily had as much rhythm as an arrhythmia. Playing the piano was the only thing that I was better at than my sisters. By the age of nine, I'd taught myself to play rather well.

It is fourteen-year-old Rose's turn to take the stage next. She was just about young enough to still take part in the family play, although I doubt she would have told her friends at school about it. Rose is dressed as a ghostbuster, and I think it was by far the best home-made costume that year. I play a little bit of the film's theme tune as she walks out, and Lily glares at me when I get a couple of the notes wrong. I remember how bad that made me feel, even though I had practised for days. The story we were trying to tell – about a princess, a gremlin and a ghostbuster – makes as little sense to me now as it did then. But I get goosebumps when teenage Rose starts to sing.

> 'Hush, little baby, don't be afraid,
> The beds we lie in are the ones we made.
> And if that means you can't sleep at night,
> Remember that wrongs are sometimes right.
> And if you fear you're all alone,
> You'll always have me and a place to call home.
> Hush, little baby, don't you cry,
> Sometimes we live, sometimes we die.'

I find myself looking at Rose in the present. If she feels me staring at her, she doesn't show it. Instead she continues to watch her younger self on the screen. Conor and Lily are staring at her now too. Rose was always changing the words of nursery rhymes when we were growing up – swapping the real lyrics for something a shade darker. Not unlike the poems in Nana's children's books. Or the chalk poem written on the kitchen wall tonight.

'Who is that?' asks Trixie, and we all look back at the television, just in time to see fourteen-year-old Conor perform his part in the play. She's right to wonder; he is almost unrecognizable from the man he grew into. Teenage Conor stands on the upturned boat and raps about the freedom of the press, dressed as the Karate Kid – one of our favourite films that year. He tries to balance on one leg, whilst doing a rather comical impression of the crane kick.

Then it is my turn. My first and – because of what happened – last speaking role in the Darker family play. Nine-year-old me looks terrified as she steps onto the old blue boat, and stares out at the audience of four adults and several toys. I clench my fists and squeeze my eyes closed, as I try to overcome my stage fright and remember the lines that my sisters had written for me. I remember that the Gizmo costume was very itchy, and made me want to sneeze. I caught Nana's eye, and she smiled at me. *You can do it*, she mouthed. Her belief in me outweighed my inability to believe in myself.

'Daughters are like gremlins, and there are three rules you mustn't break,' I say.

'One: keep them out of bright light . . .'

Conor and Lily shine torches at me, and Rose throws a white sheet over my head, which was always part of the plan. The sheet had holes cut into it, so that I could still see.

'Two: never feed them after midnight,' I say.

Lily throws an egg at me, which was *not* what we had rehearsed, but everyone laughed so I carried on.

'Three: do *not* get them wet . . .'

Lily throws a bucket of cold water over me, which was also not part of the plan, and I struggle to remember my final line. I watch myself spin around, revealing a scary hand-drawn face on the back of the white sheet I was beneath.

'Or they'll turn into ghosts!'

There is a slight pause before all of Nana's clocks start to ring and ding and chime in the past. It must have been midday when we gave our little performance, because they seem to go on forever. She had a new one that year that looked like an owl. Its eyes turned as it ticked, as though it was watching us.

When the clocks stop, Rose – the ghostbuster – aims her cardboard proton pack in my direction, shooting a hidden can of squirty cream. When the show is over, we all hold hands and take a bow. I watch as our mother congratulates us and hands me a towel – so even she knew I was going to get wet – then I disappear inside the house.

The static camera picks up some of what the adults are saying, but I have to lean a little closer to the TV in order to hear. Conor's dad and our dad seem to be fighting for Nancy's attention. Bradley Kennedy was completely in love with my mother by then, and anyone who saw them together knew she felt the same way. My dad – who'd had more girlfriends than any of us could keep track of – didn't seem to like my mother having a 'friend' of her own, even though they'd been divorced for years.

'I have to leave first thing, my orchestra is playing in Paris next week,' Dad boasted.

'That sounds wonderful,' Mr Kennedy replied, sounding genuinely pleased that my dad was leaving.

'Bradley has written a book about grief and gardening,' Nancy said to my dad, as though it was some sort of competition.

Dad shrugged. 'Sounds . . . delightful.'

'I think so. Nana is going to put him in touch with her agent,' my mother replied. 'I've read it, and the writing is beautiful. The book deserves to get noticed,' she added, beaming with pride as though she had written it herself. But the smiles didn't last for long.

There is a scream from inside Seaglass on the TV, which makes everyone here, then and now, jump. The scream belonged to Lily. She had just found me lying on the floor at the bottom of the stairs, still dressed as Gizmo the gremlin, and I wasn't breathing.

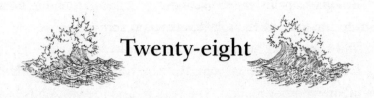

# Twenty-eight

*31 October 2:55 a.m.*
*less than four hours until low tide*

My mother said that it was nobody's fault that my heart stopped that day, but I think being so scared on that stage might have had something to do with it. I have never liked people looking at me, which I think is because of all the doctors who stared at me when I was a child. They would look at my face, then stare down at the scar on my chest, then shake their heads and frown their frowns, and look very disappointed indeed. When people stared at me, it was almost always for the wrong reasons, which was why I would rather they didn't look at me at all.

There were months of hospital visits the fifth time I died, including a trip to see yet another specialist in London the following February. The private hospital fees were paid for by Nana, who always refused to believe that there wasn't a way to fix me. Most memories of my times in hospital have faded around the edges over the years, but I remember that week for two reasons. Firstly, it was Valentine's Day, and the boy in the bed opposite me on the ward gave me a card. I had never received a Valentine's card before and didn't know quite what to make of it.

'Why does it have a heart on the front?' I asked.

'Because I love you,' he said, pushing his jam-jar glasses a little higher up his nose. He was eleven, I was nine, and I'm not convinced either of us knew too much about love.

'Well, don't get any funny ideas. I have a boyfriend,' I lied.

'No boys have ever come to visit you,' he replied. 'What's his name?'

I didn't hesitate. 'His name is Conor Kennedy. But even if I didn't have a boyfriend, which I definitely do, given the ward we're on, we might both be dead by morning. So please don't spend what might be your final hours having fanciful thoughts about me.'

From the boy's expression, I thought maybe I shouldn't have said what I said. But his freckled face soon recovered from the shock of my words, and he smiled, revealing shiny silver braces. 'God will watch over us, and I'm sure we'll both still be here for breakfast.'

I've never been religious, nobody in my family is. Nancy said that she believed in God until the day she found out I was broken. They had a bit of a falling-out after that, which resulted in her not speaking to God for several years, so in some ways her relationship with God wasn't unlike her relationship with my father. I suppose the doctors were like gods to me; it was up to them whether I stayed alive. They always seemed to find a way to fix me, so maybe I should have been more optimistic about living long enough to endure another hospital meal. But I wasn't – optimistic, that is – it's something I've always struggled to be. I have a highly active imagination, and it's been self-taught to imagine the worst.

The boy was still staring at me with a dreamy expression on his face, holding the home-made Valentine's card. I didn't much like the look of him, or it.

'Why do you think you love me? You don't even know me,'
I said.

'Yes, I do. I've read all the Daisy Darker books,' he replied
with a grin.

It was my first taste of fame, and I didn't like the flavour.
Just because someone has read a book with my name on the
front, it doesn't mean that they know who I am.

I put the card on the little table, said that I needed to sleep,
and asked the nurse to pull the flimsy curtain around my
hospital bed. Then I tried to pretend that the boy and the rest
of the ward weren't really there. I didn't like sleeping in a room
full of sick strangers, I don't suppose anyone does. I stared at
that Valentine's card, wondering why the red heart on the front
looked absolutely nothing like the heart inside my chest. I'd
seen enough posters on enough doctors' office walls to know
it was a very poor likeness. And I wondered how and why this
rather ugly internal organ had become the universal symbol
for love.

Over the next few days, I asked all of the doctors – who
were supposed to be clever – and all of the nurses – who
seemed even cleverer than the doctors to me – but nobody
seemed able to answer my question. When Nana came to visit,
I asked her, because Nana knew *everything*.

'You're far too young to start worrying about *love*. I suggest
you concentrate on getting better,' she said, pulling the curtain
around my hospital bed before perching on the side of it. She
was wearing a purple coat with a matching purple hat and
gloves, and I could tell from her rosy cheeks that it must have
been cold outside. 'Here,' she whispered, opening up her huge
pink and purple patchwork bag. 'I brought you a snack.' The
red-and-white tablecloth made another appearance. She laid
it across the bed between us, then produced two parcels of

takeaway cod and chips wrapped in newspaper. She set the makeshift table with wooden cutlery, sachets of salt and vinegar, and a pot of mushy peas mixed with green Jelly Tots. The memory still makes me smile.

'Why do you let your sisters treat you the way they do?' Nana said, dipping a chip in ketchup.

'What do you mean?' I asked.

'You need to stand up for yourself, or life will always knock you down.'

I thought she might be right about that. Nana was almost always right about everything. So I decided things would be different with my sisters from that day on Nana was as wise as an owl, she even had a new owl-shaped clock to prove it, so I asked her the question again.

'*Do* you know why the heart is a symbol of love?'

'Well, that is an interesting question and therefore deserves an interesting answer,' Nana said. 'The ancient Egyptians thought that the human heart epitomized life, the Greeks believed that it controlled our thoughts and emotions, and the Romans declared that Venus, the goddess of love, set hearts on fire with Cupid's help. The Romans also believed that there was a vein connecting the fourth finger on the left hand directly to the heart. There isn't, but that's why people traditionally wear wedding rings on that finger, even today. In the Middle Ages, Christians agreed that the human heart had something to do with love, and hundreds of years later, the familiar red shape still appears on greetings cards, playing cards, even T-shirts. The heart symbol became a verb in the 1970s, with I Heart New York. Does that answer your question?'

'I think so. How do you know the answers to everything?' I asked.

She laughed. 'I don't, nobody does! But if I do know more

than most, it's because I read. Books will teach you anything you want to know, and they tend to be more honest than people.'

We finished our fish and chips as the sun was setting outside. Then we read *Alice's Adventures in Wonderland* together, which has always been one of my most favourite books.

'Speaking of love . . .' Nana said. 'I hope you know how much I love you.'

I grinned. 'How much?'

She looked out of the hospital window and pointed at the full moon. 'I love you from here to the moon and back.'

'I love *you* from here to the moon and back twice,' I replied.

It was her turn to smile now. 'I love you from here to the moon and back three times and once for luck.'

Later that night, when I was alone again and tucked into my hospital bed, I started to wonder if my heart being broken meant that I could never truly love someone. The human heart beats eighty times a minute, one hundred thousand times a day, and about thirty-five million times a year. In an average lifetime, a heart will beat two and a half billion times. Maybe it had something to do with endurance, something which hearts and love have in common?

The second reason I remember that particular hospital stay so well was because my mother cried the next day when she came to visit. It was something she rarely did – the crying part, I mean – and as I watched her talking to a doctor on the other side of a window on my hospital ward, I wished I could lip-read. She never told me what that doctor said, or why it upset her so much.

We all hear the sound of the lounge door creaking open, and I spin around.

Rose looks as startled as we do as she lets go of the handle, the key still in her hand.

'I just need to pop to the loo,' she says, as we continue to stare at her.

'You're going to go out there again? Alone?' Lily asks.

'Yes. Or do I need a hall pass? You told Trixie off for being scared to go to the bathroom earlier. I'm a lot older and I have a gun. There's no need to worry about me. I'll be two minutes,' Rose says, and leaves the room before any of us have time to reply.

'*Conor*,' Lily whispers.

He looks up like a startled meerkat, then whispers himself. 'What?'

'Do you think it was a bit strange how quickly Rose knew what was wrong with Trixie? Finding the blood between her toes like that?'

'She was missing a sock . . .'

'I know, but still . . .'

'When was there blood between my toes?' asks Trixie. 'And who was that man in the audience on the lawn in the home movie?' She has a habit of asking too many questions, sometimes not waiting for the answer to one before asking another.

'That was Conor's dad,' Lily says.

'That's weird,' Trixie mumbles. 'I thought I recognized him. Also, on the video, Nancy said something about his work getting *noticed*. And the Scrabble letters on the tape's cover said NOTICE ME.'

'She's right about that,' I say, and Lily stares at her daughter as though she is a child genius.

'Why was Conor's dad at Seaglass?' Trixie asks next.

Lily shrugs. 'Because he became friends with Nancy.'

'Are they still friends now?'

'No,' Conor says, without further explanation.

Rose returns, slots the key in the door, and locks us all inside the room once more. She sits down on the sofa, a little too close to Conor again for my liking. None of us say a word, but she was gone longer than a couple of minutes.

'Shall we finish the tape?' she asks, aiming the remote at the TV and pressing play without waiting for any of us to reply.

'What's happening? Is it broken?' Trixie says, staring at the screen.

She's too young to remember what it looks like when someone tapes over an old recording on VHS. The picture looks stretched and distorted while one image replaces another, as though wiping away the memory of what was there before. We all stare at the screen now, but Conor is the first to say anything about what we see.

'Oh my god, that is terrifying.'

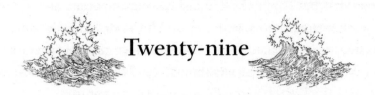

# Twenty-nine

## SEAGLASS – 1985

'What happened to your hair, Mum?' asks Trixie.

It's a good question, and 'terrifying' is the only word to describe Lily's 1980s hairstyle on the TV screen. To be fair, I'm sure everyone has at least one haircut from the past that comes back to haunt them. I'm guessing it must have been 1985. It's the same tape, but what we're seeing now would have been filmed a year or so after the family play on the lawn. Lily has very short, *big* hair in this home movie, and it doesn't suit her. But it definitely got her noticed.

'I had a bad haircut,' is all she says to Trixie.

'There is a tape in the camcorder already,' says the younger version of herself on the TV, like a whining echo from the past.

The seesaw of power constantly changed between my sisters and me as we grew older, but even on the rare occasions when it was my turn at the top, Lily still seemed to look down on me. Rose blossomed as a teenager, in looks and personality, and became a kinder version of the person she had been before. It's her fifteen-year-old smile that we all see next. She has taken the camera from Lily and turned it to face herself before speaking.

'This is Rose Darker, reporting for Crazy Town News . . .' The sight of her looking so happy shocks me. Her beauty has never faded, but her happiness diminished over the years, and it's rare to see her smile. 'I'm joined now by Mr Conor Kennedy,' she says in a deep voice, imitating a newsreader. The camera swings around to show Conor, clearly going through his Michael J. Fox lookalike phase. I think *Back to the Future* must have come out that year, because he's dressed like Marty McFly. I remember him becoming slightly obsessed with the scientific theories about time travel, and writing about the space–time continuum for his school newspaper every week until the teachers begged him to stop. 'Tell me, Conor Kennedy, why are you celebrating Lily's birthday with the Darker family this year, and has it been fun so far?'

'Because I was invited, and thought it would be an interesting social experiment to witness. As always.'

'Was it interesting because my little sister, Daisy Darker, somehow won a game of Trivial Pursuit this afternoon? Even though she's never been to school!'

The camera turns to where childhood me is sitting, on the other side of Conor. I watch myself stick my tongue out at Rose, but then I smile, in both the past and the present. I look happy in 1985. We all do. I was almost ten, and had become even more of a bookworm by then. I liked teaching myself about things other people didn't seem to know. I remember wanting to vanish, and books helped me to escape. I longed to disappear inside a dream of the world that was less cold and lonely than the life I lived in. I read more and more, hiding inside my room and my books for hours. Mostly murder mysteries, while dreaming of one day writing my own.

'Or . . . are you really here as a secret detective?' Rose asks Conor. 'Trying to solve the mystery of what will forever be known as . . . Hairgate.'

'That's enough, Rose,' says my mother.

In this home movie, we are all sitting in the music room, on our individually painted chairs from the kitchen, waiting for someone to play the piano. We might not have been able to perform family plays on the lawn anymore, in case my problematic heart couldn't take it, but there was never going to be a way to stop Lily wanting to show off. She craved attention like oxygen, and because it was her birthday, we all had to watch and listen. Belinda Carlisle was her firm favourite that year. I'd been forced to hear 'Heaven Is a Place on Earth' so often, I'm surprised she didn't wear out the cassette tape.

Teenage Rose continued her family news report. 'I'm now joined by Nancy Darker, a.k.a. my mother, but she doesn't like to be called that because it makes her feel *old*. Nobody knows how *old* my mother really is, but scientists say she was probably born in the *Dark* Ages. Any words of wisdom for the next generation, Mrs Darker?'

'Yes. Make sure you film Lily or I'll never hear the end of it. You've caused quite enough trouble for one day,' said Nancy, before smiling for the camera. She was sitting next to Conor's dad, and the shot zooms in on them holding hands, then returns to the front of the room.

My dad appeared then, walking out through the door that connects the music room to the kitchen. He sat down at the piano as though he had just stepped onto a stage. My father seemed to make more of an effort to attend family birthdays, and come home for the holidays, after my mother started dating other men. Lily walked through the door next. Then Nana followed her, which was a complete surprise for most of us, because Nana was actually painfully shy when it came to performing. Even around her own family. Just like me.

Dad started to play the piano, and I recognized the song immediately, it was another of Lily's favourites. 'I Know Him So Well' was always blaring from her bedroom, behind the permanently closed door. She was in love with the performance by Elaine Paige and Barbara Dickson, so much so she had twisted Dad's arm to play it and Nana to sing it with her as a surprise for the rest of us on her birthday. And it was a surprise. Because it was really very good. I didn't even know Nana could sing. They hit every note and every harmony, and when the song was over, we all clapped in genuine admiration.

I remember how Lily sang the lyrics staring at Conor the whole time, and now that I've seen the video evidence, I know I didn't imagine it. Lily got goggle-eyed whenever Conor walked into a room back then, and she had started blushing whenever he spoke to her. Which was one of the many reasons why I was pleased to see her looking so ugly with her short hair.

The night before this scene from our family past was filmed, Lily's hair had been down to her waist. She had gone to bed in the room she shared with Rose, with two long plaits just like always, so that she wouldn't wake up with a head full of tangles. But when she sat up the following morning, on her fourteenth birthday, she screamed. Her two plaits were on her pillow. Someone had cut them clean off her head in the night. Nana's kitchen scissors were on Rose's bedside table. But Rose didn't cut off Lily's hair. I did.

The people who love us the most hurt us the hardest, because they can.

When I found Nana and Lily secretly rehearsing together the day before, something inside me *snapped*.

Lily was always my mother's favourite daughter.

Rose was my dad's favourite because she was beautiful and clever.

But Nana was supposed to love *me* the most. She said *I* was her favourite.

Seeing Nana and Lily together felt like some kind of betrayal.

Lily and I had had a squabble a week earlier, and Nana said something I've never forgotten.

'You should always fight, especially if you think you are going to lose. That's when you should fight the hardest.'

So I did. Fight. But I did it quietly and carefully, and planned the whole thing so that I wouldn't get caught. I stole some of my mother's sleeping pills, I put them in my sisters' hot chocolate before they went to bed that night, then I crept into their room and cut off Lily's hair. Everyone thought that Rose had done it in her sleep – she was studying for exams, had been exhausted for weeks, and had already sleepwalked once before. I could tell that Rose – the clever daughter – didn't believe she had done it. But she didn't have an alternative explanation either. I'm not sure Lily ever really forgave her or trusted her again. Nobody suspected me. *Nobody.* As though a good person is incapable of doing something bad.

No one ever noticed *me* in my family except for Nana. Lily couldn't have her too; Nana was mine. I hated her for trying to steal the affection of the only person who really loved me. And people can make a hobby out of hate. The more they practise, the better they get.

The rage I felt when Lily and Nana sang together was all-consuming. And it wasn't just jealousy. I wanted revenge for all the horrible and unkind things that Lily had said and done to me over the years. I decided that cutting off my sister's hair was just the start.

# Thirty

*31 October 3 a.m.*
*three hours until low tide*

The tape comes to an abrupt end and ejects itself. Then the eighty clocks out in the hall inform us that it is three a.m. We all wait for the noise to stop.

'I don't think we learned anything at all from watching that nonsense,' says Lily when it is quiet again.

'Maybe not,' says Rose, putting down the remote. I stare at it and can't help wondering if *she* stopped the tape just now, and whether there might have been more to see. 'But this will be the first hour that someone didn't . . . go missing. So I think we did the right thing by staying together in one room.'

'What do you mean?' asks Lily.

'Well, Nana was . . .' she looks at Trixie and censors herself '. . . *found* at midnight. Dad at one a.m. We . . . found Trixie at two—'

'You can all stop pretending. I'm not a child,' says Trixie. Though in pink pyjamas and with her mess of curls, she does look like one. 'I've guessed that I didn't just faint and that something happened to me too.'

'We didn't want you to be scared,' says Lily.

'Why not? It's obvious *you* all are,' Trixie replies, staring at her mother.

'If Rose is right, and someone planned to do something to one of us on the hour, every hour, then we're due another . . . incident,' says Conor.

'Well, I make it three-oh-three, so maybe we're safe now,' says Lily.

'Maybe,' Rose replies, sounding uncertain. She stares at Poppins, who is lying upside down, stretched out in front of the fire. It's one of the old dog's favourite spots in the house. Poppins hasn't moved or made a sound for quite some time. We exchange looks, and then Rose speaks in that special voice she only uses for animals.

'Poppins?'

The dog doesn't move.

'Poppins?' Rose tries again.

Nothing.

'Wakey wakey, Poppins,' says Trixie.

Rose turns a whiter shade of pale when there is still no response.

'Poppins,' she tries one last time. 'Do you want din-dins?'

The dog goes from upside down to up on all fours and wagging her tail in seconds, and we breathe a communal sigh of relief.

'Thank god,' says Rose. 'It's less than three hours until low tide now. We just have to stay calm, then we can all get out of here. Together.'

Conor starts checking that the doors and windows are locked again, it's Lily's turn to pace up and down the room, and Rose sits in Nana's purple armchair, quietly playing with the ring on her right hand. It's made of three interlocking bands, of bronze, silver and gold, and was a gift from Nana on Rose's sixteenth birthday. It's something that I've always been jealous of, like so many of the things my sisters had that I didn't. I remember that birthday and that year very well. It was 1986.

Nana and Nancy were both wearing aprons – which was a recipe for disaster seeing as Nana didn't like anyone else in the kitchen when she was cooking. But Nancy insisted on helping with her daughter's sixteenth birthday cake. Lily – the lover of all things sweet – marched into the room where I had been sitting quietly and stuck her hand into the bowl of chocolate icing, before licking her finger clean. Lily still had short hair, but it had grown into a bob by then, so she looked like a miniature version of our mother.

Rose was allowed to have a sleepover at Seaglass with some of her closest friends for her sixteenth birthday. She would soon be attending a different school, and I think in many ways it was a chance to say goodbye. Things were never quite the same between my sisters after the hair-cutting incident. But Lily was not looking forward to life at boarding school without Rose, and clung to her side that summer like a barnacle. She was our sister's shadow but was never in it. She followed Rose everywhere, always wanting to be one step ahead. But she couldn't follow Rose to a school for gifted students because she wasn't one.

I remember the conversation Nana and Nancy had about my dad, and for the first time I didn't really care whether he made an appearance or not. He wasn't there for all of *my* birthdays.

'If he said he'll be here, he'll be here,' said Nana, defending her son.

Nancy sighed. 'Well, it isn't long before the kids arrive, then

the tide will be in, and then he'll be too late. You can't be there
for one daughter's birthday and not there for the other. Rose
will feel so let down if he's a no-show again.'

'Just be patient,' Nana said. 'And as for the other one, he'll
be back. Men don't like being told off; it makes them sulk like
the little boys they're pretending not to be.'

'All I asked was for Bradley to wipe his feet before trudging
in mud from the garden. It's as though he can't see the dirt.'
I remember my mother and Conor's father squabbling about
the strangest of things when they were 'friends'. Being neat
and tidy frequently seemed to be high on their list of differ-
ences: she was, he wasn't. Nancy was always tidying things
away and putting them in cupboards. Conor's dad's inability
to remove his muddy gardening boots before stepping inside
made her crazier than normal.

'Daisy!' Nancy said. 'Leave the cake mix alone!'

'Lily stuck her finger in the bowl, why can't I? And why
can't I stay up for the party? I'm almost eleven,' said ten-year-old
me.

'Because I said so. Rose wants to have a sleepover with
some friends. They're all a bit older than you, sweetheart. You
can stay for the food, then straight up to your room. Nana and
I are forbidden from staying downstairs too,' my mother said.
'You'll understand one day.'

I didn't believe her.

Like all children whose parents get divorced, my sisters and
I learned to adapt to our new lives. Rose and Lily learned to
love going to boarding school, and soon seemed to resent their
long summers back at Seaglass with me. Despite the unpleasantness they unpacked with their bags, I always longed for
their return. I missed them. They shared a life that I had little
knowledge of, filled with teachers and friends and lessons. I

would listen to their stories with little understanding of what they meant. For years I thought that a spelling test was something only trainee witches had to do, to check they had learned their magic spells. I wondered if that's what my sisters really were: witches. There had been plenty of evidence to suggest I was right. I resented their relationship, and was jealous of their education, and the older I got, the more being left behind bothered me.

My mother's idea of home schooling was to allow me to read the books Nana gave me. She wouldn't even let me watch the news on TV, only cartoons like *Bugs Bunny*.

'Daisy doesn't need to learn about the horrors of the real world,' Nancy would say, depriving me of the joy of learning. So I tried to teach myself. This Daisy was a self-raising flower. But my life was too quiet without my sisters in it. I was almost always alone, with nothing but novels and an overactive imagination for company.

Books can take you anywhere if you let them, and reading proved to be a big part of my education. But my sisters learned a lot of things that I didn't. Things about real life, and social skills, and *boys*. I have always been a little awkward around real people. I don't know how to talk to them, and even now, I still prefer the company of characters in books. I suppose it is a hangover from my childhood, when I was so often drunk with solitude. 'Doesn't play well with others' is to be expected when playing with others was rarely an option. And I have always been a little over the limit with my own opinions, without the views of others to dilute them.

'Can I watch *Labyrinth* again?' I asked Nancy, when she tried to shoo me out of the kitchen for the tenth time. It was my favourite film that year, and Conor had managed to get me a bootlegged copy, but my sisters only wanted to watch

*Top Gun* and drool over Tom Cruise, so I had to watch it on my own.

'Yes, but not tonight, because the only TV is downstairs, as you well know. Go on, skedaddle,' she said, wearing her enormous shoulder pads – a very strange invention, then and now. She started blowing up a blue balloon and left the room.

'Don't waste your life being sad about things you can't change,' Nana said when my mother was gone.

'I'm just sick of being such a loser,' I replied. Lily had started calling me that name on a regular basis, and always made an L-shape on her forehead when she did. She called me a loser so often I had started to believe that I was one. 'Rose will go off to university one day, Conor will probably be a brilliant journalist . . . and I want that to happen for him, he's so talented, he deserves it—'

'Don't spend all of your ambition on other people's dreams,' said Nana.

'Why not? What kind of future do I have to look forward to? I'm a nobody.'

She smiled and shook her head. 'The only nobodies in this world are the people who pretend to be somebody; the people who think they are better than other people because of the way they choose to look, or speak, or vote, or pray, or love. People are not the same but different, they are different but the same.' I was too young to understand what she meant at the time, but I think I do now.

'And Daisy . . .' Nana said, as we heard the sound of people arriving at the front door.

'Yes, Nana?'

'Best to leave the scissors in the drawer this family birthday.'

She *knew*. Nana knew that it was me who cut off Lily's hair, but she had never said anything about it before. I've no idea what my face did – I've never had much control over the expressions it pulls – but the rest of me froze.

Nana smiled. 'I'll always keep your secrets, my darling girl. And you'll always be my favourite. You just have to prove all those doctors wrong for me. As for your sisters . . . Albert Einstein once said that weak people revenge, strong people forgive, and intelligent people ignore. It was one of the few things he was wrong about. *Success* is the best revenge. Try to remember that.'

Before she could say any more on the subject, a small but perfectly formed group of fifteen- and sixteen-year-olds arrived at Seaglass. They had been shepherded across the causeway like lost sheep by Rose before the tide came in. Every one of them was dressed to impress. The only teenager I recognized amongst them was Conor, doing a not bad impression of Tom Cruise in *Top Gun*. He wore aviator sunglasses indoors even when it got dark, so was constantly bumping into things and people, but he thought he looked cool.

I was allowed to stay downstairs until Rose blew out the sixteen candles on her birthday cake. Nancy, with a lot of help from Nana, had created a magic-looking Malteser cake, which looked like the bag of chocolates was hovering in mid-air. The number sixteen was spelled in chocolate balls too. It really was very impressive. When the bowls were all cleared away, Rose started opening her presents, surrounded by friends and people who loved her. My mother gave her a beautiful pale blue designer dress, and I felt the jealousy growing inside me until it hurt. But I wasn't the only one. Lily looked at that dress as though it should have been hers, which might be why Rose immediately put it away in her wardrobe upstairs. When Rose opened Nana's present – the bronze, silver and gold ring that Rose still wears today – I remember how hard it was not to cry. The ring was so beautiful, just like my sister. I wished it was mine.

'Time for bed now, Daisy,' my mother said in front of everyone, and I hated her a little bit. I didn't feel like a child, even though I was one, and I didn't like the way she spoke to me in front of everyone else. I was old enough by then to notice that my mother always wanted to hide me away from the world, as though I were something to be ashamed of. At least that's how it felt.

Ten-year-old me did go upstairs, but I didn't go to bed as instructed.

Instead I sneaked into my sisters' bedroom, while everyone else was having too much fun downstairs to realize. I opened their wardrobe and found the pale blue dress my mother had given Rose for her birthday. The tags were still attached. I didn't care that it didn't belong to me, or that it was several sizes too big. I was sick of wearing hand-me-downs that were years old and faded from being washed too many times. I put the dress on and admired my own reflection.

Disappointed by what I saw, I borrowed one of Lily's bras, stuffed it with socks, and pulled the dress over my head again. I looked better, even if one fake boob was bigger and higher than the other. Next I stole a pair of shoes, kitten heels that were too big and impossible to walk in, but that didn't bother me. I never knew my shoe size as a child because I always just wore the shoes Rose and Lily had grown out of.

I borrowed some of my sisters' make-up. Applying it wasn't something I was good at – having never been shown – but I'd give myself an A for effort. Then I backcombed my hair. I'm still not sure why anyone ever thought this looked good, but in 1986, big hair was *cool*. I sprayed a can of hairspray all over the creature on top of my head until I made myself cough,

and admired the finished result in the mirror. My face was a
shock of pink lipstick and blue eyeshadow, my hair looked as
though I had stuck my fingers in a socket, but the blue dress
was beautiful, and I liked what I saw.

Not sure what to do next, but still in the mood to do things
I knew I shouldn't, I opened Rose's diary, which she kept by
her bed. I understood that what she wrote inside was private,
but I wanted to know everything about the lives that my sisters
got to lead. I found one of Rose's 'Hush' poems scribbled on
a scrap of paper, hidden between the pages, and I sang it out
loud.

*Hush, little baby, don't say a word,*
*Mama's gonna buy you a mockingbird.*
*And if that mockingbird does scream,*
*Mama's gonna trap you inside a dream.*
*And if that dream is a scary place,*
*Mama's gonna put a pillow over your face.*
*Hush, little baby, don't you cry,*
*Sometimes we live, sometimes we die.*

There were magazines spread across Lily's side of the room
– she loved *Just Seventeen* – and there was a pair of scissors
on top of an open page, where she had been cutting out the
faces of her favourite boy bands and sticking them to the wall.
Lily was obsessed with boys by then, and to be fair, they were
fairly obsessed with her in return.

I could hear my sisters and their friends playing a game
downstairs in the hall, so crept out onto the stairs so that I could
listen. The game involved striped drinking straws; the kind Nana
normally used for home-made lemonade. The rules of the game
seemed hard to follow, but the boys picked blue-and-white

straws, the girls picked red-and-white ones, and the boy and girl
with the shortest straws were locked in the cupboard under the
stairs for one minute. The cupboard with no light. And mice.
And spiders. But spiders aren't the only ones to spin webs to
catch their victims.

I peered down at them all through the banister, and it didn't
look like a fun game to me. When Rose and Conor chose the
short straws and were locked inside, Lily looked very upset.
The group of ten or so teenagers were all counting down the
seconds, and giggling, and I couldn't resist slowly creeping
down the stairs to get a closer look. When the clocks in the
hallway all struck midnight, the kids all screamed.

Lily unlocked the cupboard.

But Rose and Conor didn't come out, they were too busy
kissing.

'Look! It's the *real* Daisy Darker!' said a boy I'd seen staring
at me earlier. He looked like he ate too many chocolate bars.

Nobody else noticed me at all, they were too busy staring
at Rose and Conor. I guess I'm one of those people who other
people just don't see. Lily was crying in the corner of the
hallway for some reason; the mascara she had been wearing
had leaked down her cheeks in a series of inky tears. Rose and
Conor were still kissing – as though the rest of us weren't
there – and I decided that it was time for bed after all.

I ran up the stairs and back into my sisters' bedroom, pulling
off the blue designer dress. I could still hear all the clocks
striking midnight down in the hall, and they sounded louder
than normal. That's when I noticed the scissors on top of Lily's
pile of magazines again. I didn't really think about it, didn't
hesitate. I shredded that blue dress so that Rose would never
ever get to wear it. Then I put the thin strands of silky blue
material in her bed, hiding them beneath her pillow. I put the

scissors on Lily's bedside table and left everything else exactly as I found it.

Lily got the blame, and a silent war started between my sisters.

Everyone thought it was an act of revenge.

They were right about that part.

 # Thirty-one

*31 October 3:15 a.m.*
*less than three hours until low tide*

Back in the present, I think I'm the first to hear a noise spoiling what should be silence. It's the sound of ringing in the distance. Like an old-fashioned alarm clock.

'Can anyone else hear that?' I whisper.

'What *is* that?' Lily asks.

'I don't hear anything,' says Conor.

'I can hear it,' Trixie says.

'So can I. Shh. Listen,' says Rose.

We all strain to hear the sound coming from somewhere outside the lounge, possibly outside the house. Nobody has left the room since Rose went to the bathroom.

'I'll go,' she says.

The gun in Rose's hand is a surreal sight to see.

Conor shakes his head and picks up the torch.

'No. We'll all go. We should stay together,' he says.

Without another word we all leave the room, except for Poppins, who is fast asleep again by the fire. Conor and I lead the way, with the rest following close behind, so close that Rose nearly walks right into me. Lily is holding Trixie's hand; I doubt she'll let her out of her sight again after what happened earlier.

We follow the sound of ringing to the kitchen. The back door is open, letting in the rain. The door bangs loudly, and the gust of wind that is battering it blows a swirl of dead leaves inside. One by one we all look up at the chalk poem on the wall and see that, once again, some lines have been struck out.

*Daisy Darker's family were as dark as dark can be.*
*When one of them died, all of them lied, and pretended not to see.*
~~*Daisy Darker's nana was the oldest but least wise.*~~
~~*The woman's will made them all feel ill, which was why she had to die.*~~
~~*Daisy Darker's father lived life dancing to his own tune.*~~
~~*His self-centred ways, and the pianos he played, danced him to his doom.*~~
~~*Daisy Darker's mother was an actress with the coldest heart.*~~
~~*She didn't love all her children, and deserved to lose her part.*~~
*Daisy Darker's sister Rose was the eldest of the three.*
*She was clever and quiet and beautiful, but destined to die lonely.*
*Daisy Darker's sister Lily was the vainest of the lot.*
*She was a selfish, spoilt, entitled witch, one who deserved to get shot.*
~~*Daisy Darker's niece was a precocious little child.*~~
~~*Like all abandoned ducklings, she would not fare well in the wild.*~~
*Daisy Darker's secret story was one someone sadly had to tell.*
*But her broken heart was just the start of what will be her last farewell.*
*Daisy Darker's family wasted far too many years lying.*
*They spent their final hours together learning lessons before dying.*

The wind outside howls like a choir of ghosts.

'Why is my name crossed out?' Trixie asks in a small voice.

'Nancy has been crossed out too,' Lily whispers.

Rose tries to reassure them both. 'It might not mean anything . . .'

'Of *course* it means something!' Lily snaps. 'And I think we all know what that might be. We should have looked for Nancy.

We should have done something. Oh my god,' Lily says, staring at Rose and taking a step away from our sister. 'It was *you*. You're the only one who left that room, and now more of the poem has been crossed out. You were always making up weird rhymes when we were children. It was *you*, all of it. *You* injected Trixie and then pretended to fix her! *How* could you? *Why* would you?'

'Injected me with what?' whispers Trixie.

'It wasn't me!' says Rose.

'Where is Nancy?' Lily shouts.

'I don't know!'

'I don't believe you! *You* were the one who said we shouldn't look for her and now I know why!' Lily steps in front of her daughter, who looks terrified. Rose takes a step towards them and we all stare at the gun in her hand. 'Stay. Away. From. My. Child,' says Lily.

'I didn't do anything!' Rose replies, hiding the gun behind her back.

'Wait!' says Conor.

'You stay out of this. You're probably helping her. I don't trust any of you,' Lily says.

'This isn't the time to start turning on one another,' Conor replies gently.

'Why not?' Lily snaps.

He holds his hands up in surrender. 'Because look at the footprints.'

We all stare down at the floor then and see what he is talking about. There are muddy footprints leading to and from the back door. It reminds me of all the times Conor's dad forgot to take off his gardening boots when he came to visit. The dirt Bradley Kennedy dragged inside drove my mother mad. I look at Rose's feet and the small, pristine white trainers she is wearing. Only a pair of large muddy boots could have made this mess. The sound of an alarm keeps ringing in the distance, and the open kitchen door that leads to the garden bangs on its hinges again, battered by the wind. We all watch in silence as Conor starts walking towards it.

'Please don't go out there,' I say.

He hesitates, but then steps outside into the rain, turning on the torch. He picked it up when we were all still in the lounge, even though the power is back on now. Almost as though he knew he might have to go out in the dark.

My sisters and I watch from the doorway as Conor walks out onto the patio, slowly shining the torch around the garden. The beam is too faint to light up the sea crashing on the rocks beyond the wall, only illuminating a metre or so ahead. The rain is light but persistent now, as though the sky is spitting in Conor's face, but he moves through the gloom until the torchlight stops on the bench in the distance. It's where my mother always liked to sit and admire her flowers, beneath the magnolia tree she planted here with Conor's dad. The tree that Nana thought was a symbol of hope always looks a little bit dead in winter.

The old magnolia is the only tree on our tiny tidal island, and has grown quite big over the last twenty years. Fat raindrops cling to its bare branches, giving an illusion of miniature lights, and it's so cold I wonder if they might freeze before they fall. I can't quite process what I am seeing when I spot my mother sitting on her garden bench. Wearing her black silk eye mask on her face, the one she always wears to help her sleep. Outside. In the dark. In the rain.

'Nancy?' Conor calls, his voice a little strangled by the sound of the sea. He walks towards her and the rest of us start to follow.

'What's wrong with her? Why is she sitting in the rain wearing an eye mask?' Trixie asks.

'Go back inside,' Lily says. 'Stand in the doorway where I can see you and don't move.'

Trixie does as she is told and the rest of us walk towards my mother. The rain is relentless now, much heavier than it was only a few moments ago, and so hard that the water seems to be falling up as well as down. Nancy's normally perfect hair is dripping wet and clinging to her face. Her clothes are soaking too, she's clearly been out here for a long time. The rain must have smudged the thick black eyeliner and mascara she always wears; it looks as if she has been crying black tears behind her mask. Even stranger is the sight of her red alarm clock. It is balancing between the branches of the magnolia tree just above her head, and still ringing.

Conor reaches up to turn it off. The clock says three a.m. but it's already twenty minutes past. I can't help wondering if that was why Nancy was never on time for anything; maybe the clocks she used were wrong. Or maybe someone just wanted to make a point. It seems my mother was late for her own murder, because I think we all know that's what this was and that she is dead.

Nancy's hands are by her sides and her sleeves have been rolled up. Her left hand is holding onto her beloved copy of *The Observer's Book of Wild Flowers*, the little green book that she always carried around like a Bible, and used to choose our names. Her right hand is holding what looks like a small bunch of lilies, roses and daisies tied to her fingers with a red ribbon. A string of ivy is wrapped tightly around her neck, not quite covering the silver heart-shaped locket she always wears. It is unclasped to reveal the pictures inside. All this time, I had presumed that it contained two tiny photos of my sisters. But now that it is open, I can only see a tiny black-and-white picture of myself as a child on one side, and a pressed daisy on the other.

Rose slides her gun into her jacket pocket. I find myself replaying Lily's words in the kitchen – when she accused Rose of having something to do with all of this – and for a moment I do wonder, as my eldest sister, once again, takes charge of a situation most people would be overwhelmed by. She leans over Nancy on the bench as though she were a stranger, not our mother, and I can't help noticing that the gun is within my reach. I could take it. Not that I'd know what to do with it. I've never even held a gun before.

'She's dead,' Rose confirms, having checked for a pulse.

Lily starts to wail, staring up at the night sky. It is a level of grief and despair that none of us have seen her display before, and nobody knows what to say as a mix of tears and rainwater stream down her face. The sound of ticking is still so loud, it makes me think of a cartoon bomb. Conor is holding the red alarm clock that was in the tree, and as he shines the torch on its face, we can all see that something has been written on it: *THERE IS ALWAYS TIME FOR TRUTH*.

'What does that mean?' I ask.

'I don't understand what is happening here tonight. Who is doing this and *why*?' says Lily.

'I don't know,' Rose replies. 'But I think this confirms it.'

'Confirms what?'

'Someone *else* did this. It couldn't have been any of us. There is someone else here at Seaglass, and they're killing us one by one.'

# Nancy

*Daisy Darker's mother was an actress with the coldest heart.*
*She didn't love all her children, and deserved to lose her part.*

*An unexpected pregnancy resulted in marriage and three girls,*
*But instead of loving her family, Nancy longed to see the world.*

*She had wanted to be an actress, but life cast her as a mum instead.*
*Her leading role took its toll, and made her want to stay in bed.*

*Her favourite daughter was pretty, and the eldest one was smart,*
*But the youngest child was always a burden, having been born with a*
*broken heart.*

*Nancy blamed herself for this tragedy, though no one understood why.*
*Her guilt made her lonely, bitter and sad, but she was still unable to cry.*

*When the time came, no one knew who to blame when she was*
*poisoned by her own flowers.*
*By the time she was found, in the rain-soaked grounds, Mrs Darker had*
*been dead for hours.*

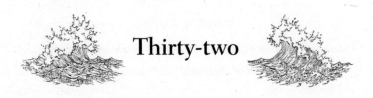

# Thirty-two

## SEAGLASS – 1987

We are getting soaked by the relentless rain as we stand and stare down at my dead mother, and the weather reminds me of the last terrible storm at Seaglass, almost twenty years ago. Nana was planning a big launch for her tenth book at her favourite bookshop. We were all invited, but my father was very busy – as usual – and said he might not be able to be there. So when the telephone rang, we all presumed it was him, calling to apologize from whatever corner of the world he was in with his orchestra. But it was a call from the hospital instead, and not about me for a change. My parents were long divorced, but Nancy was still registered as my dad's next of kin, and he'd been in an accident.

Most people in the UK can remember the great storm of 1987. We've all laughed about the BBC weatherman, Michael Fish, who got the forecast so spectacularly wrong and never lived it down. There's a fantastic clip of what he said that day: 'Apparently a lady rang the BBC and said she heard that there was a hurricane on the way. Well, don't worry, if you're watching, there isn't.' But he was wrong. There was. That October, a hurricane devastated huge parts of the country, and Seaglass nearly disappeared beneath the waves for good. Dad had been on the way to join us to celebrate Nana's latest children's book when his car was hit by a falling tree. His visit was meant to be a surprise, but the storm had a bigger one in store.

'I'll be there as soon as I can,' Nancy said when the hospital called. Love always trumps hate when you fear you might lose someone for good. She and Nana left immediately, the book launch was cancelled, and Mr Kennedy came to look after me and my sisters for the night, along with Conor.

One night turned into several. Mr Kennedy soon ran out of things to do with a house full of children – even though one of them was his own – so when the weather allowed, he encouraged us to spend as much time as possible outside. He taught us about the flowers and plants he and my mother had introduced to Seaglass – the magnolia tree wasn't much taller than him back then – but our interest and concentration soon started to fade.

'Gardening is *boring*,' declared Lily, who never liked Conor's dad. She called him 'the narrow man' because he was tall and had grown thin. In some ways I agreed with her assessment. He did look as though life had squeezed him into wearing only narrow thoughts, jumpers and jeans, almost all of which had pockets and holes in. His words were coated in cynicism, even the kind ones, so I could sort of understand why Lily wanted to stay inside and play on her computer.

'Gardening isn't boring,' said Mr Kennedy with a strange smile. 'One day you might regret spending your life staring at a screen instead of seeing the real world.' Then he told us a story that was unlike anything I'd heard before. 'Did you know that spies use plants?'

'Like James Bond?' Conor asked.

His father nodded. 'Yes, but in real life. You were all probably too young to remember, but in 1978, a BBC journalist was killed by a poisoned umbrella.'

There was a brief silence while we processed his unfamiliar words.

'An umbrella isn't a plant,' said Lily.

'Did he open the umbrella indoors?' I asked. 'Nana says it's very bad luck to do that.'

'No, Daisy,' Mr Kennedy replied. 'Someone walked up to him on Waterloo Bridge, pointed the umbrella at his leg, and then the journalist felt a sharp pain.'

'Why did someone want to hurt him?' asked Rose.

'Because he defected to the West.'

'What does defected mean?' Lily asked.

'Cornwall is in the west . . .' I started to say.

Mr Kennedy shook his head. 'It means that he . . . decided to change sides.'

'Like when people get divorced?' I asked.

'Yes. I suppose defecting is a bit like divorce, but even more deadly. The journalist became very ill, very quickly. He was taken to hospital but he died. The point of this story is *what* was on the tip of that umbrella?'

We all stared at him, feeling a little clueless, but then Rose's hand shot up as though she were in class. 'Poison.'

'Yes, but where did the poison come from?' None of us knew the answer to that one. 'The poison on the tip of that umbrella was called ricin, and it came from the seeds of a castor bean plant. The castor bean plant isn't a rare species, or terribly difficult to grow or find. In fact, it can sometimes be found in gardens. Just like this one.'

Mr Kennedy pointed at the red and green plant in my mother's garden, and there was a collective – and rather dramatic – intake of breath.

'So I hope we can all agree that gardening is *not* boring,' he said, looking at Lily. 'Plants can be the perfect partners in crime. Do you know why?' We all shook our heads again. 'Because they'll never *grass*. Get it?' His dad jokes were even worse than our father's. 'Don't forget to wipe your feet and take your shoes off before going inside the house. You know how much your mother hates muddy footprints.'

Later, when we were all back indoors, Mr Kennedy made himself busy in the kitchen, trying to cook us some sort of dinner. We ate a lot of fish fingers, chips and beans when he was left in charge. As he rummaged about in Nana's freezer, I heard Rose and Conor whispering about him.

'My dad is really upset about your dad,' Conor said.

'We're all upset. The doctor Nancy spoke to today said it was serious. Apparently, Dad's car is a write-off and he's lucky to be alive.'

'My dad isn't upset about your dad being in hospital. He's upset that Nancy rushed to be by his bedside. They're *divorced*. They basically defected from each other years ago. She's supposed to be with *my* dad now.'

'I don't think it works like that,' Rose said. 'When you love someone, you can't just turn it off, there isn't a switch. Even if you hate someone that you once loved, there is still a little bit of love there. Love is like the soil that hate needs in order to grow. I think it's rare in relationships to have one without the other.'

Sixteen-year-old Rose was ridiculously mature, but I think she might have been born that way. She and Conor were in a relationship of their own. It was almost as though she wanted him to know that she would always love him, even if she hated him one day. Just like our parents. Lily and I watched as Rose held Conor's hand. I could tell it made Lily feel uncomfortable too.

When Nancy returned two days later, our dad was with her. He needed to rest, and Seaglass was where he wanted to do it. His head was bandaged and he had a broken arm. He could have gone to his London home – a flat in Notting Hill – just like my mother could have gone to hers, but she chose to look after him and he chose to let her. My sisters and I were delighted to have him with us for so long. Rose and Lily even put their feud to one side.

They decided to cook together one night – a meal for the whole family – and chose to use one of Nana's recipes for spaghetti bolognaise. I wasn't allowed to help them *at all*, for reasons I didn't understand, but I watched from the doorway. When Lily shouted at me for the tenth time to go away, I sulked in the garden. Rose did almost all of the cooking: chopping onions, carrots, garlic and chilli, adding all the herbs to the meat, tomatoes and stock. She grated cheese and – because this was one of Nana's recipes – had a bowl of hundreds and thousands ready to sprinkle on top. All Lily did was open a packet of dried spaghetti and pour some boiling water over it in a saucepan.

We sat down in our individually painted chairs when dinner was served, but I didn't take a bite. Instead I just waited. My mother put a fork full of spaghetti into her mouth and spat it out seconds later. My father swallowed his, but then drank an entire glass of water. Nobody took more than one bite. I'd helped with the meal after all, adding a full jar of hot chilli powder and a bottle of hot chilli sauce to the spaghetti. Lily blamed Rose, and Rose blamed Lily. I think only Nana guessed that it was me.

Apart from the occasional sibling-shaped squabble, we were happier than we had ever been before. But not everyone was pleased to see the Darker family reunited. It was the beginning of the end for Nancy and Mr Kennedy. He was furious about the new living arrangements and didn't hide it well. He stayed away from Seaglass the entire time that my dad was there. Days turned into weeks, and weeks stretched into months. Nancy's garden was neglected, the flowers faded, wilted and died. But she barely noticed.

During that time while my dad recovered, we were like a real family again. We spent time together playing board games (Cluedo was a firm favourite), went for walks along the coast, and watched old movies. Dad – unable to play his beloved piano – completed lots of jigsaw puzzles with just the one hand. And Nana cooked *a lot* of her 'special chicken soup'. It was what she made whenever one of us was ill. The secret ingredient was mashed banana, and the soup was always served with home-made crusty bread slathered in Nutella.

We were a real happy family for a while, and I thought we might stay that way forever. Christmas in 1987 was very much a Darker family affair, and everyone was a little more grateful for what we all had. Not that the sentiment lasted . . . gratitude tends to go off quicker than milk in our house.

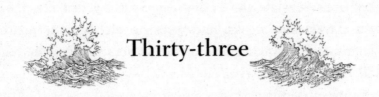

# Thirty-three

'We need to get Nancy inside,' says Conor. 'We can't leave her out here in the rain.'

I realize I have drifted back in time again. Life feels a bit like a movie at the moment. Maybe when the present is too painful, it's only natural to disappear inside flashbacks of happier times. It reminds me of something Nana used to say: if you spend your present focusing on your past, you will never change your future.

'Why is someone doing this to us?' Lily asks again, and Rose is the only one to answer.

'We need to keep it together for just a couple more hours until low tide. You and Trixie are going to be okay. Do you hear me?' Lily looks more vacant than usual. 'Lily, do you hear me?' She still doesn't answer. 'Do me a favour and go inside. I want you to find your diabetic kit and check your blood sugar. We all need to be well enough to leave when the tide goes out.'

'Okay,' says Lily. She looks like a person who has had their plug pulled out, and is surviving on a dwindling battery. 'Can you wait a couple of minutes before you bring Nancy indoors? I don't want Trixie to see her like this – she's already seen far more than she should have tonight – I'll get her back into the lounge and keep her there while you do whatever you have to do.'

Rose nods and Lily walks towards the doorway, where Trixie is waiting. Then Rose stares down at the small bouquet tied to Nancy's hand. 'I sometimes think our mother named us all after flowers because that's what she wished we were. Flowers are much easier to pick, and arrange, and cut down to size than daughters.'

I can tell I'm not the only one who thinks that was a strange thing to say given the circumstances. Conor looks equally puzzled.

'We need to move her inside,' he says again.

'Are you sure we should?' Rose asks, and Conor looks a little shocked. 'Shouldn't we be trying to preserve evidence for the police? Isn't that what a *crime correspondent* would say next? You're probably getting some kind of sick thrill out of all this. I bet you can't wait to call the news desk. Maybe this will help your career?'

'I know you're upset, but none of this is my fault,' he says.

'Isn't it?' Rose asks. She looks at him for a long time, then shrugs. 'Fine, let's move her. She's dead. We can't really make matters any worse. Where do you suggest we move her to?'

They stare at each other, and I feel as though I'm intruding on something I don't fully understand.

'We could put her with the others?' Conor suggests.

Rose doesn't reply straight away. Apprehension is the mother of our mistakes, and tries to warn us before we make them, but we don't always listen to our mothers.

'I suppose that makes sense,' Rose says eventually, sounding as though she doesn't really believe it. She's quietly crying now. 'We can keep them all together . . . but out of sight until the police come. I'll take this end, you take the other,' she says to Conor, and we all bow our heads against the rain as we make our way towards the house. Carrying my mother seems to slow Conor and Rose down more than it should, and they fall behind. I can hear the two of them whispering again, but the sound of the wind and waves in the distance steals their words from my ears.

Something is different when I step into the kitchen, and it takes me a moment to realize what. The muddy footprints have been mopped up. It's a strange thing for Lily to have done; she's the untidiest person I've ever met, and I'm not convinced she'd know what end of a mop to use if I gave her one. Maybe she is just trying to protect Trixie from everything that has happened tonight, in whatever way that she can. I can hear them quietly talking in the lounge.

Rose appears in the kitchen doorway behind me. She is holding my mother's feet and Conor is carrying Nancy beneath her arms. They are soaked to the skin, and I feel as though I am not doing enough to help. I step aside as they struggle past me, heading for the cupboard beneath the stairs. We all try not to look at Dad and Nana's bodies as they carefully lower Nancy beside them. When Conor's hand accidentally grazes Rose's fingers, she pulls away as though he has burned her.

'Rose, I . . . I just want to say that I'm so very sorry.'

'For what?'

'All of it,' Conor says, and she frowns at him. 'I just mean that I know what it's like to lose a parent, and it's okay to be . . . upset.'

'This is not the same as what happened in your family,' she replies, and Conor looks like he's been slapped in the face.

We never knew for sure whether Conor's dad started drinking again because he thought my parents were getting back together. The tree that fell on my dad's car during the great storm of 1987 did more damage than anyone first thought. Dad ended up staying at Seaglass for a couple of months while he recovered, which meant Mr Kennedy stayed away. Nancy spoke to him on the phone, but the next time we all saw him, he was very different from the man we thought we knew. He arrived uninvited and unexpected at Seaglass one day, demanding to see Conor. We all heard what he said.

'*This* is not your family. *I* am your family, and I don't want you coming here anymore.'

I was too young to understand that he was drunk. We found out afterwards that he had lost his gardening job with the National Trust. It wasn't long before Conor started regularly running away from home again, and turning up at Seaglass at odd times. But he was almost eighteen by then, and better able to defend himself. Nancy ended her relationship with Mr Kennedy, and I think that everything that happened afterwards broke what was left of her heart. A few months later, Conor left home for good, and none of us ever saw his father again.

'Are those your boots?' Rose asks, looking at the front door.

Conor and I both follow her stare and see the pair of large muddy men's boots in the hallway. I'm sure they weren't there before.

He shakes his head. 'No.'

# Thirty-four

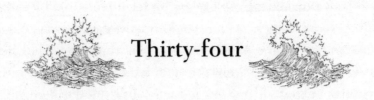

*31 October 3:45 a.m.*
*less than three hours until low tide*

'Someone clearly left them here deliberately,' says Conor. 'These boots are not mine.'

'Someone mopped the kitchen floor too,' says Rose.

Conor frowns. 'What?'

'There were muddy footprints in the kitchen, before we all went outside and found Nancy in the garden. Now the floor is clean,' Rose replies.

'I thought Lily might have done it,' I say.

'It would have been easy enough for Lily to come back inside, send Trixie into the lounge to watch TV, then clean up the mess while we were still out there,' Rose agrees.

'But . . . why would she?' Conor says. 'Have you ever known Lily to clean or tidy anything before?' Rose shakes her head. Conor takes a step closer and lowers his voice. 'Maybe you're right. Maybe there *is* someone else here. But what if there isn't?'

'You can't possibly think that Lily is behind all of this?' Rose whispers.

'I don't know what to think anymore,' Conor replies. 'It's only fifteen minutes until the top of the hour. I say we keep a close eye on Lily until then. I think she's been acting strangely all night.'

'I think you're wrong, but okay. I need to get dry first though,' Rose says.

Conor stares at her wet clothes, then at his own. 'You sure you'll be okay alone?' She gives him a look involving one raised eyebrow. 'Fine. Shall we meet here in five minutes?'

We all go our separate ways, and something feels wrong as Rose disappears inside Nana's little library where she slept last night. I wouldn't want to be alone right now. But I suppose she does have a gun, and Rose has always been very good at taking care of herself.

Conor and I head towards the stairs, and the wooden punch clock by the front door catches my eye on the way. The cards in the cubbyholes next to it remind me of old-fashioned paper library cards. They are not just for visiting family and friends, there are some other names written on them too. Nana made everyone punch in and out . . . it was one of her many quirks. It was also something that used to annoy Conor's father, along with all the other things that he got so upset about. I spot a card with another familiar name. It's sticking out and at an angle. According to the time and date stamped on it, Nana's agent was here at Seaglass yesterday. Just a few hours before I arrived. There is no stamp for when he left, but maybe he just forgot to punch out.

Upstairs, Conor grabs some dry clothes from his bag, then disappears down the hall, presumably to change in the bathroom. Seeing him in my bedroom is still a surreal experience, and I'm relieved to have a couple of minutes to myself. I try and fail to gather my thoughts, but I'm scared of what might happen next. I don't say a word when Conor returns and starts packing his things as though getting ready to leave. He forgets his laptop though, and I see that it is still open on the desk in the corner of the room. The word *Boo* that I typed last night seems in poor taste now, even if today is Halloween.

I could tell that Conor was genuinely worried about Rose when we were downstairs, even after all these years, and don't quite know what to make of it. He doesn't ask if *I'm* all right, but I try not to hold it against him. Sometimes other people can see when a couple are in love long before they can see it for themselves, and that's how things were between Rose and Conor for years when we were children. But they were insep- arable after that first kiss in the cupboard under the stairs. A long-distance relationship followed, and it continued even when Conor was stuck here in Cornwall and Rose was away at school. They were always writing and calling each other, and I confess I felt jealous. I wonder if we are all just echoes of the people we might have been if life had unfolded differently. The by-products of a crease in time.

Sometimes I think Rose and Conor fell in love the first time they saw each other on the beach, when they were both nine and Nana invited him to come to Seaglass for lemonade. Something happened that day. It wasn't something you could see or explain, but it was there. You could feel it. I often wonder whether we are born with love in our hearts, and whether life just slowly erases it, eating it away little by little, until all the empathy and warmth is completely rubbed out. We learn to love regardless of whether there is anyone in our lives to teach us how. Love is as instinctive as breathing, but we don't have to give it away. Like our breath, we can hold onto it if we choose to. But not forever. Because then it starts to hurt.

I wasn't the only one who was jealous of their relationship. When Conor turned eighteen, Rose gave him her virginity as a birthday gift wrapped in black lace underwear. Lily – who already felt a bit abandoned – was *furious*. Conor was the only boy in Blacksand Bay who Lily really wanted to fool around with, and the only boy she hadn't. And she wasn't the only one secretly in love with her sister's boyfriend. The eldest sibling inevitably wins most of life's unspoken races. Rose was the first to fall in love, but also the first to experience the sorrow and grief of breaking up.

When Conor says something in the present, it's so unexpected, I jump.

'Daisy, I can't imagine how awful it would feel to see what is happening to your family tonight.'

*He's speaking to me.*

After all these years of him acting like I don't exist, I am overcome with emotion. I just wish it hadn't taken something so awful for him to forgive me.

'Thank you,' I say.

Conor sits down on my bed right next to me, and I'm a little girl again, in love with a boy who never really noticed her.

'I blamed you for what happened all those years ago for such a long time,' he says. 'But it wasn't your fault. I know that now. Deep down, I always knew, and I'm sorry for everything that has happened since.'

Tears are streaming down my face. I've waited so long for him to say these words.

'It's okay,' I say, and consider reaching for his hand. But the sound of a door slamming downstairs interrupts the moment and it is lost. Conor's face is now filled with fear, and I imagine my own must look the same.

We hurry back down the staircase and see that the muddy boots are gone. Conor knocks on the closed library door, where Rose said she was getting changed, but nobody answers. I feel a strange sensation, like when your heart skips a beat, but it's more than that. He's about to knock a second time when Rose opens the door. She has changed into a white T-shirt – and clearly isn't wearing a bra – along with another pair of skin-tight jeans. The jacket is gone, and she has untied her long dark hair so that it falls down past her shoulders in damp, wavy curls. Something unspoken passes between the two of them, and I feel like a spare part again.

'We left the back door open and I think the wind slammed it shut,' Rose says, answering the question before we ask it. Then the clocks in the hallway start to chime, and they sound even louder than before.

'What is that?' Rose asks, looking over my shoulder.

Conor and I turn and see what she is staring at. The door on the front of the grandfather clock – the largest of the eighty different varieties of clock in the hall – is open. And there is what looks like another VHS tape covering its face. My mind whirs like all the clocks I'm surrounded by, and just as loudly. Lily and Trixie could have put the tape there while the three of us went to get changed. Or Rose could have put it there while Conor and I were upstairs. Or Conor could have put it there when he left the bedroom. Or someone else could have done it while we were all distracted, then let themselves out the back door. For a moment I can't decide what is worse: the idea that a stranger is here doing this to us, or that it might be one of the family.

Unpleasant thoughts tend to outstay their welcome, just like unpleasant people. I stare at Conor and Rose and can see that they are thinking the same thing: wondering if they can trust each other or anyone here at Seaglass. They both reach for the tape at the same time, their hands grazing just like they did before. I'm not imagining the chemistry between them, and it's making me feel a bit peculiar. I know I have no right to feel anything at all, and there are far more important things to worry about. But the last of my nerves are being gotten on, and I feel sick with fear.

When Rose picks up the latest VHS tape, I feel even worse. The cover has a new message spelled out in Scrabble letters stuck to the front of it:

**SEE ME.**

'There's no time to explain or argue,' says Rose, speaking at Lily as she marches into the lounge. 'We've found another tape . . . or rather another tape was left for us to find. I think we need to see what's on it as soon as possible, before anything else happens to anyone here.'

Lily doesn't disagree. I think all the fight has gone out of her because she doesn't say a word. She and Trixie are huddled together on the sofa nearest the television, and I can tell that my niece has been crying again. An image of one of Nana's birthdays here at Seaglass fills the screen, and I instantly remember that night sixteen years ago. It's a night I've always wished I could forget.

# Thirty-five

## SEAGLASS – 1988

It was Halloween 1988. My mother had slowly withdrawn from the world after her break-up with Mr Kennedy – who seemed intent on drinking himself to death again – and there was a strange, melancholy mood at Seaglass that October. The sorrow and sadness seemed to seep out of the cracks in the walls. I remember walking into the room that evening and finding my family all there, sitting around the kitchen table, seated in their individually painted chairs.

Nancy was sitting in her tall, thin white chair, looking beautiful but uncomfortable as always. My dad, then fully recovered from his car accident, sat at the other end of the table, as far away from Nancy as possible. Just because she didn't want to be with Mr Kennedy, it didn't change the status of *their* relationship; Nancy didn't want to *be* with Dad either. Not in that way. Not then. His chair seemed a little wider, and rounder, and darker than before, as though it had aged with him. Eighteen-year-old Rose sat in her red chair, next to Conor, who visited so often by then that Nana had painted him a chair of his own. It was sky blue with little white clouds, because she said he was a dreamer. Seventeen-year-old Lily looked sulky and jealous in her green chair.

She'd had an audition for a drama school in London the day before and didn't get in. Lily couldn't handle the knock-back, so gave up on her dreams of performing on stage after just one rejection. I guess they didn't like her rendition of 'Eternal Flame'. Even at thirteen, I understood that if you really wanted something, you had to fight for it. Always. But my mother, who had also dreamt of being an actress, did nothing to encourage Lily to try again. Almost as though she couldn't stand the possibility of her daughter succeeding when she had failed. That thought might be unkind, but I think it might also be true. She spoilt Lily even more than before after that – unlike Rose and I – which only made matters worse. The problem with growing up with parents who say 'yes' to everything is that it doesn't prepare you for the real world, which often says 'no'. I've never known my sister to work hard for anything or anyone, not even herself. The reality of hard work being a prerequisite for success meant she was doomed to fail.

There was one other guest at the kitchen table that day, but he didn't have a chair of his own. I've always presumed that Nana's agent was roughly the same age as my father. When I was a child, anyone over thirty looked the same age to me: old. But staring at the screen now, and seeing Nana's agent again for the first time in years, I notice he was surprisingly young. Early thirties at most. I remember that she was his first real client, and the success of *Daisy Darker's Little Secret* launched his career as well as hers. She took a chance on him, he took a chance on her, and it paid off in a big way . . . until she stopped writing a few years ago. Nana's agent was sitting next to her that night, on a dark blue chair covered in shooting stars reserved for special guests. My chair – decorated with hand-painted daisies – was next to his.

I hadn't met him before. It sounded strange to my ears when she talked about having an agent – to me, she was always just my nana – but I was curious about this man who she was clearly rather fond of. Her birthday party was normally a family-only event. Nana said that she could count the people she trusted on one hand, and that she didn't need all of her fingers to do it. Her agent was the person she trusted most. He wore a smart suit and a kind smile. I had always imagined him carrying books inside all of his pockets, but I couldn't see any.

'It's such a pleasure to finally meet the real Daisy Darker,' he said as I sat down at the table. He held out his hand for me to shake as though I were a grown-up, and that – along with his posh voice – made me smile. He pronounced all of his words properly, which made me want to do the same. I found myself imitating the way he spoke without meaning to. Nana's agent was like a character in a book or a film, and I wasn't entirely convinced he was real until I touched him. 'That's a good, firm handshake,' he said.

'Thank you,' I replied, rather pleased with myself. As a slightly awkward thirteen-year-old, I took compliments wherever I could get them. 'What do you mean, the *real* Daisy Darker?'

'Well, I work with your nana. Her book *Daisy Darker's Little Secret* was the first book we worked on together a few years ago, and it sold all over the world. Which means there are copies of a book with your name on it in bookshops in America, and Spain, Australia, Poland . . . even as far away as China. It's quite a thrill to finally meet your nana's muse.' I didn't know what a muse was, but didn't want the nice man to think that I was stupid, so I nodded. I might be misremembering things – it was a long time ago now. There was a twinkle in his eyes as he spoke, and I wondered if the nice man was secretly made of stars. His chair was covered in them after all, and Nana was right about most things.

Every family is a fortress that few outsiders get to see inside. Especially ours. Sometimes people are invited in for a period of time, but they only ever get the public tour, they never really see behind the scene. 'Access All Areas' is a myth when it comes to human relationships; we can never really know another person because we rarely know ourselves. Knowing that Nana's agent was one of the very few people on the planet who she trusted, I always wondered and wanted to know why. But whenever I asked her, she could never explain. Maybe she didn't really understand it herself.

'You do know that my nana's stories aren't real, don't you?' I asked him. 'What she writes is called *fiction*.'

The agent smiled. 'Yes, I am aware of the term.'

'Then you should really understand that I am *not* the Daisy Darker in the books. Nana just borrowed my name, that's all. A book about the *real* me would be far more interesting.'

He laughed at that, and it made me cross because I thought it meant he didn't think that I was. Interesting. But then Nana's agent gave me something wonderful, which made me like him again. He reached into the top pocket of his jacket and took out a silver pen. Then he took out a business card and wrote on the back of it:

*Looking forward to reading
about the real Daisy Darker.*

What was most remarkable was that, with a simple click, the pen could write in different colours: red, green, blue and black. I'd never seen anything like it. He gave me the business card, and when he saw me staring at the pen, he gave me that too.

'Here you go. Write your own story with this if you like, and I'll read it if you do.'

Then Nana tapped her champagne glass to get everyone's attention, and our conversation was over almost as soon as it had begun. I put the pen and the card in the top pocket of my dress. I see on the video that it was a dress of my own – rather than a hand-me-down – a denim dungaree dress, not unlike the ones I still like to wear today. I also had my first shoes that had only been worn by my feet: a pair of white trainers that Nana had painted with daisies.

'Now then, I know it's Halloween, and *some people* have a party to go to,' Nana said, looking at Rose and Lily. 'But I'm glad we could be together for a little while. It means a lot to have my family in one place all at the same time for my birthday. Cheers to all of you, and special congratulations to Rose for getting into Cambridge University. We're so proud of you.'

I was only thirteen, but even I was allowed a glass of champagne. I liked it, and tried to sip it as slowly as possible to make it last.

'Shall we do presents before dinner?' Nana asked, and everyone looked uncomfortable. It had always been her rule that nobody was allowed to buy proper presents on her birthday, only sweets, with it being Halloween. I'd already given her a Cadbury's Dairy Milk miniatures dispenser, which she had seemed thrilled with, and Rose gave her chocolate frogs. Dad brought an expensive box of chocolates all the way from Switzerland, where he'd spent the summer with his orchestra. Lily forgot as usual, so Nancy pretended her gift of Milk Tray was from both of them. 'Don't panic, I'm only teasing. You all being present is present enough,' Nana said.

Her agent cleared his throat. 'I didn't know about the "no big gifts" rule, so I'm afraid I did get you something, I hope you'll forgive me.' He reached beneath the table, and put a large, beautifully wrapped gift box on it.

'Oh my goodness!' said Nana, beaming like a child. 'What is it?'

'Open it and see.'

Nana lifted the lid, revealing the hand-carved wooden Scrabble set that Trixie and I were playing with earlier this evening. Her agent even had some of the small square letters made with real sea glass on the bottom and driftwood on top, with a letter and value carved into each one – I thought they were beautiful. 'It's hard to know what to get someone who loves words but already has all the books they want in their own little library. You always say it's important to use your words, and I know you like the game,' he said, sounding more like Nana than himself. His eyes seemed to twinkle again, and I noticed how very blue they were, just like hers. They wore similar smiles on their faces too. They looked like a mother and her son celebrating a special moment together.

'It's the most wonderful gift I have ever received,' she replied, and I think we all felt a bit sheepish about what we had given Nana. Her agent had made more of an effort than her own family. I had forgotten until now that he gave her the beautiful wooden Scrabble board. Before I can think too long about the significance of that, the home movie continues.

'Thank you, I'll treasure this always,' Nana said. 'I actually bought myself a gift this year too, and I wanted to share it with all of you before we start eating,' she added with a mischievous grin, then shuffled out of the room. I noticed that her slippers matched her new dress, which was pink and purple and covered in tiny hearts. We all watched from the kitchen table as she wandered out into the hall before disappearing inside her library. She continued to talk to us the entire time, shouting a little in order to be heard.

'Now, as all of you know – because I've complained about it often enough – things can get a little lonely here at times, when none of you come to visit and I am left alone with just my characters for company. I've checked the dates on all of your cards by the punch clock, and I'm not imagining being on my own more than before. So my gift to myself this year is a rather special one. I'd like you all to meet Poppins.'

The puppy on the TV screen is ridiculously cute, and so small, it's hard to believe that she grew into the giant Old English Sheepdog currently sleeping in front of the fire, with hair so long now that it is plaited with ribbons to keep it out of her eyes. It's also hard to believe that she first arrived at Seaglass all those years ago. The old dog managed to outlive Nana, which is something nobody would have predicted, not even a palm reader in Land's End.

Miniature Poppins was passed around, and we all made a big fuss of her. I watched Nana's agent as he smiled at the puppy, and decided that if Nana trusted the man with stars in his eyes, I would too.

'If I write a story about the *real* Daisy Darker, will you *really* read it?' I whispered.

He smiled again. 'Yes. I promise that I will.'

'Daisy, stop bothering the man with your silly stories,' said my mother, passing Poppins to Rose – Nancy never had any real interest in dogs *or* books.

'Oh, I don't mind at all,' Nana's agent said with that kind smile of his. 'Finding the stories hidden inside people's heads is my most favourite thing to do.'

We look like a happy family on the screen, and it's a nice memory to be reminded of. As usual the Halloween/birthday menu Nana had prepared for us all catered to her sweet tooth. That year we had chocolate chilli con carne for the first time, along with chicken and hot chocolate gravy, jelly babies and sweetcorn, chocolate-filled ravioli, fish fingers with sherbet lemon, white chocolate lasagne and cola bottle trifle. It all tasted a lot better than it sounds.

I watch, transfixed, as seventeen-year-old Lily picks up the camera from its tripod and films some close-ups of Poppins the puppy. Then there is a shot of Nana hugging me and whispering in my ear. I can still remember what she said.

'I love you from here to the moon and back three times and once for luck.'

It was something she only ever said to me, and the memory of that moment haunts me.

The picture on the screen turns black. I've never seen anything that happened that evening captured on camera before. I didn't know this tape existed until now, so I wonder if that's all there is. But then an image of a beach at night appears, and a bonfire, and I don't want to see any more. I don't want to remember what happened next, or what I did. That night is why they all stopped speaking to me. It was the worst night of my life.

# Thirty-six

*31 October 3:55 a.m.*
*less than three hours until low tide*

'Maybe we shouldn't watch any more of this tape,' says Rose in a voice that doesn't sound like her own. She remembers what happened that night too. So does Conor.

'I agree. Several members of this family have died tonight, this isn't the time for home movies,' he says. But that isn't why Conor doesn't want to watch anymore.

I ignore them both and cross the room to take a closer look at the Scrabble board Nana's agent gave to her that year. When I see what is on it the room seems to spin.

'Did you do this?' I ask Trixie, and she comes to stand by my side. We tend to be the only ones to play the game these days. Rose joins us to see what we are looking at, and frowns at the board.

'Was this you?' she asks our niece. 'It's really important that you tell the truth.'

Trixie shakes her head and stares wide-eyed at both of us.

Someone has spelled out our names.

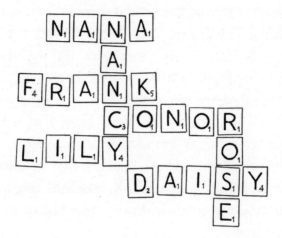

Rose starts pacing again. 'I don't understand the connection to Nana's agent, or the link with Scrabble letters . . . *someone* has been sticking them to the covers of our old home movies. But why would *he* be involved in any of this? Nana loved her agent.'

'Because she couldn't write any more new books after what happened in 1988?' Conor says, staring at the floor. 'She didn't publish anything ever again after that. What if *he* trashed her studio last night, looking for her latest work? If an author can't write, that's got to be bad for their agent too, right? I mean, she *was* his biggest client.'

'His first and only client for a while,' I say, remembering how much I liked the man.

Rose shakes her head. 'We must be missing something.'

She turns to Lily, as though hoping she might have the answer. But Lily continues to face away from us all, staring at the TV screen, as if hypnotized by what she sees. For now, all it shows is an image of a bonfire on a beach at night. The fire in the room crackles and spits again, and I see what looks like a chair leg burning on top of the logs. It's painted blue with white clouds. I turn to Conor, and there is a scribble of a smile drawn on his face for no more than a second, before a frown erases it as though it were never there. But that doesn't mean anything. Sometimes our faces don't know what to do with themselves when we are scared.

When I look back at the TV, I know that a lot of what happened after Nana's birthday meal and before the bonfire on the beach is missing – moments that definitely weren't captured on camera because Lily wasn't filming at the time. Unfortunately, my mind remembers that night well enough to fill in the gaps.

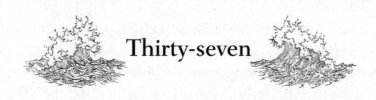

# Thirty-seven

SEAGLASS – 1988

'Why do *they* get to go to a Halloween party and I have to stay *here*? I *always* have to stay behind. You never let me do *anything*,' I said to my mother, hoping that the vast amount of alcohol she had consumed that night might have made her change her mind. Saving an alcoholic seemed to turn her into one. Albeit the functioning variety who people aren't as quick to condemn.

'Because you're only thirteen,' Nancy said, pouring another glass of wine.

'So? You let Rose and Lily go to parties when they were my age.'

'You know as well as I do that your sisters aren't as—'

'What? Unhappy? Lonely? Bored?'

Nancy tutted, and it made me so angry. It was the bad habit she was always so good at. The sound of people tutting still makes me cross. Sometimes my mother would tut for the benefit of nobody but herself, when she thought she was alone and no one could hear her. *Tut. Tut. Tut.* It was her response to everything that irritated her, including me. Nancy steered me out of the room, as though I were an embarrassment that Nana's agent shouldn't have to see.

'Your sisters aren't as *delicate* as you are,' she said, with a level of satisfaction that made *me* want to tut.

'I'm not—'

'Daisy, I have spent my life protecting you from the world and looking after you . . .' That sounded like a joke to me. By then, my mother was a woman who could barely look after herself. After the break-up with Conor's father, she seemed smaller and had become a bit introverted. London was too loud for her, and our tiny town house was too claustrophobic with no real outdoor space. So we spent more time at Seaglass than ever before. Nancy sat alone in the garden for hours with her precious flowers, because they were all she had left of Conor's dad, and her only *friends* came in bottles. My mother had less time than ever for me, and she resented the pity and guilt I seemed to cause her to feel. 'I am never going to let anything happen to you,' she said, holding my shoulders a little too tight. Sometimes it felt like she *wanted* me to stay sick and vulnerable forever.

A lifetime of my mother 'protecting' me meant that I didn't have much of a life or any friends of my own, not real ones. I didn't go to school, or Brownies or swimming lessons like my sisters. I didn't get to hang out with any other children my own age. Even now, I find it hard to make friends, and sometimes I think it's because I never got taught how to do it. That was something neither Nancy nor Nana knew how to teach, because they didn't have any either. My childhood friends were Agatha Christie and Stephen King.

When I look back, I think being home-schooled deprived me of so much more than anyone realized. I can understand why my mother didn't see the point in me learning algebra – that was something we did agree on – but there were plenty of things I couldn't teach myself by reading books. I didn't just miss out on the lessons most children learn in a classroom. There were life lessons I never knew about.

I gave up demanding to be allowed out that night. There was no point arguing with my mother. You can't win an argument with someone who refuses to have one. I left them all to it and went up to my room, furious about being treated like a child when I no longer felt like one. Nancy wouldn't even let me read the letters from the hospital, even though they were about *me*. I thought about the last doctor I had seen, and how happy and cheerful he was compared to all the others. 'Now go and live your life,' he had said with a big smile on his face, as though there were nothing wrong with me at all. Living was all I wanted to do, so I couldn't understand why Nancy still insisted on locking me away and treating me like a porcelain doll.

An hour or so after Nana's birthday dinner, the tide was almost low enough for Rose, Lily and Conor to leave. They had changed into fancy dress for the annual Halloween beach party and, like always, I was going to miss out on all the fun. Whenever the three of them attended local parties, there was normally some coordination when it came to their costumes. That year they were going as the Lion, the Witch and the Pumpkin. Rose was the lion, Lily was a witch – a role she was well rehearsed in – and Conor was dressed in what looked like an orange sack.

I sat at the top of the stairs, watching them put on their coats and say their goodbyes. Then I heard the front door slam, and listened to the adults return to the kitchen and their drinks. In my fury at the injustice of it all, I stumbled into the old wicker hamper on the landing, the one that we used for dressing-up games when we were younger. I kicked it in frustration, then had an idea. I opened up the hamper, pulling out home-made ghostbuster and Gizmo costumes, along with witches' hats and wigs, but realized none of it would be enough to change my appearance and hide my face. Then I found the old sheet from my performance as a ghost a few years earlier. I pulled it over my head, lined up the two holes with my eyes, and looked in the mirror. Then I put the sheet in my backpack and hatched a plan.

After using cuddly toys to make a me-shaped lump in my bed, I crept downstairs and let myself out of the front door. I ran across the causeway as fast as I could with the moon lighting my way, constantly checking over my shoulder to see if I'd been caught escaping. Then I scrambled up the cliff path, until my sisters and Conor were only a few metres ahead of me. They were taking the long route – which was safest when it was dark – but I knew a shortcut and reached Conor's car before they did, just in time to climb inside the boot. Nobody ever used to bother locking their cars when leaving them behind the sand dunes back then. Things have changed so much since 1988. These days we are taught to suspect others of doing us harm at all times.

Conor had borrowed the old blue Volvo from his dad, without Mr Kennedy's knowledge or consent. Forgiveness is easier to ask for than permission, but Conor no longer asked his father for either. The car was already as battered and broken as its owner. Since his return to drowning his sorrows, Conor's dad had driven home drunk from the pub on more than one occasion, often driving into a wall or a tree along the way, but at a speed that luckily only dented his pride and the vehicle.

Conor had only recently passed his test – a few days earlier – and was keen to impress Rose before she went off to university. He opened the passenger door for his girlfriend, leaving Lily to help herself to the back seat. She sprayed on her Poison perfume, stinking the entire car out – she was already wearing more than enough to scare a skunk – and the smell made me want to sneeze. I covered my nose and mouth with my hands, and stayed as quiet as I could in my hiding place.

'Nice wheels,' Lily said unkindly, and Conor slammed his door so hard I'm surprised it didn't fall off its hinges. As he started the engine, I wondered whether there was enough air in the boot for me to survive the journey. The car coughed and spluttered a few times before coming to life, and I began to panic. My heart was thudding in my chest, and I could feel a sneeze trying to escape my nose, which it did, but luckily Conor turned on the car stereo at the exact same time. He pushed a cassette tape inside, and a song called 'Don't Worry, Be Happy' started to play, replacing the noise of the radio. My sisters knew all the words, and they sang along as Conor pulled out from behind the sand dunes and started driving down the winding cliff road.

It was a bumpy ride and I felt carsick, but it was only a five-minute drive to the other end of Blacksand Bay where the Halloween gathering was being held. I was thirteen, but the only parties I'd ever been to before were hosted at Seaglass by Nana. The excitement I felt outweighed the fear. It was exhilarating. When we finally stopped driving, I waited for them all to get out, then I tried to open the boot. It wouldn't budge. Conor had locked the car. I imagined them walking away and me running out of oxygen, and my sense of panic went from zero to a hundred before I could take another breath. I screamed.

Conor's face when he opened the boot was not one of his happy ones. He was busy inflating his Halloween costume, and I had clearly interrupted him halfway.

'Have you lost your tiny mind?' Lily asked, blowing a bubble of gum in my face.

'What were you thinking, Daisy?' Rose said, sounding just like our mother. 'If anything had happened to you—'

'Come on, credit where credit is due. She wanted to come to the party and she came,' said Conor with a kind smile. He reattached a nozzle to his costume and started stepping on a foot pump.

'She'll ruin this year's theme,' Lily moaned. 'The Lion, the Witch, the Pumpkin and the Daisy doesn't have quite the same ring to it.'

Conor ignored her. With every enthusiastic foot pump, I could see that he was wearing an *inflatable* pumpkin costume.

'This is an *adult* party,' whined Lily.

'Then you should probably go home,' I said.

'Watch it, pipsqueak,' Lily snapped. My dad's nickname for me morphed from a term of endearment into an insult whenever she used it.

'Lily's right,' said Rose. 'Some of the others might feel a bit funny about a thirteen-year-old being on the beach and seeing what they get up to.'

'I brought this,' I said, pulling the white sheet ghost costume out of my bag.

I was allowed to stay, because none of them wanted to leave, but only if I promised to remain hidden under my makeshift costume for the entire evening. I didn't mind. I was just excited to be out with other people, witnessing a snapshot of humanity first-hand instead of reading about it in a book or seeing it on TV. It was a big step for someone who rarely went *any-where* without her mother. Peering through those two holes in the sheet felt like looking at life through a tunnel. A bit like the View-Master my dad gave me one Christmas. I liked the imagined safety of my disguise; it meant that I could see everything without being seen. And I wanted to make the most of it because I knew that the things, people and parties that had always been out of reach before were within touching distance for one night only.

Everything that happened next was a real education.

After so many years of feeling like I'd been missing out, I actually missed being at home. It was cold on the beach at night, and curling up in an armchair in front of the fire, with a good novel and a mug of hot chocolate, suddenly seemed a lot more appealing. The 'party' consisted of fifteen or so boys and girls – some of whom I'd seen before but were still strangers to me – all sitting around a small fire on the beach, drinking cheap cider and white wine.

Conor – our designated driver – drank Coke to begin with. I knew better than to drink alcohol with the cocktail of drugs my mother made me take every day to keep my heart ticking, but I did have an occasional sip of Rose's wine when nobody was looking. I didn't like the way it tasted – it was nothing like Nana's birthday champagne, which I'd tried earlier that evening – but I wanted to know what it was like to be like the others. How it felt to be *normal*. After an hour of sitting on the beach with a sheet over my head, all I felt was cold, and tired, and a little bit sick. I concluded that being normal might be overrated. Lily drank more than the rest of us combined, and it was her suggestion to play spin the bottle.

'You have to kiss whoever it points to when it stops spinning. I'll go first,' Lily said, with a naughty grin stretched across her pretty face. The other kids smiled too; everyone except Rose seemed to be having a good time. We all watched as the bottle spun, a zoetrope of drunken teenage faces lit up by the flickering light of the fire. It seemed to spin forever, but then it stopped, and the bottleneck pointed at the boy next to Conor. Without hesitation, Lily took out her bubble gum, then leaned over and kissed him. There were tongues involved and it looked unpleasant. She popped her gum back in her mouth afterwards and smiled at everyone.

Sex was a mystery to me back then. I'd read about it, and thought about it, but the idea of actually doing it seemed both unnecessary and unhygienic. Watching Lily kiss a random boy only made me feel more queasy.

'Conor's turn next,' Lily declared.

'I don't really want to play—'

'Man up. Perhaps you can write about it for the local newspaper,' she said when he tried to refuse.

Conor – a now slightly deflated orange pumpkin – leaned forward and reluctantly played the game. He stared at Rose the whole time the bottle spun, but it stopped on Lily.

I've never seen her look more delighted.

Sometimes when we think we know what we want but don't get it, we look for something or someone else to fill the gap. Lily had always been jealous of Conor and Rose being together. Not because she really wanted to be with Conor, but because she always wanted whatever Rose had. Lily couldn't stand being left out of anything. She marched around the fire and kissed him before he had a chance to protest – or run away – and I noticed Rose drink from her bottle of wine until it looked half empty.

'Delicious,' Lily said with a drunken smile as soon as their lips parted. That was the year she started smoking, so I imagine it wasn't delicious for him at all. 'Who wants to go skinny-dipping?' she asked everyone and nobody in particular. Then she stood up and removed her witch's hat, black dress and shoes, before running towards the sea in just her underwear. It looked whiter than white in the moonlight. Despite the cold, a few of the boys from around the fire followed her. Lily had made more than a bit of a name for herself by then. Her variety of fun was mostly harmless, and only ever born out of a desperate need for affection, but rumours ruin far more reputations than reality. Despite the unpleasant things that people sometimes said, in that moment I would have given anything to have been my sister. Everyone seemed to adore her. She was fun and beautiful, full of life and free. While I was only ever me.

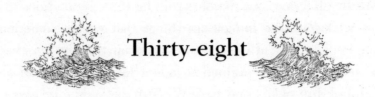

# Thirty-eight

## SEAGLASS – 1988

Rose stormed off in the other direction, disappearing down the beach, her lion's tail swinging as she walked. And Conor the pumpkin chased after her. If I didn't feel so ill, I might have found the whole scene funny.

'You're the youngest Darker sister under there, aren't you?' asked a boy I recognized from Rose's sixteenth birthday party at Seaglass. He sat down next to me, so close that I could smell the beer on his breath. The wine had made me very sleepy, and I didn't try to stop him at first, as he attempted to remove the sheet from my head and peek underneath. I was tired of pretending to be a ghost and of being treated like one all my life, but part of me wanted to stay hidden. I pulled the sheet back down. 'I wish it *was* Daisy Darker under there,' he said, backing off a little. 'I was hoping that the bottle might land on her if I spun it,' he whispered, even though there was nobody else left by the fire to hear.

I didn't know what to say to that, so said nothing.

'Or maybe we could play a little game of trick-or-treat if you don't like spin the bottle?' he suggested innocently, as though we were discussing what board game to play on a rainy Sunday afternoon.

'I don't know how to play trick-or-treat,' I replied.

'It's easy, I'll teach you. But come a little closer first, you're shivering. I'll keep you warm.'

I looked around for my sisters, but they were nowhere to be seen. Everyone else had wandered away from the fire except the boy. And me. I shuffled an inch closer and he smiled.

'First, the trick,' he said. 'If you can guess which hand I'm holding this chocolate coin in, you can eat the treat, but if you guess wrong, you have to take the sheet off your head.'

I looked at the chocolate in its shiny gold foil wrapping and nodded. The game seemed simple and harmless enough. He put his hands behind his back, then held two closed fists out in front of me to choose from. The hand I chose was empty, so I took off the sheet and he smiled.

'That's better, and look how beautiful you are. No wonder your sisters always want to leave you at home, you outshine them both. Play again?'

I think that was the first time a stranger had ever paid me a proper compliment. I knew I wasn't really beautiful, not compared to Rose or Lily, but I confess that I liked someone saying that I was, even if it wasn't true. I nodded a silent agreement to play again, and he held out two closed fists. I chose wrong a second time.

'I'm afraid that means one of these comes undone,' he said, unhooking one of the clips on my dungaree dress. When I lost again, he unhooked the other. Then he tried to kiss me and I tried to let him. I had never been kissed before. It was cold and wet, and I kept my mouth firmly closed as he tried to stick his tongue inside it. I closed my eyes too, as though I didn't want to see what was happening.

I'd always dreamt of Conor being the first boy who I kissed, perhaps because he was the only boy I really knew. I'm sure

I wasn't the only girl in the world to fantasize about their sister's boyfriend, and it was him I imagined as I let this eighteen-year-old stranger kiss thirteen-year-old me. I don't expect people to understand, but according to all the doctors I spent my childhood visiting, I only had a couple of years left. I didn't know then what the most recent doctor had said to Nancy, about a dramatic change in my life expectancy. And I didn't want to die never having been kissed. When you know you can't make long-term plans, it's easy to let yourself make short-term mistakes.

'Try to relax,' the boy whispered, kissing my neck, and I noticed the shiny foil chocolate on the black sand behind us. It was never in either of his hands. Those lying fingers were busy instead sliding up and under my top, before pulling it off over my head. I was wearing a hand-me-down training bra and felt nothing but shame. The cold air stole my breath from me, tiny clouds of it escaping from my mouth. It reminded me of the cloud creatures I used to try to see in the sky when I was a little girl, and I imagined seeing a lion, a witch and a pumpkin as the boy reached behind my back, trying, and failing, to unfasten my bra.

I saw someone dressed as a devil run past laughing and I felt afraid, even though I knew it was just a costume. Nana taught us that the devil is not a fictional man with a red cape and horns, he's the voice inside our heads that tells us to do things we shouldn't, he's the eyes that pretend not to see, and the ears that pretend not to hear. He's you, he's me, he's all of us. The full moon was a flirt that night, teasing the sky with little glimpses of itself, only occasionally coming out from behind the clouds. They all started to look like devils too. The boy kissed me again, still trying to take off my bra.

'Wait, stop,' I said, feeling very sick all of a sudden.

'You're so beautiful, I just want to see it,' the boy said, staring at my chest.

'See what?' I asked.

'Your scar. You won't die if we do this, will you? Can I touch it?'

I knew there and then that if that was what it was like to be normal, I'd rather be me.

I pushed him away, covered myself up, and fled.

'Freak!' he called after me, then laughed.

I cried, because he was right: I was a freak. A freak with a broken heart, who would never love, or be loved. A freak who had been kissed for the first time by a horrible, disgusting boy. A freak who wanted to disappear. But first, I wanted to go home.

I couldn't see Rose or Conor anywhere on the beach, but I thought I could hear Lily laughing with one of the boys behind the rocks. She has always craved attention, especially from men. Little girls who lose their fathers spend their lives looking for them in every man they meet. In my tired, slightly drunken state, I thought Lily would look after me. The rocks were covered in barnacles and seaweed, but I kept climbing until I was high enough to see without being seen.

I was right, Lily was talking to a boy. The boy was Conor.

'Rose is upset with me,' he said, then took a swig from what looked like a bottle of whisky, just like the ones his dad liked to drink.

'She'll get over it, pumpkin,' Lily replied, grabbing the bottle from him and taking a swig herself. She screwed up her face as though she hated the taste, but then drank some more. 'Besides, Rose is going to university, you've got a job on the local newspaper . . . it was never going to be forever. You'll be breaking up soon anyway when she meets some brainiac at Cambridge. May as well rip off the Band-Aid now if you ask me.'

'How can you say that? I *love* Rose,' Conor said, sounding like he might cry. 'And she loves me.' Denial is often a down payment for future heartbreak.

'Then why, deep down, do you already know she's going to dump you?' said Lily. She was still in her underwear, but had a towel wrapped around her. 'I know the truth hurts, and I'm sorry to be the one saying it, but we both know Rose is out of your league. I understand how you're feeling, Rose is leaving me too,' Lily said, taking a step towards Conor. 'Maybe we could help each other feel better?'

'How?' he asked, taking another sip of whisky.

I stared at Lily's feet as she took another step towards him. Her toenails were painted red, and I knew the varnish must have belonged to our mother. I had stolen all of Lily's nail varnishes a week earlier, when she refused to let me borrow any of them. There were ten in total, and I used them to paint each of my toenails a different colour, before burying each tiny glass bottle in the sand outside Seaglass. I imagined the crabs that lived in Blacksand Bay finding them, and taking it in turns to paint one another's claws.

Lily's towel dropped onto the ground and she took one more step towards Conor, until their lips were almost touching. Her white underwear seemed to glow in the moonlight against a backdrop of black sand.

'Rose might be the clever one in the family, but there are all kinds of things I know how to do that she doesn't,' Lily said, not taking her eyes off his. 'I could show you if you like? Or we could just kiss it better?' she added, pressing herself up against him. 'Just tonight, then never again? It could be our little secret?'

But they didn't just kiss.

I watched from my hiding place above the rocks while they did what they did beneath them.

*One Mississippi . . . Two Mississippi . . . Three Mississippi . . .*

Conor accidentally called Lily 'Rose' at one point. But she didn't seem to mind.

*One Mississippi . . . Two Mississippi . . .*

I think it was the toxic mix of shock, and revulsion, and heartbreak that prevented me from moving or saying a word. There are times when we all stand still while the ghosts of our pasts run by. And that's how I felt: like a ghost. I watched, unable to look away, just like people rubbernecking at a car crash, until it was over.

*One Mississippi . . .*

Then I slipped on the rocks, and they both looked up and saw me.

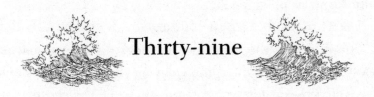

# Thirty-nine

*31 October 4 a.m.*
*two hours until low tide*

The clocks out in the hall start to chime four o'clock, and nobody says a word. My memories of that night did not appear on the TV screen. All we saw just now were some teenagers sitting around a bonfire on a beach in 1988. But it's a night both of my sisters and Conor and I would rather forget. We've never really spoken about what happened after I caught Conor and Lily together. And none of them have ever forgiven me for what happened next, even though it was not my fault.

'I don't want to see any more of this,' Conor says. He crosses the room and ejects the tape. 'It's only two hours until we can leave – less if we don't mind getting our feet wet – I vote we just sit in silence while we wait. No more home movies. No more unhappy trips down the Darker family memory lane.' He crosses the room and throws the VHS tape on the fire. When it doesn't catch light straight away, he adds another log to the flames. But it isn't a log in his hand, it's another sky-blue chair leg painted with white clouds. Someone has chopped up the chair Nana once painted for Conor and left it here to burn. He turns to stare at us.

'I don't know which one of you is responsible for all of this, but I'm not playing along anymore. It's sick. That's the only word for what is happening here tonight. This ends now.'

'I don't remember anyone putting you in charge,' says Rose.

'Someone needs to be. For Trixie's sake. The poor kid doesn't stand a chance growing up in this family. It isn't as though Lily will ever win mother of the year.'

I'm shocked by Conor's outburst, I think we all are, but most of all I'm shocked that Lily doesn't respond. It's not in her nature to stay quiet. She's still just staring at the TV screen, even though there is nothing on it. Rose finds it strange too.

'Lily?' she says.

Trixie, who has been sitting next to me since I called her to the Scrabble board, walks over to Lily and taps her gently on the shoulder. 'Mum?'

Lily's head bows, as though she has fallen asleep. Her face twists towards us at an unnatural angle, and she looks a little faded. Like a watercolour painting of herself by someone who got bored halfway through.

'Lily!' Rose shouts, as our sister falls sideways onto the sofa. She pushes Trixie out of the way and leans over Lily, checking for any signs of life. 'Oh my god. She's not breathing.'

'Mum!' Trixie screams, trying to get closer.

It gets very loud in the room very quickly.

'Don't you dare die,' shouts Rose, starting CPR.

The words seem to detonate inside Trixie's ears, and she covers them with her hands as Conor pulls her out of the way.

'There are strange marks on Lily's neck,' I say, trying to help in any way that I can.

'Are those bruises?' Conor asks, noticing them too.

Rose shakes her head. 'No. They look more like . . . burns to me. Come on, Lily. If you can hear me, I need you to breathe.'

The rest of us watch in silent horror as she continues with
chest compressions and mouth-to-mouth. Trixie is crying, so
am I, and I can't process any of what I am seeing or hearing
as I try to comfort my niece.

Eventually Rose stops and shakes her head. 'It's too late,'
she whispers, tears streaming down her face. 'She's gone.'

'Are you sure?' Conor asks Rose.

'Of course I'm bloody sure.'

We all stare at Lily in silence, while the fire crackles and
spits, and the VHS tape of that terrible night burns. Rose takes
a woollen throw from the sofa and uses it to cover Lily's body.
Although I'm sure we've all seen them, nobody mentions the
two objects that have been tied to her hands, which are still
visible. We were in the same room as her, and we didn't even
notice. In one of Lily's hands there is a bottle of perfume, in
the other there is a hand mirror, both held in place with red
ribbons.

# Lily

Daisy Darker's sister Lily was the vainest of the lot.
She was a selfish, spoilt, entitled witch, one who deserved to get shot.

Lily was a jealous woman, too quick to complain and moan.
She wanted too much, but gave too little, and chose to make hate
her home.

When she slept with her daughter's father, it was never a
question of love.
It was to settle a score, that boys liked her more, even though they all
gave her the shove.

Nobody was more shocked than herself when Lily became a mother.
She wasn't clever or kind, and was really quite blind, when it came to
the feelings of others.

But the child was her best achievement, and somehow grew up
to be good.
It proved that apples do sometimes fall far from the tree, and grow in a
different wood.

When the time came, no one knew who to blame when she was
poisoned by her own perfume.
With her skin so cold, and the rash on her neck rather old, she was a
long time dead in that room.

# Forty

*31 October 4:10 a.m.*
*less than two hours until low tide*

'I think there might have been some kind of poison in her perfume,' says Rose.

'What?' asks Conor. 'Why would you think something like that, let alone say it?'

'People have been killing each other with perfume for centuries. Everyone in this family knows that Lily is constantly spraying herself. Look at those marks on her neck and wrists . . . and the perfume bottle has been tied to her hand. You don't have to be Poirot to work it out.'

'What could possibly have been in a perfume bottle that would have killed her?' Conor says, almost as though he is accusing Rose.

'I don't know. I'm a vet, not a chemist. My sister has just died. Someone is killing my whole family. Stop asking me stupid questions!' she says.

Conor frowns, backs off a little. 'I'm sorry.'

Rose doesn't reply. I've always thought that the best way to truly know a person is to listen to them. Not just to what they say, but to what they don't. All sorts of secrets are neatly tucked inside the silent gaps between words. The simple act of listening is a forgotten art in our loud world. I don't think Conor has ever really forgiven Rose for breaking up with him after what happened that night, and I don't think she has ever forgiven him for what he did.

I don't mean him sleeping with Lily.

'I said, I'm sorry,' Conor repeats, and Rose turns on him.

'Are you? Which part are you specifically sorry for? And why are you even here? Nobody in this family has spoken to you for years except for Nana. *She* might have still cared about you, but the rest of us don't. You were dead to me, to all of us. Whenever people are stupid enough to care about you, bad things happen. You should have stayed away!' Rose leans over Lily's body and holds her close before crying again. 'You should have stayed away,' she repeats as her tears continue to free-fall.

They both seem oblivious to the child in the room who has just lost her mother. Trixie is trembling, and sobbing so hard she can barely breathe. I try my best to comfort her.

'I think whoever has been killing off the family is in this room,' says Conor, looking at Rose. 'It's the only option that makes sense now.'

'Is that so?' she replies. 'And who do you think did it? *Me?*'

'Well, who else could it be? Do you think it was a fifteen-year-old child? Or perhaps sweet little Daisy has decided to finally get revenge for what happened *that night*,' Conor says, looking wilder than I've ever seen. I ignore them both because looking after Trixie is more important than their childish accusations at the moment.

'It's going to be all right,' I tell my niece, who is still covering her ears with her hands.

I don't know what will happen to Trixie now – who she will live with or who will take care of her – but I'm determined to do everything I can to play my part in keeping her safe.

None of us know who Trixie's father is, Lily never told us, and I sometimes wonder whether that was because she didn't know.

'You're going to be okay. Sit down here with me,' I say, and Trixie does. 'I won't let anything bad happen to you, I promise.'

She nods, but doesn't look up. I don't think she believes me. Given everything that has happened tonight, I worry whether it is a promise I will be able to keep. I can't help wondering what witnessing all of this horror might do to a child long term. As Rose and Conor continue to accuse each other, Trixie hugs her knees to her chest and closes her eyes, but I can still see the steady stream of tears falling from them. I look at the Scrabble board on the table behind us, with all of our names intertwined, just like all families are in real life. Even if they wish they weren't.

'I agree with you,' Rose says to Conor. 'I also think it is only logical now that the person responsible must be in this room. My money is on *you*.'

'Me?' Conor replies. 'How on earth did you reach that conclusion?'

'All the terrible things that have happened took place after *you* appeared, unexpected and alone in the middle of the night. Allegedly by boat, not that any of us saw one. You could have been here the whole time, waiting for us to arrive, and waiting for the tide to come in so we couldn't leave. If anyone should be under suspicion right now, I'd say it was you.'

He doesn't get a chance to reply, because a floorboard squeaks above us.

Everything stops and we stare wide-eyed at one another, as the sound of someone walking in the room above our heads continues. Trixie stops crying, and peers at the ceiling in silence. I can't even hear the clocks ticking out in the hallway. Time seems to pause for a little while, politely waiting for us all to catch up. Rose, Conor, Trixie and I look at one another, confusion and fear on our faces, as we try to understand who is upstairs.

 # Forty-one

*31 October 4:15 a.m.*
*less than two hours until low tide*

'We've got to get out of this house and off this island,' Rose whispers.

'How? Are you going to swim to shore?' Conor whispers back.

'If I have to. There *is* someone else here at Seaglass. We just heard them walking around upstairs! I don't plan to hang around and wait for someone else to die.'

It's all quiet up above again now. Almost as though we imagined it.

'Maybe it was Poppins upstairs? She's already given us a fright tonight?' I suggest.

Poppins, having heard her name, appears from behind the sofa, where she sometimes likes to sleep. She stares in my direction and wags her tail. The dog never stopped loving me, despite what happened. Animals don't know how to hate or hold a grudge.

'At least we have the gun to defend ourselves,' Conor says.

'That's true,' I say, but Rose turns a paler shade of white.

'What?' Conor asks.

Rose shakes her head. 'I . . . I left the gun in the library when I changed into some dry clothes. It was in my jacket pocket. I don't have it.'

'Well, that's just great,' Conor mutters.

'I put it on the chair. Then I took off my wet things. I must have put them on top of it and then I just . . . forgot. You knocked on the door when I was still getting changed and distracted me.'

'Of course it's my fault,' says Conor.

'We should get out of here anyway. We're sitting ducks if we stay in this room. Nana's library is smaller, safer. We can lock ourselves in there and I can get the gun. We need to move. All of us. Now,' says Rose.

She takes the master key from her pocket and opens the little door that joins the lounge and the library. All the down-stairs rooms have these doors connecting them – it reminds me of the times when Lily used to open them up and roller-skate through the house, lap after dizzying lap. But I don't remember seeing any of the internal doors open since we were children. It amazes me how Rose can still think so quickly and clearly, and stay so calm.

'Maybe whoever is out there doesn't know about these doors?' she whispers.

'Or maybe they do,' says Conor. 'It must be someone who knows the place pretty well. How else would they be able to sneak around Seaglass all night without being seen?'

We stop for a moment, as if thoughts can only surface when we are still.

'The sound of the storm would have drowned out the noise of someone creeping around the house. But who would be familiar enough with this place to know it so well? Nana was super private, she rarely had visitors,' I whisper.

Rose nods. 'The only people I can remember Nana ever inviting here, for years now, were the people she thought of as family.'

'What about her agent?' Conor says.

'Yes. She trusted him, and there's the Scrabble connection . . .' Rose replies, almost to herself. 'What makes you think a man is behind all of this?'

'Your dad. Frank was a big guy . . . moving his body from the music room to the cupboard wouldn't have been easy. I think even I would have struggled to lift him. Remember how hard it was for us to move Nancy? And she weighed nothing at all.'

'You have a very morbid sense of logic,' says Rose. 'I understand your theory about Nana's agent, but we all know she hasn't written a new book for years. I don't know if they are even still in touch.'

'He was here yesterday. I saw his card in the cubbyhole by the punch clock. Either he forgot to punch out, or he didn't leave,' I whisper, wishing I'd thought to mention it earlier. I only met him that one time, but he seemed like such a lovely man.

The footsteps above our heads resume, and we all look up in terror.

'Hurry, come on, into the library,' Rose says. 'You too, Poppins,' she adds, and the old dog gets up and trots behind her. As soon as we are inside, Rose starts locking all of the doors, trapping us in the small room. Conor starts pacing, and Trixie stands on her own by the window in the corner. She looks so small in her pink pyjamas. Trixie might be fifteen, but she's still a child who has just lost her mother. I rush to her side but she barely notices, and I doubt she'll ever get over this. I suspect none of us will.

Rose starts throwing her things into her bag, almost hitting Poppins with a wet jumper in the process. Then she freezes.

'What's wrong?' I ask.

She turns back to stare at us all. 'My gun was right here on the chair earlier.'

'And?' Conor asks.

'And now it's gone.'

# Forty-two

*31 October 4:20 a.m.*
*less than two hours until low tide*

'So what you're saying is that the killer has a gun?' Conor whispers.

'It's possible,' says Rose.

'Great. What now?' he asks.

She shrugs. 'We barricade ourselves in here and wait?'

'Wait for what? There is no way to call for help. Nobody is coming to save us!' I say, feeling just as hysterical as I'm starting to sound.

Rose ignores me and checks that all three doors in the library are locked again – the one that leads to the lounge, the one to the music room, and the main one leading out to the hall – until she is sure that we are safe – or trapped – inside. Trixie looks exhausted and a little out of it. Her eyes are half closed. I remember that she's been drugged with sleeping pills, injected with insulin, and witnessed the horror of her mother, grand-parents and great-grandmother being murdered tonight. Her knees buckle as if she can't stand any longer, and she slides down against the wall before I can catch her. I'm amazed she's lasted this long. I sit next to her on the floor and try to hold her hand, but Trixie pulls it away. Her fingers form two little fists, and she wraps her arms across her chest as though hugging herself. I suppose if I were her, I wouldn't trust anyone left here either.

Three of the four walls in Nana's library are covered in shelves crammed full of books, but the one at the far end of the room, which has an old sash window, is what she liked to call the 'Wall of Achievements'. It makes sense that Rose chose to sleep in this room this weekend because most of the achievements are hers. There is a picture of Rose – the clever one – winning an award at school, some of her prizes and certificates for 'best this' and 'best that', and a photo of her wearing a graduation gown and cap at Cambridge. Nana was always so proud of Rose for going to university and pursuing her dreams. Unlike Lily, who she described as devoid of ambition. *Your dreams can't come true if you don't have any.* Nana used to say that to me and my sisters all the time. But she did frame a newspaper clipping of Lily winning a beauty pageant when she was ten, probably to keep my mother happy. *It's important to celebrate life's small successes; like most things, they need to see the light in order to grow into something bigger.*

There is a framed picture of Dad conducting his orchestra at the Albert Hall in London. Next to it, there is a childhood picture of me sitting with my father in the music room here at Seaglass. I'm holding up my Grade Five piano certificate, and we're wearing matching smiles. Nana also framed a poem I wrote when I was eleven, perhaps because writing was her passion, and she secretly wanted someone in the family to follow in her footsteps.

*Here's what I think*
*About people who drink*
*Then say mean things to others*

*Without even a blink*
*Of an eye*
*Make them cry*
*Or worse, wonder why*
*They exist in this death we call life.*

*I think those who tittle and tattle*
*Or give the fears of others a good rattle*
*Should be wary of making smiles fade.*

*For what goes around comes around*
*And kills you without a sound*
*Leaving you dead in the bed that you made.*

I confess it is rather dark, but I was a child living with a death sentence at the time. Perhaps if I'd known back then that I'd still be around now, I might have had a more cheerful disposition.

But I didn't know I was living in a family full of liars.

My mother lied to me – and everyone else – about how long I had left to live. The doctor who made her cry at the hospital hadn't given her *bad* news about my life expectancy. It was the opposite. Thanks to medical advances, that doctor thought I could go on to live a lot longer than everyone previously believed. He was right. My death sentence had effectively been revoked thanks to science. I just needed one more operation. But my mother didn't tell me at the time. She didn't tell anyone at all at first. And she didn't sign the consent form. It was as though she *wanted* me to be broken forever.

Some secrets really shouldn't be shared.

There are no other Daisy-shaped achievements to see on the wall. Maybe some members of this family didn't think I

amounted to much – volunteering at a care home for the elderly
might not seem like an accomplishment to people who have
spent their lives reaching for the stars. But I was always happy
to keep my feet firmly on the ground, and watch the stars
sparkle in the sky where they belong. I'm proud of what I do:
helping and caring for people who can no longer care for
themselves. Being there when it matters most.

Framed book covers decorate the rest of the library wall –
some of Nana's own favourites, including *Daisy Darker's Little
Secret*. Nana had Conor's first cover story on the front of the
*Cornish Times* framed too. His father disappeared the day after
the Halloween beach party in 1988, and Nana let him move
in with her at Seaglass for a while. The start of Conor's career
in journalism did not go well – he seemed to spend more time
making tea than writing stories – so Nana let Conor do a rare
interview with her, which made the front page. Then she framed
it so that he would know that she considered him one of the
family and that she was proud of him.

Conor has worked so hard to get where he is today. He's
done more working than living for the last decade. I imagine
an exclusive story about the murder of the celebrated children's
author Beatrice Darker and her family, in an eccentric house
on a remote tidal island, would be good for his career. Making
the jump from a local newspaper to local TV, to London and
network news, before finally achieving his dream of becoming
a BBC crime correspondent was not easy. I think his success
has exceeded even his own expectations. But success is a drug:
the more people have, the more they want. And Conor has
always been a man with something to prove, if only to himself.
Sometimes when people try too hard to be more than they are,
they end up being less than they were.

The frame on the Wall of Achievements that belonged to

Conor is still there, but the faded newspaper article that had been inside it for over a decade is gone. I'm not the only one to notice.

'Someone stole my front page,' he says, taking a closer look.

The frame isn't empty. Rose and I step forward to read the piece of paper that has taken the newspaper's place. It's an official-looking typed letter, with only a handful of words. But those words change everything.

Dear Ms. Darker,
Test report for case ref: DAR2004TD
Your supplied samples have been analysed and our results can be summarized as follows:
**Alleged father:** Conor Kennedy
**Mother:** Lily Darker
**Child:** Trixie Darker

Based on our analysis, we can conclude without reasonable doubt that Conor Kennedy is the biological father of Trixie Darker. Please call us for further details if you would like to discuss these results.

I stare at the words printed on the paper for a long time, trying to make sense of them. Then I remember Conor and Lily on the beach in 1988 and do the maths. I'm sure I'm the only person in the family who knew that they'd slept together, but I can't believe how stupid I've been never to have put the pieces of the puzzle together before. Lily was always very casual about sex. I thought Trixie's father could be just about anyone. It never, ever occurred to me that it was Conor. We all have to compromise between the ideas we can afford to live inside and the ones we hope to inhabit.

Rose stares at Conor. So do I. He stares at the framed letter for a very long time before turning to look at Trixie, who is still sitting on the floor staring into space. She hasn't said a word since Lily died.

Having a niece is as close as I'll ever get to having a child of my own. Most doctors I met over the years said that people with my condition should never risk getting pregnant; that if I did, a pregnancy would put so much pressure on my heart that it would almost certainly kill me. Trixie is my world in some ways. I've never felt anything but love for the child since the first time I saw her. I think some people might presume that she was *my* daughter if they saw us side by side, we look enough alike, but now I turn to stare at her as though she were a stranger.

'Why are you all looking at me like that? What does it say?' Trixie asks, a new frown forming on her tear-stained face. Nobody answers, because we can hear someone walking around upstairs again. Someone who shouldn't be.

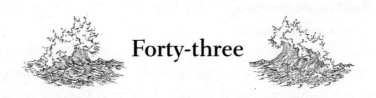

# Forty-three

*31 October 4:55 a.m.*
*just over one hour until low tide*

I turn to stare at Conor and see that his face has drained of colour. He looks at Rose, then at me, then at Trixie again.

'I didn't know,' he whispers. 'I was drunk. I presumed she was on the pill. If I'd known . . . Why didn't she tell me?' I look at Rose and wonder if she has done the maths too. There's something strange about the expression on her face. Lack of surprise, perhaps? 'I always wanted to be a better father than my own,' Conor says to nobody in particular, before turning away. I think he might be crying.

He never talks about what happened with his dad, none of us do.

Emotional blows leave invisible bruises that can hurt just as much as the physical variety. Growing up, Conor had more than his fair share of both. All I remember about what happened to Mr Kennedy is that the police found his car parked at the highest point of the cliff the day after the Halloween beach party, and he was never seen again. There was a note on the dashboard, but it didn't make a lot of sense:

*My dead wife stole my heart and the Darker family stole my son.*

*I'm sorry for the man life and death turned me into, and for the mistakes I made.*

*There is nothing left for me here.*

Conor was eighteen when it happened, and he wasn't the same afterwards. There was a funeral for his father – not that I went, I was left behind like always – but the coffin must have been empty, because I know the police never found the body.

Conor turns to look at Trixie again, then opens and closes his mouth a few times, like a goldfish. Whatever words he wants to say are too scared to come out. He shakes his head and stares up at the ceiling.

'I don't know what is going on here, but I'm going to put an end to it.'

Conor snatches the key from Rose's hand, marches towards the door that leads to the hall, but then stops. He stares at the handle for a long time, as though it is something very complicated that he can't remember how to use. Then he opens the door, as slowly and quietly as he can.

'Lock yourselves inside,' he whispers, giving the key to Rose before leaving the room and closing the door behind him.

Trixie starts to cry again and Rose rushes to her side.

'Everything is going to be all right,' Rose says, putting her arms around the girl in a slightly awkward fashion, as though needing to keep her at a distance.

Trixie stares at her before wiping her tears away with the sleeve of her pyjamas. Then she shakes her head of brown curls. 'I don't believe you.'

I don't believe Rose either. I'm not sure who to trust anymore. All I feel is afraid: of what I know and of what I don't. Anxiety builds a series of roadblocks inside my mind until it seems like there is no way out.

You can hear everything in this old house. If there is no chatter, or storm, or TV or music to muffle the sound, it is possible to hear the creaks and groans of the building whenever someone moves inside it. With the constant soundtrack of the sea, being here often feels like being on an old ship. One that might sink at any moment. Seaglass has thin walls that like to eavesdrop, and tired floorboards that like to talk. This house has never been good at keeping secrets. The rain outside has stopped, as has the howling wind, but I almost wish they hadn't. It's *too* quiet now. We can hear things I wish we couldn't. And not just the eighty clocks ticking in the hall.

Rose, Trixie and I listen as Conor walks across the hallway to the bottom of the staircase. We hear him walk up the stairs and along the landing until his footsteps seem to stop right above our heads. I think about the geography of the place, and realize he must be in Lily's room. We hear him go back out on the landing, probably to look inside another room, maybe mine. The sounds repeat themselves as he checks each bedroom: slow, methodical footsteps moving from one end of Seaglass to the other, before stopping on the landing directly above us upstairs.

'There's nobody up here,' Conor says from the first floor, barely loud enough for us to hear his words. 'Maybe it was our imagination, or just the noises an old house makes in a storm?'

Then we hear what sounds like someone falling down the stairs.

And a loud thud.

Right outside the library door.

Everything is silent for a few seconds. Rose, Trixie and I stare at one another, then at the closed door, all too afraid of what might be on the other side of it.

'Did you remember to lock the door?' Trixie whispers. She looks terrified.

Rose rushes forward, her hands shaking so much that she struggles to slot the key in the lock. Then she flicks off the light. Our eyes don't have much time to adjust, but it's possible to see the outlines of one another thanks to the moonlight from the window. The clocks in the hall start to strike five a.m., and Trixie covers her ears trying to block out the sound. It reminds me of me and my sisters when we were children, closing our eyes and counting the seconds to help us feel less afraid.

*One Mississippi . . . Two Mississippi . . . Three Mississippi . . .*

We didn't only do that when there was a storm *outside*.

*One Mississippi . . . Two Mississippi . . .*

Sometimes we did it to distract ourselves from what was happening *inside* Seaglass.

*One Mississippi . . .*

Just like now.

When the clocks stop, we all sit in silence again. In the dark. Huddled together against the fear as well as the cold. Then we hear more footsteps.

*Someone* is coming down the stairs.

 # Forty-four

*31 October 5:05 a.m.*
*less than one hour until low tide*

Rose and Trixie both look terrified, as the slow, steady footsteps continue along the hall, stopping right outside the library door. The handle turns very slowly, then the door shakes when the person on the other side realizes it is locked. We all hold our breath as the door rattles, until the house is silent again. The sound of footsteps resumes, and I hear the squeaky hinges of the door belonging to the cupboard under the stairs. None of us speak. I think true terror always tends to steal its victim's words.

Time passes, I'm not able to tell how little or how much. We listen to someone walking from room to room, and the sound of them dragging something behind them, twice. Then the house is silent again. We strain to hear something else – anything else – but our ears can only find the sound of eighty clocks still ticking in the hallway, and a few seagulls out for an early morning fly.

'I think they might have gone,' Rose whispers, then looks down at Trixie. 'The tide should be far enough out for us to wade to shore now. We just have to get to the front door. Maybe we should be brave and take a look?'

'You don't have to speak to me like I'm a child,' Trixie whispers back, looking and sounding like one.

'Or we could wait?' I suggest. Bravery has never been one of my strengths.

Rose ignores me – as though she might know something I don't – and takes one last look at the Wall of Achievements. She appears to be reading the poem I wrote. Then she says something I find so hard to comprehend that, at first, I can't answer.

'I'm only going to ask this once. And I feel ridiculous and ashamed that I'm asking at all. But are you behind all of this, Daisy?'

I stare at her for a long time, but she can't even look me in the eye. I don't know how or why she would think such a thing.

'No,' I say, wiping a tear from my cheek. Rose stares at the floor, looking sorry. But words don't come with gift receipts; you can't take them back.

'Daisy would never do something like this,' whispers Trixie, and I'm glad someone in this family sees me for who I am.

Rose turns to her. 'Whatever happens, I want *you* to stay back behind me. Okay?' she says, and our niece nods while standing perfectly still, literally scared stiff. Rose creeps towards the library door, leaving me no choice but to follow. Poppins tries to do the same, but my sister shoos her away.

'No, Poppins. You stay here for now. We need to be as quiet as possible.'

The dog looks at Rose as though she understood every word and sits back down on the rug.

Rose slowly turns the key until the door clicks unlocked, and I notice that her hand is trembling. Then she opens the door quickly, as if there might be someone behind it, but there is nobody there. 'Stay back,' she whispers over her shoulder, as she steps out into the hall. I watch from the library as she creeps towards the cupboard under the stairs, already knowing that whatever she finds inside will be something none of us want to see. Rose reaches for the handle, hesitates, then opens the cupboard door.

I can't see what she can from here, but her body language isn't good.

'Stay there,' I whisper to Trixie and she nods. I step out into the hallway to look over Rose's shoulder, and what I see shocks me more than anything else tonight. Lily's body is on the cupboard floor, her head is hanging down as though she is staring at the mirror tied to her hand. She has been left next to Nana, Dad and Nancy. And Conor. His neck looks broken, and there's a yo-yo wrapped around it. What looks like a newspaper page has been stuffed inside his open O-shaped mouth, and there is a red ribbon holding it in place. I have to look away when I see him.

'He died eating his own words,' whispers Rose.

'What?' I say.

'I'm guessing that is what stuffing his own newspaper article in his mouth is meant to mean?' I take a step back, no longer able to process any of the horror I have witnessed tonight. I think I'm going to be sick. I rush to the kitchen and lean over the sink but nothing happens. Then I look up at the wall and see that the chalk poem has changed again.

*Daisy Darker's family were as dark as dark can be.*
*When one of them died, all of them lied, and pretended not to see.*
*~~Daisy Darker's nana was the oldest but least wise.~~*
*~~The woman's will made them all feel ill, which was why she had to die.~~*
*~~Daisy Darker's father lived life dancing to his own tune.~~*
*~~His self-centred ways, and the pianos he played, danced him to his doom.~~*

*Daisy Darker's mother was an actress with the coldest heart.*
*She didn't love all her children, and deserved to lose her part.*
*Daisy Darker's sister Rose was the eldest of the three.*
*She was clever and quiet and beautiful, but destined to die lonely.*
*Daisy Darker's sister Lily was the vainest of the lot.*
*She was a selfish, spoilt, entitled witch, one who deserved to get shot.*
*Daisy Darker's niece was a precocious little child.*
*Like all abandoned ducklings, she would not fare well in the wild.*
*Daisy Darker's secret story was one someone sadly had to tell.*
*But her broken heart was just the start of what will be her last farewell.*
*Daisy Darker's family wasted far too many years lying.*
*They spent their final hours together learning lessons before dying.*

'Why is Rose's name crossed out?' I whisper. '*She's* not dead.'

'I can see you breathing,' I hear Rose say to someone in the hallway.

I rush out of the kitchen, but not in time to see who she is talking to. The confusion I experience is sickening when the sound of a gun shatters the silence. I watch in horror as Rose falls to the floor in the hall, and I feel as though my whole world is breaking, not just my heart.

# Forty-five

*31 October 6 a.m.*
*low tide*

I rush to Rose's side and kneel down on the floor beside her. There is so much blood, too much. I don't know what to do, but I don't think it would make any difference if I did. I try to focus on Rose's beautiful face instead of the puddle of red spilling out beneath her. The clocks in the hall all start chiming that it is six o'clock, and I wish that they would stop. I want it *all* to stop. Time never heals anything in this house, it just hurts. I'm sure Rose must be dead, but then she opens her eyes, stares at me and frowns.

'Daisy?' she whispers.

'I'm right here, Rose. Everything is going to be okay,' I say.

She smiles, but it's an inadequate disguise for her pain. 'You always were a terrible liar,' she says.

Then she closes her eyes, her head falls to one side, and I know that she's gone.

'Why?' I scream, no longer afraid. 'What have you done?' I stand up and turn to stare at the person who shot my sister, no longer caring what might happen to me. 'You were always so loved by all of us. I loved you more than I think I've ever loved another person. Why did you shoot Rose? Answer me! Why?'

But Trixie doesn't answer.

Rose's veterinary gun looks very big in her small hands.

Her eyes are wide and wild. She wipes a tear from her cheek, then she runs.

# Rose

Daisy Darker's sister Rose was the eldest of the three.
She was clever and quiet and beautiful, but destined to die lonely.

She spent her childhood with books, despite her good looks, a smart little
worker bee,
But achieving your dreams isn't always quite what it seems, and
heartbreak is rarely funny.

Becoming a vet meant more to Rose Darker than listening to her
lonely heart.
But there's a price to pay when you push everyone away, some of her
choices were not smart.

Preferring pets to people is not a crime, in many ways it was the
right choice.
So Rose worked alone, made the vet's practice her home, until no one
remembered her voice.

When the time came, even she knew who to blame when the gun was
fired at her chest.
All work and no play meant there was little to say, as she took a first but
final rest.

 # Forty-six

*31 October 6:10 a.m.*
*low tide*

I can't believe that Trixie shot Rose, but I saw her holding the gun in her hands before running up the stairs. I don't understand anything that is happening, but I am afraid, and even more confused than before. I try to remember what I was like when I was fifteen years old, but I can't imagine what on earth must be going through my niece's mind right now. *My* mind is blank. A child I thought I knew so well that she could have been my own is really a stranger to me. A dangerous one.

The house is eerily silent as I head upstairs, one step at a time. Even they don't creak. I find Trixie in her bedroom, but she isn't crying or curled up in the corner as I thought she might be. Instead my niece is searching for something in her little pink suitcase.

'Hello, Aunty Daisy,' she says, looking up as I enter the room.

'What are you doing?' I ask.

'Getting dressed,' she replies, as though it was a ridiculous question. 'Can't stay in my PJs all day long when we have so much to do.'

She's still crying. I wonder whether she is suffering from some form of post-traumatic stress. Maybe she shot Rose by accident, we were all so scared. Then I remember the sleeping pills, and wonder whether this might be a terrible reaction to the drugs Lily gave her.

'Your mum . . . she put some pills in your drink earlier. Trying to help you sleep . . .'

'I know, it's not the first time my own mother tried to drug me. I didn't drink the tea. I tipped it into a potted plant in the lounge when none of you were looking,' Trixie replies, unfolding some clothes and laying an outfit on the bed. Right next to the gun she shot Rose with.

'Do you remember what you just did?' I ask very slowly.

'You are funny, Aunty Daisy. I'm not the one who has trouble remembering things,' she says. Her tears have stopped.

*One Mississippi* . . .

'What does *that* mean?' I ask.

'You always do this . . . forget what really happened,' she replies, with a strange look of pity on her face. I don't understand anything she is saying.

*Two Mississippi* . . .

'Are you telling me that you didn't kill Rose and the rest of the family?' I ask, desperate for there to be some other explanation.

'Of course I didn't . . .' Trixie starts to say, and I feel a brief moment of relief. Maybe this is just a bad dream and I'll wake up soon. But it isn't. 'I couldn't possibly have killed them all by myself. I had help.'

I feel dizzy and strange.

'What are you talking about?' I ask, losing my temper. 'What have you done? Why would you murder the whole family? And why didn't you kill me too?'

*Three Mississippi* . . .

'Stop being silly, Aunty Daisy. I couldn't kill *you* because *you're* already dead.'

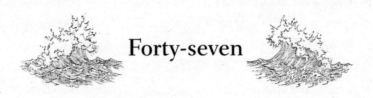

# Forty-seven

*31 October 6:30 a.m.*
*low tide*

It feels like I'm falling.

'What did you say?' I ask Trixie, but she turns her back on me and starts to get changed. She takes off the pink pyjamas, neatly folding the cotton fabric before placing them beneath her pillow. I watch as she calmly dresses in a pink cotton shirt and pink dungarees instead.

'Why don't you sit down on the bed?' she suggests. 'You sometimes faint when you remember that you're dead. I've seen you do it a few times now.'

I am dreaming. That's what this *must* be . . . a nightmare. Nothing else makes sense. Which means I just have to wake up.

*Wake up. Wake up. Wake up.*

'You're not dreaming, Daisy. You've been dead for years,' Trixie says, as though she can read my mind. I do sit down on the bed, but only because it feels like I'm falling again.

'I can't be dead. I have a job. The old people's home . . .' I whisper.

'So you always tell me. But how much do they pay you these days?' Trixie asks.

'They don't *pay* me . . . I volunteer there. I—'

'You *visit* the care home. You don't volunteer. None of the staff have ever heard of you. And most of the residents have never seen you. You go there because it's one of the few places you do occasionally feel *seen*. People seem to see you just before they die – like Rose did a few minutes ago – and you like comforting the residents when they're scared and alone at the end. It's sweet really, but it's not a job. It's just something you do to convince yourself you're still alive.' She sighs and looks genuinely sad. 'I do love you, Aunty Daisy, and I hate seeing you so upset. Try to remember that night, after the Halloween beach party in 1988.'

My train of thought has derailed. The child has lost her mind.

'What are you talking about?'

'*Please* try to remember. Concentrate,' she says, sounding impatient. 'You were on the rocks, you saw my mum and Conor doing something they shouldn't have been doing – although if they hadn't, I guess I wouldn't exist. Then what happened?'

I remember exactly what happened after that. I ran.

Conor and Lily were both pulling on their clothes and yelling at me, but my heart was thudding so loud in my ears, I couldn't hear what they were shouting. All I knew was that I never wanted to see either of them ever again.

People should be more careful what they wish for.

I ran along the beach in the dark until I ran straight into Rose. She was holding a bottle of wine, and I noticed it was almost empty.

'There you are!' she said. 'I was getting worried; I've been looking everywhere for you! We all need to leave soon or the tide will be too far in to cross the causeway. Where did you go?'

'She was with me,' said Conor, out of breath from trying to catch up.

I stared at him, then at Rose. Then at Lily, who had also been running. She was still only wearing a towel over her underwear, after swimming in the sea, and her lipstick was a little smudged. The look she gave me made me want to run again.

'I didn't see anything,' I blurted out.

Rose frowned. 'What *didn't* you see, Daisy?'

I could feel my cheeks start to burn. The cheap wine I'd been drinking made my head feel fuzzy. I didn't know *what* to say. So I opted to tell the truth.

'I just saw Conor and Lily having sex behind the rocks.'

For a moment, nobody said anything. Then Rose laughed.

'Daisy, you are a terrible liar,' she said.

*She didn't believe me.*

Conor started to laugh too. 'Wow, Daisy. That is quite an imagination you've got!'

'Do you even know what sex is?' Lily slurred. She was drunk. They all were. 'Look at the lies little Daisy tells when she's had a couple of drinks!'

'I'm *not* lying. Lily is in love with Conor,' I said.

They all laughed some more. Then Rose stopped. At first, I thought she'd realized that I was telling the truth, but then she smiled. It was her puzzle-solving smile. The expression her face always wore when she had solved a difficult sum.

'Was it you?' she said, staring at me. 'Did you shred my new blue dress on my birthday and pretend it was Lily? Have you been telling lies for years and getting away with it? Trying to start little fights between us?'

'Oh. My. God!' laughed Lily. '*Daisy* has a crush on Conor! That's what all this is really about!'

Rose laughed again too. '*Do* you have a little crush on Conor?' she asked, and her unkind smile made her beauty turn ugly.

'No,' I whispered.

'As I said, you really are a terrible liar, Daisy,' Rose replied, still smiling.

I stared at Conor and saw the look of pity on his face. The humiliation was worse than the heartbreak. Then Lily's face turned dark. 'Was it *you* who cut off my plaits when I was asleep? The night before my birthday? When *everyone* – including me – thought it was Rose?'

I ran before anyone could say or do anything else. Cutting off my sister's hair was the worst thing I ever did to anyone, and the guilt was never a good fit for me. I still loved my family, even when I hated them. I just wanted them to love me too.

'Daisy, wait!' Rose shouted, but I ran and didn't look back.

I must have been running – and crying – for over ten minutes, mostly uphill, along the coastal road to the cliffs overlooking Blacksand Bay. That was the fastest way home when the tide was that far in, above and around the rocks down below that prevented me from just walking across the sand. I felt so alone. I kept thinking about the boy who had kissed me, then called me a freak, and how he was right. I was a freak and nobody loved me. Nobody even liked me, not even my own family. My heart felt as though it was trembling inside my chest.

I was over halfway home when it happened. Right at the very top of the cliff, but so close to the sand dunes and the hidden path that would have led me to our part of Blacksand Bay, and the causeway that would have carried me home to Seaglass. All I wanted in that moment was to get back to my bedroom without being seen, close the door behind me, and lock myself away from the world forever.

I heard the music before I heard the car. I knew it was

Conor's because of the song: 'Don't Worry, Be Happy' I stopped in the middle of the road, thinking that maybe he had come to rescue me. That maybe he loved *me* after all. My imagination started working overtime, just like always, and I pictured Conor telling me that Rose *and* Lily had both been nothing more than mistakes, and saying that he too wished that he had been the first boy to kiss me.

But the car didn't slow down.

'Don't Worry, Be Happy' blared out across Blacksand Bay as the blue Volvo got closer. But I *was* worried, and I *wasn't* happy. I remember how the sky was an inky black, and the stars were shy and sometimes hiding. I remember the sound of the sea crashing on the rocks below, and I remember how very cold I was. My teeth wouldn't stop chattering.

All I had on was a denim dungaree dress, a stripy long-sleeved T-shirt, my rainbow tights and my daisy trainers, and it was a particularly cold Halloween. I had pulled my last-minute sheet costume over myself, trying to keep warm as I walked along the cliff road. I didn't care whether I looked like a ghost; I already felt like one. Maybe a ghost was all Conor saw when he drove his dad's car into me at thirty miles an hour. Otherwise I'm sure he would have hit the brakes.

I remember the sensation of flying through the air. So high, like a bird. It didn't hurt a bit. Not even when I landed on the road. The white sheet flew too, then fell on top of me, covering my face as though declaring me dead. The car skidded to a sudden and violent stop, the twin beams of its headlights shining at the sheet, and me hidden beneath it. Then everything was perfectly still and silent and calm.

Until one of the car doors opened.

It was Lily's voice I heard first. She sounded very drunk. 'What was that?'

Then two more car doors opened.

'Conor, I think you hit something,' said Rose. 'You should have been watching the road instead of playing with the stereo.'

'I can't believe this is happening,' Conor said, sounding even more drunk than my sisters. 'It came out of nowhere.'

'It?' said Rose. I could hear her slowly walking towards me. The way she would have if I were an injured animal on the side of the road. 'Is that Daisy's ghost costume?' she whispered. 'Oh my god, did you hit Daisy?'

'No!' said Conor. 'No, it's just a sheet.'

'Sheets don't bounce off bonnets,' said Lily.

One of them pulled the sheet back. I think it must have been Rose, because I heard her scream first. It was a gentle scream, if there is such a thing. I wanted to reassure her that I was fine. But that was the moment when I realized that I couldn't speak, or open my eyes, or move at all. I was only thirteen years old, but I had already died eight times before. Even if my heart had stopped beating, I knew there were ways to make it start again. There always had been in the past. They just needed to get help.

'What have we done?' Rose whispered. 'What. Have. We. Done?' She screamed the words a second time, sounding hysterical.

'We didn't do anything,' said Lily, sounding more sober all of a sudden. 'Conor was the one driving.'

'This isn't helping,' said Rose. 'We have to help Daisy.'

She checked for a pulse, and I remember that her trembling fingers felt so warm on my cold skin. I wanted her to hold my hand and tell me that everything was going to be all right.

'She's hit her head. It's very bad. There's a lot of blood . . . a lot.' Rose leaned down over me, and I could smell the alcohol on her breath. 'I can't find a pulse and . . . I don't think she's breathing.' Rose started to sob loudly. 'We need to find a phone and call an ambulance.'

'How?' said Lily, and I could hear that she was crying too.

We all knew that they couldn't call for help without either driving into town or driving to Seaglass, then scrambling down the cliff path and across the causeway to use Nana's landline. Both options would take at least twenty minutes, by which time it might be too late if it wasn't already. None of us had mobiles in 1988. Even now, there is no phone signal on this corner of the Cornish coast.

'Wait,' said Conor. 'We should think about this before we do anything we might regret.'

'What are you talking about? Haven't you already done something that you regret?' Rose screamed at him. 'You've killed Daisy!'

'I didn't pass my driving test,' Conor said quietly.

'What did you say?' Rose asked.

'I didn't pass my driving test, but I didn't want to tell you that I'd failed. How could I confess to my genius girlfriend – who was about to head off to Cambridge – that I couldn't pass a simple test? I lied. For you. And I didn't ask to borrow my dad's car tonight because he would have said no – *he* knows I don't have a licence.'

'Oh my god,' Rose whispers.

'I'm going to jail,' Conor says. 'They'll say it's manslaughter. I've been drinking. They're going to lock me up. My life will be over . . . I'll never get a job after this. I just wanted to drive my girlfriend to a party before she left for university, a girlfriend who was probably going to dump me anyway, and now I'm going to jail.'

'I was never going to dump you, why would you think that?' Rose says. 'This was an accident—'

'An accident I am going to regret for the rest of my life.'

Silence followed. All I could hear was the sound of the sea. It was like a lullaby, and I could feel myself drifting away to somewhere else. Then Conor spoke again.

'Do we have to make things even worse than they already are?' he asked.

'What do you mean?' said Rose. 'Daisy is dead. *Nothing* could be worse. I'm sorry that you lied about having a licence, and I'm sorry that you're going to get in trouble, but this *is* your fault.'

'Is it? You both knew that your little sister was at the party tonight when she should have been safe at home. Your parents will find out that neither of you looked after her, or tried to take her back to Seaglass. You let her drink alcohol, then left her alone on the beach, despite her being underage and having a heart condition. You bullied her and made her run away. Your family will hate you just as much as they will hate me, for the rest of your lives.'

I wanted to tell them that I was fine. That they didn't need to worry. But I still couldn't move.

'He's right,' said Lily. 'They *will* hate us.'

'Have you both lost your minds?' said Rose. 'What are you suggesting? That we leave her here on the street like roadkill?'

'No,' Conor said, and I felt such an overwhelming sense of relief until he spoke again. 'I'm suggesting we throw her over the cliff.'

Even if I could have spoken at that point, I don't think I would have been able to.

'Think about it,' he said gently. 'I know how upsetting this is, but Daisy really didn't have much longer to live anyway. We all know that. Every doctor she ever saw said her broken heart wouldn't last forever. She was a good person. She wouldn't want you, or me, or Lily to have *this* hanging over us, like a noose around our necks for the rest of our lives. Her life is over whatever we do, but ours don't have to be. It will look like an accident. All we have to do is go home and keep quiet. Say that she wandered off and left the beach without us realizing.'

I could hear my sisters crying. Both of them. I imagined myself sitting up and us all hugging, with our arms wrapped around each other. I knew they would never be mean to me again, not after this. I thought maybe we would become the best of friends, and that one day we might even laugh about the night Conor accidentally hit me with his dad's car.

But that isn't what happened.

'Come on, before another car comes along and sees us. I'll take her feet,' Conor said, picking me up by my ankles.

'No! What are you doing?' Rose screamed at him.

I didn't think my sisters would let it happen, but then Lily held my hands in hers. I could smell her favourite perfume: Poison.

'I think he's right,' Lily said. 'We're all going to be in so much trouble otherwise.'

'We can't do this. Stop it, put her down,' Rose argued, and I could hear a scuffle.

'She's already dead. What difference does it make?' Lily replied.

Until that moment, I never really believed that they were going to throw me off the cliff, onto the rocks and into the black waves below. I wanted to kick and scream and bite them to make them let go, but I couldn't. And they didn't.

'Are you sure you want to do this? She's your sister,' I heard Rose say.

'I don't know,' said Lily, starting to cry again.

'We don't have a choice,' said Conor.

It was a lie. Life is only ever a series of choices; we all have them and make them and regret them every single day. The ability to choose between right and wrong is a fundamental part of being human. But Conor's humanity got lost that night, and I fear he never found it again.

'On three,' he said, and Rose sobbed. I could feel Lily's hands trembling as she held onto mine. The waves crashing on the rocks below sounded like thunder in my ears. Conor started to count, and they swung me back and forth as though I were the old skipping rope we used to play with on the beach.

'One.'

*Mississippi.*

'Two.'

*Mississippi.*

'Three.'

*Mississippi.*

When they swung me the third time, I could hear my heartbeat in my ears. It was louder than Conor counting, louder than my sisters crying, and louder than the cold dark sea crashing on those rocks beneath me. Looking back, I wonder if the fear I felt produced so much adrenaline that it restarted my heart.

Just as they let me go, I opened my eyes.

I was flying again, and I smiled at Rose, Lily and Conor. Because I was alive, and everything was going to be okay. But they did not smile when they saw my eyes open. They stared back in horror as I disappeared over the cliff, and fell down, down, down into the icy-cold black sea.

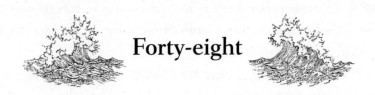

# Forty-eight

*31 October 6:40 a.m.*
*low tide*

Everyone you know is both good and bad, it's part of being human.

Nana used to say that, and I think she was right.

'Are you okay?' Trixie asks. 'I can see you're lost in those thoughts I know you'd rather forget. But everything will be all right now, you'll see.'

I don't know how to respond to that, but I am *not* okay. I have been hoaxed by my own memories on more than one occasion, but I have never felt this lost to myself. I feel like I just watched a scene from my past, performed with a new backdrop. It looked out of place, left there by someone else, so that the memory seemed all wrong. I've tried so hard to exchange it, to give it back. I don't want to remember what really happened that night. But then I have always found fiction more attractive than real life.

'They killed me. Rose, Lily and Conor *killed* me,' I whisper.

'Yes. We've had this conversation many, many times. But for reasons I don't understand, you always forget,' says Trixie.

There are surreal moments after any tragedy when you forget

what has happened. The mind often tries to delete files it can't process. When you remember, it's as though whatever caused that grief happens to you all over again. And I feel as though I am falling. But I never *really* forget, I just choose not to remember.

'If I died that night, why am I still here?' I ask. 'How can you see and hear me?'

'I'm not an expert in the afterlife, but I'm guessing this has something to do with it.'

I look up and see that Trixie has undone the top few buttons of her shirt. I stare at the pink scar down the middle of her chest, almost exactly like my own.

'I was born with a broken heart too,' Trixie says with tears in her eyes. 'They think it might be hereditary, but nobody knew about mine until I was ten. I was at school when it happened. Mrs Milton, my bully of a PE teacher, made us do cross-country on a really hot day. Around the school field and through the woods. After the first lap, I said I didn't feel well. I tried to tell her that my chest hurt and it felt like I couldn't breathe. But Mrs Milton is one of those women who only sees what she wants to see, and only hears what she wants to hear. She made me keep going even when I said I felt a bit broken. I didn't want to let anyone down, so I kept running. I collapsed beneath a huge oak tree, and it was a few minutes before one of the other girls found me. They thought I'd fainted from the heat, but then my heart stopped. The next thing I remember is waking up in the hospital two days later with this scar down my chest, and seeing you sitting at the end of my bed, watching over me. I died that day in the woods, and I think that's why I can see you. I was only dead for a couple of minutes before an ambulance arrived, but that's when I saw you for the first time. I've been able to see and hear you ever since.'

It still feels as though I am falling, again and again, and nobody is ever going to catch me.

'Can anyone else see me?' I ask.

'No. Except Poppins the dog! She can see and hear you too. I bet she ran out to greet you when you arrived at Seaglass yesterday! People seem to see you just before they die. Like the residents in the care home you visit – I know how much you like to comfort them in their last few moments – but there have been other instances. You visited the hospital once, and sat talking to a little girl who had been in a car accident. Her parents were killed in the crash, she was in a critical condition, and you stayed with her until it was time for her to . . . leave. But seeing children die made you too sad, so maybe that's why you only visit the elderly these days. We both know that Rose saw you downstairs, briefly, just before she . . . passed away.' Something like remorse makes itself at home on Trixie's face. 'I told my mum when I first started seeing you, and she got super cross about it. She didn't believe me and said she never wanted to hear me say your name again. That's why she tipped the Scrabble board on the floor last night, because she was scared that I was playing with you. Sometimes if she heard me talking to you, I would pretend that you were an imaginary friend. She was more comfortable with that than the idea of me talking to her dead sister. The one she threw off a cliff.'

I know what she's telling me is true. All the times my family ignored what I said this weekend were because they couldn't *hear* me. Nobody hugged me when they arrived because they couldn't *see* me. My family has treated me like a ghost for years because I am one. Clarity comes like one of the waves I can hear outside Seaglass, crashing all around me, over me and into me, before knocking me down. The lucidity of the moment cannot be ignored or forgotten. I believe it, but still can't quite accept what happened then, or has happened now.

'But *why* did you kill them? I don't understand why you would do such a terrible thing? You've been crying all night, as though you were as scared as the rest of us!'

'I *was* scared and I did cry. What I did tonight was truly horrible, so of course it upset me. I'm not a monster.' Trixie stares at the floor. 'I didn't mean to scare *you*. I really thought you'd figure it out once you saw the Scrabble letters stuck to the VHS tapes: WATCH ME, HEAR ME, NOTICE ME, SEE ME. Those are all the things you wanted your family to do since you died. But even before you died, they didn't really *see* you. And Scrabble was a game we always played together, so I thought you might guess it was me. Try not to be too sad about all of this, Aunty Daisy. Some people are ghosts before they are dead.'

I stare at her and notice the open suitcase on the bed again. There are some things inside that I couldn't see before: a reel of red ribbon, some Scrabble letters – including a square B made from sea glass and wood – the missing B piano key, a handkerchief with the letter B stitched onto it, a bumblebee necklace, and some pages torn from my mother's *The Observer's Book of Wild Flowers*: buttercups, bellflowers and bluebells. I understand now that B is for Beatrice, Trixie's full name. She was leaving clues the whole time, as though she wanted someone to know that it was her. Maybe she wanted someone to stop her.

'What's that?' I ask, seeing something else in the suitcase.

'This book?' she replies, picking up a battered-looking old novel. 'It's *And Then There Were None* by Agatha Christie, one of my favourites. Would you like to borrow it?'

'No. And I meant the sheets of paper with all of our names on.'

Trixie smiles. 'Poems. About each member of the family. Like the one written in chalk on the kitchen wall last night, I wrote that too. Did you like it? I've written one about everyone except you. I even wrote a poem about myself as a little red herring! But I decided not to share them in the end. Would you like to read them?'

I feel as though I am staring at a monster and have to look away, but she still takes the sheets of paper and lays them out on the bed for me to see. Each page is a poem about a member of the family. I don't want to read them, but can't seem to stop myself.

'You said you had help. Who?' I ask.

'I did say that. Come on, let's put you out of your misery.'

I follow her in stunned silence as she hurries down the staircase. But I hesitate when she walks past the cupboard beneath the stairs. The door is closed again, and Rose's body has disappeared from the hallway. I'm not as good at herding my thoughts as I used to be, they tend to come and go as they please. But the ones inside my head right now are loud, and clear, and frightening. I follow Trixie into the kitchen.

Only a moment ago, I believed that the rest of my family were all dead.

But now one of them is sitting at the table, smiling at me.

Once again, it feels like I am falling.

'Hello, Daisy.'

 # Forty-nine

*31 October 6:45 a.m.*
*low tide*

'Hello, Daisy,' Nana says, with a smile I spent my whole life trusting.

It takes a while for me to think of anything to say, and even when I do, it isn't terribly articulate. 'I don't understand what is happening.'

'Nana can't see or hear you. Do you want me to tell her what you said?' Trixie offers.

'Yes. I'd like you to ask Nana if she has completely lost her bloody mind.'

'Did she swear?' Nana asks, and Trixie shrugs. 'Daisy, you know I don't like any bad language under this roof. You must remember to use your words. But I do understand why you might be feeling a bit upset,' she says.

Nana stands up from the kitchen table, careful not to disturb Poppins, asleep at her feet. I see that she is wearing a new pink and purple dress covered in a pattern of birds. She starts to shuffle towards the sink, in her pink and purple slippers. 'I'll explain everything if you'll let me. But I might just put the kettle on first. I'm a little parched, and it is officially my birthday!' she adds. Nana still has a bit of blood and brain matter in her hair, and a big bloody gash on the side of her face. She looks like a ghoul.

'I'll make the tea. You two have a lot to talk about,' says Trixie, going to fill the kettle.

'Well, I suppose it's always best to begin at the beginning,' Nana says, sitting back down in her pink and purple chair at the table. 'It began when Trixie told me that she could see and hear you a couple of years ago. At first, I presumed she was making it up. But then she started knowing things, things that she couldn't possibly have known unless someone had told her. I thought about all the times after you were gone, when books went missing from my library and then would sometimes turn up in your bedroom. Pages folded down just the way you used to when you couldn't find a bookmark. The clues were always there. They always are.' She smiles. 'One day – Halloween last year – I saw Trixie playing Scrabble, and I watched the pieces move all by themselves on the board when it was your turn! But then she told me what really happened the night that you died. You told her your secret, and she told me.' Nana's face darkens. 'That's when we started to plan all of this.'

'What *did* you think happened to me that night?' I say.

'Daisy wants to know what you thought happened the night she died,' Trixie relays without waiting to be asked, then puts the kettle on the stove.

Nana looks so sad. 'Your sisters came home from the Halloween beach party and went to bed without saying a word. Your parents and I didn't even know that you were missing until the next day – we thought you were in your room the whole time, and had no idea that you had sneaked out to join them. My agent was still here. Do you remember that he gave me the Scrabble board that night? It was a birthday gift, and you played a game with him after dinner. It was the last time I saw you alive. He and I found you the following morning. Your broken little body had washed up on Blacksand Bay. The tide at the time when you fell – which was what we thought had happened at first – should have dragged you out to sea and along the coast. But there you were, face-down near the causeway, almost as though you had tried to swim home to Seaglass.

'The police were called, and we were all questioned. They visited Conor and his father too . . . that's why the silly fool killed himself soon afterwards. Mr Kennedy found a streak of your blood on the front right headlight of his Volvo. Conor had taken the car without his dad's knowledge or permission, so Bradley Kennedy thought he'd accidentally hit you himself when driving home from the pub. He was too drunk to remember that he hadn't driven anywhere the night before, and threw himself off the cliff in a tragic case of misguided guilt. His body was never found. Even the police believed that he was responsible for your death. That's when I invited Conor to move in here for a while. His father had just committed suicide, and Rose had just dumped him – though none of us knew the real reason why – and he had nowhere else to go. I didn't know *he* killed you.

'I really wasn't sure if Conor would come when I invited him here this weekend, but I'm glad that he did. Nobody else outside of this family knows the worst things about ours, and there are some things I would prefer to take to my grave. Anyone who lives long enough starts to worry about their legacy, and I didn't much like the look of mine. The Darker family will be remembered for the right reasons now, instead of the wrong ones. Conor arriving by boat was a surprise, but I just cut the rope attaching it to the jetty once you had all gone to bed.'

'I wondered what happened to the boat,' says Trixie. She smiles, but Nana doesn't.

'When I first found out what really occurred the night that you died, I confided in my daughter-in-law, your mother. I invited her here to Seaglass and said there was something very important we needed to talk about. I didn't tell Nancy *how* I suddenly knew the truth – she was already waiting for any excuse to call the men in white coats – I just told her that I was sure. That's when she confessed that she already knew. Lily had told her. Years earlier. Your mother started sobbing, and revealed that one of the last doctors she took you to see in London thought you had a chance to live a longer life. It involved groundbreaking heart surgery, but she never shared that information, the choice, or the opportunity with anyone else, for reasons I still don't understand. If you'd had that surgery, everything might have been different. You might still be alive now.'

'I know,' I whisper, but Nana doesn't hear me.

I was here at Seaglass when they had that conversation.

That's how I knew.

I remember Nana and my mother sitting at the kitchen table, drinking tea, and talking about the doctor who might have changed my life. I remember Nancy crying, I remember Nana sounding so upset, and I remember how neither of them noticed me sobbing in the corner of the room.

Because they couldn't see me.

They behaved as though I wasn't there.

But maybe I was always here. Maybe I never left.

'It turned out *everyone* knew what really happened that Halloween, except me,' said Nana. 'Even my son, your father. They all kept quiet to protect your sisters, the Darker family reputation and their future inheritance. Which is why none of them deserved a penny of it. I am not foolish *or* blind. I knew that my family were selfish and unkind. But they took you away from me, then they lied about what happened, and I could never forgive them, or Conor, for what they did. You were always my favourite, my darling girl. You inspired me to write my own stories, you gave me something to live for, and you made me want to be a better person. They *had* to pay for what they did to you.'

The kettle boils and it sounds like a scream.

Nana glances up at the chalk poem on the kitchen wall.

*Daisy Darker's family were as dark as dark can be.*
*When one of them died, all of them lied, and pretended not to see.*
*Daisy Darker's nana was the oldest but least wise.*
*The woman's will made them all feel ill, which was why she had to die.*
*Daisy Darker's father lived life dancing to his own tune.*
*His self-centred ways, and the pianos he played, danced him to his doom.*
*Daisy Darker's mother was an actress with the coldest heart.*
*She didn't love all her children, and deserved to lose her part.*
*Daisy Darker's sister Rose was the eldest of the three.*
*She was clever and quiet and beautiful, but destined to die lonely.*
*Daisy Darker's sister Lily was the vainest of the lot.*
*She was a selfish, spoilt, entitled witch, one who deserved to get shot.*
*Daisy Darker's niece was a precocious little child.*
*Like all abandoned ducklings, she would not fare well in the wild.*
*Daisy Darker's secret story was one someone sadly had to tell.*
*But her broken heart was just the start of what will be her last farewell.*
*Daisy Darker's family wasted far too many years lying.*
*They spent their final hours together learning lessons before dying.*

'Did you like Trixie's poem?' Nana asks, but I don't answer. 'She wrote more – one about each of you – but was too shy to share them all. When I told Trixie my plan, she agreed to help me. The two of you have a lot in common, and she loves you, just as much as I do. I wanted, no, *needed* to make things right for you and for her before it was too late. While I still could. I killed Frank. He was a terrible son and a dreadful father. Being the only one in the family who ever touched whisky made him surprisingly easy to poison. As soon as your dad locked himself away in the music room, I revealed that I wasn't dead after all. I told him the whole thing with me on the kitchen floor was nothing more than a Halloween prank. We had a bit of a laugh about it, I encouraged him to drink even more of the whisky, then I had the piano play a pretty tune while he died choking on his own blood.' Nana looks down at the floor as though avoiding eye contact, even though I know she can't see the way I am staring at her. She wipes away a tear, and I'm relieved that telling this story is making her feel as sad as I do hearing it. 'Frank was too heavy for me to move by myself, so Trixie helped me drag his body into the cupboard. Nancy was busy ransacking my studio at the time – I think she was worried I might have written about her in a new book – and you were all upstairs, looking for Trixie.

'I was worried about people suspecting Trixie – she's always been a little too clever for her own good – so the additional red herrings seemed necessary. She stole Lily's diabetic kit, took what she needed, then left it in Nancy's bedroom for someone else to find. She sneaked out of the lounge while you were all watching old home movies and joined me in the cupboard under the stairs, locking herself inside with a spare key. Injecting herself with insulin was her own idea after Rose mentioned it at dinner, but I would never have let anything bad happen to her. We had a spare shot of glucagon in case none of you found her in time.'

Trixie puts a cup of tea down on the table in front of Nana.

'The rest was easy,' Nana says, taking a sip. 'Nancy was busy looking for her missing granddaughter when I called her out into the garden. When I told her the whole thing was an elaborate Halloween joke, she got very upset. So I suggested a cup of tea – that was almost always her answer to everything. It was poisoned using plants that she grew herself here at Seaglass. She died a little later than she should have, but punctuality was never Nancy's strong point.

'Everyone else died on time, and they were found once an hour, just like we planned. That part was one of Trixie's ideas. She was full of them, after reading so many murder mysteries. Lily killed herself by spraying her neck with perfume, which we had replaced with a deadlier poison than the one she preferred. Conor took an unfortunate topple down the stairs, then suffocated on his newspaper article. Trixie shot Rose with her own gun. I had no idea she would bring one this weekend. That changed our plans and we improvised—'

'Rose did nothing wrong, she was a good person,' I interrupt. 'She helped animals and I don't understand how or why—'

'Did Daisy say something?' Nana asks Trixie, who is frowning at me.

Trixie nods. 'She thinks Aunty Rose didn't deserve to die. *Rose* shot ponies on the way here. *Rose* only liked to help people and animals if helping them was easy. *Rose* only ever did good things to make herself feel less bad. *Rose* let Lily and Conor throw *you* over a cliff. She witnessed something truly terrible and did nothing to stop it. Then lied about it. That makes her just as bad as the rest of them.'

Nana nods in agreement. 'In some ways, they were all killed by what they loved the most:

Frank was killed by his desire to be alone with his music.

Nancy was killed by her precious plants.

Rose was killed by something to do with her work, which she always put first.

Lily was killed by the stench of entitlement she wallowed in.

And Conor died eating his own words. Being a journalist is a privilege. The stories they tell should always be true.'

'Have you got any idea how crazy you both sound?' I say, but Trixie doesn't reply and Nana can't hear me. 'There is still so much I don't understand. At midnight, when this nightmare started, Trixie found you on the kitchen floor. Rose examined you and said you were *dead*. The head injury . . . I saw the blood . . . the gash on the side of your head still looks serious . . .'

Trixie repeats what I've said, and Nana nods.

'The blood and brains were thanks to Amy and Ada . . .' I have to think for a moment, before I realize that she means her chickens. The chickens that the rest of the family ate for dinner last night. 'They died naturally this week, almost as though they wanted to help with the plan, but I confess that plucking them and preparing props from their remains was horribly messy. I bought a latex gash from a joke shop in town, it peels right off, see?' she says, removing it with a smile. 'And the grey skin was just make-up. I've always had a weak pulse, and it's not the first time Rose thought someone in this family was dead when they weren't. To be fair, I've practised breathing very slowly when meditating – I learned from the best at a monastery in Bhutan – I can breathe *so* slowly that your sister thought I wasn't breathing at all. People tend to believe what they want to, so maybe that's why the whole family were so willing to believe I was dead.'

'But I still don't understand *why*,' I say. 'Why do it at all, and why like this?'

'Did she ask why again?' Nana says, and Trixie nods.

Nana takes another sip of tea, as though thinking very carefully about the answer.

'I did what I did, the way that I did it, because I wanted them all to feel the fear you must have felt before you died that night. And, if I'm going to be completely honest, because I wanted to be proud of what I was leaving behind after I'm gone. I'm proud of you and Trixie. I'm proud of all my books. But I wasn't proud of any of them. Not dealing with them before I died . . . it would have been selfish and irresponsible, like leaving litter on the beach. If that silly old palm reader in Land's End is correct, then I'll die when I'm eighty. Today is my eightieth birthday . . . so I didn't have very long to put things right.' She adds some sugar to her tea, something I've never seen her do before, and takes another sip. 'I don't understand why you're still here, Daisy. Why you haven't . . . moved on. After you died, I couldn't sleep. Sometimes it felt like I couldn't breathe, and I've struggled to draw, or paint, or write. Grief can change a person into someone even they can't recognize. I haven't published a new book since. I thought my agent had completely given up on me, but he still came to visit yesterday to wish me a happy birthday. We talked about you. I think he knew that you were always my favourite grandchild.

'I kept asking myself the same question when you were taken from my life. Where does the love go when someone dies? Their last breath disappears into the atmosphere, their body gets buried in the ground, but where does the love go? If love is real, it must go *somewhere*. And maybe *that's* why you're still here, because the love got trapped? I wanted to set you free . . . and I hoped that if I put things right, you would be. But you're still here. I so badly wish I could see you, the way Trixie can. That's why I asked Conor to take a picture of the whole family last night, hoping perhaps then I might be able to see your face again.'

I take a step closer to the fridge, where she stuck the Polaroid photo of us all. Everyone is there: Dad, Nancy, Rose, Lily and Nana. But where I was sitting, all I can see is an empty chair. Nana continues, and I try my best to keep up.

'Yesterday, my agent said that the night you died, you told him that you wanted to tell your own story. Do you remember that? He said that you wanted to write a novel about the *real* Daisy Darker and asked if he would read it. That's what I think you need to do.' She stares around the room for a moment, as though waiting for an answer. 'Did she say anything?'

Trixie shakes her head.

Nana drains her cup of tea, then looks straight at me as though she really can see me. 'Daisy?'

'Nana?'

'Oh my goodness! My darling girl, look at you! Just the same as you were before, with your plaits and your denim dungaree dress. Oh, how I've missed you!'

'You can see me?' I whisper, wondering how and why now.

Nana starts to weep. 'Yes! I can see you and I can hear you, and this proves I was right to do what I did because here you are and now we can say goodbye. Properly this time.' She puts her cup down with trembling hands. 'That last book I wanted to write, the one about a dysfunctional family not unlike ours, I've realized it is not *my* story to tell. It's *yours*. You have to write your own story, that is the answer to everything.'

'I can't write a book—'

'You can and you must. I believe that telling your own story, the truth about what happened, might set you free. I wish I could be here to help you, but that palm reader in Land's End was right.'

'I don't understand—'

'Your mother was always the only one to take sugar in her tea; the poison I used to kill her was in the bowl. It seems to have worked more quickly on me. I just had to see you again, and I knew this was the only way to do it. I'm so sorry I didn't do more to protect you from this awful family when you were a child. I know I let you down. But everything I did tonight, I did for you. Forgive me, and take care of each other, my darling girls. You are the only good future this family ever had.'

'Don't go,' I say, holding her hand. 'Don't leave me again. Not yet.'

It feels like I'm falling once more.

'I'll always be here,' she says, gently putting her other hand over my heart. 'The people who truly love us never leave us. And you were *never* broken. In my eyes, you were always perfect. I love you from here to the moon and back three times and once for luck.'

'I love you too,' I whisper, new tears streaming down my face.

Nana smiles at me one last time before resting her head on the kitchen table. She closes her eyes, and I know she has gone. Poppins starts to whimper, and the ocean continues to serenade every unsettled thought inside my mind, as though trying to silence them with the relentless *shh* of the sea.

# Fifty

*31 October 6:55 a.m.*
*low tide*

The tap of grief never turns off completely. It allows a person's sorrow to slowly drip inside them until they are so unbearably full of sadness, they have no choice but to let it flow freely and pour out. Drowning every other thought and feeling.

'She's dead,' says Trixie with tears in her eyes. 'Why would she do this?'

The eighty clocks out in the hallway seem to tick more loudly than ever before.

'Because it was her time,' I say. 'I think she always planned to take her own life when it was over. She could never live with what she had done. I understand why she did what she did now, but I still don't know why you went along with it.'

Trixie sits down at the table, on her little chair covered in stars, and she looks so small to me again. Like the child she used to be, not the woman she is growing into.

'Do you remember what it was like when they all realized that you were broken?' Trixie asks in a quiet voice. 'The way they treated you? Well, it was the same for me. My mother stopped letting me go out with my friends, wrapped me up in cotton wool, and every time she looked at me, all I could see in her eyes was pity and resentment. Not love. My mother and Nancy didn't think anyone else should know about my heart condition – as though it were a dirty secret, something to be ashamed of. They didn't even want the rest of the family to know. Let's be honest, they really were horrible people. All of them. Look what they did to you.'

'They all thought I wouldn't live beyond fifteen.'

'Your mother knew that you might, if she'd let that doctor try to help you. I had the surgery that you didn't. There were some complications, but the doctors think I might live until I'm twenty now. Twenty-five if I'm lucky. And that's all I want: to live what is left of my life. I'll be sixteen soon, I can leave school, I can travel the world. I just want to live while I still can. Surely you must understand that? The only people in this family who ever really loved me were Nana and you. And you're a ghost. She couldn't forgive the rest of the family for what they did to you. Neither could I. We killed them so that you and I could both be free. You shouldn't still be here, it isn't right. Nana thought your soul might have got trapped because you died on Halloween. That's why we did it tonight.'

I stare at her, but don't know what to say.

'What Nana said was true: you haven't aged,' Trixie continues. 'I know you can't see your own reflection, but you must be able to see that you're still wearing the same clothes you did that night? The denim dungaree dress, the stripy rainbow tights, the trainers covered in daisies? You're still a thirteen-year-old girl. You might be my aunt, but I'm really two years older than you now.'

I can't process her words anymore. I am trapped inside a nightmare, one in which I've been dead for years. Poppins starts to whimper again, and I want to do the same.

'I might give you some space, take Poppins for a quick walk,' says Trixie, as though this were a normal day. 'I can see this is a lot to take in. You should have a think about what Nana said. Her theory about why you're still here might not be as crazy as it sounds. And if she *was* right, maybe there is a way for you to leave.'

'What are you talking about?'

'She thought you should write your own story. Think about it: using your words is the only thing you can still do. Death isn't like the movies, at least not for you. I've never seen you walk through walls or even a door unless someone has opened it first. But you can move Scrabble letters, and books, and type on keyboards.'

Trixie walks out into the hall.

'Wait!' I say. 'Don't leave me here alone with . . . them!'

'I'll be back soon, I promise,' she says, attaching Poppins' lead to her collar. 'The pen Nana's agent gave you the night that you died is still in your dress pocket,' Trixie adds. She's right. I take out the special silver pen with four colours, and find Nana's agent's business card too. I stare at his name and the address of his office in London. 'Perhaps writing your own story *is* the only way you get to escape this life? Maybe telling the truth about what happened is your unfinished business? Nana's agent told you he'd read a story about the real Daisy Darker if you wrote it, do you remember? I won't be long, Aunty Daisy. Come on, Poppins!'

I retreat inside the darkroom of my mind, trying to develop a picture of a future that would be more appealing, but all I see is black. I rush to catch up with Trixie, but she closes the front door behind her and I can't seem to open it. She's right; I can't walk through walls. I bang on the door, but it doesn't make a sound. I peer out of the tiny round window in the hallway; it's like a porthole on a boat, and I do feel as though I am trapped on a sinking ship. My view of Trixie and Poppins gets smaller and smaller as they walk across the causeway, leaving me behind. I don't know if I'll ever be able to love my niece the way that I used to. Sometimes we love monsters without knowing that's what they are.

I love this house too. I never wanted to leave it. Until now.

The eighty clocks surrounding me in the hallway start to strike seven and the noise is deafening. I stare at the punch clock and see the faded card with my name on. The last date stamped on it says 1988. I run up the stairs to my bedroom and find Conor's laptop on the desk where he left it. The cursor is flashing on the screen, and the word that I wrote last night is still there:

*Boo!*

The letters disappear one by one, and are replaced with something new:

DAISY DARKER

My fingers tremble when I have finished typing what I hope might be the title of my story. I feel for the business card in my pocket, take it out and stare at the agent's name again.

I wonder if I could really write a book.

I wonder if I could really tell the truth.

There is so much we don't know we don't know.

The tide is out now and the sun is just starting to rise above Seaglass, casting the sky in streaks of pink and purple. I've always thought that dawn is the most beautiful time – shining a light on the clean slate of a new day. A chance to start again. The birds are swooping and singing above the waves in Blacksand Bay, and as I look out towards the ocean, I spot a pod of dolphins in the distance. The sound of the sea is serenading what feels like my final scene.

I *want* to be free.

I wonder if anyone will ever read the story I want to write?

The eighty clocks downstairs are quiet again, and I enjoy the silence as I type the first few words on the blank page: *I was born with a broken heart*. I spent my whole life hiding inside stories when the real world got too loud. I don't know if anyone will ever read mine. There are some stories only time will tell.

# Acknowledgements

Books are a bit like children for authors, we're not really allowed to have favourites, but *Daisy Darker* is mine. I first had the idea for Daisy in 2015 and it took me over five years to write her story. I wouldn't have been able to write it at all without the following people.

Forever thank you to Jonny Geller for being the best agent in the known universe and one of the best humans I know. And forever thank you to Kari Stuart, my Mary Poppins, and agent extraordinaire. I don't think I can remember how to exist without these two people, and I feel very lucky and eternally grateful to have them in my life.

Thank you to Kate Cooper and Nadia Mokdad for all the translations of my novels. Seeing my books out in the world will never be anything less than magic, and Kate and Nadia are my favourite magicians. Thank you to Josie Freedman, Luke Speed and Anna Weguelin for the screen adaptations of my stories. And thank you to everyone else at Curtis Brown and ICM who do so much for me and my books, especially Viola Hayden, Ciara Finan and Sophie Storey (a.k.a. the Geller Office Book Club!).

Huge thanks to my editor in the UK, the one and only Wayne Brookes, and the rest of the brilliant team at Pan Macmillan.

Thank you for believing in Daisy, and for turning this story into such a beautiful book. And huge thanks to my US editor, Christine Kopprasch, and the brilliant team at Flatiron. I feel so lucky to be working with the best in the business on both sides of the pond. I'm also very grateful to all of my foreign publishers who take such good care of my novels.

Thank you to everyone who helped with the research for this book, with special thanks to the loveliest vet in the land, Louise Ketteridge, for letting me shadow her at her practice. The experience changed the plot in more ways than one. Thank you to the beautiful Cornish coast for inspiring the setting of this book. I have been visiting the same secluded spot on my birthday for years, and I picture Daisy and Seaglass there every time.

Thank you to the librarians, booksellers, journalists and book reviewers who have been so kind about my books. And thank you to all the book bloggers, and bookstagrammers . . . I love seeing your beautiful pictures from all around the world. My books travel far more than I do these days, and I am quite jealous.

Thank you to my Daniel who is my first reader, my best friend, and my favourite human. Thank you to Diggi, for being the most wonderful writing companion and the best dog in the world. My final and biggest thank you is to my readers. I wouldn't be here without you. This book is for you.